sleep softly

GWEN HUNTER

sleep softly

MIRA®

MIRA

ISBN-13: 978-0-7783-2464-5
ISBN-10:   0-7783-2464-8

SLEEP SOFTLY

Copyright © 2008 by Gwen Hunter.

www.MIRABooks.com

Printed in U.S.A.

Acknowledgments

FOR HELP ON MUSES:
S. Joy Robinson, who did research and brought me wonderful books on the subject.
And Misty Massey, who gave me the idea in the first place.

FOR MEDICAL HELP:
I have tried to make the medical sections of *Sleep Softly* as realistic as possible. Where mistakes may exist, they are mine, *not* the able, competent and creative medical workers in the list below.

Susan Prater, O.R., Tech and sister-in-love, in South Carolina
Earl Jenkins, Jr., M.D., in South Carolina
James Maynard, M.D., in South Carolina
Eric Lavondas, M.D., in North Carolina
Randall Pruett, R.N., in South Carolina

As always, for making this a stronger book:

Miranda Stecyk, my editor, who had a massive editing job in this one! Kisses!

Jeff Gerecke, my agent.

Lynn Prater, esthetician and owner of Serenity Spa in Rock Hill, South Carolina, who gave me all the skin info (hope I got it right) and who keeps my skin glowing.

My husband, for answers to questions that pop up, for catching so much in the rewrites and for his endless patience.

My mother, Joyce Wright, for editing as I work.

To the love of my life who
Handles all the details
Is never boring, though is often hard to keep up with
Writes wonderful songs
Didn't laugh when I wanted to learn to whitewater
    kayak
Fixes the trucks and the RV and anything that
    breaks in the house.
Painted my dining room and didn't balk at the dark
    garnet color
Learned to dance just for me
Rubs my feet when they hurt
Works 16 hours a day because he loves it
And who is a man of honor. There are so few in the
    world today.

Prologue

He spotted his landmark, a lightning-blasted tree, its bark peeled back to expose pale, dead wood, and turned left onto a little-used tertiary road. The pavement was pitted and cracked, and the old Volvo shuddered as the right front wheel slammed into a particularly deep pothole. The girl who hadn't been his daughter shifted on the seat beside him, her head hitting the window with a thump and whipping toward him.

He caught her one-handed and eased her back to the seat. Her earrings tinkled softly beneath the music on the CD player. Violins harmonized the heartbreaking melody of a Mozart sonata.

Slowing, he pulled the black velvet throw over her again and patted her shoulder. She didn't respond. He didn't expect her to. She had been dead nearly an hour.

There were no streetlights here, the road disappearing into the darkness. A doe stood on the verge of dead grass, watching the car. She was unafraid, her jaw moving as she grazed on the coarse vegetation. "Did you see that deer?" he asked the girl. "You like deer." She said nothing. He patted her shoulder again.

The old graveyard appeared just ahead, the damaged bronze horse beneath the Confederate soldier casting a bizarre shadow. The nose of the horse had broken off when vandals had thrown the statue to the ground in 1998. The cost of repairing the monument had been more than the local historical society had been able to acquire, and so the horse, while returned to its perch and secured to its base, remained a half-faced mount. He knew all this and much more; he'd done tedious, fatiguing research into the family tree and this graveyard. "Research is paramount, right, honey?"

The girl was still silent. When he braked in the grave-yard, she slid down the seat, her body curling limply on the floor. "Sorry, sweetheart. But we're here now."

Leaving her in the car, the motor running, he took a flashlight and walked the perimeter of the graveyard from the monument clockwise, until he reached the horse again. The New York Philharmonic continued to play the Mozart piece as he paced an approximate ten feet to the family plot. Six generations of Shirleys were buried here, several with Confederate memorials on their headstones. Others were heroes of the First and Second World Wars. A husband and wife were buried side by side, though they had died two decades apart in the late 1800s. The husband, Caesar Olympus Shirley, the wife, Susan Chadwick Shirley. Five children had died and been buried within one week. Flu? Cholera? Strep? There had been no historical documentation.

The girl would like the Shirley children. He had seen an old daguerreotype of the family. They looked like nice people.

Back at the Volvo, he changed the CD to Vivaldi, opened the trunk and removed a shovel, a second flashlight and four small statues made of polished brass. They shone like gold in the light, each of them dressed in Grecian robes with arms lifted high, fingertips touching so their arms made a circle, as if they held the world. Each had devices at her hip, delicately molded brass instruments. He tucked a Bible under one arm and carried a small pink box by its plastic handle. A child's lunch box he'd obtained on eBay. The girl had been delighted.

To the quickening pace of Vivaldi, he chose a place at the feet of the Shirley children, set down the funeral items, and shoved the shovel, blade first, into the ground. In the headlights, a long shadow created by the shovel was thrown across the graves, undulating as if seeking a place to secrete itself among the night-dark stones. Using his body weight, bruising his foot on the shovel, he dug the grave. Long minutes passed as the strains of the music soared and fell. The shovel acquired a rhythm that matched the music. A small blister rose on one palm. He worked up the sweat of a peasant, perspiration trickling down his sides in the unseasonable warmth. He dug deep enough to keep out scavengers. Deep enough to keep her safe. She hadn't been his daughter, but she had tried. She deserved a decent resting place and someone to mourn her passing.

When the grave was satisfactory, he threw the shovel to the side and went back to the car. Using the damp cloth he had brought in a Ziploc bag, he pulled off his shirt and washed himself. Then he removed a clean shirt from its hanger and forced his hands through the heavily starched arms, tied his tie and put on a suit coat. Funeral-black.

Properly attired, he pulled the velvet throw over her snugly. Lifting the precious bundle from the floor of the car, the black velvet tangled around her, he carried her to the narrow pit. He laid her gently on the grass and eased her down into the raw earth, the small grave illuminated by the headlights. Vivaldi played softly now, the strains drifting through the car windows into the night. A whip-poor-will sang in the distance.

One last time, he checked her pulse, two fingers on her wrist. Just to make sure. She wasn't supposed to still be here, but there could always be unexpected problems. Nothing. Nothing at all. Leaning into the grave, he pressed his fingers against her cool throat and studied her in the earthen cavity. She was so beautiful. He had hoped she would be the one.

Using the utmost care, he bent over the grave and eased the velvet throw smoothly away from her, over her torso, down the hollows of her arms. Dragging it from her feet.

As he rose up, his body bent at an unnatural angle, his back wrenched, an excruciating tremor. Shock rippled through him. *She had done this.* This little girl. How could she hurt him? Angry, he held his breath against the pain, grunting when he tried to breathe, cursing her in his mind. *Little piece of trash!* Long minutes later, the spasm eased. He sat up, stretching his spine. The tremor worsened for an instant, then slid away.

He tested its return, bending and tensing. Satisfied, he bowed back over the grave and felt for a pulse a final time. Two minutes passed. There was nothing. No pulse. His anger of the moment before evaporated.

She was gone. A sob tore his throat. It wasn't supposed to end like this. She was supposed to be the one.

Folding the velvet cloth, he tossed it to the side, opened the child's lunch box and took out a blond ballerina doll. He placed the doll in the crook of the girl's arm, smoothed the doll's long hair with a tender hand, then tested once again the knot that decorated the doll's waist over its pink ballerina outfit. Beside his daughter's hip— No, not his daughter. *The girl.* What was her name? It didn't matter. She had failed. Beside her hip he set her flute. She had forgotten how to play the flute in the last months of her life. Her loss of talent had saddened them both. But she was free now. On the other side of the grave, her gift was restored. And the girl would find his daughter, tell her that he was trying, that he loved her.

Vivaldi's sonorous melody lifted on the night air, rising like a promise. She had loved Vivaldi. Or had that been the other one? For a moment, his confusion stirred and grew, but he pushed it away. All that mattered was that she hadn't been his daughter. He had to remember that. It was all that mattered.

In the front of her leotard, the lavender and pink bleached gray in the moonlight, over her heart, he tucked the folded piece of heavy paper, paper they had made together so long ago. The poem this one had inspired would go with her to paradise, a gift she could pass along to his daughter when they met. He checked her tights, adjusted the pink tutu and retied one pointe shoe in the knot he preferred. Grief gathered as he tied the knot. It was always so hard.

He folded her hands, the flesh cold but still limber, maintaining the appearance of life. Her bound hands had slid out of place as he'd moved her to the earth. He pulled on both ends of the fine rope, tightening the complicated knot.

The engraved silver ring had slid backward. It was a bit too large for her slender finger and he straightened it. That was odd. The ring had fit when he'd bought it. He was sure of it.

A silver bracelet gleamed in the moonlight on the same wrist. He turned it just so. In her pierced ears were silver knots that jingled when she moved her head, the earrings hanging back onto her pale neck. Each piece of jewelry contained Celtic knots, not the kind he wanted, but he hadn't been able to find the right style of knot. He was still searching. After this last failure, it was becoming imperative that he find the right earrings. He stroked the cool flesh of her neck, the skin so soft, so young and innocent. He wiped his face, found tears on his fingers.

"Sweetheart?" She didn't answer. A second sob tore from him. He stooped over the small grave and wept softly. Why did she fail? She could have been the one.

When his grief abated, he opened the Bible to Psalm 88. It was a wise and insightful selection, one he had researched for hours. She would have liked the poetry of Psalms. He wished he could have read it in the original Hebrew, but he didn't know the language. It looked like painted strokes. Perhaps he'd study that tongue. He brightened a moment. When his daughter came back to him, when her soul found its way back to her body, they could study it together.

Dropping to his knees in the damp earth so that one of the flashlights illuminated the page, he placed the brass statues around the small grave, one at the head, one at the foot and one to each side. He began to read. "O Lord, the God of my Salvation, I have cried to You for help by day; at night I am in Your presence…."

Warm night breezes caressed his skin. Vivaldi and the whip-poor-will called into the darkness as he spoke the holy words. The ceremony was exquisite. Grief fluttered in his chest like a dying bird. Tears gathered and trickled down his cheeks, causing the text to waver. By the tenth verse his voice was broken, his anguish so acute he feared his heart might burst and he might die before he finished the last rite. A heart attack would put an end to his pain. Perhaps he should welcome it. But death didn't come.

The psalm finished, "Lover and friend have You put far from me; my familiar friends are darkness and the grave." Putting the book aside, he bent over the grave and touched her face once more. She was as flawless as he could make her. She must remain so.

Tears still falling, using his hands so that no metal would bruise her, he scooped dirt over her feet. His knees pressing deeply into the damp earth, he was careful not to move too much soil with each scoop and disarrange her clothes or position. Scattering only a thin layer, he covered her legs, her thighs, her hips. Lastly he covered her face. She was gone from sight now. Regret scoured his soul. He wiped his face again with the damp rag. It showed traces of darkness in the dim light. He'd have to shower when he got home.

He set the statues aside where they were protected and wouldn't accidentally fall in the grave, took the shovel, and finished filling the hole. Within a minute, sweat trickled down his back in the unexpectedly temperate air. It hadn't been this warm when she'd left him. He'd have to remember that. Another variance he would have to work through. The last of his tears dried as he plied the shovel, the act of closing the grave bringing him back into control. It was always this way.

When the grave was full, he tramped on it, walking back and forth before walking a final time on the blade of the shovel to remove any shoe prints. With gentle hands, he smoothed the top of the grave. From the lunch box, he removed a rose bud. It was wilted, a bit bruised, but she had been pleased this morning when she'd woken to find it beside her face, on her pillow. She had smiled and sniffed the bud, had seemed for a moment less melancholy. Gently, he placed it atop the soil. Good memories.

Gathering all the tools he had brought with him, he tucked the statues, which he had purchased from a Grecian antiquities dealer, beneath an arm. He walked from the ancient family plot past the statue of the Confederate soldier mounted on his maimed horse, through the graveyard to the car. He drove into the night, the symphony leaving mournful notes on the air.

Back on the highway, he removed the Vivaldi CD and inserted a Beatles album. John Lennon singing about a flawless world.

It wasn't too soon to start looking. Before long he would have it perfected. Perhaps he had worked out all the variables this time. Next time, the method of selection, enticement, abduction might be perfect. Then again, he might have to try, try again. He smiled at the whimsy but knew it contained an ultimate truth. There was no goal in life, in art, but perfection. The Greeks had understood that concept far better than any other people.

He sang into the night about an ideal world. He was prepared to spend an eternity to get it right. Eternity to bring his daughter back to him, perfected.

On the seat beside him was a Sunday edition of *The State* newspaper, open to the sports section. A girl's face smiled at the photographer. She was beautiful. She was perfect.

1

Monday Morning

Parking behind the house, I crawled out of the battered SUV, slung my canvas bag of forensic nursing supplies over a shoulder and blinked into the early morning light. Jas ran from the house and jogged over to me. Bending, she kissed me once on the forehead. "Bye, little mama. I haven't fed the dogs."

"You never feed the dogs anymore," I grumbled, feeling the age difference as she loped to her truck, looking lithe and nimble. And skinny in her size-five jeans. Waggling her fingers at me through the driver window, she gunned the motor of her new little GMC truck and spun out of the drive, heading to early class at the University of South Carolina. "And good morning to you, too. How was Sunday night at the hospital, Mama? It was lovely, Jasmine. Thank you for asking," I said to the trail of dust in her wake.

Thinking I was talking to them, Big Dog, Cheeks and Cherry yapped at my hips, thighs and knees according to their height, demanding attention, which I absently gave while I yawned, a pat here, an ear-scratch there. Abandoned dogs needing a home made the best pets, and I took in as many dogs as I could, even adopting some from the county, when K-9 dogs became too old to work. The well-behaved animals romped and writhed in delight as I trudged to the house. They reeked of something they had rolled in, probably dead rabbit or squirrel, and wanted me to play a game of fetch but the shoe they brought was stinky.

"Bring me a stick. That thing is nasty." I nudged it away with my white nurse's shoe.

Big Dog, my half moose, half monster protector nudged it back, his floppy ears dangling, long tail wagging. Cheeks stopped my progress, a wriggling clot of hound-dog muscle in front of me. Cherry bounced up and down on her front feet, still yapping her high-pitched bark. "Hush. Okay. One toss," I said, "then I bury this thing."

I bent and lifted the shoe. A smell gusted out, sickly, almost sweet. I knew that scent. The scent of old death. The world seemed to slow as I held the small red sneaker. It was no longer than my hand, filthy, laces snarled with leaves and twigs. Reeking of the grave.

A child's shoe.

Turning it over, I looked inside. Tissue. Something soft and rotten. A sycamore leaf twisted into the laces. A deep scuff along one rubber sole, some gummy substance ground into the uneven ridges. Decayed-meat smell. The early morning air shivered along my shoulders.

I returned to the SUV and opened the hatch, placing the shoe on the floor. This was dumb. This wasn't…

It couldn't be. I was too tired and not thinking straight. I moved the photocopies of the family genealogy charts to the side so I wouldn't dirty them or contaminate the evidence. If there *was* evidence.

I dumped out everything from the canvas tote I still carried and dropped the bag beside the spare tire attached to the sidewall. From the pile, I pulled a pair of blue non-latex gloves, tweezers, evidence bags, a tape measure and a sterile plastic sheet on which I set the shoe. I added a small handheld tape recorder and my new digital camera, part of the tools of the trade for a forensic nurse. I checked the time. Then I hesitated. I felt the chill air beneath my scrub shirt as I rested my hands on the rubberized ledge of the hatch. "This can't be what I think it is."

Big Dog huffed at my words and finally brought me a stick, sitting politely, with one paw raised. Though I called him part moose, he was part mongrel and part Great Pyrenees, and his head was higher than my waist. I tossed the stick once and the dogs ran, baying.

Should I call the cops? Stop right here and call the sheriff's office? If I contaminated evidence after graduating with honors from the forensic nursing course, I'd feel like a failure as well as an idiot.

I blew out a breath of air. Okay. I knew how to preserve evidence.

I was too tired to think and my feet hurt and my lower back ached. All I wanted to do was drop the shoe and go to bed. The smell from the shoe permeated the SUV as I stood there, hesitant, staring at the red sneaker.

What if I called the cops and it was just a shoe from

the illegal dump near the new development at the back of the farm? And the tissue was an old half-rotten hamburger that had gotten shoved inside, or a dead mouse? I'd feel even more like an idiot. I didn't waste much effort on pride but I'd be embarrassed if I called law enforcement all the way out here to look at trash brought up by the dogs. The guys on the call would never let me live it down. I had worked as a volunteer for the Dawkins County Rescue Squad long enough to know I'd receive a new nickname and it wouldn't be flattering.

It was probably nothing. A mouse. The remains of someone's lunch. My chill subsided. I pulled on the gloves and dated, timed and initialed two evidence bags. I marked one bag FOLIAGE FROM LACES. Just in case. I snapped two shots with the digital camera and checked the viewer, making sure the sneaker would be visible, acceptable in a court of law. Not that I would need it. I was absolutely…I was almost sure.

Turning on the tape recorder, volume up high, I set it to the side, gave the time, date, my name, location and a short account of how I came into possession of the shoe. Extending the tape measure, I held it against the bottom of the shoe and took a photograph of the two together so the size could never be lost.

At the same time, I said the dimensions aloud for the recording and noted that it was a left shoe. Somehow that seemed important, though I was certain that was the mother in me reacting, not the forensic nurse.

With the tweezers, I pried apart the shoelaces, putting the leaves and twigs in the first paper bag. Using my fingers, I worked the snarled knot from the laces, gathering the material that fell out and adding it to the evidence bag, even small grains of dirt and grit and what looked like pale yellow sand. When the laces were unknotted, I pushed apart the stiff sides, exposing the tongue curled deep into the toe.

I snapped another photograph and labeled the second evidence bag CONTENTS: SHOE, TONGUE. Prying with the tweezers, I pulled on the cloth tongue, easing it out, gathering the scant granules and vegetable matter that escaped and put them into the second bag. The tongue twisted out, awkward and unyielding, wrapped around something, and I stepped back, letting the early morning sun touch the thing I had exposed.

Painted a bright, iridescent blue, the nail was separated from the surrounding tissue by decomposition. A lively shade, bright as the Mediterranean Sea. Blackened tissue. It was a child's toe.

In the distance the dogs barked, a horse neighed, a door slammed. A crow called, the sound like mocking laughter, grating.

After a long moment, I found a breath, strident, harsh. The air ripping along my throat. My vision narrowed, darkening around the edges, focusing on the bright blue toenail. I leaned forward, catching my weight on the tailgate. I wanted to throw up. I sat down on the dirt at my feet, landing hard, jarring my spine.

The cool air now felt unexpectedly warm and I broke out in a hot sweat. My breath sped up, hyperventilating from shock. A mockingbird song I hadn't heard until now sounded too loud, too coarse. In the distance, a horse tossed her head and snorted. Cherry, the small terrier, nudged my leg and romped around the SUV, yapping. I hadn't been practicing forensic nursing a month yet, and here I had a toe in a shoe. Nothing I had studied told me what to do next.

Where had the dogs found the shoe?

There was no doubt. I had something important, something horrible, in my truck. A part of a little girl… I shuddered. *A part of a little girl…*

And I had tampered with evidence. "Well…" I said, wanting to say something stronger. I added another, softer, "Well," not knowing any appropriate swear words that might cover this situation. What do you say when your dogs bring you part of a little girl? I fought rising nausea, swallowing down vile-tasting saliva. A shudder gripped me. *Part of a little girl…* I dropped my head and tried to slow my breathing.

When my vision cleared and the faintness passed, I stood again, pulling up on the tail of the truck, my knees popping as they had started to do in the last few months. Nausea rolled through me and faded. "Okay," I said. "Okay. I can do this." I wasn't convinced, but I also knew it was far too late to stop.

With surprisingly steady hands, I rewound the tape in the recorder, found the place where I'd last spoken and took up my narrative. I turned to the shoe, describing what I had discovered. Forcing myself to breathe deeply and slowly, I took digital photos and checked to see that all the shots so far were in focus. That the shoe measurements were clear, that the toe was visible in the tongue of the shoe. I added the length and depth of the toe to my recording, doing the job I had learned in the forensics and evidence-collection class. I pulled a Chain of Custody form out of the pile of my forensic supplies and filled it out, comparing the times with the time on the photos.

Carefully, still narrating, I curled the tongue back into the shoe and placed the shoe into a third evidence bag I labeled SMALL RED SHOE/TOE. I gathered up the plastic sheet and placed it into another bag. I placed all the evidence bags into a large plastic bag labeled EVIDENCE in big red letters.

I pulled my gloves off, one at a time, gripping the wristband of the left, pulling it down and inside out, over my fingers. Holding the left glove in the right fist, I pulled that one down over my fingers and over the other glove, securing it inside the right, to keep the evidence I had touched in place. The scent in place. They went into a final evidence bag with a separate Chain of Custody form. I switched off the tape recorder and repacked my forensic supplies, setting the final bag on the top of the truck.

Closing the SUV hatch with the evidence inside, I took the bagged gloves and COC with me into the house, then washed my hands thoroughly at the kitchen sink, carrying the last bit of evidence with me as I moved.

With Jas already gone for the morning, the house was empty and quiet. Her bowl, smeared with yogurt and blueberry cereal, was in the sink, filled with water, next to her glass. I wasn't interested in eating, though my daughter had left a box of Cheerios on the table with a clean bowl and spoon. My baby taking care of me, as she had since Jack had died, reminding me to eat.

The transition from child to caretaker had come early in Jas's life, forced on her by her daddy's death four years ago and my withdrawal into grief. I had spent the last two years letting her know I was fine now, but the habits learned in fear in the weeks after Jack's funeral had proved impossible to break. I touched the bowl, almost smiling, took a deep breath and let it out slowly, letting my fingers fall away. I breathed again. Stress management. Sure. That would work. I took a third breath and forced it out hard.

There were a lot of things I had to do. The first one was to stop and think clearly. Not an easy task after a twelve-hour shift that had included two gunshot victims from a gang-related shoot-out, a three-car pileup and a near-drowning. But there wasn't a hurry. No one was going to die if I paused and took the time to collect myself.

So I showered, slathered on sunscreen, dressed in jeans and tank top, then pulled one of my husband's old flannel shirts over it, letting the tail hang out. Riding clothes. Things I could wear all day, if needed. I paused once to sniff the fabric. I had washed the few things of Jack's I wanted before packing all the others off to friends and relatives. The shirt no longer smelled of him. I slipped on heavy socks and short-heeled western riding boots, found my hat, grabbed outdoor supplies and went back into the morning, feeling better now that I had decided what to do.

In the sunlight, still carrying the gloves, I made my way to the barn and checked on Johnny Ray to make sure he had done the chores. There were days when the stable hand was so far gone in the bottle that he never woke up, which had happened in a permanent way to his twin brother not so very long ago. Today Johnny Ray was sober, which could mean DTs tomorrow, but he was capable at the moment, and that was all that mattered. I had other constantly sober help, but Johnny had no place else to go. If I fired him, it would toss him down into total ruin faster. And when he was sober, he was an excellent stable hand. "Morning, Johnny Ray," I said. "Saddle Mabel for me, will you?" I asked, choosing an old Friesian Jack had purchased years ago.

"You're gonna ride?" he asked, surprised. "For *fun?*"

I hated to ride, so the question was legitimate. "Not for fun," I said.

Though huge enough to pull a fully loaded wagon or carry a knight wearing a suit of plate armor and weapons, Mabel was a placid mount and took easily to saddle and bit. She was too old for much work, but I needed her calm nature this morning. When he was done, I told Johnny Ray to lock the other dogs in the tack room with water and food and put a long leash on Cheeks. If he thought my orders peculiar, he didn't say, just moved from task to task with an unrelenting, steady pace. While he worked, I made the first call to law enforcement.

"Sheriff's Department."

"This is Ashlee Davenport and I'd—"

"Hi, Ash. How you doing?"

"Buzzy?"

"'At's me. Miss you at the hospital. Ain't been the same since you left and went to the big city to work. What can we do for you?"

"Thank you, Buzzy. I'm at the farm, and the dogs brought something to me this morning. A child's red sneaker with a part of a human foot inside."

Buzzy went dead quiet. As his silence lengthened, I walked from the barn, cell phone held close to my ear. Buzzy was a paramedic who worked part-time for 911 and in various dispatch jobs for law enforcement. One could call dispatch any time and stand a chance of having Buzzy answer the phone. "You hear me?" I asked.

"Yeah, I hear you. You joking? Something about this new forensic course you took?"

"No joke. I wish it was. I found it at 7:52. The shoe and evidence are in the back of my old SUV in evidence bags, timed and dated, with audio description and a Chain of Custody."

"You got a shoe with part of a foot. No body?"

"Not with me, no," I said, managing to sound wry and jaded instead of near tears. "But I have a couple ideas where it might be."

"How…? Never mind." I could almost see Buzzy scratching his head as he pondered how to investigate and interrogate a toe. "I'll get an investigator out your way ASAP. And maybe a crime-scene crew?" He was still perplexed. I'd had longer than him to figure out what came next and understood that I didn't have a crime scene. All I had was a toe.

"Dogs, Buzzy. The canine team. To find the body. I've got four hundred acres here. There are farms on the east and the south, and an illegal garbage dump nearby. Not to mention I-77 close by, where a body could be tossed."

"K-9's up near Ford County helping track a suspect

of a bank CEO shooting and aborted robbery. But I can send a crime-scene team out."

I sighed. "Buzzy, I'm going to look for the body. I've got one of the Ethridge boys' old tracker hound dogs—it's done work for the K-9 unit—and we'll be heading west from the barn. Cheeks has worked with horses before, so I'll be on horseback. I've got my cell phone with me."

"Why west?"

"Sycamore leaf," I said. "There was a sycamore leaf in the laces." I hadn't even thought about my reasons for heading west until he asked and I paused, surprised. "I don't have many sycamore trees on the property, but there's a small stand of about four…. Just head west from the barn, Buzzy. And have your crime-scene crew take the shoe in the evidence bag and the voice tape in the back of my truck. I'll provide digital photos later."

"Gotcha. Cavalry's on the way."

Snapping the phone shut, I stuffed it in a pocket. Clicking to Mabel and Cheeks, I took up reins and leash. Together, we ambled to my truck where I removed the tote of forensic supplies, added in bottled water, a compass, sunscreen and a box of Fig Newtons, and looped the bag over the saddle horn.

Satisfied that I had what I needed and that the old dog would stay out from underfoot properly, I looked up at the saddle—up and up. My stomach fluttered at the thought of sitting up there with all that power beneath me. I braced myself. I could wait here like a good little girl and let the cops handle it. I could never get up on that horse and never go scouting to find the rest of the little girl. I could be a coward. Or I could do what needed to be done.

Wrapping the long leash around the saddle horn, I accepted Johnny Ray's hand to mount the huge horse. I threw my leg over the saddle and paused, waiting until my stomach settled. I had been raised on a farm and lived for years with horses, but I had only recently learned to ride. I still didn't like the height from the ground, and Mabel stood over eighteen hands high at the shoulder. Maybe I should have taken a smaller, less tranquil horse. Too late now. Bending, I held the glove in its open evidence bag down to Cheeks. "Find!"

Cheeks stood up on his hind legs, balancing, and sniffed the gloves. The scent of vinyl was strong, a source of confusion to the dog and he looked up at me dolefully. "Find," I said again, and again Cheeks dutifully sniffed before dropping back to all fours with a pained grunt. I led him to the back of the SUV and out a ways, moving west. Again, I held the gloves out to the hound and commanded him to find.

The dog had been retired for two years, accepting a home on the farm because he could no longer keep up with younger dogs working as trackers. He was as old as dirt; he had an arthritic hip and his nose wasn't the best anymore. But in his prime, Cheeks, named after his long, drooping facial skin, had been one of the best, and he hadn't forgotten how to find a scent. Jowls dragging the ground, he put his nose down and walked in a large circle, sniffing. I turned Mabel as Cheeks circled once, twice, in a widening pattern. After a moment, he paused, his tail held erect, the ruff on his shoulders standing slightly stiff. "Yeah. Good dog," I said. "Find."

With a satisfied woof, Cheeks headed west, toward the stand of trees I had unconsciously thought of as soon as I'd seen the sycamore leaf twisted in the laces of the small red sneaker.

2

I held on to the saddle horn as Cheeks walked west, the reins twisted in my right hand. The saddle was an old western cutting saddle Jas had found at a sale when she'd started badgering me to learn to ride. The high cantle held my hips securely, the horn keeping me upright and in place when I wanted to slide left or right. I had never really understood how riders managed to stay on a flat English saddle. I was graceless on my own two feet, and any sense of balance I had on the ground was lost when perched up high. If I could have convinced someone to tie me in place on horseback, I'd have done it.

Cheeks pulled hard against the leash in a straight line west until we were over the first low hill, and then he seemed to have a problem. He moved left and right and back again, ignoring the hooves of the huge horse, so intent on his task that Mabel snorted and stomped in warning. "Easy, girl." I pulled back on the reins, bringing Mabel to a halt. With my other hand, I gave Cheeks more leash, the dog's movements pulling the nylon cord from the reel with a whirring sound.

The old dog was excited, moving left and right,

around and back. I could envision the other dogs playing with the shoe, tossing it high and catching it, a game of tag and fetch all at once. Cheeks stopped, his haunches quivering, his nose buried in the tall grass. I knew what I'd find. More parts of the little girl.

Unexpected tears filled my eyes. Some mother and father's special little girl… Using Jack's cuff on my wrist, I dashed the tears away and tried to figure out what to do next.

I hadn't considered what might happen if I needed to dismount. Blowing out a breath, I said, "Well, this is peachy." Having no choice, I shifted my weight to my left leg, swung my right over the mare's back and dropped down—and down—to the ground, where I landed hard. Mabel looked back over her shoulder with placid eyes, her thick black lips moving as she chewed on her bit. "Now what?" I asked the horse. Mabel sighed, her huge barrel chest expanding and contracting. Mabel clearly had no suggestions.

Cheeks looked up from the grass, his woeful eyes on me, wanting me to come see what he had found. I couldn't figure out how to get to him and still keep the horse with me, too. Bad planning. "Some forensic nurse I'll be," I muttered. "Two hundred yards from the barn and I'm already useless." Mabel dropped her head and chomped at the long grass. "How about you staying here awhile? Okay?" The huge black horse ignored me, munching on. With no choice, I dropped the reins, lifted the forensic tote off the horn and moved to Cheeks.

In the eight-inch-high grass, liberally coated with Cheeks's drool, was a second toe. The digit was blackened, the toenail half off, its iridescent blue polish shining in the morning sun. Fighting tears, I took photos and marked the site with the spray can of garish orange paint in my bag, making a two-foot ring on the grass. I should leave the toe in situ for the crime team, but I worried a scavenger might make off with it. I added the toe to an evidence bag, labeling this one TOE 2, WEST FORTY PASTURE, with the date and time, and dropped it into my tote. I didn't have a GPS device, so crime scene would have to document the exact location by the orange spray paint.

I called Cheeks to me and flopped on the ground beside him, giving him a thorough scrub along the ears and neck. "Good dog," I said, my voice thick with misery. "Yes, you are. Good, *good* dog." I cleared my throat and forced my shoulders to relax, talking to the dog for the comfort it gave me. "Those stupid men didn't know what they gave up when they put you out to pasture, did they, Cheeks? Yes, Cheeks is a good dog." I was supposed to give a tracker a treat when he was successful, but I had forgotten to bring dog treats. Cheeks didn't seem to mind, pleased with the praise I heaped on him until I felt able to stand again.

Mabel looked at me and seemed to smile when I hooked the tote back over the horn and tried to lift a foot to the stirrup. I was several inches from success. Mabel's shoulder was a full six feet from the ground. I stood five feet four. In shoes. And I wasn't as limber as I used to be.

Leading the mare to an old fence post, I hooked Cheeks's leash to the post and pulled Mabel around. She kept going; around and around. "You think this is funny, don't you?" I said as I tried to position her for mounting. Cheeks sat and watched, his canine grin only egging Mabel on, I was sure of it. I climbed down off the post and tried again to get her into position, then climbed back up the cedar post. Mabel moved again, stopping just out of reach, her eyes on me over her shoulder.

I laughed, the sound shaky. Cheeks woofed happily at my tone. And suddenly I was okay again, or okay as one got when carrying a child's toe in a bag. "Let's try this again," I said to Mabel, making my voice more commanding and less imploring.

When I got the Friesian to pause long enough for me to throw a leg over her back, I slung my body up and landed half in the saddle. Mabel was moving again, around in circles. By the time I got both feet settled in the stirrups, she had circled away from Cheeks, who sat panting in the rising warmth, but I had done it. I had retrieved evidence that might have been destroyed by rodents or birds, and gotten back on the mare.

Taking control of the situation and the reins, I retrieved Cheeks's leash and ordered him once again to find. An hour later, after a meandering traipse through the west forty and onto fallow land, the old hound stopped near a creek and lapped at the water, as did Mabel. In horse and dog years, they were both in their seventies, content to be working as long as they didn't have to move fast and there was plenty of water and liniment at day's end.

The sycamores were just ahead, pale green leaves and curling bark and spinning seeds just released from the stems. It was spring, and everything was sprouting out green. As if he sensed that the day's work was nearly done, Cheeks pulled on the leash and headed directly to the trees. The earth beneath the stand was stripped of growth, windswept, the center tree ancient, bigger around than I could reach, its bark curled and hanging loose from the trunk like pages of a book.

There were no toes on the bare ground. There was no sign of a body under the copse of sycamores. But there was a strong, musky odor, skunk-like, rank and bitter. Cheeks lost the scent.

Enough time had passed that I thought the Crime Scene team had probably arrived at the farm, so I tied off dog and horse under the trees and checked the cell phone. There were four bars of reception this close to the I-77 corridor, and I called the barn number. The phone had a loud outside bell with a distinctive chime and Johnny Ray picked up on the fourth ring.

"Davenport Downs," he said. I could tell he had started drinking and I wasn't really surprised. Johnny Ray didn't much like cops. The thought of law enforcement on the premises would drive him to the bottle.

"Johnny Ray, are the cops there yet?"

"They're here," he said sourly.

"Let me talk to the officer in charge."

"It's your boyfriend."

"I'm sorry?"

"Your boyfriend. The FBI agent. He's done took over. And let me tell you, the sheriff's stomping around, cussing under his breath. He's mad as a dead hen."

"Wet hen."

"Huh?"

I shook my head in frustration. "Let me talk to Jim." A moment later I heard his voice in the background as Jim directed the unloading of some sort of equipment. Closer, directly into the old black receiver, he said, "Ramsey."

I felt an unreasoning sense of relief at the single word, as if someone had given me a hug and told me he would take care of me and any problem I might have. That was a feeling that didn't last. "Hi. I'm glad you're—"

"Ash? What the hell do you mean, taking off and ruining a crime scene. Damn it, don't you know how hard it's going to be find this body?"

"You have dogs?"

"Do what?" Jim said.

"Dogs. Do—you—have—tracker dogs?" I said it sweetly, so sweetly my mama couldn't have sounded more sugary. Jim Ramsey knew what I sounded like when I was ticked off. About like I did now. "You know, to find this body? Or does the FBI have another way to locate a body in the rough? Like, oh, I don't know, psychics?" When Jim didn't answer, I said, "No. You don't have any dogs. Because the dogs are up near Ford County. But I have one of the best tracker dogs in the state on my farm and he's managed to follow the trail to the edge of my property. And he found another toe while he was at it. The site is marked clearly with bright orange paint."

Jim sighed. "I'm acting like an ass, aren't I?"

"Yes, you are," I said pleasantly.

He chuckled. "I'm sorry. I have a good reason." His

voice lowered. "Guess what local is running this gig, because the county investigators are up at the bank thing in Ford County. Sheriff C. C. Gaskins, himself."

"Johnny Ray told me. Gaskins is a bona fide male chauvinist pig, but you didn't hear it from me. It's been years since the sheriff had to do fieldwork."

"And it shows, but you didn't hear it from me. Couple deaf folks talking on cell phones. Head west, huh?"

"Yes, and while you're at it, I'll try to get Cheeks to find the scent again. We ran into polecat scent and his sniffer shut down."

"Polecat..."

"Oh, yeah," I grinned into the morning light, knowing Jim would hear the laughter in my voice, "and it's quite, ummm, potent. Hope you brought overalls and boots to put over your fancy FBI suit and tie. It's aromatic and a mite damp out in the west forty."

"Well, hell."

"Yep. I reckon that says it all fairly well. Bring some Tylenol and Benadryl, will you? I've been up too long, the glare is giving me a headache, and the dog is going to be sore from the exercise."

"Will do. On the way."

It was only after I cut the connection that I wondered why Jim was on the farm. What was the FBI's agent coordinator of the Violent Crime Squad, from the Columbia field office, doing answering a call about a red shoe and two toes? On first glance, I would have assumed that someone in local law enforcement, probably C.C. himself, had called him in. FBI worked only on cases at the behest of local law, unless there was a task force already in place. Yet Johnny Ray had said C.C. was unhappy at Ramsey's presence. Interesting.

I drank bottled water and shared the Fig Newtons with Cheeks, munching as I thought about the implications of a task force that had something to do with the red sneaker. There had been nothing in the local *Dawkins Herald* or the Ford County paper about a special task force. I only read *The State* newspaper on weekends, but there had been nothing there either.

Placing the food and water back into the tote, I studied the surrounding countryside. The farm was a bucolic setting in a rural county, though only half an hour from Columbia, the state capital, a sprawling city with big-city problems and big-city prices. Long, low rolling hills stretched out before me, pasture for Davenport Downs's horse stock and acres sown with hay, alfalfa, soy beans. A few strategic acres were planted with mold-resistant sweet basil, parsley and other herbs, tomatoes, summer squash and zucchini. Most were only half-sprouted this early in the year. The smell of fresh-turned earth, pollen, horse and polecat; the sounds of birdsong; the far-off roar of a tractor carried on the wind—all were part of Chadwick Farms, my family home.

I didn't like the conclusions I was drawing about what a task force might mean when combined with this isolated location and a kid's shoe. A hidden grave, perhaps tied in with other graves. But I couldn't seem to stop putting two and three and maybe forty-six together and coming up with… This was bad. This was very, very bad.

"Cheeks. Come," I said, reeling the old dog in. "We have work to do." I bent and searched the hound's rheumy eyes. "Have you had enough time to get that polecat scent out of your nose yet?"

Cheeks looked back at me with his usual mournful expression.

"Let's give it a try." Leaving Mabel tied by her halter in the cool beneath the sycamore trees, her saddle loosened, her bridle pulled from her mouth and draped across her neck, I shouldered the evidence bag and held the sneaker-scented gloves out to Cheeks. He sniffed, black nostrils fluttering slowly. He looked up at me, his lower lids drooping, showing red rims. He sniffed twice more, securing the scent in his memory. "Find."

Cheeks meandered out into the pasture and circled back. Out and back. I let him sniff again, trying not to encourage him in any particular direction. Again he moved out, nose to the ground, lifted, back to the ground. Around and around in an ever-widening circle.

Some hounds are air dogs, meaning they are so sensitive they can pick up a scent left on the air, carried on the breeze. Cheeks was a ground hound. Not a cadaver dog, either, one trained to find only dead bodies. But he'd searched for a little of everything in his years in law enforcement and I hoped he'd be able to find the scent again. Ten minutes of wandering away from the sycamores, he succeeded. His ruff bristled, his tail went tall and stiff and he pulled hard on the leash, his nose puffing at the earth.

On foot, we crossed the pasture, a field of hay to my left, fenced pasture to the right, separated by the grassy verge between. Cheeks's nose followed a convoluted path. On the other side of the field, we entered a darker, cooler place, earth-brown and loamy, mixed trees, oak, maple, scrub cedar, swamp hickory, tulip poplar with its yellow blooms still turned toward the April sun.

Cheeks pulled me left into a slight depression and the earth changed beneath my feet, turning pale and sandy, the remains of the ancient river that once had flowed through the state and now was no more. I remembered the grit that fell out of the laces and the curled toe of the shoe. There had been yellow-white sand in the mix. No red mud, no yellow tallow—a poorly draining clay-like soil, which would be typical of the area—but grit and pale sand. I had recognized it but not placed it, not consciously, yet I had known that Cheeks would head in this direction when he found the scent again. Because of the sand.

My breath came harsh and fast as the old dog's pace increased. "Good boy, Cheeks," I muttered, stumbling along behind him. "Good old dog."

He pulled me down a dip, past a lichen-covered grouping of boulders cluttered with rain-collected debris from a recent storm. Back up over a freshly downed tree, its bark ripped through by lightning, its spring leaves withered.

We were surely near the edge of Chadwick Farms property by now, over near the original Chadwick homestead, close to the old Hilldale place. I could see open land through the trees off to one side and the tractor I had heard earlier sounded louder. Cheeks sped up again, his gait uneven as his degenerating hips fought the pace, and I broke into a sweat.

And then I smelled it. The smell of old death.

I reeled the leash back short, keeping Cheeks just ahead. The hair on his shoulders lifted higher and his breathing sped up, making little huffs of sound. His nose skimmed along the sandy soil. The old dog put off a strong scent of his own in his excitement.

Rounding two old oaks, Cheeks quivered and stopped. He had found a scrap of cloth, his nose was planted in it. Just beyond was a patch of disturbed soil, the fresh sand bright all around, darkened in the center. More cloth protruded from the darkened space.

"Oh, Jesus," I whispered, pulling back on Cheeks to keep him close. "Oh, Jesus." It was a prayer, the kind one says when there aren't any real words, just horror and fear. Cheeks lunged toward the darkened spot in the sand, jerking me hard.

"No!" I gripped the leash fiercely and pulled Cheeks away, back beyond the two oaks. With their protection between me and the grave, I stopped. Legs quivering, I dropped to the sand and clutched the old dog close. I was crying, tears scudding down my face. "Someone's little girl. Someone's little girl. Oh, Jesus."

Cheeks thrust his muzzle into my face, a high-pitched sound coming from deep in his throat, hurt and confused. I'd said no when he'd done what I wanted. Shouted when he had found what he'd been told to find.

"I'm sorry, Cheeks." I lay my head against his face and he licked my tears once, his huge tongue slathering my cheek into my hairline. My arms went around him, my body shaking with shock, fingers and feet numb. "Good Cheeks. Good old boy. You're a hero, yes you are. Sweet dog. Sweet Cheeks."

I laughed, the sound shuddering. "Sweet Cheeks. Jas would tease me all week if she heard me call you that. But you are. A sweet, sweet dog."

The hound stopped whining and lay beside me, his front legs across my thigh. The pungent effluvium of tired dog and death wrapped around me. The quiet of the woods enveloped me. I breathed deeply, letting the calm of the place find me and take hold, not thinking about the death only feet away.

After long minutes, the tingling in my hands and feet that indicated hyperventilation eased and I stood. I checked my compass, dug out the spray can of orange paint and marked both trees with two big *X*s.

"Okay, Cheeks. I hope you can get me back to Mabel. Home," I commanded. "Let's go home." When Cheeks looked up at me with no comprehension at all, I held my jeans-clad leg to him so he could sniff the horse and said, "Find. Find." He was a smart dog, and without a single false start led me back along the sandy riverbed. With the bright paint, I marked each turn and boulder and tree on the path, back into the sunlight and the pasture.

3

I shared more Fig Newtons with Cheeks—not the best food for a dog, but not the worst, either—took the animals to the creek for water, and used the quiet time to compose myself before moving horse and dog to the edge of the woods near the sandy depression. Once there, Cheeks and Mabel and I remained in the shade of the trees and waited for law enforcement.

Cheeks had developed a bad limp and wouldn't make it back to the barn on his own four feet. His medication was in the kitchen, too far away to do him any good, and I could tell he was in pain. Not much of a reward for a job well done. "There's a price to be paid for every good deed, sweet Cheeks," I said, stroking the hound. "You find a body, you get aching joints. And I'll bet you the cops are going to be mad at us for finding the body in the first place."

Cheeks just panted in the rising warmth, his huge tongue hanging out one side of his mouth. In the distance, I heard the unmistakable sound of engines. Standing, I tied the dog off near Mabel and waited at the edge of sunlight.

Johnny Ray led the way along the fence that marked

the pasture, driving his old truck, a seventies-something battered Ford pickup that he couldn't seem to kill, though the motor sounded like a sewing machine that was missing a beat, and the paint was rusted and dulled out to a weary, piebald brown. Behind him came unfamiliar vehicles, a white county van, two four-wheeled all-terrain vehicles, a sport utility vehicle. For the most part, they stayed off the crops and on the verge of mown grass, but Nana would lose some hay. I figured she would have a few words to say to C.C. about that, words he wouldn't like, and that would force him to apologize, at the very least.

The vehicles pulled up near the trees and killed the engines, pollen and dust swirling around us all. Special Agent Jim Ramsey unfolded himself from Johnny Ray's pickup, wearing that distinct air of the FBI, suit pants and a heavily starched white dress shirt that glared in the sunlight. We were dating. Sort of. As much as I would let us. Jim was divorced, with a young daughter I hadn't met yet. I liked Jim a lot, far more than I admitted, but he was nearly nine years younger than I. It was the age difference that I was having trouble with.

The sheriff, Johnny Ray and five cops, some in uniform, followed Ramsey from various vehicles. All were men except for one of the crime-scene techs, and I nodded to Skye McNeely, who waved back, holding up a box of Benadryl. She was my height, plump from motherhood, and newly married to the father of her child. I knew most the other cops from the rescue squad, where I volunteered. "Thanks," I said, catching the box Skye tossed.

"Ashlee," Sheriff Gaskins called, swiping an arm over his sweaty forehead. His pale skin gleamed in the bright sun, and sweat already stained the western-style suit coat he removed and tossed into the van. "The crime-scene guys say you did a good job with the shoe. Very thorough. Listen, thanks for getting us this far."

"Welcome," I said, watching the cops stack equipment and bags of fast-food breakfast. The smell of bacon and eggs made me salivate.

"That the tracker dog?" Ramsey asked.

I glanced at the animals and found Cheeks standing, straining at his leash, tail wagging. I realized he might know some of the cops, too.

"I know Cheeks," Gaskins said. "Best tracker in the state at one time. Caught those bank robbers on motorcycles back in ninety-seven. Tracked them twenty miles to their homes."

"That's Cheeks. He's still got a nose, but his hips are going," I said.

I took two small pink and clear capsules back to my pack and buried them in the center of a Fig Newton. "Here you go, boy." Cheeks took the treat instantly. Benadryl was an old veterinarian's trick. It worked to combat all sorts of problems in older dogs and they could take it every day without upsetting their digestion. The dog rubbed his jowls up and down my leg in thanks and I gently smoothed the length of his ears. He sighed in ecstasy, a trail of drool landing on my boot. I'd reek by day's end.

"Okay, people, we need to spread out, get as much work done as possible until the investigators get back from the bank scene," Gaskins said behind me. I hid a smile at his officious tone. C. C. Gaskins was the highest elected law enforcement official in the county, but, while a trained investigator, he didn't usually handle fieldwork. It was very likely that this was his first independent investigation in years. And he had an FBI guy watching.

"We'll make a grid," he continued, "and when the rest of the crew get here, we'll go over it foot by foot until we find the body or rule out its presence."

"It's here." I stood straight and walked back to the group of cops.

"Woman's intuition is a wonderful thing, Ashlee," C.C. said, his tone gently patronizing as he spread out a map of the county on the hood of Johnny Ray's pickup, "but we need more to go on."

I stood as tall as God had made me and put my hands on my hips. "Woman's intuition?" I repeated. "I beg your pardon?"

"We need to go about this search in an approved manner until the dogs get here, Ash. That way we don't mess up the crime scene. Not that we don't appreciate all the help you've been to this point." He turned his back to me in the sharp silence and concentrated on his map.

"So I can take myself home and knit awhile?" I asked softly. "Maybe bake cookies?"

Skye snickered before she caught herself and the back of C.C.'s neck burned a bright red. Johnny Ray's eyes grew big and he hitched up his jeans, disappearing behind his truck. Ramsey glanced curiously at me.

I turned into my mother, God help us all. "I don't

think so. You see, C.C., I've had a course in the approved method of evidence collection and preservation, so I don't think I'll be messing up anyone's crime scene." I turned big, innocent eyes to the cops. "But *if* I were using woman's intuition, I'd say the body is *thatta* way—" I pointed "—about a half mile into the woods, the path clearly marked with bright orange paint."

C.C. shoved his cowboy hat back on his head and turned slowly from his map to me. He wasn't happy. "I don't think you're—"

"Cheeks found the body," I clarified sweetly. Skye glanced between us, then busied herself at the passenger seat and a big denim bag planted there. The other cops were promptly busy as well. Ramsey crossed his arms over his chest, cocked out a hip and watched me a little too closely for my comfort level, but I was mad. I hadn't been anyone's easy-to-dismiss little woman in four years and wasn't about to start now.

"You took a dog to the body?" C.C. growled.

I smiled with all the force a Southern woman can offer such a simple act. "C.C., how is Erma Jean?" It was a polite way of telling a grown man that you know his mother and if he kept talking like a fool, she'd hear about it sooner than later. "She and my nana are on that county homeless-shelter committee together."

C.C. cleared his throat and repositioned his cowboy hat yet again. Probably to keep the steam rising off his bald pate from curling the brim. My grandmother was a big contributor to local political campaigns. So was I. He wanted to shout at me, but there were witnesses. After a moment, C.C. said, "Well, I reckon we got ourselves a crime scene, boys and girls. Miz Davenport, would you please be so kind as to guide us in?"

There were a lot of other things I would rather have done than return to the wooded grave, but my hackles were up and I wasn't about to head home now. "I'd be happy to, Sheriff."

Raising my voice, I called, "Johnny Ray?" The stable hand lifted his head so only his cowboy hat and his eyes showed above the back of his pickup bed. "I want you to ride Mabel to the barn, see that Elwyn rubs her down with that liniment Nana made up, wraps her legs, and gives her some TLC. You can leave your truck here and when the other cops get to the farm, ride back with them to show them the way. Then drive your truck to the barn and take Cheeks with you."

"Yes, ma'am, Miz Ash."

I wasn't sure Johnny Ray'd remember all that, so just in case he was a long time returning, I took the Tylenol and gave Cheeks the last of the water from my bottle. "Me and my big mouth," I muttered to the hound. Cheeks rolled his eyes up to me in sympathy. Johnny Ray set the bit back in Mabel's huge mouth, adjusted bit and bridle, gathered the reins and climbed into the saddle, sending Mabel's huge hooves into a slow, stationary patter. Mabel didn't like men, but she tolerated Johnny Ray well enough.

"Effective technique. Exactly who were you channeling just now?"

I closed my eyes hard for a moment and took a deep breath before turning to face Jim. "My mother. Josephine Hamilton Caldwell. She's a debutante socialite in Charlotte."

"A *what?*"

"Well, she's a socialite who thinks she's still a deb. Josephine is sixty-something going on sixteen, with a mouth so sweet, candy won't melt in it."

"And she's why you get sugary as rock candy when you're pissed off?" He was laughing at me, staring down from his nearly six feet in height, brown eyes glinting.

"As a technique for getting my way, it seemed just as effective as grabbing the sheriff by his privates and has fewer side effects than violence. Being Mama has never resulted in a lawsuit or my being arrested. At least, not so far."

Jim barked with laughter, the sound startling Mabel, who jerked up her head and blew hard. She wasn't happy about the stable hand being on her back and was looking for a reason to startle or kick. "Be good, Mabel," I said. The mare flattened her ears and looked around at the human planted on her back, as if pondering how much effort it might take to dislodge him.

"I said, *be good.*" She rolled her eyes at me and seemed to consider my command. With a grunt, the mare lifted her tail and dropped an aromatic load, seven distinct plops before she moved away, into the sunlight, and headed toward the barn. The cops found it funny, but I knew when I'd been dissed. "Thank you, Mabel," I muttered. But at least she did as she was told.

"You want to tell me about the land around here?" Jim asked, controlling his laughter admirably as we walked deeper into the shaded wood.

"The better part of valor?" I asked.

"Retreat isn't a cowardly action. Not when dealing with a woman who can channel her mother."

I decided I should let that one go and moved with Jim to the first orange paint mark, set waist-high on a poplar. Behind us, the cops shouldered equipment and followed. One cop complained about having to walk when there was a perfectly good four-by-four right there. C.C. handled that one, growling that the deputy needed some exercise and if he didn't take off a pound or two, he'd be out of a job.

I didn't know what Jim was asking about, so I decided on a tutorial. "We're at the edge of Chadwick Farms, heading toward the eighty acres, give or take a few, of Hilldale Hills. The property between the farms is partial wetland, marked by a sandy riverbed left over from the Pleistocene Age, I think. Anyway, the Chadwicks haven't farmed this area in decades and the Hills acres were left to go fallow for ten years."

"Why?"

I told Jim that Hoddermier Hilldale had lain fallow himself in a nursing home, the victim of a stroke that had left him in a vegetative state. His son lived in New York and was less than interested in being a farmer. "Hoddy died in early winter," I said, "about sixteen months ago. The son, Hoddy Jr., came home and leased out most of the acreage to my nana, who bush-hogged it and put it into half a dozen crops. Hoddy Jr.'s in the middle of investing heavily in the house, out-buildings and grounds as part of a bed-and-breakfast-slash-spa he and his gentleman friend think they can make a go of. Why do you want to know?"

Instead of answering, Jim asked, "Any graveyards nearby?"

It wasn't an idle question. The man who walked beside me had morphed into a cop as I spoke, his face unyielding, warm eyes gone flat.

"Graveyards? I'm not… Wait a minute." I stopped and turned slowly, looking up the old riverbed and back down, orienting myself. "I wasn't thinking about where I am, but yes. This land's been a family farm since the 1700s. The first Chadwick settled here because of the access to creeks and several spring-heads. When the original cabin burned down, the family moved closer to where Nana's house is now. Somewhere near here are the old foundations and a small family plot. Why?"

Jim glanced back at C.C. and the men nodded fractionally. The cops seemed abruptly tense, as if I had said something important, but I had no idea what part of my soliloquy it might have been. Why would my family plot make them react? I pointed off to the left and jumped over a ditch, leading the crew to the next mark, this one on a low boulder buried in the earth. "What's up, Jim? Why are you here?" I asked softly.

"The sheriff asked me in on this."

"And?"

He seemed to consider what he wanted to say. "The red sneaker."

"You've got a missing child, one who was wearing red sneakers?"

"Something like that."

I figured that was all I was going to get from him so I just pointed to the next marker, but Jim surprised me. "You might remember that Amber Alert in Columbia last September?" When I shook my head no, he went on. "We've had four preteen blond girls go missing in Columbia in the last twenty-four months. The girl in September was one of them. Blond. Wearing red sneakers."

Which explained why the coordinator of the Violent Crime Squad was traipsing through the countryside with mud on his polished black shoes. The air in the shadowed woods grew colder as I again considered what a body buried here might mean. "Why are you looking for a graveyard?"

"We found one of the missing girls in December, buried in a Civil War-era graveyard. So I was just curious," he said as we rounded the pile of lichen-covered boulders.

"Putting together a profile," I guessed.

"We're working on it." His voice lost inflection. Cop voice, giving away nothing.

"But keeping it out of the media," I suggested.

"Not so much keeping it out as not sure whether we have a serial thing going here. Other than the general hair coloration and age, the missing girls have nothing in common."

"I was trying to stay away from the evidence. I didn't get up close to the burial site so I'm not sure if it's near the old homestead. I looked one time and backed away. But it may be. And if so, we'll see a family burial plot, gravestones lying on the ground where they were washed by a big storm before I was born."

We moved the rest of the way in silence, the birds

flitting through the trees as we walked, chasing one another in spring courtship, preparing for nesting time, an occasional squirrel making a leap from tree to tree. A hawk circled overhead in lazy spirals, searching for prey.

Not far beyond the fallen tree, its bark ripped away by lightning, we caught the smell of old death carried on the breeze. It had been bad before, but with the rising heat, the putrid scent had grown fetid and pungent. One of the cops swore, and I had to agree.

4

I stayed behind the two old oaks when we arrived; Jim stood at the edge of the grave site only a few feet away, hands on his hips while cops ran crime-scene tape from tree to tree at the sheriff's direction. Though the scene was far from pristine, Jim obviously wasn't going to add tracks or evidence to it until the photos were finished. Skye and Steven, another deputy, set up cameras and began to take digital and 35mm shots. Steven was giant, an African American with a shaved head and biceps as big as my thighs. Well, *almost* as big as my thighs.

"Ramsey?" Skye said almost instantly. "Headstones. I count three, lying flat."

"Where?" he demanded.

"With this marker as six, we got one at two o'clock, one between ten and eleven, and a broken stone that looks as if it's been moved recently at five and eight."

I looked where she pointed, my gut tightening.

"Got it. Keep your eyes open for any other signs of grave markers," Jim said. "Ash says this is nearly three hundred years old. A plot like this might have some uncarved markers, too, or some carved stone that's so old it's not easily recognizable as a grave marker."

She nodded and began removing equipment from the cases they had toted in.

After the shots, Skye passed out protective clothing, paper shoes and coats that shed no fibers. Then she handed out gloves, evidence bags, small cans of orange paint, a one-hundred-foot tape measure for marking a grid and string to run from one spot to another, indicating straight lines. Together, working like a precision team, she and Steven measured the circumference and diameter of the space between the trees, marking off specific intervals around the vaguely circular area. They mapped it out on a pad, creating a visual grid to prevent the crime-scene guys from tripping, adding measurements and other indicators. Skye took more photographs while Steven recorded the dimensions into a tape recorder and on a separate spiral pad.

I had seen cops mark a grid on television using spray paint, and in class we had been lectured extensively on the proper way to handle a scene, but I had never seen one detailed in person. It was very clean and geometrical. I noticed that Skye and Steven walked carefully, studying the ground before putting down a bootie-clad foot. They avoided the center of the area, where clothing peeked from the makeshift grave. The *alleged* makeshift grave.

I knew that, until they saw human remains, it would be only a suspected grave. All this effort and we didn't even know for certain if there was a body or if it was human. The toe could have come from somewhere else. This grave could be a dog, buried in a pile of rags. Not a child. It could be anything. I wanted it to be anything, anything but a little girl.

All the cops seemed to have a job except the sheriff. Gaskins stood back and looked important. Jim was out in the trees, walking a course around the site in a spiral, marking things on the ground with painted circles. A quiet hour passed during which I found I could disassociate myself from the meaning of the scene and watch. Perhaps that was part of my nursing training, being able to put away normal human feelings and simply do a job. The cops moved in slow, studied precision, touching nothing, recording everything on the detailed evidence map that would be one result of today.

Into the silence that followed I said, "Cheeks buried his face in that strip of cloth right there. There'll be drool and hair on it. And I think my other two dogs—" I paused, breathless as the meaning of my words slammed into me. I licked lips that felt dry and cracked. "I think they actually dug up the body and rolled in it. You'll want to take samples from each dog, I'm sure." The cops were looking at me. I thought I might throw up. I pressed my hand to my stomach. "Johnny Ray has Big Dog and Cherry both locked up in the barn."

The cops went back to work without a word. Gaskins called in my information to one of the investigators driving in from Ford County and told him to take care of the dog samples before coming out to the site. No one said anything much after that.

The preliminaries over, Jim donned fresh gloves and booties and tossed several evidence bags into a larger bag he marked with black ink. With the digital camera slung over his shoulder on its long back cord, he followed a straight line he referred to as CLEAR. Walking slowly from the two oaks into the center of the small clearing, back hunched, eyes on the ground, he marked evidence as he moved but left each item in place, a paper bag beside it. When he reached the scrap of cloth that Cheeks had drooled on, Jim looked up at me with a question on his face and I nodded. "That's the one."

He photographed the scrap of cloth where it lay and took another shot in relation to the total scene. "Document contaminant information," he said to Steven, "with the year, case number and item."

"Got it," Steven said.

Jim marked the photo with the same numbers and continued his slow methodical pace to the center of the circle. Taking several shots, he backed out the same way he'd gone in, and handed the photos and camera off to Skye. "You the acting coroner today, too?"

"I have that pleasure," she said, her tone belying the words. It was common in poor counties for law-enforcement officers to be trained in several different fields. Skye was a trained crime-scene investigator and also worked as part-time county coroner. She moved closer to the edge of the clearing. "What do we have?"

"Protruding from sandy-type soil, I see part of a small skull," Jim said, "presumptive human, part of what looks like a femur and lower leg bones, and clothing."

· "Ah, hell," Steven said.

Skye's expression didn't change. Stone-faced, she stepped to the denim bag I had noticed earlier on the passenger seat of the county van and removed a folder marked Blank Coroner Forms. "Could it be from the 1700s?" she asked.

"No," Jim said. "Connective tissue is still in place. In this kind of soil, well draining but under a canopy of trees, I'd guess it's not more than a year old."

Something turned over in my belly, a slow, sickening somersault of horror. Silently, I walked away, along the length of the old riverbed, back out of the shadows. When I reached the pile of boulders, a single shaft of noontime sunlight found a way past the foliage, falling on the topmost stone. Without thinking, I climbed up the pile, pushing off with booted feet against the slick rock until I was perched on top, my arms wrapped around my knees.

There was a body buried in the woods near my house. The body of a child, taken by someone intent on evil and buried in the shadows, alone and isolated. I had discovered it.... Most likely a little girl. I had discovered *her*.

My family would be questioned by the police, possibly by the FBI. My house and grounds would be overrun by cops. And I had nothing to tell them that would explain how the body had ended up on Chadwick Farms property. Nothing to tell the parents, if I ever met them. Nothing to tell her family or mine.

I was trained to gather forensic evidence but my forte was nursing, gathering evidence on living human bodies, evidence that police would need in later investigations and trials. Such evidence was often lost during medical procedures, especially during emergency medical treatment where dousing the victim with warmed saline or Betadine scrub washed away vital clues to the perpetrator, and cleaning skin for IV sites, bandages, or application of fingertip epidermal monitors hid defensive wounds and damage—evidence that should have been preserved for standard and genetic testing.

I wasn't trained to work a crime scene where the victim was dead.

A child. Dead in my ancestors' family plot. And my dogs had surely rolled in her grave. I put my head on my knees and cried, trying to keep my sobs silent. An early mosquito was attracted to my position and I killed it as it punctured the back of my hand for a blood meal. A squirrel chittered at me from a low branch. Long, painful minutes passed. Finally, I took a deep breath.

I heard the sound of vehicles and voices in the distance and knew that the other investigators had arrived. Sheriff Gaskins had been keeping in touch with the men and they would know already that there was a body. They didn't need help to follow the trail, and I didn't especially want to be caught sitting on top of a pile of big rocks crying my eyes out, so I wiped my face, slid back to the ground and returned to the site.

Jim met me partway, his eyes tired, face drawn, his paper clothing left at the site to reveal the dress shirt, tie and slacks, his entire lanky frame speaking of exhaustion. "You okay?" he asked.

"I'm lovely. Just hunky-dory. You?"

His smile was crooked. "I've had better days. But I need your help."

"What for?"

"I need you to tell me about that homestead and grave plot."

"Yeah, that's what I figured would happen." I turned my back, shoulders stiff and angry. "You're going to have to question all my family, aren't you? My nana, my daughter. All the help."

"Like I said. Better days." I could hear the strain in his voice, but I still didn't turn around, even when he put a hand on my shoulder, the first comfort he'd offered. "But not me. I'm too close to you." His tone softened, as if to both warn and console me at once. "It'll be one of the other agents. It needs to be thorough to rule out your family, so it won't be pleasant."

I wiped my eyes again, fighting tears that were half selfish, half for the child buried in the sand just ahead. "That's just great. Do you have any idea how many Chadwicks know about this site, either by family history or by actually coming out here to see it? Do you know how big an investigation you're talking about?"

"Tell me."

I looked up at him. He wavered in a watery pattern of tears. "At the last family reunion back in 2005, over 225 people attended. Lots more couldn't make it. My family is scattered all over the nation. We're two races and all ages, from the late nineties to not yet born. We started on a family genealogy chart last year, and it points to dozens of other family members—dozens, Jim—that are lost or missing. Hundreds of us live in this state alone."

"You're kidding."

"Do I look like I'm kidding? You're going to have

to talk to all of them, aren't you? And before you ask, yes, we've had our share of spotted sheep."

"Don't you mean black sheep?" he said, amused.

"Not with my family's ethnic mix. And some of our spotted sheep have done jail time."

Jim swore, his amusement gone.

"Don't let my aunt Mosetta hear you swear. She won't care if you're a cop or not, you say that in her presence and she'll wash out your mouth with good lye soap. Why concentrate on just the Chadwicks? Anyone could locate this place."

"Not likely."

"Yes, likely." I swiped at my face with the flannel cuffs. "You said the last body was buried in a Confederate graveyard. Was it easy to find?"

"A lot easier to find than this one." The comforting tone was gone from his voice. That hadn't lasted long.

"Well, this one's not impossible to detect either."

"Ash—" Jim stopped himself from whatever he was about to say and took a deep breath. "Why don't you tell me how anyone outside of your family would know about this burial plot."

I jerked my head at the grave site just ahead. "The South Carolina State Library has information on graveyards across the state. The information is available online at the library's Web site, and also in the South Carolina reference room. I know, because at that family reunion I mentioned, we looked it up one rainy day for fun. You can click on 'counties' and find any graveyard thus far discovered in any county." The whole time I talked, tears fell, dripping off my chin in dual steady streams. My nose was clogging.

"The Chadwick plot is registered with the state in historical records. It's listed in county records, on some old county maps, and frankly anyone who wanted to find it could, with a little work. Any teacher, student, historian, politician, librarian or professor could pinpoint it on MapQuest. Anyone looking for genealogy information. Anyone doing research for any purpose could find it. It's easy. Just as easy as finding the Chadwick family Web site."

Jim looked at me thoughtfully. "Your family has its own Web site?" I just looked at him. "What is it, www.Chadwicks.com?"

Grudgingly I said, "Chadwickfamily.org."

"So we may not be dealing with a history buff. Just someone who can use the Internet," he said tiredly.

"That narrows it down for you a lot, I guess. Only eighty-something percent of the citizens in South Carolina have Internet access. Even my nana uses the Internet these days, to get the best prices on her crops."

"But the problem with the farm and your family is this—the perpetrator would have to get here somehow, carrying a body and digging implements. He had to drive straight through your family farm."

"Hilldale Hills is closer than Chadwick Farms. A lot closer. In fact, if I'd known where the body was in the first place, I'd have driven over and walked in. It's no more than a quarter mile thatta way." I pointed. "There's another farm about a mile thatta way." I pointed off toward the Iredells' llama farm. "Have you even figured out what direction the perpetrator came from? Have you found a trail? Have you asked me any questions to determine the most likely ingress and egress? No." I sniffed. I decided to give up fighting the tears. I couldn't seem to stop them.

"You're not channeling your mother anymore."

"Josephine doesn't cry. It ruins her makeup. Causes lines in her skin and dehydrates the horny layer of her epidermis. Or maybe it negatively affects the acid mantle or something. I don't remember exactly."

Jim chuckled. "Horny layer?"

"I'm not kidding. Josey is a youth obsessed, skin-treatment-aholic. A plastic surgeon's professional financial sleep-induced orgasmic pleasure." The more I talked, the more I cried and the more Jim laughed. At least someone was happy.

"Would that be a wet dream?" Jim's tone was half-disbelieving.

"Not in front of my family, it wouldn't."

"I have to meet this woman."

"You will." I scuffed at my cheeks. "She'll be a suspect, remember? Maybe you can drag her to an interrogation room and visit for a while."

"Well, hell." Jim's laughter was gone.

I looked at him and my eyes ached, tears flowing as if I had opened a faucet. "And I wasn't joking about my aunt Mosetta. The worst thing you better say in her presence is *dang* or *dantucket*. Even my nana is careful about her language in front of Aunt Moses, and Nana could cuss the bark off an oak in her younger days."

"I thought it was *Mosetta*," he said, his tone half laughter.

I shrugged. "Mosetta, Moses, she goes by either. The old ones mostly call her Moses."

"Please stop crying, Ash." That tone was back in his

voice again, the tone that said he was my boyfriend-sort-of-maybe and didn't want me to cry.

Boyfriend. I was facing fifty in a few years and I had a *boyfriend.* What in heck was I going to do with a boyfriend? It made me cry harder, and the sobs felt as if they were raking my throat with claws. "I can't…I can't seem to stop crying."

"Why not?" He put his arms around me and pulled me close.

I had the feeling that most cops didn't hug most suspects. I snuggled my face into his dress shirt and wrapped my arms around him. I hadn't known how badly I needed a hug until he tightened his arms. *"Why not?"* I repeated. "There's a dead child buried about twenty yards ahead, a huge group of investigators and crime-scene people behind me, my entire family's a suspect in a murder case and I haven't slept in over thirty-six hours."

"That sounds like a good group of reasons. You worked last night?"

I nodded, my face against the starched fabric. It smelled of laundry detergent and man-sweat, an altogether satisfying scent. Amazingly, my tears slowed. I pressed into Jim's shoulder with my aching face, my skin feeling burned and salty. If she saw me, my mother would drag me to Charlotte to her aesthetician for an emergency session, probably screaming that my epidermis and lipid layer were permanently damaged. She'd done it before. I sighed into Jim's shoulder, the sound muffled.

"Feel better?"

"Yes. Thank you. Now all I want is a nap."

"Me, too. Feel better, I mean. I needed this." His arms tightened a moment and we stood in a shadow, birds tweeting nearby, and a squirrel scampering through dry leaves. Jim released me, easing me away. "Company's coming." He brushed a strand of my hair back from my face. "I need to get back to the site."

I took a breath that still burned down my throat and dropped my hands away from him. "Okay. Thanks for the hug."

"There's water in one of the bags at the site." A half smile raised his lips on one side. "Wash your face so your horny layer does whatever a horny layer is supposed to do."

"Prurient epidermal thoughts, Agent Ramsey?"

"Thoughts of skin have been known to give me sleep-induced orgasmic pleasure."

I laughed softly, the sound almost normal as we walked back to the two old oaks and the body buried beyond.

"So. Tell me about Hoddermier Hilldale Jr. and his gentleman friend."

I sighed. I had a feeling that my neighbors were going to be as abused as my own family.

I considered Hoddy Jr., a slight, delicate man who listened to classical music, wore cashmere in winter and silk blends in summer, and offered cooking classes through the Episcopal church. He looked as if he couldn't hurt a fly. Could Hoddy be the killer? Surely not.

But how many other friends and neighbors would the cops target? And would they find the killer among them?

5

He entered the mega-store, whistling Vivaldi. The notes were classic and quick, spare and tripping. A good omen for today's business. He trailed through the grocery aisles, buying things she liked. Blueberry yogurt, bagels, soft cheese in a wheel, pears, caramels, frozen pizza. Because he had to keep her healthy, he added baby spinach—organic, of course—and tomatoes, apples. Big, red, seedless grapes. For himself, he tossed in a bag of shrimp and a couple of thick steaks, baking potatoes. Sour cream. A bottle of merlot, an underappreciated label but a very good year. Surprising to find in a superstore.

Dawdling, enjoying himself, he pushed the buggy through the clothing section, picking up a pair of jeans, a few T-shirts in vibrant pinks and purples. Satiny nightclothes. The ones in her room were getting worn. He wasn't sure what underwear size she had worn, so he added three packets in different sizes, each containing several pairs. Socks. There were athletic socks with pink stripes and fuzzy socks for sleeping. He selected a half-dozen packets. She had no need of shoes.

In the toy section, he picked through the dolls until he found a nine-inch-tall, plastic, teenage doll wearing a soccer outfit. He added casual clothes and dress clothes for the doll and a new lunch box with a picture of a girl kicking a soccer ball on the top. Perfect. She would love it.

A quick trip through the cosmetic department allowed him to replace the shampoo and bubble bath the other one had liked. This one was independent, outgoing. She'd probably like a fresh scent, not floral. He added a perfume with a sporty name.

And finally the jewelry section. He bought the bracelets. The rings and earrings had already been delivered from eBay. All he had to do was pick up the black velvet throw from the cleaners and he would be ready to begin. This time he had managed all the variables. This time it would work. He was quite certain.

Paying cash, he exited the store and stowed his purchases in the back of his Volvo, still whistling Vivaldi.

The afternoon wore away as all the surface evidence was collected in bags, labeled and stored. As the hours passed, my eyes grew heavy, gritty from lack of sleep, and my limbs seemed to take on a distant buzz, as if they had a current flowing through them. Exhaustion was setting in.

The numbers of federal investigators grew and diminished as the need arose and as Jim dispatched them to question neighbors. With the discovery of a human body, a child, this had officially become an FBI investigation. The locals were here because it was their turf, but everyone knew they were mostly errand boys, not the stars of the investigation. Jim disappeared once to question Hoddy Jr. and his significant other. Hoddy had been out shopping earlier, when a special agent had gone by, and the second attempt fell to Jim.

He left again to oversee the questioning of my nana and Aunt Moses. He was gone a lot longer that time but was back by the designated hour the grave was to be opened and the body recovered. I didn't ask about the session with Nana. I knew she'd tell me soon enough and would want to know why I hadn't warned her about the problem on her land. The fact that I was trying to protect her would not be an acceptable reason. Nana wanted her finger in every Chadwick Farm pie.

Around 4:00 p.m., they were ready to open the grave. I might have felt a spurt of excitement or fear except I was too tired to feel energy of any kind. Skye looked up from the ground in her position two feet from the body. Her knees were protected from con-taminating the evidence by a layer of special paper and she had an open evidence kit beside her. She was gloved, her blond-streaked hair pulled back and secured. Across from the body knelt Steven, his pate glistening, though the heat of midday had passed.

It was warmer than usual for April, the temperature near eighty in the sunlight. Under the canopy of trees, leaves still not at their summertime fullness, it had reached the seventies. As the sun moved off to the west, it grew cooler fast, and I was glad of the flannel shirt I wore. On the damp earth, Skye shivered.

Using a brush that looked a lot like one I had under my sink to sweep up dry spills, she began pushing the sand away. Behind her squatted another cop, holding what looked like a huge sieve. As Skye moved the earth, he scraped it up and placed it in the sieve. When it was full, he handed it off to yet another cop, who took it to the sidelines, held it over a plastic mat and shook it till all the soil was gone.

Everything that remained after the dirt passed through the sieve was placed in an evidence bag marked with the square of grid from which it came, the depth, the date and time, and the initials of everyone who had touched it. Anything that looked interesting was mentioned and tagged for special attention. Paperwork in triplicate, the Chain of Custody forms were carefully filled out and proofread by one of the cops on the periphery.

It was remarkably like an archeological dig. The evidence collection seemed much more intensive and comprehensive than what the local cops were used to doing, the action choreographed by Jim and another FBI man named Oliver.

"Got something," Skye said several times. Once it was a hair; once it was a fold of foil, the kind gum came wrapped in. Twice it was an unknown, something she shrugged over without identifying. After an hour, the loose soil around the child was gone, all of the earth that had been disturbed by the person who had buried her removed, sifted and set aside. An indentation remained around a small mound, far too small to be a human. Yet, clearly it was a child. One with blue-painted toenails.

The skull and left leg bones had been disarranged by whatever had dug her up—I assumed by my dogs, although the cops wouldn't accept that without more evidence—but the rest of the body was positioned carefully, hands crossed on her chest, right leg straight. She was wearing a red sneaker on her right foot, a schoolgirl's pleated skirt that might once have been blue, green and red, and a T-shirt. All the colors were darkened by death fluids and damp earth except the red in the skirt, which was still vibrant. Scraps of blond hair still clung to the skull. Her hands were folded around a book and other objects.

The buzzing along my nerves that marked an advanced case of exhaustion seemed to grow, becoming almost a sound, like bees in the distance, a hornets' nest nearby when there was nothing. I sat down just outside the crime-scene tape, rubbery legs folding under me.

When the body was fully exposed, two dozen photographs were taken, some close-ups, some to document the remains in situ. Jim and the other cop, so slender he was almost emaciated and who dressed and moved like FBI—meaning expensive and as if he walked on water—stepped to the center of the site and knelt down on paper mats as well. They looked like pagan supplicants bowing before a little godling, hoping for enlightenment or worldly gifts.

I could hear some of the conversation between Jim and the other FBI guy. My exhaustion seemed to improve my hearing, the buzzing in my ears seeming a magnet for sound waves, drawing them in, clarifying words and phrases I might have missed were I more alert.

"Same positioning of hands and feet," Jim murmured. "Same binding of the wrists."

"But none of the missing girls were wearing this style of clothing."

"We don't know how long he keeps them. Maybe he buys them new clothes when he buys them the dolls."

"What about the book? The other one didn't have a book. And the clothes are ordinary—"

"The other one was wearing the leotard when she was taken from the dance rehearsal. What's this?" Using tweezers, Jim lifted something off the body to get a better look at it and returned it to its place.

"Looks like a pointed stick. And maybe a melted candle on a tray?"

"I don't see a wick. And why bury her with a candle?"

"Why the flute on the last one? She didn't play the flute but was buried with one."

"This one had schoolbooks when she was taken. There's a book." Jim tapped it.

"Can you see the title?"

"Too water damaged."

"What about the paper?"

Jim bent over the body as if he would kiss the rounded skull and did something I couldn't see. My hands twitched as if to stop him, before settling in my lap like broken twigs. The breath burned in my throat.

"Got something in the pocket. Folded and mashed. It could be paper." Jim sat back on his heels.

"So we got positioning, graveyard burial, ethnicity, age and the folded paper. I think that's enough. I'll get a pair down from Quantico."

Jim checked his watch. "If you book it with lights

and siren, you can upload the digital photos and e-mail them, so the analysts can study them tonight and on the flight tomorrow."

"Let's get her to the medical examiner and get a postmortem and ID process started. See what the lab can do with the folded paper."

"I'll handle that. You get on back and see about upgrading us to full task-force level."

"Who you want locally?"

Jim raised his voice only slightly, the tone too cold to be teasing. "Skye, you think Gaskins would give you part of the action?"

"Not me," she said sotto voce. "First, I got the wrong kind of genitalia. Gaskins is only going to appoint a man to a task force. And second, honestly, I got a baby at home. A 24/7 thing isn't what I'm after right now. Ask Ash. She wouldn't cost the county diddly. She did a great job getting here, preserving all the evidence on the way, and she knows the local history, the local people, everyone in law enforcement in the county. And she's trained as a forensic nurse, in case you get a splinter in your finger or find a live one as you go."

"We need law enforcement," the other cop said.

"Take Steven, too," Skye said. "He's up to take the detective test this fall."

"Steven?"

"Yeah, sure," he said, trying to sound only half as interested as his shining eyes suggested. "If the sheriff approves."

"Gaskins?" the other cop called out. "We need a local guy to liaise in Columbia with the task force. Steven's willing."

C.C.'s nose hair twitched in the lengthening shadows. "Long as you don't ask for one of my investigators, you can have who you want. But I'm shorthanded starting in the second week of May. I need Steven back by then."

"It's not full-time we're talking here. Only a few hours a week, unless more bodies show up in this county. The other one was in Calhoun County, so our killer's not sticking close to home with them."

"Even better," Gaskins said.

"Ash, you willing to take part in this?"

I wanted to say no and even opened my mouth to say no. "Yes. I'll do it."

"Let's get our vic out of here. Get everything we collected back to the lab by dark-thirty. I'll schedule a meeting for noon tomorrow. That'll give the NCAVC guys time to get to the local FBI office from the airport.

"Steven?" Jim asked.

"I'll be there."

"Ash?"

My hands twitched again and a cramp was starting in my foot. I would never make it back to the trucks. "I'll be there, too. Someone will have to give me directions."

"Get them from the agent who does your interview." Jim's expression was hard, a cop look that gave nothing away.

"Interview?" I asked stupidly.

"You'll be interviewed later on today by a special agent."

I blinked at him. Interviewed? That was a fancy

word for *questioned*. I had to be questioned in the case. "Well. I hope he can question me while I sleep, 'cause I'm dead on my feet."

"We can start now if you like, Miz Davenport."

I looked up into the blue eyes of a young looking cop. "I'm Special Agent Julie Schwartz."

"Well, dantucket," I said.

Julie Schwartz found that remark inordinately funny.

6

He heard a soft noise above him, a scraping sound like a shoe on wood flooring. Quietly, he locked all the doors, pocketed the key and went up the steps. On the way, he lifted a hammer, tested its heft and balance. Just in case. Not that he expected it to be a trespasser.

At the top of the stairs, he paused and turned off the basement lights, the door behind him open. The only light downstairs now came from the window into the pink room. It cast a soft glow in the hallway.

From the kitchen he heard off-key humming, familiar, congenial. Still silent, he set the hammer on the step and carefully stood, locking the door behind him. Again he pocketed the key. Pasting a smile on his face, he went to the kitchen.

After Special Agent Julie Schwartz left, I stood at the kitchen sink and washed dishes by hand. Neither of us had eaten all day, so I had whipped up cheese omelets with bacon, and we'd eaten while she'd questioned me. The meal obviously wasn't by the book, but we both had wanted to get the day and the interview over with, so Julie had compromised.

I put the plates in the drainer and turned to the skillet and omelet pan. I had a top-of-the-line Kenmore automatic dishwasher, so it wasn't as if I *had* to wash them by hand, but my body was exhausted and my brain needed the mindless chore of washing and rinsing. When the last dish was clean and left to air-dry on the plastic drainer, I poured myself a glass of wine and walked out to the swing on the screened back porch.

Night was falling. The cop cars were long gone. Jas would be home soon, and Nana and Aunt Mosetta were sure to come by. Even if my lack of sleep hadn't left me with a sensation of cotton wool between my ears, the coming confrontation would have. The moment Julie had left, I should have gone directly along the path through the woods to Nana's house. The woman was psychic. She would know when the last cop was gone; Nana knew everything about her land, everything except that a little girl had been buried on it. And what Nana didn't know, she would spy out through the side porch with the binoculars she had kept there since Jack had died.

In spite of what I knew I should do, I was just too tired. *Let them come to me.* I sipped the wine, smelled the fresh scent of horse and hay, watched as Johnny Ray let the last mare out into the back pasture, her form moving darkly against the setting sun, bright red on the horizon. Mabel, I figured, from the size and the way she moved, lumbering and just a bit stiff from the day's ride.

Elwyn was long gone. I hadn't even seen the horse trainer today, but I was fairly certain the cops had.

They had spoken to everyone associated with the land except Jas, and they would get to her tomorrow.

Johnny Ray stumbled and went to his knees while closing the paddock fence, pushed himself back to his feet, using the gate as a prop. Drunk as two skunks. He would sleep it off in the barn tonight.

Could Johnny Ray be the killer? How about Elwyn? Do I have a murderer on the payroll? Jas dated Elwyn for a short time after he came to work here. Did she date a murderer?

It was a silly thought. Johnny Ray was too wasted to carry out a murder except maybe one of drunken passion. If someone tried to take away his bottle before he was ready to let it go, he might do some damage, half by accident as he fell on them. Elwyn was from up north. He lived in town in an apartment. He didn't know about the family graveyard plot or much of anything about South Carolina. He had Internet access to look up graveyards, and he had enough time off to do any crime he might be capable of. But where would he keep a young girl? In his apartment in DorCity, as locals called nearby Dorsey City? In the tack room in the barn? No. Not Johnny Ray or Elwyn.

"I hope that's bourbon and you have enough for me."

I jerked, sending the swing off at a jittery angle and back. "Nana." I hadn't heard them walk up. Nana and Aunt Mosetta climbed the steps and walked onto the dark porch. "It's wine. Let me get—"

"I'll get my own liquor," Nana said and moved into the house. She knew her way around as well as I did and she saw better in the dark. The bourbon was kept on hand just for her anyway. I hated the stuff.

"I been telling that old woman she got to give up hard liquor. At her age it be going to kill her," Aunt Moses said as she levered herself into the heavy captain's chair she preferred. The chair had wide arms to bear her weight, and its legs splayed out at slight angles to make it steady. The firm cushion I had supplied supported her back and protected her thighs from the wooden seat and was pretty, according to Aunt Moses, a bright floral pattern totally at odds with the rest of the porch.

"I'll drink if I want to. Stop badgering me. I've been badgered enough today by self-important cops not old enough to drink this." She saluted us with the lowball glass, bourbon straight up, no ice, no water. The very thought made my stomach ache.

"So. Fill us in." Nana settled into a cushioned deck chair with her denim-clad legs out in front, ankles crossed, her hands warming the glass across her T-shirted middle. Even in the dark, I could tell that she had showered and pulled on tomorrow's work clothes, her steel-gray hair still wet and curling around her ears.

Aunt Moses pulled her terry-cloth housecoat closer around her shoulders and said, "You badgering the girl you own self. Whyn't you jest set and be quiet. She tell us in her own time." When I didn't respond, Aunt Moses said, "Well?"

I guess that meant my own time was now. I started from the beginning and walked them through my day, through everything I saw and remembered. After my recital, they were silent, the only sound the wind through the trees, the squeak of the swing as I moved it with a toe. "It was pretty awful," I finished, "and they seem to think it could be a Chadwick who killed her."

"Ain't none a my peoples. Ain't," Aunt Moses said. "But I answer all they questions and lets 'em look around all they wants. They gots to clear my peoples 'fore they can find the real suspect."

"She's been watching *CSI* reruns. Thinks she can help the cops," Nana said.

"I *can* help the police. They sends a real nice black woman to the house to ax me questions. I 'member time when a black woman woulda been cleaning the toilets at the police station. This gal was a special agent with the FBI. She treat me real nice when she ax me questions and I answered her. You was mean and rude to the man who talking to you. I hear that tone on your voice when he axing you questions."

"The so-called man talkin' to me was young enough to be my great-grandson and had a disagreeable manner. He never once called me *ma'am*. My grandsons speak to me without a 'yes, ma'am' and a 'no, ma'am' and I wouldn't be polite to them either. I didn't have to be polite, I only had to answer his questions, that little officious, pipsqueak Yankee."

I smiled into my wine and wished I had brought the bottle. I caught a whiff of Aunt Mosetta's latest favorite perfume, night-blooming jasmine, a gift from my daughter for Mother's Day last year.

"You look all done in, Ashlee," Nana said.

"I haven't slept in two days. I'm worn out. In fact, I'm not sure I'm not dreaming right now."

"You come to your senses about that new forensics job? It ain't you, girl. It ain't you."

"Ash can do that job and any other one she want. I seen how they gather up all the evidence and find the killer. Ash can do that iffn she want."

Nana shook her head. "Ash has been like a boat with no rudder since Jack died. First trying to run his business, then selling it."

"She made a fortune. Ash no silly girl."

"Then leaving the Dawkins County Hospital and going to that new, big hospital in Columbia. Now this forensic stuff. She doesn't know what she wants. Hasn't, since finding out Jack had cheated on her with that worthless best friend of hers."

Something twisted painfully deep inside, burning. It was a familiar pain, one I always felt whenever I remembered that I had lost Jack and my best friend Robyn, all in one fell swoop. Whenever I remembered that he hadn't loved me as he should. As he'd promised. "I am sitting right here with the two of you, if you'll remember. And I'm not deaf." My voice sounded cool and controlled, not as if it were burning a hole in me. "If you'd like me to go inside so you can gossip over me in private, I'll be happy to."

"Sounds jist like her mama, don't she."

"Josey is not what I'd call a good influence. But at least she knows what she wants."

"Nana," I said, to stop the bickering. "You are absolutely right." That shut them both up. "I have no idea what I want to do with the rest of my life. I'm still trying to get it all together inside. I know you think I should have it all figured out by now, but I haven't."

Jack's heart attack and my subsequent discovery of his affair with Robyn had indeed played a huge part in my inability to direct my own future. I hadn't told my family about the affair. I wouldn't ruin my daughter's vision of her father. But Nana had her own ways of discovering the truth, and she had eventually found out. I pushed thoughts of the past away.

"All I can say is, I always wanted to be a nurse and I'm still nursing. I'm just not nursing exactly the way you wanted me to, working in the county hospital with Wallace Chadwick as my boss and surrounded by family. I want more, and I'm not sure what kind of more. So I'm trying new things, going new places. And I'll find myself."

"Jack left you enough money to sit and play pinochle all day if you wanted to. You don't have to drive into that dangerous city to work. Next thing you'll be moving there, taking Jas with you."

Ahhhh. Understanding nestled in me. Nana was worried about my health a lot less than she was worried about the possibility that I might move to the state capital. Leave home in my midlife crisis. Cleave a chasm in her comfortable world "Crime is everywhere, Nana," I said softly. "Even on Chadwick Farms. We can't hide from danger or troubles. And I promise I'll find myself. Without moving away."

"Tole you she figure out what you doin'. Ash got your number."

"Shut up, old woman."

Before the bickering could start up again, a small truck pulled into the yard and cut its lights. Jas was home. I felt something inside lighten as she slid from the truck, something tight and frightened that I hadn't even been aware of. Jas skipped up the steps and stopped when she saw us. "What's up?" she said, trepidation in her voice. My Jas was smart. Smart enough to know that there was trouble just by reading our body language in the deep dusk light.

"Nothing. We going home. Jist stop by to say goodnight to your mama." In a slow and ponderous process, Aunt Moses stood, crossed the porch and enveloped Jasmine in a mama-bear hug. Nana hugged right behind her and they were both gone, slow steps crunching across the gravel, leaving me to explain to my daughter about a body, cops and a task force.

Once she got over the shock of hearing that a child had been buried at the old family homestead, my daughter thought it was cool to have a crime scene on the property and even cooler that she would be questioned by the FBI. Youth, I thought, disgusted. So tired I weaved when I walked, I made my way to my room, showered the stink of the grave off me and fell into bed.

7

Tuesday

By noon I had found my way through horrid traffic to the South Carolina FBI field office. Luckily, I discovered a parking spot close by, not that easy in a metropolitan area that was growing so congested. The inner city had been designed with gracious living and farming in mind, rather than good use of government resources, and many of its streets were narrow and twisting. And I was sure its belt loop and interchanges had been designed by a caffeine-charged five-year-old with a box of crayons.

Inside the entrance, my ID was carefully checked, twice, my photo compared to my face, and my reason for coming to feeb headquarters questioned by a guard with the personality of a block of stone. Finally I was given a name badge with a security locator device attached so I couldn't get lost or misplaced, and directed to a room on the second floor.

I passed large rooms, some full of frenetic activity and ringing phones, and offices with closed doors. I heard a variety of languages, though most conversations were in English or Spanish, and foreign-sounding names interspersed with names Bubba might have been born with. Everyone I passed or glimpsed wore a look of intense concentration or anger or some combination of the two. The expressions seemed unrelieved by even brief moments of levity or relaxation, and I was glad I didn't work here.

As a forensic nurse, I was expected to work with law enforcement. I had toured the local LEC—law enforcement centers—in three counties surrounding Dawkins, and had even taken a tour through SLED, the State Law Enforcement Division. But no one who set up the training had envisioned a forensic nurse needing to work with FBI, so that locale had not been on my list of suggested places to visit.

I entered a conference room and nodded to the officers gathered around a coffeepot and three boxes of glazed Krispy Kremes. How trite was that? Cops and doughnuts. As I walked across the room and looked out the dirty window into the street below, they inspected me from head to foot, cataloged and filed me under Not a Cop, and promptly went back to their muted conversation.

I was glad I had opted for basic khaki-green woven trousers and a hip-hiding darker brown jacket with short-heeled pumps. With an amber necklace dangled between my breasts, and with my ashy-blond hair up in a French twist—which pretended to give me some height—and gold hoops instead of pearls, I blended, at least, though the cops seemed to go for black and blue with power-red ties. Even the women wore dark, subdued clothing. Unlike the TV heroines, none of these women showed cleavage or wore Armani. Jas would be distraught.

I caught sight of Jim as I took a seat at the long table in the room's center. He looked secure and confident, even when wearing the same intense look as the other cops. His suit coat was tailored and his own power-red tie was knotted in a full Windsor. I recognized it for several reasons, chiefly because Jasmine's father had had difficulty knotting his ties himself and I had always tied them for him. But Jim wasn't Jack. I felt some unidentified tension begin to uncoil inside me at that thought.

"Afternoon, Ash," Steven said, pulling out the chair beside me and easing his frame into it. The big cop was a weight lifter, the kind who went into the sport with the intention of building muscle mass, not simply getting into shape. Beside him, I looked like a matronly housewife, something he might break in half with two fingers and thumbs. Steven passed me a cup of coffee, a cream and pink packet of sweetener.

I didn't drink coffee often as it upset my digestion, but I mixed, stirred and sipped to have something to do with my hands. Steven bit into a glazed doughnut and washed it down with half a cup of coffee, copstyle. "We should have driven up together," he said. "Traffic is worse today than downtown Charlotte."

"I thought about it, but I'm on call this afternoon and might have to leave at any time."

"You're like a combination of nurse and cop now, aren't you? Doing both jobs?" The chair groaned as he shifted around, trying to find a comfortable position.

"Sort of," I said. "I still have my job at CHC in the Majors Emergency Department, but the forensic nursing position is taking more and more of my time. My callback hours are starting to look like another full-time job."

"Welcome to my world," he sighed, sounding tired. "But you're making big bucks, not a lowly cop salary."

Steven was fishing, and I grinned sourly. "Yeah. Mega bucks. Call time for forensic nurses is about what you made as a first-year beat cop."

"Now that sucks."

Of course, that was on top of my nursing salary. I wasn't hurting, at least not financially.

"Thank you all for coming." Jim Ramsey stood at the front of the room, which had filled up while Steven and I talked. He bent forward, hands flat on the table, a position that said, *I'm offering you all I have. I'm just one of the guys*, and then he stood and seemed to take over the room. Nice ploy. Effective. I had seen Jas's father do the same thing in business meetings. I wondered for a moment why I was thinking so much about Jack, but I pushed the question away. I wasn't ready to look at the fact or the question, knowing both were snarled up with my evolving feelings for Jim Ramsey.

"The investigators from the Criminal Investigative Analyst Unit from the National Center for the Analysis of Violent Crime in Quantico are in the building, being escorted up, so let's get started. We hope this will be the only time we all gather in this room, but we may be back. We will be, if we find another body before we catch the person or persons responsible for these crimes. Tacked to the corkboard to my left are the photographs of the missing girls."

I looked back over my shoulder and saw eight-by-ten photos of girls, all blond or strawberry-blond, with blue or possibly gray eyes. Below each photo was a list of personal statistics: height, weight, eye and hair color, age, distinguishing characteristics, where they'd been abducted, time and place. Not all the girls had been recovered. For two of them, the date and location where their bodies had been found was on the bottom of the form. One had gone missing after a school event, the other after a dance rehearsal. I remembered Jim and the other cop saying something about a tutu.

I could remember Jasmine in a pink tutu at age ten, long bangs curling over dark eyes and hair tumbling down her back. My daughter had hated dancing. I turned back, having missed part of Jim's message.

"—introduce ourselves briefly. I'm Jim Ramsey, agent coordinator of South Carolina FBI Violent Crime Unit."

Introductions went to Jim's left. A woman, wearing a black suit with a white blouse that featured a bow beneath her chin, stood and nodded. Emma something, her title had *supervisory* in front of the words. A VIP in the South Carolina FBI office, I was sure. The man beside her was thin enough to be ill. On around the table, all the cops spoke their job titles and what they'd be doing with the task force. When my turn came, I stood and said, "Ashlee Caldwell Davenport, forensic nurse."

As I was sitting back down, Jim amended that for me by adding, "And the woman who discovered the red sneaker belonging to the second victim and tracked the body."

That won me an even better scrutiny from the gathered cops. I smiled sweetly at Jim, my expression promising retribution for that. He lifted his brows fractionally and smiled sweetly back. I wasn't quite sure what that might mean but it didn't bode well for our relationship if he was going to turn my psychological ploys back on me. Jack Davenport had never been that sly or that smart. *Men.*

The introductions continued around the room and I heard the name Julie Schwartz, the special agent who'd interviewed me. I liked Julie. That might not be a smart thing to feel for a cop who was hoping to arrest a member of my family for serial murder.

A small, slightly rounded white man and a taller black man stepped through the door and stood behind empty chairs. Jim nodded, and the small man said, "Haden Fairweather, Ph.D. in behavioral sciences and a master's in criminal justice. I've worked with the Federal Bureau of Investigation for fifteen years, the last seven as a supervisory special agent, field-office program manager and violent-crime assessor with the National Center for the Analysis of Violent Crime, or NCAVC."

This was the profiler. Not a very charismatic man for such a fancy title.

Haden introduced his junior partner, whose name sounded like Joshua Timmodee. Joshua nodded to us, spoke greetings with a South African accent, and sat down beside Haden. Jim passed out folders as Haden stood again.

Haden nodded to the room. "Last night and on the flight down, my partner and I studied all the information e-mailed and faxed to us, including many of the crime-scene photographs, the preliminary postmortem autopsies and all the physical evidence available before our flight took off. I will be meeting with the team leaders of the ERT, the medical examiner and various others of you to garner information as needed. We will also be studying the grave sites, and we appreciate you keeping both as pristine as possible for us."

Haden touched a forefinger to the bridge of his nose as if pushing up sliding glasses, his gaze taking in the entire room. "However, from the evidence reviewed thus far, we have drafted a preliminary victimology profile. A very hasty, inadequate, preliminary report. Please remember that. A detailed report takes time, and much more information than we now have, most importantly the cause of death and any evidence gathered that might point to physical or sexual assault on the victims.

"While I know you all are eagerly awaiting the final, full report, I'm unable to give you much this morning that you don't already know." Haden blinked and put a fingertip to his eye, as if a contact lens was sliding around on his cornea.

"Our perpetrator is likely to be a white male, age thirty-five to fifty, with a very organized mind, a competent understanding of South Carolina state history, Chadwick family history, and/or the ability to use the Internet to research complex state records. He has very specific preferences in his criminal methodology, as per the placement of the bodies and the sites chosen for burial, though he appears to be inventive and creative, as indicated by the implements buried with each victim."

Haden shuffled two papers and centered a third on the podium that stood at the front of the room. "At this time, we believe your perpetrator has a higher than average IQ and a minimum of four years of higher education, likely more, possibly with a liberal arts or history emphasis. Your subject has a need to dominate the victims, as is evident in the tying of the girls' hands. However, the lack of gross physical damage on the victims, no evidence of prolonged violent physical abuse, neglect or sexual abuse may indicate that the perpetrator feels he is being kind to the girls for as long as he keeps them, perhaps even fatherly."

The attention level in the room went up a bit. I noted that even Steven, who was likely the least experienced man in the room from an investigative standpoint, angled his head in interest. "This, however, may be revised or negated by any future information on the COD or evidence acquired by the forensic PMs," Haden again reminded the group.

"Until we receive the report from the forensic pathologist, my partner and I can offer you no more of a psychological profile, though we hope to have something substantive within twenty-four hours after the final ME report."

"For the purposes of this orientation for our new members," Jim said, "we have two folders before us. Please open the red folder to page one."

I opened the folder and looked into the eyes of a pretty little girl. I had seen her photo hanging on the wall behind me. With cold fingers, I touched the matte paper of the small, grainy, color copy.

"We'll give an overview now, but take and study each file to bring yourself up to date on the first body recovered. The volume of evidence tested on the first victim is obviously much greater than what we have so far on yesterday's victim," Jim said. "Our first vic's name was Jillian LaRue, a twelve-year-old student taken from a dressing room immediately following a dance rehearsal eight months ago. No witnesses, no evidence at the scene.

"There was some reason to believe that the victim went willingly. Initially it was suspected she left with her biological father, who had been spotted several times by the instructor in the past few months, trying to speak to her. However, he was located in the county jail two days after Jillian disappeared, having been pulled for DUI and resisting arrest. He had been locked up for five days prior to the LaRue girl's disappearance. We lost two days. It won't happen again. Now that we know we have a serial case, Amber Alerts will go out if a child takes too long in the bathroom or hides too well while playing hide-and-seek. We won't lose any more children through technical glitches or inattention."

I noticed Emma purse her lips across the table. She didn't like that comment at all, as if it reflected badly on her, but she kept quiet. I looked at her name badge. Emma Simmons, SAC. I wondered if she was Jim's boss. I closed the folder on the photo of the lost little girl. I would read it tonight, and knew I'd have nightmares for days after.

"Her body was discovered partially buried in a Confederate-era cemetery in Calhoun County, dressed exactly as she had been in rehearsal, lavender-and-purple leotards, tights, pink tutu and pointe shoes. Best estimates are that she was in the ground a little over two months, which means he kept her for six months."

The body in my family cemetery had been in the ground for at least that long. Had the red-sneaker girl been taken and killed just before the dancer? Or had there been others in between? I closed my eyes.

Six months in the hands of a stranger. Six months.

Haden took over from Jim. "Like our latest victim, she was buried with a doll—a blond, nine-inch-tall ballerina doll—which she did not have in her possession when taken. In the front of her leotard, placed over her heart, which placement appears to be significant, was a folded piece of heavy paper with writing on it. Unfortunately, it was so heavily damaged by the elements and the conditions of the grave site that only a portion could be read. You'll see a partial transcript on page eleven, though the lab is still working on it."

"The paper was handmade, which I understand is still possible," Jim said, sounding skeptical. "The lab is tracing the paper and the dyes used in the ink back to the manufacturers. We hope one of the manufacturers will be able to pinpoint where the ingredients were purchased."

I waited patiently for someone to tell Jim that papermaking was all the rage now in the arts-and-crafts crowd, that products could be purchased in every craft store, every Michaels, every Wal-Mart and Garden

Ridge store in the nation. No one did. Unless the maker had put something very odd into his paper or used a rare ink, it would be nearly impossible to trace who had bought the paper ingredients. But no one pointed that out. Maybe I could tell him later, after the meeting.

"Fiber evidence is finally back from the lab, revealing a wealth of information. It appears the leotard and tights may not have been washed following the abduction and were not continually worn in the intervening months. This allows us a visual of specific moments in the victim's life. The victim's bedroom, the short ride to the dance studio, the fabric fibers picked up in the dressing room, the immediate moments after the abduction. And the last hours before her death.

"The most common fiber not originally from the victim's own environs and the dance studio was a short, smooth, black fiber, most likely nylon. The analysts speculate the fibers are from velour or velvet, as if she was wrapped in a black velour robe or blanket. Fibers were found head to foot, even under the dance shoes she was wearing."

Other people in the room were following along in their red folders, most taking notes. From my peripheral vision I could see Steven's color copies of microscope photos of the fibers and his pen, writing fast, firm comments on a yellow legal pad. But my mind was seeing something else entirely. A little girl goes to the bathroom, perhaps walking down a long corridor. A man tosses a black throw over her, silencing her screams, and runs out an exit into the darkness, holding her down while she screams and struggles.

My maternal instincts were kicking in as they never had when taking the forensic nursing course. As they never did when dealing with victims in the emergency room. I understood my own reactions. In the E.R., I was helping, doing something to make it right, to make it better. Here, I was on the sidelines. And no one had helped the victims. Little girls had been stolen and kept by a stranger, killed. I wanted to cry and rage and I couldn't.

Someone at the front of the room stood and someone else sat, and I realized Jim and two other suited types had covered the rest of the fiber evidence while I wool-gathered and grieved. Knowing I was missing important parts of the meeting, I forced my emotional reactions down into a dark hole inside of me. I pulled myself back to Jim's words. Breathed deeply to center myself. Watched my hand as it flipped pages in the red folder.

Jim was listing the physical evidence, the most important things available to the police to convict the guilty man when they caught him. Hopefully, that same evidence could be used to locate and stop the perpetrator before he took another girl. It was all they had, and the only thing I could do for these little girls was pay attention. But the ache in my chest was a sharp burn.

About half an hour later, Jim instructed us to turn to page thirty-five, to the lab and medical-examiner photos of Jillian LaRue's postmortem. It was weird, but these photos were easier to look at than the photos of the body in the shallow grave. They were clinical, medical, and I was able to focus tightly on the information.

"When we recovered the body, one of the odd things was the knot that bound the hands," Jim said. "It's the main item of physical evidence that ties this victim with the victim discovered in Dawkins County yesterday. The knot doesn't seem to do anything. It's complicated, it looks pretty, but it comes apart so easily it's a waste of time to make it. Our knot expert says it's similar to a thief knot or a granny knot, but works less well than either. When we know more we'll update you."

Leaning forward, I took Steven's pen and wrote on the margin of his pad. *Grief knot.* He looked at me, a question in his eyes. I tapped the words with the pen and handed it back. Steven raised his hand. "Ash says it's a grief knot."

I had meant for Steven to just say the words himself and leave me out of it. My face instantly burned and my skin went all blotchy. I could feel it. The fate of light-skinned women everywhere, the dreaded fluorescent effect. All eyes turned to me, especially Joshua Timmodee, who bent over the table to fasten his eyes on me with liquid intensity. "A grief knot?" he asked.

I shrugged, feeling the blotches worsen. "I was raised on a farm. Farmers use them to bind garden trelliswork, hold up roses, that sort of thing." I searched for something else to say. "The photo shows a locked version with the ends levered up on opposite sides, but before it's locked, you can adjust the tightness of the knot by just pulling on both ends."

"Why is it called a grief knot?" Joshua asked.

"I'm not sure. Probably because it comes apart so easily if you're not careful."

His dark eyes rested a moment on me, then he inclined his head and sat back.

I kept my mouth shut through the rest of the information dissemination and the subsequent discussion between law-enforcement types. I was pretty sure my blotches didn't fade. A grief knot. Me and my big mouth.

8

"Open the blue folder," Jim said later, "and let's go over the evidence we have so far on yesterday's case. We have an ID by dental records as of eleven this morning. Her name is Lorianne Porter, she was twelve years old, abducted from a schoolyard after school where she was playing with friends. A man had been watching them from his car. There was an MVA across the street and the girls ran to see. Later, they found Porter was missing. None of the girls remember what the man watching them looked like or what color the car was. Some of them thought he might have been bearded."

I watched as my fingers reached out and opened the blue folder. This was my victim. The one found in my family plot. She stared up at me, artless and vibrant, a mischievous expression on her face.

"—and so I'll turn it over to Ashlee Davenport to tell us how she discovered the shoe and subsequently the body of the second vic."

Me? Jim wanted me to…? How nice of him to share that information with me ahead of time. I gave him a look that must have said exactly how I felt, because his eyes went wide and innocent. I was pretty sure the evil man was laughing at me. But I had taught third graders in Sunday school for several years. After that, a bunch of federal agents would be a piece of cake. I could feel my neck retaking its splotchy, rosy hue.

"How many of you are native South Carolinians?" I asked. Only a few hands went up as I bent to see both directions down the table. From the front, Jim made a small "stand up" gesture. Reluctantly I stood, smoothing my jacket.

"Often people from the North say the South has a small-town feel, even in the bigger cities. What they're sensing is a perception of rural roots, a slower pace that comes from the land. The Carolinas were predominantly agricultural states until long after the Civil War, a widespread smattering of small cotton or tobacco industrial towns or educational centers surrounded by cultivated land." I watched the cops' eyes glaze over as I spoke, but I needed them to understand why I had reacted as I had, even if my reasons had been subconscious.

"Farmers know their fields, what kind of soil is where, what the drainage problems are, how surface water moves across the property. We know where certain types of trees are likely to grow and where large copses of trees of a particular variety are." I opened my notes, transcribed from the tape I had made when I'd first found the shoe.

"My dogs brought me the shoe at approximately 07:52," I said, giving the time in military numerals. "I had worked all night and was standing at my vehicle holding my forensic nursing supplies, which includes equipment for evidence gathering and preservation. The shoe smelled…" I paused, remembering the fetid stink. I started over. "I knew from the smell something was wrong. However, my initial thought was that the dogs had been to the illegal dump northeast of the farm and brought back a shoe that had been buried with food or some other decayed matter.

"Just to be on the safe side, I took the shoe and began treating it as evidence I might gather in the emergency room. Most of the soil on Chadwick Farms and the surrounding property is red dirt with a smattering of yellow-tallow or black-jack, which are both types of poorly draining clay. The shoe had not been in contact with either." Several cops looked up at that. They were beginning to understand.

"There was a sycamore leaf crushed into the laces. Sycamores grow only in a few places on the farm, and only in red clay, except for one area of the farm where an ancient, dry riverbed runs through. The riverbed soil is white or yellow sand. There was sandy grit in the tongue of the shoe."

Emma leaned forward in her chair. "You're telling us you knew where the body was the moment you saw the shoe." Her tone was faintly disbelieving, which made my face blossom even redder.

I straightened my shoulders and lifted my head. A short woman's trick for looking taller. "I didn't know there *was* a body when I *first* saw the shoe." I smiled pleasantly at Emma and let the sweetness flow through me like honey. "When I examined its exterior, I *assumed* it hadn't been taken from the illegal dump, which is located northeast from the farmhouse on red clay, and I *assumed* that because the shoe had no red clay stains. Sounds simple once you think about it, doesn't it?"

I looked around the table and made eye contact with the cops as I spoke. They were listening now, which could be a good thing or could mean more interest in Chadwick land and Chadwick family members. But I did owe law enforcement an explanation of my decision-making processes the day before.

"When I opened the tongue and saw the toe, I *assumed,* mostly subconsciously, the general direction it had come from, which is near the stand of sycamores, which are near an old creek bed, due west. I *assumed* it was from a little girl, because the toenail was painted blue and most little boys don't paint their toenails." I looked at Emma. "And I *assumed* she was dead by the smell."

Steven started coughing. I resisted the urge to pound him on the back—a mother's urge, not a nursing one, as that never helped unless food was trapped, and he had finished the doughnut long ago—and leaned in toward Emma.

"At that point, everything was an assumption except that there was a body nearby, likely within two square miles because that's the range my dogs have been known to wander. Frankly, I was hoping I wouldn't find it. But I did. And you have an entire report in the blue folder. You might want to read it," I said pointedly. I sat down.

"Thank you, Mrs. Davenport," Jim said. His lips had a natural tendency to curl up, but he seemed to be having more trouble than usual keeping them straight.

"You stated for the record, when you gave your report to the officers at the scene and afterward to the agent during your interview, that you do not actually work the land on Chadwick Farm."

My eyes met his. "Chadwick Farms. Plural, not singular. No, I don't work the land. My maternal grandmother is the farmer. She makes the decisions, hires the help, works the soil, handles the harvesting and the sale of all the crops. Occasionally, I will over-see a specific job, especially during haying, though I no longer work the land myself. But I was raised helping Nana and have lived on the farm for most of my life. We Chadwicks know our land."

Jim nodded and turned to the side. "Let's take a look at the physical evidence and the items recovered with victim number two, Lorianne Porter. If you'll turn your attention to the wall at the head of the room, we have 35mm slides just back from the lab and they are much better quality than the digital photos in the blue folder.

"Let's rearrange the chairs up here." He pointed to the head of the table. "Schwartz, would you get the lights?"

Julie stood and dimmed the lights as Jim and the others seated at the head of the table moved to the sides with a scraping of chair legs and huff and puff of breath. A photo was projected on the wall against which they had sat. It was an in-situ close-up shot of the skeletal remains of a child's hands. I blinked once to settle myself in reaction. The hands were bound at the wrists in a grief knot. A ballerina doll was under the left wrist. A pointed stick seemed to be clasped in the skeletal right fingers. A black wooden tray was under the right hand, liberally coated with wax that had softened and run across it at some point. There was no wick.

"The lab has determined that this doll, like the doll found with Jillian LaRue, is the same brand ballerina doll, but the ballet clothing has been replaced by two men's white handkerchiefs, tied in artistic knots," a female voice said from the back of the room. "Silk embroidery thread holds them together at the doll's waist like a makeshift ball gown. I'll have to compare, but I believe that the thread is tied in a grief knot, too.

"Notice the jewelry," she continued. A silver ring engraved with intricate knots was on a left finger and a silver bracelet gleamed in the photograph on the same wrist. The PowerPoint presentation switched to a second slide showing side-by-side photos of her ears, where silver pierced earrings hung. Silver knots on dangly chains pressed into the desiccated flesh. Possibly Celtic knots, though I looked away before I could be sure.

"Lorianne Porter's family says she didn't own jewelry of this type and her ears were not pierced. She had wanted to have her ears pierced for over a year and the piercing had been planned for her next birthday. As you recall from the red folder, similar, though not identical, jewelry was found on Jillian LaRue."

I swallowed down a second reaction that brought tears. I closed my eyes a moment in the darkness and breathed deeply to calm myself. It wasn't working. Tears still gathered. The PowerPoint blinked again.

The third shot was of a filthy and partially decomposed pink cloth backpack on a table, with what must have been its contents placed neatly around. Water-damaged schoolbooks, pencils, spiral notebooks and several three-ring binders with lined paper inside. One binder was open, showing words arranged in verse like a song or poem. I hadn't seen them removed from the grave. I squeezed the bridge of my nose to stop my tears, knowing I would be the only person in the room showing such a reaction. The cops would simply be analytical, cold or angry.

"We aren't certain what this next item is," the woman's voice said. "The quarter is there solely to show dimension. The coin was not on the child's body."

A new visual was on the wall, showing a shiny quarter and beside it a deep-brown rock. It, too, was shiny on all but one side; the top was rough as if it had been broken off.

"We think it's composed of pottery or dark ceramic clay with a brown glaze, but the lab hasn't had time to analyze it. It was in the girl's jeans, the tiny short pocket that is part of the usual larger right pocket in the Levi's she was wearing. Nothing similar was in the other vic's possession. It may be something, or it may be nothing."

Again I borrowed Steven's pen and quickly sketched the rock-like thing in the margin of his page. He nodded in approval though I couldn't draw worth a toot. When he took the pen back, he redrew over my image, adding shadows, roundness. The woman kept talking as I watched him work, and the shape resolved into something common. I knew what the object was. Maybe.

Pulling the pen from Steven's hand, I wrote beneath his sketch *Hoof?*

He nodded slightly. Looking at the picture, he redrew it from another angle. It could be a horse's hoof, with the leg broken off. The woman had said it was pottery or ceramic. Her voice was droning on, but I had ceased to listen, ceased to watch the photos being zapped on the wall. It was a hoof. I was almost sure.

Into a momentary silence, Steven asked, "The broken piece of pottery from the girl's pocket, was there a flat side that was glazed? Opposite the broken side?"

From the dim room, the woman said, "Yes. We have a photo right here." She flashed a group of photographs onto the wall, perhaps thirty of them at once, searching.

"Why do you ask?" Emma said from across the table.

"Did it look like this?" Steven pushed his legal pad to her.

"Yes. It does," she said flatly, raising her eyes from the pad. "From another angle which we haven't shown. Rachael, do not put that up on the wall. Blank the screen. Lights," she demanded. The screen on the wall flickered into white as bright overhead lights came on and we all blinked in the glare. All of us except Emma, the supervisor with the silly little bow under her chin. She was staring at me, though she seemed to be addressing Steven when she asked, "Why?"

I answered her. "I think it's a horse's hoof. A broken-off horse's hoof, like maybe from a ceramic or pottery statue."

She smiled and it wasn't a pretty smile. "And you have one of these in your home."

Though shocked, I smiled back, and I was very sure that my smile was everything Emma's wasn't, gentle and kind, in contrast to my words, which sounded both too soft and too hard for the room. "What an interesting, if erroneous, conclusion to jump to. If I did own such a statue, and if I were the killer, or a member of my family were the killer and I an accessory, I wouldn't have been so stupid as to bring attention to myself by telling you it was a hoof." I gave Emma my best Princess Di smile, all sweetness, no teeth.

Someone up the table started to speak but I kept going, raising my voice a notch to override him. "However, if you feel the need to satisfy your mental calisthenics, you are welcome to send someone to my home to look. My nana will happily let you in so you don't have to break down the door." I narrowed my eyes slightly. "Just don't frighten my daughter or I'll bring you up on whatever excuses my very expensive lawyer can find."

"We have your permission to search your house." The words were flat and clipped, neither statement nor question.

I shrugged by lifting a hand and turning it palm up, just the way my mother had taught me a lady always did, especially when in the presence of one who had no concept of the niceties. "The cleaning crew hasn't been in two weeks. It's dusty. But you have my permission to look for a broken horse statue," I said, as sugary as corn syrup. I could feel the heat on my skin, this time because I was angry and not bothering to hide it. "Anything else you wish to search for, of course, will require a warrant," I said.

"Mrs. Davenport doesn't have a horse statue, broken or otherwise," Jim said.

Emma's eyes slashed to him. "Oh?" The word was loaded with insinuation and some threat I couldn't identify.

"I've been there a number of times," Jim said easily. I could hear the smile in his voice and knew he was about to give away our secret to the world, trying to protect me from the bow-tied barracuda across the table. "As you know from discussion yesterday, we're dating."

Emma's eyes rested on me with crushing weight, as if she had planted her feet on my chest. When she spoke, her soft tone was corrosive. "Of course, since you're dating her, the entire Chadwick family must be innocent."

"Simmons—"

"Stop," she said. Her cheeks were blazing with an anger all out of proportion to the situation. The air in the task-force conference room was brittle. No one said a word. The boss was pissed and looking for a boxing bag to bash. If that person happened to be an agent she could bully, so much the better. Steven started to speak, but I silenced him with a touch on his elbow, my hand below the table. Emma noted the movement.

"Who did the preliminary interview of this woman?" Emma asked, her eyes still on me.

"This woman has a name," I said distinctly, the

sweetness dissolved. "It's Ashlee Davenport, and Special Agent Julie Schwartz had that honor."

Without taking her eyes from me, Emma said, "Agent Schwartz, please escort Mrs. Davenport to an observation room."

"And see that my lawyer is notified immediately," I added. "Macon Chadwick, of Chadwick, Gaston and Chadwick, Attorneys at Law. I will not be speaking to any of you until he is present. I'd like water and a trip to the ladies' room." I dropped my wallet in front of Steven without looking at him. "Please make sure my car isn't towed while I'm being *observed,* Steven."

"Why do you need a lawyer, Mrs. Davenport?" Emma asked. The woman had a smile like the barracuda she had become, all teeth and intent to do damage.

And I'd had enough. "Because you are an ass, Ms. Simmons."

Beside me, Steven choked. I smiled sweetly again. And was escorted from the room.

9

Macon Chadwick was from both Aunt Mosetta's side *and* Nana's side of my family. He was half brother to my first cousin, Wallace Chadwick, which made him a…half cousin? All this convoluted genealogy gave Macon astonishingly beautiful skin tone—chocolate and milk, heavy on the chocolate—hair in soft locks, lashes long and curling over very dark green eyes. A one-hundred-percent gorgeous man.

Wearing a hand-tailored black suit, Macon pushed in the door of observation room 27. "They treating you all right, cousin?" he asked, his dark eyes seeming a deeper green in the light of the barred window. I nodded as he set a sweating Diet Coke beside me and opened his briefcase on the table. "You need anything?" I popped the top on the can and swallowed deeply. The fizz roared against my tissues on the way down, just the way a good cold Coke is supposed to.

"Not anymore. Thank you for coming."

"Sorry you had to wait. I was in court," he said, his deep voice bouncing off the walls of the narrow room. Macon could captivate a jury by the power of his voice alone, the tone so rich it reminded me of a big brass bell, sonorous and powerful. He propped a hip on the table. "What's this about you giving the feds permission to tear apart your house? Nana is pissed. Her words, not mine."

I narrowed my eyes. "I gave them permission to search for a broken ceramic or pottery horse, the hoof of which was found in the grave of a little girl. I did so in front of more than twenty witnesses, all of them cops. If they are tearing apart my house, they better be prepared to deal with the consequences."

"Figure of Nana's speech. I don't really know what they're doing from personal observation." He sat and pulled out a pen and pad. "Why did you give them permission?"

Briefly I told him why the FBI considered me a murder suspect or a material witness or a conspirator or an accessory after the fact. Sitting across from me, Macon took copious notes, his pen flying across the page.

When I finished an hour later, he tapped his expensive pen on the page with little bouncing motions like a snare drummer and said, "They're fishing. They need to do two things. One is to look busy for the press, which has been informed about the task force, the kidnapped girls and the hunt for the kidnapper. They're gathering out front in a rabid clump. The other thing the feebs have to do is to eliminate the obvious."

"The third thing they have to do is get me back for calling Supervisory Special Agent in Charge Emma Simmons an ass. In front of the same witnesses."

Macon's eyes glowed happily. "You didn't."

"She was and I did. Don't ask me to be sorry for it.

I'm not," I said, feeling guilty but unrepentant. I sat straight in my chair.

"For a such a sweet-looking little thing, you got a lot of Nana in you. There's no law against calling an ass an ass. At least not yet, anyway. But you could be considered as obstructing justice."

"I am not a sweet-looking little thing." I glared at him. "And I gave them permission to search my house without a warrant. How can that be obstructing justice?"

A knock came at the door and Macon opened it, said something to someone on the other side and closed the door, dropping a paper into his open brief-case. He sat on the table edge, hands clasped in his lap. "Sure you are. Always were, even when you stole the boys' clothes that summer at the pond and made Wallace and his friends walk home naked." Without segue, he added, "Feebs got a warrant. Probably because you called her an ass."

I put the two subjects together just as he had and answered them as one. "They deserved to have to walk home naked when they ran the girls off and wouldn't let us swim. What does the warrant say?"

"An agent on the scene very kindly faxed me a copy." Macon handed me the paper he had received at the door. It was an old-fashioned fax, the kind that used special thin paper and heat to mark it. "They are looking for basically everything. You ever finish selling Jack's guns?"

"Most of them. The only weapons left in the house are a double-barrel shotgun, one hunting rifle to use if I ever have to put down an injured horse myself, my pearl-handled 9 mm, which Jack gave me when we were first married, and another small caliber handgun, a pretty little steel-blue, short-barreled .38. Both the shotgun and the .38 are loaded, in my bedroom closet. The hunting rifle is in the fireproof vault room in Jack's old office, and my 9 mm is locked in my SUV. Jas keeps the little .32 Jack gave her in her closet, I think. You'll have to ask her where it is for sure."

"Cops may think that's a lot of guns for two women."

I could tell that Macon thought it was a lot of guns, and maybe it was for a city dweller, but not for someone who lived in the country. "Jack collected weapons. We sold off most after he died, but kept a few of his favorites."

"They'll likely confiscate all of them."

"For what reason?" I ticked off my irritation on my fingers. "They all are properly registered. Jas and I took courses in handgun safety. The girls weren't killed by guns, that much I understood." I dropped my fingers. "There's still no COD. That's cause of death, right? So why take my guns? That leaves a single mother at the mercy of any crime that might come her way. I want my protection back."

"Right. But you dissed the special agent in charge of the Columbia Field Office, a VIP with something like thirty agents under her." Macon showed his teeth happily, a vulpine grin that got wider when I narrowed my eyes at him. "I'll see what I can do, maybe pull your 'the little woman alone' routine."

"You don't like her either, do you? Emma Simmons."

"No one likes Emma Simmons. Look up 'wicked witch of the west' and you'll see her photo in the encyclopedia."

"Is she listening in now?"

"I wouldn't put it past her, though I requested privacy to confer with my client."

"Good." I clasped my hands in my lap, crossed my ankles and in my best Mother-Teresa-cum-finishing-school voice said, "I wouldn't want Ms. Bow-tie to hear that she dresses like a 1970's schoolteacher, or that her hair is twenty years out of date, or that chewing one's nails is often a sign of poor white trash or uncontrolled obsessive-compulsive disorder. It might also hurt her feelings to learn that she needs serious attention from a good aesthetician and a style expert. If she apologizes, I might direct her to a really good day spa, and I know this woman at Harbison Mall who can do wonders with clothes, even for someone as frumpy and styleless as Emma."

Macon laughed, throwing back his head, the voice that captivated juries and judges alike ringing like a bass-toned bell. "God, I love being a member of this family. And I don't think it likely that Emma will offer up any apologies. Don't think she has the balls."

I shook my head at him and sighed theatrically, knowing we were digging ourselves deeper if Simmons was listening, but I didn't care. "I agree, cuz. And if she gives us too hard a time, please feel free to ask Nana to call in the big guns."

"You mean political favors?" His eyes were glinting with evil humor, enjoying our exchange.

"I happen to know one or two of her pals personally. You know as well as I do that Nana has a judge and politician or two in her pocket. See if she'll dust off the pocket lint and get me out of here. I'm hungry, tired and have been locked in this room and treated like a suspect, while not being informed of my rights. I'm on call starting at 6:00 p.m. and I need to be free. I'd tell you how long that gives me, but they confiscated my watch."

"You'll get it back." Macon stood when a second knock sounded. Special Agent Julie Schwartz entered, glanced at him and set a large envelope on the table. Her face held a peculiar expression and she gestured at the door. "You're free to go, Mrs. Davenport. We thank you for being so helpful, and apologize for keeping you so long."

"The FBI doesn't apologize for anything," Macon said, his voice harder. Lawyer tone.

Julie quickly searched the length of the hallway, swiveling long legs and arching her back and neck to see down both ways. Macon followed her with his eyes, interest in his gaze. "They do when a member of congress calls to ask why his personal friend is being held without charges. They do when someone leaked to the press that the woman who discovered one of the bodies and who provided two of the most important clues in the case—four if you count finding the shoe in the first place, the toe in the field, the grief knot and the hoof—is held and questioned."

Julie pushed a strand of dark hair back behind her ear and smiled. "You have friends in high places, Ashlee Davenport. And one or two here. I managed to keep the last bit of repartee between you and your lawyer off the tape that was accidentally left running in the next room." She grinned, her eyes seeking Macon's again.

"That's a shame," Macon said. "That a tape was accidentally left running while an attorney was conferring privately with his client. I bet it gets destroyed, too."

Julie glanced at him and back at me. "Bet it does."

"I thought you wanted to question my client."

"Mrs. Davenport, did you kidnap and/or kill and/or bury the girls Lorianne Porter and/or Jillian LaRue?"

"No."

"Do you know who did?"

"No."

"Are you withholding any evidence or information from me or any law-enforcement officer or officer of the court that might speed us to the discovery and identification of the perpetrator of these crimes, or are you in any way impeding the resolution of these crimes?"

"No."

"Do you have any reason to think that you might know who perpetrated theses crimes, either acquaintance, friend, member of your family or stranger, for that matter?"

"No, I do not."

"Do you intend to discuss with friends, family or the media anything regarding the ongoing case?"

That one was a surprise but I figured cops had the same confidentiality issues as hospitals. I could treat this as I would patient information. Keep it to myself. Totally. "No."

"Good." Julie looked at Macon for an instant. He was watching her with a little half smile on his face. She looked back to me. "Ashlee, we're asking you to stay on as part of the task force, in a limited capacity. Though we're calling in a specialist, one or two of the agents want you to look over all the physical-evidence photographs for other signs that the perpetrator has rural roots. We're now looking for indications that he is a longtime Carolinian with interests in history and literary poetry, and perhaps in gardening."

"I don't want my guns confiscated. I want them all left at the house." When Julie hesitated, I pushed it. "I'm a woman alone in a remote part of the county. I need protection both from rabid animals and interlopers."

Julie chuckled at my choice of words. "Interlopers?"

"Trespassers." I'd been shot once by a man who wasn't welcome in my home and had been forced to defend myself. I had survived. The man hadn't.

Macon lifted his brows and watched us, seeming content to let me handle this one small thing on my own.

Julie sighed. "I'll see what I can do." Her eyes darted back to Macon, though she kept speaking to me. "You won't be needed on the task force full-time—in fact, you aren't wanted full-time, and your participation will be scaled back to zero if a link is found to your family. We won't divulge any evidence to you that might implicate or exonerate any member of your family, and will likely not share much with you at all. But my boss's feelings notwithstanding, most of us think you might be a help. We hope you'll tell us something else we didn't know, like you did today with the grief knot and the hoof."

"Grief knot?" Macon asked.

I hadn't mentioned the name of the knot in my rendition to Macon. "I'll show you later," I said. "Aunt Mosetta uses them to tie up her climbing roses. Has for years. So do lots of farmers and flower gardeners across the South." I looked at Agent Schwartz, who was looking at Macon, who was looking at her. "That doesn't mean my aunt Moses killed the girls or knows anything about them." Macon smiled faintly at Julie while I watched them. "I assume that it's still necessary to interview the rest of my family."

Julie turned to me. Her face was flushed and her eyes just a bit wide. Macon was a good-looking man, one of the rare ones who knew just how to look at a woman; he often caused them to lose composure, forget what they were saying, become a little lost for a second or two. But Julie seemed to be having the same effect on Macon. Interestinger and interestinger, as my daughter had said when she was a child.

"Yes," Julie said, sounding more composed than she looked. She flicked her eyes back at him. "In fact, Macon is on my list. I'll be interviewing you today, if you have time." She sounded a bit breathless, as if she were asking him over for drinks instead of an interrogation. "Then I need to track down other members of your family. Maybe you'd be willing to help me with that?"

"After you clear me as a suspect, and after we have dinner, I'd be happy to." Macon gave her *the look*. The one that melted women's hearts.

Julie rocked back fractionally under its weight, her blue eyes glued to his. "Dinner? I'm not sure that would be appropriate."

"You can pay your way if that would help resolve any ethical dilemma. Special agents and attorneys do have to eat. And my condition for offering to assist in contacting my family and aiding the FBI in whatever way possible is dinner with you." He smiled and Denzel Washington didn't have a thing on my cousin. Macon's smile was pure, hundred-proof, liquid sex. "After I answer your questions, of course."

"Of course." Julie looked a little shell-shocked. "Would you like to step into my office? We could start now." Her blush deepened, as if the activity she was starting in her mind was something different from and more heated than a simple interview.

I had the feeling that Special Agent Julie Schwartz didn't want to let my charming cousin out of her sight. Both of them seemed to have forgotten I was in the room.

"When do you want to let my client see the photographed evidence?" Macon asked, his voice a low purr, like a very large cat.

"Now would be fine. If she has the time." That breathless tone was present in Agent Julie's voice again. Shame on Macon.

Breaking the spell, Macon glanced at his watch. "It's quarter to five. You have over an hour before you start forensic call, Ashlee. Is now okay with you?"

"Now is fine. I'd like my belongings back. I left my tote bag of forensic supplies in the conference room. This is just my jewelry," I said, opening the large shipping envelope and removing my watch, amber necklace and gold hoops. I guess the cops had been afraid I'd hang myself with the necklace or slit my throat with the earrings. I stuck the earring hooks back through my pierced holes.

Power plays by the cops. Silly Emma Simmons. But maybe something was going on with the woman that I wasn't privy to.

Special Agent Julie looked at me, her eyes wide, pupils slightly dilated. "I'll assign someone to go with you to look over the photos of the physical evidence in the folders. Yours are still in the conference room. So is your bag. Everything should be there."

"Meaning everything has been gone through with a fine-toothed comb," I said.

"Never," Macon and Julie said at the same time. They both laughed—together. Sort of in harmony. It was so cute, Jas would have gagged as a matter of principle.

I spent the better part of the next hour going over photos of physical evidence and crime scenes. I drank another Diet Coke provided by a twelve-year-old boy masquerading as an FBI agent. I suspected he didn't even shave yet, but he stayed by me, watching me like a hawk. I was pretty certain he had been put up to the constant scrutiny by Emma Simmons. It was almost amusing. Only almost.

When I closed the final folder, I sat for a time rubbing my eyes. I hadn't cried. Hadn't given away by the slightest expression that I was horrified by what I looked at, that fighting tears was a constant battle. But when I closed the folder for the last time, tears sprang to the back of my lids and I sat, holding them in place until I found control.

I turned and stared at the wall of photos behind

me, memorizing each face, each name. Wanting to know them as little girls, not as victims, even if only for this moment.

Little girls. Two of them dead, the photos of their graves scorched into my memory. I had nothing to offer to help solve the crimes. Not a thing. Except a niggling suspicion in the back of my mind that I knew something but didn't know what I knew. Big help that was.

"Anything?"

I heard a soft scuffing sound and looked up at Jim, who was leaning one shoulder on the doorjamb. One hand was in his pants pocket, as if he had been there awhile, watching me, his face solemn and drawn. He looked as tired as I felt, dark five o'clock beard showing over an expression that said he really wanted to be at home or at the golf course, the shooting range, grocery store, getting his yearly bend-and-cough physical, or anywhere but here.

"Something. But I'm too tired to know what," I said. "Maybe it'll come to me after some rest. I'm sorry about the 'Emma the ass' line. Hope it didn't get you in trouble."

"Nothing I can't handle. I understand that a certain tape was damaged when it was left running in an unoccupied observation room."

"Oops."

He gave me a tired smile. "Got time for supper? I have an hour."

And my forensic call beeper went off. Lucky me.

10

He watched the girls playing, the soccer ball arcing off an elbow. The movement was effortless, clean, the goalie rejecting the attempted point with ease. His daughter caught the ball and pivoted, sending it back to the other end of the field with a single kick, the team instantly repositioning for attack. She was grace and beauty, her dark hair flying. Of course, the hair was a problem. He'd have to dye it back blond. The dark hair was her mother's fault. Had to be. He would never have allowed her to darken her hair.

As he waited for the end of the game, he sketched words and phrases on a legal pad propped on a small portable writing desk, finding a meter and rhythm as lyrical as the girl flying on the sporting field. It was coming quickly this time, the words flowing faster. *Perhaps this was the one.* Yes. This one. When inspiration waned, he stopped and watched his daughter. Another thought drew him back to the pad.

A referee's whistle sliced the air. He turned up the CD player, Vivaldi rising above the raucous sounds of the game, over the traffic. Words drifted onto the paper, linked to one another and to history and to art in a seamless flow.

"Lovely music," a voice said. He jerked, losing his place in the meter of verse.

The lyrical words that had been so brilliant dimmed and ebbed, slid away from him in a relentless rush. The poem... He took a single breath, the air bitter in his lungs.

"What is it?"

He looked up, bemused, and blinked back to the day, with its lengthening spring shadows and dull yellow sun. A soccer mom, bored, rich, a diamond bracelet glittering on her wrist. He struggled against rage climbing his throat. No one *ever* interrupted the muse.

Fury swallowed back like acid and he said, "Vivaldi."

"Oh. I like it."

When he offered nothing else, she pulled away from his car door and walked off, looking back at him once. Smiling. *Smiling!*

She should have been afraid. She had interrupted the muse. *No one interrupted the muse. It is not allowed.* Breath gusted from his lips in a little pant. *No one. Not ever.*

She waved at him. A little trill of her fingers.

A thin sweat broke out on his brow, under his arms. *It is* not *allowed.*

On the field the team started to play. The woman moved out of sight. His daughter crouched, her knees bent, her hands at the ready. She darted left, right, her body quick and lithe, her movements economical and graceful. She dove hard, straight to the side, and seemed to hang suspended, as if she could fly, arms outstretched, toes pointed.

The words that had fled returned as his daughter blocked a fast shot. He laughed happily. She had the gift. And she shared it with him, as always. The verse poured onto the page.

Near the end of the game, he pulled a single sheet of heavy paper from a folder and uncapped a fine black calligraphy pen. He opened the small vessel of ink and transposed the poem from the ugly yellow legal pad to the fine handmade paper they had created together. He finished the poem just as the CD finished the last strains. The sun would set soon; already it was tossing shadows over the field. In minutes, the game would be over and practice session would start, and soon after that it would be fully dark. Perfect.

Shutting off the CD player, he placed the poem in the small writing desk, away from prying eyes, and opened the car door. Locking the vehicle, he sauntered to the playing field to congratulate his daughter on a game well played. Over his arm he carried a black velvet throw.

She was jumping up and down in a small group of girls, their squeals slicing the afternoon air. Their excitement heated his blood. The pulse pounded in his head, roared in his ears. One girl hammered her back, resounding victory blows. He winced, but she only laughed and beat the other girl in return.

"We won! We're going to the finals!" she shouted.

He marveled at her. His huntress. So full of life and verve. How had she come from his genes, from her mother's genes? How had they, such an ordinary pair, made this incomparable perfection? But he knew the answer. She was a gift of the gods.

She threw her fist in the air, her feet coming off the ground in her exuberance. A taller girl grabbed her up in a bear hug and slung her around once in a tight circle. Three others joined in the mad dance and hugged, giggling, shrieking.

A push in the darkness sent him stumbling. He caught himself on the park fence, warm metal biting into his fingers. It was the woman who had stopped at his car. Fury flared in him. His fists clenched and he turned his head away to hide the reaction.

"Oh, I'm so sorry. I tripped. I'm so clumsy in heels. Are you okay?" She touched his arm in a casual gesture, her perfume floating over him. "Wasn't it a great game? Vivaldi, right? Which one is yours?"

"I'm sorry?" he managed to say, the words little more than a whisper as he harnessed his rage, leashed his voice.

"Which girl? Which is your daughter?" Excitement lit her eyes, but she said the words slowly, as if she found him pleasantly amusing or not quite bright enough to understand the questions. As if he were not in his right mind or was abstracted to the point of stupidity, his mind elsewhere.

The thought brought a rare smile to his face. "The goalie."

"Oh. Right. I remember that Carolyn's father travels a lot. It's good to meet you at last. I know you and Meagan don't get along very well, but believe me, we all know she's a difficult person. No one blamed you at all for the divorce." She put out a perfumed hand.

"Jan Krymer." She was brown-haired with long, bottle-blond streaks, her breasts firm mounds of flesh thrusting against her shirt, straining the buttons. She seemed friendly, but her words baffled him.

Meagan? Hesitantly he took the hand she offered. *Who was Carolyn?*

"My Julie and she are best friends. Maybe she's told you about me?"

He managed to shake his head as he withdrew his hand from her grip. *Carolyn?*

"You're Sam, right?" She hooked her arm through his as if they were the dearest of friends and gave a gentle tug toward the group of girls. "They have a sleepover next week at my place. You can rest assured that I'll keep an eye out." She tilted heavily mascaraed eyes to him. "No beer, liquor or guns in the house. Well, except for my Baileys but I keep that over the fridge and it's just for me. Special occasions only, like Christmas, New Year's and my divorce anniversary. I celebrate that every year. I bet you will too, huh? Glad to be out of that madhouse."

He nodded again, his breath speeding up, growing shallow and thin. This was not going well. He tried to pull his arm free, but she held on, pressing her body against his side. His heart rate accelerated at the sensation of a trap closing about him. What did she want with him?

"Maybe you'd like to come by the night of the sleepover? Check out the house, make sure it's secure enough for your comfort level?"

"I'm out of town that day," he said, the words coming abruptly to his lips.

"Oh? Where to this time?" She looked at him expectantly, a smile on her face. Why was she smiling at him? A rush of panic shot through him, an electric bolt of fear. He fought to keep his hands from fisting.

After a moment, he said, "Cleveland." The lie felt peculiar in his mouth, uncertain and foreign. He had never lied well. The syllables of the city carried a note of panic, the word breathy, the tone doubtful. "Yes, Cleveland." Surely she would hear the falsehood. But she accepted it completely.

"Well, maybe we'll just have to get together next game." She released his arm and patted her pants pocket, finding and holding out a card. "That's my private number. You give me a call when you're in town for the next game and we'll sit together, maybe go out for a quick drink after?"

He nodded and took the card. It was a business card for a local realty company. At the bottom was a number. He closed his hand on the embossed paper, fumbled for a pocket and inserted it. She ruffled her fingers at him again and went on to tap on the shoulder of a young redhead who turned quickly, a squeal on her lips. They hugged.

Seeing the gesture, the way the girl wrapped her arms around the woman's neck, he wondered if he had made a mistake not choosing this one. She was so loving. But it was unlikely she would have all the qualifications. His daughter ran across his line of vision, drawing his eyes. Her grace a magnet. No. She was the one. The poem proved it.

She ran to a woman with dark hair, and the two slapped palms together. Ugly, manly gesture. Her mother had never had an artistic spirit about her. He still could not believe he had married the cow. Before she could spot him and turn their daughter against him again, he made a quick right angle and moved back up the hill toward his car. He'd have to claim his daughter later. Later, she would be his. The way she was meant to be.

He went to his car and pulled out of the lot. There was a practice session before the girls could leave for the night. He had plenty of time to set up his arrangements.

11

I called the number on the cell's readout to let the hospital know I was on my way and opened the car door. Steven had added enough quarters to the meter so that I actually wasted half an hour of parking time as I raced away. Well, crawled away, through rush-hour traffic toward I-77 and the brand new trauma center where I worked, Carolina HealthCom.

Traffic was bumper to bumper, all lanes stopped in the quickly falling dusk. I looked at my watch. I'd be late to the call. I had a yellow emergency light perched atop my car to speed me past most obstructions, but it was pretty useless against several thousand cars all heading in different directions on the same freeway system.

I craned my head out the car window and tried to see around the eighteen-wheeler ahead. I wondered if I could blame the FBI for my tardy appearance. Probably not. Frustrated, I turned on a National Public Radio station and tried to relax.

It took me forty-three minutes to get to the Emergency Department. I made it to the hospital, parked in the employee lot, maneuvered past seven cop cars blocking the door at irregular angles, swiped my card through the security box and jogged toward the Minors ED. I was late. When on call, I was supposed to make it to the hospital needing my services within half an hour of the page.

In a large, well-appointed, modern hospital, the Emergency Department is divided into sections. The Majors section, where I usually work, is for big-ticket injuries, gunshots, codes, strokes, heart attacks. The Minors is for cuts, fevers, problems that could wait awhile if needed, but still had to be attended to. Ambulatory section was for walk-ins, things like headaches, bandage changing, administration of IV meds after outpatient hours. Carolina HealthCom even had a well-baby department that worked in conjunction with the county health department to administer shots and assist low-income or worried mothers.

I rounded through the entrance at the Minors and met a wall of cops blocking the hall. I slipped my forensic nursing ID around my neck on its chain and held it out to the cops as they inspected me, one by one and allowed me to pass through. In street clothes I didn't look as though I belonged there. In the background I could hear a girl crying but couldn't see where she was.

When I got to the nurses' desk, I searched out Lynnie Bee, my former supervisor at Dawkins County, who had moved on to bigger and better things and who was ultimately responsible for my career changes. She'd wooed me away from Dawkins with the promise of a $25,000 signing bonus. Money talks, and small hospitals are pretty mute. Lynnie and I had also brought over a few of the Dawkins County Hospital doctors for part-time work at a third more than they made in the smaller hospital.

"You got yourself quite a crowd, Lynnie," I said, spotting her sitting with a phone at each ear, obviously on dual hold. "What's up?"

"Thank God you're here." She slammed down the phones, shot to her feet, gripped my upper arm and pulled me away from the crowd, all as if she were moving in fast forward. Lynnie was stronger, younger and more athletic than I and I didn't bother to put up a fight. "We got a kidnapping. Claimed to be eighteen but looks more like fourteen," she said, talking at high speed. "She presented with acute abdominal pain, vaginal bleeding. Her husband was acting kinda weird, according to Clarissa, who saw them in triage."

"Husband?"

"Claimed to be. Weird bearded creep. Clarissa gave me a heads-up and I took the girl myself." Lynnie shoved back her bangs, which hung above her brown eyes and dangled over her glasses frames. The hair stuck straight up with the motion, boy-short and stiff with hairspray. "Something didn't smell right about it. She looked too young. Bruising at wrists and ankles, torso and around her neck in a choke pattern. Vaginal bleeding. She was scared. I told her husband he'd have to leave the room while I examined her. He refused. Was getting really agitated. So I asked to see some ID and he took off."

"Breathe, Lynnie," I said.

"No time. As soon as he leaves the room, the girl starts screaming that he kidnapped and raped her. A cop was in the next room talking to an accident victim and he overheard and took over. Now there are cops everywhere and I can't even get to her. Administration is dithering around trying to decide what to do besides firing me for hanging up on them just now and I haven't seen a security guy at all, not that they'd be any help against real cops."

"She's still bleeding?"

"How would I know?"

"Who's the MD in charge of Minors?"

"MacRoper just showed up, and thank God they've called Christopher in to cover the last two hours on Evans's shift. Evans's wife finally went into labor." We shared a grin. Evans was forty-two, madly in love with his wife, and a first-time dad. It had been cute watching him suffer through her pregnancy, trying to maintain a professionally composed demeanor, while chewing his nails in private. "Unfortunately, MacRoper's useless as ever," she continued. "I'm so glad you didn't date that man when he was sniffing after you."

"You pointed him in my direction," I reminded her. "MacRoper, Christopher and about three other single or separated doctors. Chart?"

"Hell, I'll find it. It's here somewhere." She began shoving three-ring binders around, checking the charts' spines for the cubical number, as she juggled subjects. "Suggesting any of them for you was a momentary case of bad judgment. And it never occurred to me to shove a young, good-looking cop your way. That girl's husband was bad news—" she interjected at whiplash speed. "Anyway, I learned my lesson. No more matchmaking." She tilted her head down and looked up at me from under her brows. "But how about Farley? He's cute."

"What are you on?" I asked, laughing. "Slow down. Farley's young enough to be my nephew, if not my son."

"Coffee. Lots and lots of coffee. You have everything I've ever wanted except a rich doctor husband," Lynnie said. "I'm just trying to live vicariously and get you one. You can't blame me for thinking you can do better than a cop,"

Ignoring the references to Jim Ramsey, I pulled a paper gown and gloves from boxes on the wall, stuck a rape kit beneath an arm, gripped my tote tighter and used my hips to wedge past the outer layer of cops, most of whom were standing around looking macho and taking up too much space.

Lynnie's matchmaking had led to a number of uncomfortable encounters, especially with MacRoper. I glanced up to see if he was around. MacRoper went by a variety of nicknames: Dr. Demerol, Dr. Death and Dr. Groper, because he overprescribed narcotics for any cause at all, because he had been known to just let people die on the code table and because he had fast and familiar hands. He was also an ass.

I had lodged complaints against him on several occasions for fast hands and for ordering meds at incorrect dosages. I avoided the man when possible. Luckily, he didn't seem to be in the vicinity.

I moved into the room slowly, smiling and apologizing each time I stepped on toes or nudged a cop a little too hard. Short women have an advantage when it comes to dealing with most male cops. Give them the helpless-little-woman look and they fall into protection mode fast. It may not last long, but I only needed to get to my patient.

"Tell me again what he said when he took you."

"He—he—he said he only wanted to talk. I didn't know he—oh! I'm hurting. I'm hurting."

"You say he was bearded? Did he have a weapon?"

I glanced at my watch as I slid between cops. It was 6:55 p.m. "Hello, dear," I said. "I'm Ashlee Davenport."

The three cops obscuring the bed shifted as one and glared at me. One was female. I smiled sweetly and slipped under the nearest one's elbow to the bed, assessing my patient instantly. Lynnie Bee was right. The girl was less than fourteen, and a small fourteen at that. She could have passed for twelve. Tears and snot were smeared on her face and her burgundy-tinted hair stuck to her skin. Fresh blood was on her hands.

Someone had gotten her into a gown before the cops had taken over and a blood-pressure machine was pumping up the cuff on her arm automatically. Blood trickled down the E.R. gurney, absorbed into the sheets. I needed an ultrasound of her abdomen, a surgeon and blood work drawn fast.

"You're going to have to wait, nurse."

I didn't look at the officer. I just pulled a rolling table over to me and placed my bag, the rape kit and my other equipment on it.

"Nurse, if you don't get out of the way, I'll have my men remove you from this room."

I turned and looked up at him. He was moderately

overweight, way taller than I, with a half beard along his jaw and sergeant's stripes. Maybe early thirties, a difficult age to deal with in men. Not a detective. Not an investigator. I'd had my fill of bossy people for the day and this one was young enough to be my son. Well, almost.

I put both hands on my hips and tapped my foot. "This is a hospital. My patient is bleeding. When medical assessment and treatment are finished, someone in authority will allow her to be questioned— with DSS or her parents present, as she is clearly terrified and underage. I am a forensic nurse, trained to preserve any evidence we might find. So, please *be quiet* and kindly get these unnecessary uniforms *out of my way.*"

The sergeant opened his mouth, but the woman grabbed his arm and said, "Sarge, the kid's bleeding. Maybe we oughtta wait."

I pulled the privacy curtain closed in front of his face, blocking them out and turned my back to them and the muttered discussion. They continued to back away, voices growing fainter as I checked my patient's blood pressure and pulse. She was losing blood vaginally. Best bet was ectopic pregnancy and/or spontaneous abortion. I checked her blood pressure and pulse— eighty over fifty-eight and 115—and I recorded the values on her gurney sheet with a ballpoint pen. Her skin paled visibly and she closed her eyes. She was breathing at a rate of thirty-two, getting shocky.

I dropped the head of the bed into Trendelenburg position, then grabbed an IV kit and ripped open the paper. I cleaned the inside of my patient's left elbow and shoved the Jelco into the antecubital vein, taping it off. To keep her blood pressure up, I gave her a bolus of Ringer's Lactate and saw an immediate response in both pulse and heart rate. Within seconds, she was more stable. I hung a bag of fluids and wet a clean washcloth at the sink. As I washed her face, she opened her eyes and looked up at me, her blue eyes vivid in the pale skin.

I felt the world slow around me. It couldn't be....

Leaning forward I brushed back her hair with my hand, parted it. A quarter inch of strawberry-blond roots reflected the light overhead. I knew this child. Knew she was—or had been—four feet ten, weighed eighty pounds, and had been missing for over eighteen months. She had grown in the past year and a half. I stroked back her hair again. Catching my breath, I said calmly, "Your name is Mari Gabrielle Bascomb, isn't it?"

Fresh tears spilled over her lids. "Yes. I'm Mari. And I want my mother."

Stepping calmly to the door, I gripped the rounded metal edge with both hands and stopped. The federal government, in its stupidity, had enacted patient privacy laws called HIPAA laws. The legislation made it a federal crime to divulge patient information. But if I didn't tell what I knew, other girls could die.

The fact that Mari was a minor worked in my favor, however. Until her parents or legal guardian arrived, I could do what I wanted. Within reason. At least that was what I told myself as I called for the sergeant. If the parents complained later, well, that's the breaks. I'd risk going to jail if it meant possibly saving a child's life. Nana may not think I knew who I was or what I wanted, but I knew that much about myself. I'd put a kid first any day. The sarge looked up.

"Call Special Agent Jim Ramsey at FBI headquarters," I said softly. "Tell him he has a…a blond kidnap victim here in the ED. She's on his list of missing girls."

"But she's redheaded—" The sergeant's eyes widened fractionally as he considered hair dye and his career all at the same moment. "The list of girls from the serial kidnapper we heard about today in shift change?" he asked, voice so soft I had to strain to hear.

"Yes." I was pretty sure there wouldn't be two different lists. "And the kidnapper was just here. Lynnie Bee," I shouted. "Get MacRoper or Christopher in here. Call an ob/gyn surgeon, and we need an ultrasound, stat." Over my words, cops were shouting orders to seal off the hospital and alert all security to watch for a man with a beard.

Turning back to Mari, I blocked out the commotion, smiled and pulled on gloves. "What's your parents' phone number and address, sweetheart?" When she told me, I wrote it on the sheet with the other information. I really needed a chart on her. "How old are you?"

"Thirteen," she sniffed and I handed her the cloth I had washed her face with earlier. "Is he really gone?"

"He's gone. You're safe. How long have you been bleeding, Mari?"

"About a week, but just like a regular period, you know? And then today it started getting worse. Charlie didn't want to bring me to the hospital but I was hurting." Her hands clasped across her middle. "It really, really, *really* hurts."

"We're going to get you something for pain, I promise." I smiled reassuringly and pushed back her hair, as I used to do with Jazzy when she was little. "Do you think you might be pregnant, Mari?" When she nodded, sliding her eyes toward the wall, I asked gently, "How many periods have you missed before this one started?"

"Two, I think. Maybe," she whispered.

Lynnie Bee appeared from behind the curtain and thrust a chart into my hands. I copied the patient's vital signs, which had changed drastically since triage, and her new ID information onto it. "Wrong name," I said as I wrote. "It's Mari Gabrielle Bascomb, age thirteen. Will you get with admitting and see that's corrected? Here's her parents' phone number and address." I handed the chart back to Lynnie. "Maybe a cop can go to the house and get the parents," I suggested.

"I'll start paperwork to give us permission to treat her," Lynnie Bee said, deliberately obscure. I nodded. The patient was underage and it was likely she needed surgery. Not that we would tell her that yet.

"Surgeon?" I asked softly.

"Ob/gyn on the way." Lynnie raced from the room.

Mari looked paler than just a moment ago, even with the head of the bed down at an angle and the LR bolus, and I didn't like the way her pulse was again increasing. It was now 107. "Sweetheart, Mari, I need to draw some blood and start another IV," I said.

Lynnie darted back through the curtain when my patient—now alert, unlike when I'd started the first IV—wailed in fear.

Almost mowing Lynnie down, Dr. MacRoper stalked in wearing wrinkled scrubs and sneakers. The man had little taste and not much personality, and I would rather see any doctor in the room than him. He jerked the chart out of Lynnie's hands and flipped through it, looking at values. Lynnie's eyes narrowed and she pressed her lips into a thin line, hiding a frown or a snarky retort, I couldn't tell which.

Diana, another nurse, moved into the room, bringing an IV pole and pump, and a second bag of fluids. She looked at Dr. Death and then at Lynnie and me, the same worried expression mirrored on both their faces. Dr. Screwup glanced up at the nurses in the room, his eyes moving from face to face. He frowned when he saw me. I raised a brow at him and he looked back at the chart.

We all sighed with relief when Christopher stuck his head around the corner. "I got this one," he said to MacRoper. "You wanted that stroke code. It's here."

"Thanks," Dr. Death said, flipping the chart at Christopher. He sent me one last look as he went out of the room. I couldn't interpret the expression, but it wasn't a jolly one. *Great.* It was clear the man knew I was one of the nurses who had complained about him.

The tension in the cubicle dropped by about thirty degrees. Under her breath, Diana muttered, "Thank God." I curled my lips under in amusement. Lynnie grinned ear to ear and slid her eyes to Christopher to see if he'd heard. His expression didn't change, but his ears turned red.

"What do we have here?" Christopher asked, his tone carrying that professionally cheery note they teach first-year doctors. He ran a manicured hand through his two-hundred-dollar haircut and shuffled closer in the six-hundred-dollar tasseled loafers from his last trip to Italy. Thousand-dollar reading glasses perched on his nose. In both his wardrobe and his demeanor, he made Dr. Demerol look like a slob.

"Possible ectopic?" Christopher asked. "Let's get an ultrasound, CBC, Beta-HCG, cath UA and BMP." Finally the doctor looked at his patient. "Hello, young lady." Christopher patted her leg through the sheet. Mari flinched.

Stretching a hand between his arm and side, I pointed to the admitting diagnosis code that designated rape. Christopher pulled his hand away from her thigh, his flush spreading in consternation. He hadn't bothered to look at the code or he'd not have touched her in such a familiar manner. He knew better.

Lynnie looked away, probably to hide a grin. There was a time when Lynnie would have insulted the man for his faux pas without a second thought. But when she'd become the Majors supervisor, she had been forced to dredge up some restraint. I was impressed with her self-discipline.

"Let's get a crisis counselor and her family in here," Christopher said. "I'll check back for the ultrasound." The doctor escaped and Diana took the chart from his hands as he went past.

"You shoulda slugged him for touching her like that," she whispered to Lynnie. "But at least he saved us from Dr. Death." Lynnie looked away, biting her lips and I chuckled under my breath. It was hard for Lynnie not to speak her mind.

According to hospital gossip, Dr. Christopher had been a pediatrician, but, like many doctors, the constant call time had been too much. He had found another specialty that required less dedication in terms of time, one more suited to his personality.

Other scuttlebutt said that his wife had dumped him, which maybe said something less flattering about him. Most doctors' wives are too comfortable to take off for less financially secure greener pastures, no matter how boorish their husbands are. But I had no problem with Christopher. He might be dull, but he was competent and capable.

I pulled the privacy curtain closed again. Bending over Mari, I soothed her, wiping her face. She managed a small smile and I realized that she had healing yellowish bruises on her face. The kidnapper had blackened her eyes recently. The anger I had controlled until now boiled up hard, my breath stuttering for a moment.

"You're going to be fine, Mari. I promise. Just fine. And your mother will be here real soon. I need to start an IV and take some blood. I know, I know," I said when she wailed again. "I'll be gentle. Okay?" The IV needle had to be big enough to administer blood through, which meant a fairly large bore. I could have lied, but I had discovered early in my career never to lie to patents, even children. I laid out my IV kit and blood collection tubes.

Mari stared at them with red-rimmed eyes. She didn't want to comply but I was good with kids and when she finally let me work, Mari barely flinched when I stuck her with the IV needle. Lynnie Bee rolled the ultrasound machine in while I obtained blood and taped the IV in place. After hooking up normal saline, I sent the blood to the lab via the pneumatic system.

In small hospitals, lab techs draw blood, radiology techs run and develop X-rays and handle ultrasounds, and nurses do only nursing. In most major trauma centers, nurses and techs do overlapping work and I was trained to handle ultrasounds. The abdominal ultrasound on Mari showed a mass above her bladder in the location of her uterus. A fetus. It looked as if it was centrally located and had no heartbeat of its own, which I verified using the fetal heart monitor. Mari's body was trying to expel a dead fetus. The radiologist checked in, agreed with my assessment and approved the quality of the ultrasonic photographs I had taken. I printed out the pictures and documented that there was no fetal heartbeat.

It wasn't my job to tell Mari she had been pregnant and was losing the baby. That was a physician's responsibility. I schooled my features so she wouldn't read the news in my face.

Knocking, the female cop stuck her head beyond the curtain. "Can I ask her if she knows the kidnapper's name and address?"

Mari turned paler than before and tears began again to run down her face. She swallowed hard. "I don't know the address. But he said his name was Tom. Tom Smith."

The cop nodded. "Thanks. No answer at your parents' home. We got a unit heading out that way. You got any other family in the area?"

"My grandmother." Mari gave her the phone number and address as I stripped off my gloves and the blood-streaked paper gown. The cop left at a dead run.

"I need to take this information to the doctor, Mari. Anything you need to tell me before I go?"

"No. Except I'm still hurting. Why?"

I touched her hand, strapped down with tape on a board. "Because you said earlier the kidnapper's name was Charlie. Not Tom Smith."

Mari jerked her hand from mine and looked away again. "You didn't hear me right."

I debated arguing with her. Stockholm syndrome was one possibility, the girl coming to love and care for the kidnapper, beginning to see things his way, wanting to protect him. Another was the possibility that she had aided and abetted a kidnapper she already knew, someone she wanted to run away with and still wanted to protect. I looked at the bruises on her wrists and ankles. She had been shackled. Her abductor had tried to strangle her, had beaten her regularly and savagely, if the fresh and fading bruises were any indication.

I checked again and Mari's bleeding had slowed. Her blood pressure was back up enough to make me happy and her pulse was stable at ninety-eight. Much better.

A tap sounded on the glass door behind me, and I saw through the crack in the curtain that the rape-crisis counselor was here. Fortunately it was Maggie, a woman I had worked with before. I held up a finger indicating I needed a moment.

"Mari, I know you're scared. And I know you were

with him a long time. I know it may feel natural to protect him, even though he hurt you and frightened you. But if you hide anything now and the police discover it later, it could cause problems, both for you and for him. Think about it, okay?"

Her face crumpled as if I had hit her, or betrayed her. And maybe I had. "I'm not hiding anything. Go away." Fresh tears trailed down and dripped into her ears.

"Okay. I understand. But you might remember something, anything, and I hope if you do, you'll tell us. Please." I stepped beyond the curtain and briefed Maggie. When I explained that Mari was hiding something, trying to protect her attacker, the counselor sighed, her massive, plaid-covered bosom moving heavily. I thought buttons might explode off her shirt and damage my eyes, but she exhaled and they stayed intact.

"It happens," Maggie said. "More than I would believe it, if I didn't see it with my own eyes. These girls are so young. So afraid."

"Yeah, well, this one may have information wanted by the FBI. Expect to be deluged by special agents and Department of Social Services and God knows who else."

"No one screws around with my kids," Maggie said. "Cops'll see her when I say they can see her. And if DSS wants a piece of the action, they can deal with law enforcement while I help with the girl. Why FBI, anyway?"

"Did you see the news today about the serial kidnapper in the region?"

"The one who's been taking girls from the city, killing them and burying them out in the country? Yeah. Why? Not—" Maggie grabbed my wrist. "Not—"

"Mari was on the list of missing girls. That's why the feds will be interested in her. It may be hard to keep them away. It may be wrong to keep them away."

Maggie swore viciously just as Emma Simmons, Jim Ramsey and Julie Schwartz blew into the ED. Great. And I'd only recently called the woman an ass. I *had* to learn to watch my tongue. Someday. But not today.

12

I pointed at Emma and got in the first volley. "This is a hospital. My patient has to go to surgery as soon as a surgeon gets here. She's bleeding. She will *not* be harassed, do you understand?" Behind me, Maggie took up position between the door and Mari, her arms crossed.

"What the hell are you doing here." It wasn't a question.

"My job as a forensic nurse."

"Get her out of the way," Emma ordered.

"I don't think so."

Emma turned blazing eyes to Jim Ramsey.

He held up a hand. "You wanted her on the task force because of her skills in nursing for just this reason. In case we got a live one. Well, we got a live one."

"And I have HIPAA laws to deal with. Federal laws you would have to arrest me over if I broke them," I said, my voice hard, but my eyes trying to tell them what they needed to know. "And you didn't give me permission to take the red folder."

Jim caught on. Turning to Julie, he pulled a red

folder out of a stack of paperwork under her arm. I took it and opened the folder to page six. The photos of all the missing girls stared out at me. His brows lifted in a question, and I didn't know how to tell him what to do. I settled on "Ask me," and pointed at the photos.

Jim looked blank.

"Is one of these girls here in the E.R.?" Julie asked.

"No comment."

A sharp silence met my reply. "Is it her?" Julie pointed at the photo of Jillian.

"No. She's dead."

"Is it her?" Jim pointed to a missing girl. He had caught on.

"No."

"This one?" He pointed at another photo.

"No."

"This one?"

"No comment."

"Mari Gabrielle Bascomb," he said.

"You did not hear that from me," I said, my voice firm.

Emma smiled at me in a way that was significantly less sharklike than before, and there was a crafty kind of consideration in her eyes. "Well, well, well. Let me guess." She pursed her lips and walked in front of me in a little half circle. The other cops backed up to give her room as if they had seen her do this before. "You were the one who told the local cops to give us a call."

"No comment," I said, watching her move. She stopped and faced me, reassessing. I hoped she was trying to forget that I had called her an ass….

"So there is a way around this 'stupid'—" Emma made little quotation marks in the air with two fingers of each hand "—HIPAA law. When can I talk to her?"

"That's not happening. She's underage and frightened and protecting the father."

"*The father?* Not *her* father?"

"No comment."

Emma Simmons swore with words that let me know she had a real problem with men in general and with rapists in particular. That last part we could agree on.

A uniformed cop ran up, breathless. "He's gone, Special Agent Simmons. But hospital security has cameras on the entrance he used and on the gate where he parked. They're pulling the tapes now for review."

"I got it." Jim turned on a heel and ran in the wake of the uniform. They disappeared around a corner.

"DSS will be here soon," I said, "and a surgeon's on the way. You—" I nodded to Emma "—need to talk to the nursing supervisor, Lynnie Bee." I looked over my shoulder at Maggie, her stout frame and dyed matte-black hair a challenge to the world. "Maggie, I know DSS isn't here yet, but we need to let someone in to talk to her."

"Like a young fresh-faced FBI agent?" She was looking at Julie. "Mari's scared. We need someone who'll go easy on her."

"Make pals," Emma said to Julie.

"This way," I said to Agent Simmons, glancing at my watch again. It was 7:15, and still no surgeon.

"You handled that well," Emma said as I led her to Lynnie Bee. "Didn't call me an ass even once."

"You didn't act like one," I said, and nearly choked on the words. Emma laughed as if she found straight talk an appealing and positive character trait. My mother would have feigned a swoon if she could have heard me. "Don't get used to it," I grumbled. "If other girls weren't missing it would never have happened."

"You're a real ball-buster, aren't you?"

My brows went up. *Me?*

"Looks like the decision to involve you in this investigation was right. As long as a member of your family isn't implicated in any way, at any point, as a suspect, we need you on this task force."

"What task force?" Lynnie asked.

"That's need to know," Emma said.

"And as long as it doesn't get in the way of our job, hurt our patients, or get us in trouble with the law, she's willing," Lynnie said. "Whatever it is."

Emma looked at Lynnie and stuck out her hand. "Emma Simmons, supervisory SAC of the Columbia Field Office of the FBI."

Lynnie Bee took her hand, gauging and measuring the woman in front of her. "Lynnette Beatrice Stubin, at the moment charge nurse of the CHC ED. Or God's right-hand woman. Take your pick."

I figured that explained the situation well enough for even Emma Simmons to understand. Two alpha females on the same turf. It would be a catfight or a remade world.

I left the sparring partners to visit, have tea and crumpets, agree on information to be shared about the task force or cuss one another, and went looking for Department of Social Services. I needed to head the

DSS officer off and explain the custody information. Hopefully that would give Julie enough time to win the trust of a frightened little girl and get whatever information my patient would share. It was 7:25. Where was the surgeon?

I still hadn't opened the rape kit. I needed to obtain the evidence for police that might lead to a conviction. And Mari was going to surgery, where most of it would be lost. Yet I didn't stop what I was doing. Not just yet. I spotted Carmella Gonzales, the DSS officer on call, before she saw me, and waved her into an empty patient room to chat. Carmella was from Puerto Rico and had married a local landscape contractor, originally from Mexico. She had two kids, both in college and a caseload longer than both my arms. She worked over sixty hours a week for way less money than I made and had more compassion than I ever thought about having.

She also knew the system inside and out and she'd skin me alive if she discovered that I had kept her from her client while a cop chatted her up. While she took notes and filled out paperwork, I told the social services officer everything that had happened up to now, including the pertinent medical information. Everything except that a fed was with her client. It took a good twenty minutes, with questions and answers in great detail. I finished with "Mari is probably losing the baby. Surgeon is on the way. OR has been notified and a surgical team is waiting for her. You won't have much time with her before she goes up."

"Thanks for the background." She added a last line to her notes and looked up, dark eyes penetrating. I hoped I didn't have the word *sneak* tattooed on my forehead. "You think it's a case of Stockholm syndrome?" Carmella asked. It had turned victims into willing helpers in the past.

"I don't know. Could be, I guess. Maybe she thinks she's in love with her kidnapper. Maybe the FBI got her on the list and she doesn't belong there. Maybe she just fit the profile of the missing girls and got lumped in with them."

"Okay." She gathered up her paperwork and shoved it back into the large canvas satchel she always carried. It had to weigh a ton. "Let's do this, then."

Over her shoulder, I spotted the surgeon entering Mari's room and knew I could relax. "I still need to open the rape kit and collect the evidence we need to take to trial," I said, "but I wanted you present when I did it. You ready for this?"

"*Chica,* I'm up for anything. Pass along my thanks to everyone for protecting the girl and getting her away from the guy. You did good." Carmella patted my arm. "I'll handle the feds and the locals once we get her into surgery. She can talk to them tomorrow or the day after if she's off pain medication."

"Good," I said, feeling guilty, but hoping Julie was finished. "She's this way."

As the surgeon swished past, we entered the room where Maggie and Julie were standing, wearing paper coats. Both looked like medical professionals. Julie smiled and said, "I'll be by later," and left, likely to update Emma. I introduced Maggie and Mari to Carmella and peeled open the sexual-assault evidence-collection kit.

* * *

Later, I leaned against the wall, rocked my head back, closed my eyes and took a deep breath of ED air. It was scented with dirty bodies, sweat, urine and old gym socks; the astringent smell of cleansers, rubbing alcohol and Clorox; and pizza from someone's supper. A wonderful mixture of smells. Hospital. A scent I loved. I'd be able to continue working here, if Mari's parents didn't make a stink about anything a judge would have to interpret, like their daughter's privacy rights.

And if they did? Well, I figured Macon would love arguing my case all the way to the Supreme Court. And my cousin would win. I didn't doubt a Chadwick.

My patient was in surgery and I had collected all the evidence I could in the rape kit. DSS was standing by; FBI was out checking leads with local law enforcement and Agent Schwartz was in the OR to collect samples from the fetus for genetic testing, so they could ID the father when he was caught. I was done for the night. I could go home. Instead I decided to wash up and wait.

I stepped back as Dr. Christopher rushed from the doctors' lounge, his starched lab coat catching the air and lifting out to both sides like gull wings. His face shifted into a concerned smile when he saw me, and he caught the door, holding it open with one hand. "I'm sorry about the little girl," he said. "I should have looked at the chart."

"Um, sure. No problem."

Christopher's blue eyes crinkled. "Next time, stop me before I do something that stupid." He pushed the door wide for me and walked off.

My mouth fell open but he turned away before he saw my reaction. One-handed, I caught the doctors' lounge door and watched him stride down the hall. I was pretty sure I had just witnessed a miracle. Doctors just didn't apologize like that. Nor did they leave their precious sanctuary open for nurses to use.

But…the lounge was open and empty, and I had been invited in. Sorta.

I stepped inside and the door swooshed shut behind me. I stretched out on one of the matching leather couches. Leather was the only upholstery good enough for doctors, and these put the worn-out plaid couch in the nurses' lounge to shame. A pillow under my neck, I watched the press conference on the wide-screen TV. An underling in the FBI told local and national media that law enforcement had a suspect in the Ballerina Doll Serial Murders and hoped to apprehend him at any minute.

They had named the case already. What a sweet sounding name for such a heinous crime.

The agent speaking to the press was the one who had watched me like a hawk in the conference room as I'd paged through the folders and studied the photographs. His knees were knocking, I was sure, as he fielded questions, answering carefully and giving nothing away. Must be part of FBI training.

A still shot taken from the CHC security camera showed the man who had brought Mari Gabrielle Bascomb to the ER and vanished. He was bearded, in his twenties, wearing a T-shirt and jeans, a baseball hat.

The man—Charlie or Tom Smith—kept his head

turned away from every security camera, the hat brim shielding his face. He looked like an angry kid, not a thirty- to forty-five-year-old man with a knowledge of South Carolina state history and the intelligence to plan and carry out multiple kidnappings and murders. Not the kind of man who could have buried a child in the ancient and difficult-to-find Chadwick Farms family graveyard. So much for profiles.

Or we had the wrong guy. I sat up slowly, leather squeaking under me as the video feed went past again, Charlie/Tom with his head down. Too young. Too country, in his boots and jeans. Nowhere near the profile. I didn't like it at all. Something was wrong with this.

The news guy was ecstatic and trying not to show it, spilling over with the urgency of the situation. Just in time for the wrap-up of evening news, this story was claiming all the public and cable news headlines. A manhunt for a child killer, and the local newscaster was making national footage. He'd combed his hair differently. He spoke with a deeper voice. Poor guy.

And yet, Mari's parents had not been found. DSS had taken Mari into custody until her family could be located. Something just wasn't right about Mari's story. I could feel it in my bones.

Using the remote, I switched off the set, stood and walked away. I left the building with worry at my heels. Something was wrong. But I didn't know what.

He found the team at their usual ice-cream parlor, the one they always went to when they won. Purchasing a malted milk shake, he took a tiny table in the back of the small dining room and sat, a periodical open beside his malt. Night had fallen, the glare of the parking-lot lights bright in the windows. The girls cheered and squealed and ran around the building inside and out, shouting with excitement. She was fast, her feet like the huntress's, swift and sure. Her face flushed with enthusiasm, her hair flying.

He tried twice to get to her when she was alone but each time missed his chance, once because another girl ran between them, the last time when her mother called to her. Frustration burned in him. He checked his watch. He'd have to try at her mother's house. This was entirely unacceptable. He had been near her too long without success.

He left the parlor, his shake untouched on the table, sweating a thick ring on the Formica. The girls were gathered at the back, talking strategy for the Saturday game. It was a waste of time for her to stay, as she would be with him by Saturday but he couldn't tell her that and spoil the surprise.

Back in his car, he folded the black throw and started the engine. He'd take a different way to her mother's house. But he'd get her back. Tonight was the night. He *must* have her tonight.

It was way past sunset when I pulled up into the farmhouse parking area and Big Dog met my SUV. He stretched, dropping his front legs down along the earth, back legs remaining upright, pulling the muscles through his chest and abdomen. His jaw opened to expose long canines and his back molars, white in the headlights. The scar from an old gunshot wound mussed the flow of fur on one side and he limped, but he was still a monster, and my guard-dog protector. Jack had given the well-trained dog to me, worried about the safety of Jas and me when he was traveling. Of course, no guard dog is a match for a bullet, and Big Dog had been injured by the same guy who'd left a gunshot wound in my thigh. Jack's poor—and illegal—business decisions had left his family open to danger no guard dog could protect against.

I cut the lights and Big Dog trotted up to my truck, happy that the last member of the household was home. I opened the door and he came close, placing his huge nose against my thigh. I scratched his ears and above his tail in the spot he liked best, and he huffed dog breath in my face as thanks. Jas's truck was parked next to mine, my niece's car on the other side, and rap music blared out the house windows at top volume.

My cell phone rang and I answered it, recognizing Nana's number. Instead of hello, I said, "Yes, the music is too loud. I'll have them cut the volume. My day stunk. How was yours?"

"Smart-mouthed kid. My day was the pits," Nana said. "More cops wandering the property while I tried to work. They wanted to *talk.*"

"And?" As I stroked Big Dog's head, the night wind reversed fitfully. He smelled of death and dog food. My stomach turned over. I had to remember to get Johnny Ray to bathe him so I could get the smell of the grave off him.

"I told them they could ask anything they wanted as long as they worked. I wore out two city boys hauling hay bales and made a woman federal agent go cross-eyed with data from the Net."

"You're an evil woman, Nana."

"Maybe so. I signed for your guns when the cops brought 'em back. They're piled on the kitchen table. Load 'em and put 'em up. And tell the girls to shut it down. Sounds like hell out here on the porch."

"Yes, ma'am, Nana. I'll tell them. Night."

The phone clicked off and I climbed the steps to the deck and into the house where I screamed up the stairs to turn the music down. Somehow the girls heard me. Young ears. I was too tired to think clearly, but safety came first. Country folk of a previous generation didn't think a thing about leaving guns lying around. These days, it was illegal with minors in the house and I had no idea who was upstairs with Jasmine and Topaz. I inspected the guns, removing the official tags indicating they had been taken from the premises and returned. Satisfied, swearing I'd clean them soon, and pushing away the guilt at the half promise, I loaded them and put them away, most under lock and key.

I hated guns, but I had needed one upon occasion. There were things I still didn't like to think about. I locked one gun, the pearl-handled 9 mm that was a present from Jack in the early years of our marriage, in the glove box of the SUV. The .32 and the shotgun, loaded with double-ought buckshot, went in my closet, behind the raised-paneled doors. The rifle I put in Jack's vault room, a tiny cubicle that once had held business papers safe from fire and casual observation but was now little more than a glorified closet off the L-shaped rec room.

I was too tired to cook supper so I poured a glass of wine, stole a slice of cold pizza from the box on the kitchen counter and started a bath. Adding some bubble bath, I crawled into the tub, the wine bottle on the ledge, and ran the jets for five seconds to make some bubbles. I had once hated baths. Now they were heaven, pure heaven. I stretched out in the tub and sipped my wine.

The small house was a pale blur in the streetlights, white paneled with real wood, not that ugly plastic stuff, blue-painted shutters on each window, a peaked roof and three steps to the front porch. The yard was neat but unimaginative, just like the woman he had married straight out of undergraduate school. Each hedge and shrub was trimmed to a rounded shape and uninspired flowers marched through the beds. Petunias. Mums. Shade-loving full-leaved plants. A straight concrete walkway to the street. Nothing creative, exciting or unusual. Just like her.

Anger burned as he thought of her and of what she was teaching his daughter about life, about art. Mediocrity. Indifferent, unremarkable, pedestrian—that was how she would turn out if he didn't intervene. And she would be taught to hate him. That could never happen. He would not allow it to happen.

Alone in the dark, the car's interior lights turned off and the door cracked open, he waited. A night breeze blew in, carrying with it a scent of ginger, delicate on the air. Ginger and vanilla, the scent of a bulb whose name he couldn't recall just now. It was a soothing scent, serene, a balm to the disconcerting sense of failure the night had brought. Calming the low-level hostility that thoughts of his deceased wife always provoked. He checked his watch. Forty-seven minutes had passed.

He had left once, to buy a burger from McDonald's and Chicken McNuggets with two different sauces for his daughter. She liked variety. Always had. Now, the vanilla shake was melted and his sandwich was cold, the nuggets rubbery and unpalatable, and still she hadn't come out to him. She always walked the dog. *Always.* He knew. He'd been watching.

Tonight, of all nights, she was late. Still, he waited.

At 10:54 the back door opened and she came through the side gate. *At last!*

His heart thumped once, a hard beat, slamming through him with potent force, settling in his ears with an erratic rhythm, in his fingers with an electric tingle. *She was coming!*

His hands slicked with sweat, his breath whistled once before he forced it under control. Even then it came in little pants, harsh and heavy, like the sounds of passion. The thought rocked him. No. *No!*

This was not like that. *He* was not like that. Not some carnal grunting in the dark, but the passion of art, of great paintings and epic poetry, of the holy things in life. The thought calmed him somewhat. This was his daughter.

Daughter.

Daughter.

The words were a muted refrain with each beat of his heart.

The ugly little mutt pulled on its leash, its bandy

legs treading a lazy, circuitous path down the sidewalk and the edge of lawn. It stopped and lifted a leg twice, once on one of the rounded shrubs, once on the garbage bin at the curb.

His daughter spoke to the dog as if it could understand her, her tone conversational. The mutt's tail wagged. It stopped to sniff at nothing on the ground.

In the car, his hands clenched on the steering wheel. Sweaty. He wiped them down his pants leg, the gesture only half-effective, the sweat like heated sludge. He lifted the velvet throw she liked so much. Its softness comforted him enough that he could take a breath, though it burned in his chest.

His daughter was coming.

Hurry up, he wanted to shout. But if he did, it would ruin the surprise. She loved surprises.

She was wearing satin pants and a tiny T-shirt, her feet in sneakers, the laces untied. Her hair was pulled back in a clip that caught the glint of the streetlight when she turned her head. She would be perfect when she washed that ugly color out of her hair and restored it to its usual blond. Her mother was a pig to dye it.

The dog led the way to his usual tree, the oak on the corner. Near the car.

He gripped the throw, taking a breath so fiery it ached. The satin of her pants caught the light, revealing a floral pattern.

The pug lifted a leg and sprayed the bark, marking territory. Disgusting. The dog looked up at him, sitting in the dark. Black eyes glittered even as he urinated on the oak. Showing uneven teeth, the dog growled low in his throat.

She looked over. Saw him. Alarm lit her eyes. She opened her mouth to speak. Or cry out.

He lunged from the car. Cast the black throw over her. She screamed. The velvet folds enveloped the sound. The dog barked. Charged. His daughter fought, shrieking, the tone shrill. Muffled. Her foot connected with his groin. He gasped, falling to one knee. Agony lanced through his leg.

"Be still. It's me. I've come for you," he said, his voice a whispered note of pain.

The pug caught his ankle. He got a glimpse of crooked teeth as it bit down. He grunted and stood. The dog held on and shook, the leg a pure, wrenching pain. He kicked. The ugly mutt flew against the tree. Rolled into a heap. In the seconds it took the pug to rebound from the blow, he had the girl in the car. The dog attacked the door, scratching the finish, jumping high, yelping. A light came on in the house. His daughter ripped the throw from her head, reared back a fist.

And hit him.

Hit him! *Him!* After all he had done for—

She screamed, hit him again, her fist connecting with his jaw. Unthinking, a reflex, he slammed his hand into her face. Her head rocked back. She gave a mewling moan and slumped to the floor.

He cursed. His breath hissed the words. His testicles throbbed. His knee fairly sang with pain. His ankle pulsated. Warm wetness filled his shoe. *He was bleeding!*

The door opened on the front porch.

Feeling light-headed, a mild nausea rising high in his chest, he started the engine. Without turning on his lights, he drove from the neighborhood, passing the house, the woman running out into the dark, wearing a bathrobe. She screamed. The ugly little pug chased him all the way to the main road before being left behind.

On the seat, his daughter moaned. He hoped she had learned her lesson.

13

I hadn't planned for the girls—fourth cousins and best friends—to join me in the bathroom, hadn't planned on the evening becoming a pj party, but it did. Two young women, one pale-skinned, one cocoa-skinned, blew into the master bath, informing me there were more friends on the way. "Class don't start till noon tomorrow and we want to partay," my daughter said. I turned on the jets again for another water-obscuring four-second cycle.

"Mamash!" Topaz shouted over the jets' roar as she draped herself across my tub and hugged my bare shoulders. "That bubble bath smell's chou!"

"And that's good?"

"The best!"

"Move over, girl. Hey, Mama," Jas said and hugged me, too.

"If you two fall in, this tub will overflow, and I will *not* be the one to mop it up," I threatened. I added bubble bath and turned on the jets one last time to preserve my privacy. The girls laughed at my modesty, high on life, college, youth and the latest gossip. Jas and Paz, friends for life. And, in the Dawkins County way of the Chadwicks, kin.

Black or white, male or female, right or wrong, good or bad, the Chadwicks had stuck together for over two hundred, forty years, sharing land, food, fortunes and opportunity, ever since Growling Jim Chadwick had married his half-black cousin and former slave just after the Civil War had ended.

Most of Dawkins County hadn't been terribly fast to integrate. I had grown up knowing my black cousins, swimming in the same ponds each summer while the city pools had still been, unofficially, segregated—and law enforcement had done what it could to keep them that way. Together we'd built snowmen in winter when school was out, sharing books and toys and playtime.

The family tradition continued in other ways as well. Topaz was Wallace's daughter, and Wallace was the result of an illicit union between my grandfather Pap Hamilton and Jonetta Chadwick, who was the granddaughter of Mosetta. Family lines all twisted around, in a way that was once typical of the South.

Topaz and Jasmine, inseparable since they were children. Jas, with her dark blond hair and dark gray eyes and pale skin, Paz with her milk-chocolate skin and green eyes and flyaway hair. Close as sisters.

He had to hit her again on the way home, hurting his knuckle on her teeth. He hadn't noticed she had braces. Dark hair and braces. His wife would pay for that—and for the wildness the woman had taught her. Desecration of his daughter, his muse. He sucked his bleeding hand for the last mile to the house. Their house.

He carried her inside, through the dark living room,

without turning on a light. After unlocking the basement door, he carried her down the stairs to the apartment, the bedroom done up in a delicate pink with a sitting area off to the side, dolls, toys and books on the shelves and in the closet. Pretty clothes. Carpet and four-poster bed. A TV and stereo system with CDs of classical music. A private bath. No windows except the one that let him look in on her without her knowing, to make certain that she was safe. No other windows anywhere below ground.

He laid her on the bed and pulled out a warm-up suit and T-shirt from the closet. Her own clothes might have to be destroyed if the blood didn't come out. That would ruin the process, but since he had already written a verse for her, perhaps it would matter less. It was, after all, the art that mattered. He checked to see that there were clean towels and toiletries in the brands she preferred.

When he reentered the bedroom, the bed was bare.

She stood at the door, her hand on the knob, a look of anger and fear on her bloodied face. But she wasn't about to cower. Her eyes flashed fire. And he suddenly understood. She was the huntress! It was true!

"What do you want with me?" she said as fresh blood dripped from her nose.

Her voice didn't quaver. Wonderful! "Art is the answer. Always. You'll come back to me. You'll wake and be whole and vibrant again, if the art is deserving, if it is worthy. I always knew it."

"You're crazy as a fruitcake. Let me out of here or I'll kill you, you sorry freak."

Something inside him snapped. He stepped toward

her, fists clenched. "You will not speak to me in that manner, without respect. I'll not have it. Now get out of those bloody clothes and into something clean. I put the outfit I want you to wear on the bed."

"You're out of your mind, you sick old bastard."

He lashed out, and the blow landed on her cheek. But then instant, breathless agony took him and he collapsed to his knees. Once again, he cupped his testicles, the pain bolting through him in electric waves of torment. His knee screamed as he hit the floor. His eyes watered. She hit him again. He saw it coming but could do nothing to avoid the kick. The blow landed on his mouth. Blood flew. Tears swelled and fell and he tumbled back. She leaned over him, her fist back.

"No!" His hand slammed her. There was a crack, a louder one as she hit the door. More blood sprayed across the room. She went still.

He fell on the bed, cupping between his legs, moaning. Long minutes went by. Slowly the agony of the testicular contusion eased. Pain like the paean of a bell sounded through him, growing softer, only slowly. Gradually the pain in his groin died away but the ache in his knee only grew worse. When he touched it, it felt bruised and swollen, as painful as the dog-bite lacerations. She had injured him!

When he could stand, he went to her. She was a crumpled heap, unmoving. He bent over her and listened for her breath, waited to feel it on his ear. He held two fingers to her throat for a pulse. Grief and fresh tears welled and he gathered her up. He cradled her on his lap on the bed and cried. It wasn't supposed to end this way. Never with blood. Never with violence. Only with love, with poetry and verse, music, art.

He kissed her temple. There was a smear of blood. Just a bit. No, it wasn't right. It was over already. Too soon. And this one had given him the verse right away. A gift of love.

He would have to make it right. When he could stand with her weight, he carried her into the bathroom and set her in the tub. In the four corners of the tub, he adjusted the positions of the brass statues, turning them so they could watch over the girl as he gathered his supplies and read the directions. As soon as she was blond again and dressed properly, he could continue. She deserved that much. A verse right away. Imagine what they could have done together had she lived longer…. Imagine.

14

The girls left me alone, finally closing the bathroom door on the way out to answer the doorbell. The other girls were here for the *partay,* the music changing to some whiny singer crooning in a minor key, the volume going up a notch. I could smell fresh pizza. I turned on the jets again and lay my head against the pillow. My muscles again began to relax. It had been a long and exhausting couple of days.

I nearly dozed off in the tub, waking with a jerk when the door opened. Jasmine stuck in her head, a big smile on her face. "What?" I asked.

"You better get out of that tub. You're famous."

"Huh?" I turned off the jets and pulled myself from the water, wrapping a huge towel around me. It draped to my calves, which was a good thing as the bathroom filled up with girls, all laughing and smelling of pizza and Clinique Happy and the newest J Lo scent. Two of the girls were chanting, arms making the circular motion of a cheer or maybe a rap singer's backup dancers.

"She famous. She famous. Jas's mama. She famous. On TV. On TV. Jas's mama. On TV."

That woke me up fast. "Okay, I got that part. What do you mean I'm on TV?"

"You made the eleven o'clock news," Topaz said, a bigger grin stretching across her face. "And we got it on tape for posterity."

"We didn't know you were working with the FBI, Mamash," one of the other girls said. She was blond with a beach-girl perkiness that made me feel old. I thought her name was Temperance, but wasn't sure. All Jas's friends called me Mamash.

"The news said I was working with the FBI?"

"And Nana called," Jas said. "She's ticked."

"Oh no."

"Oh yeah." Jas and Paz were both laughing. "Nana and Aunt Moses are on the way over for a family conference."

"At this time of night!"

The back doorbell rang, the one used by family and friends. I could have cussed. I settled on "Dantucket!"

I sighed, exhaustion pulling at my shoulders. All I wanted to do was sleep, but that would have to wait. "Turn the music off, Jas, and take your friends to the rec room. You girls go online and chat or something. And let Nana in." I shooed the girls out of the bath and went into the walk-in closet. I rested my head on the wall for a moment, savoring the brief silence. When I had dawdled as long as I could, I found a jogging outfit and socks and dressed. At this rate, I'd never get to sleep.

"Mama! Mama!" Jas screamed. I froze for a single moment. The other girls began to scream. Over the sound of terror I heard the raucous barking of dogs.

My fear shattered into fury. *No one would hurt my Jazzy baby.* I grabbed Jack's double-barreled shotgun, racing from the closet and down the hall. All the girls were shrieking, a shrill tone of real alarm.

I burst from the hallway, banging my elbow on the jamb, and followed the sound of fear out onto the porch. In the security light, I saw a fury of dogs, snarling, teeth bared, ruffs raised, darting about. Barking in sharp high tones. Above it all was an agonized squeal.

The dogs had cornered a possum.

My heart thudded in my chest, half residual fear and half frantic relief. I handed Nana the shotgun, grabbed a broom and waded in, banging dogs away, shouting, "No! Down, Big Dog. Cherry, no!"

Like it did any good. Any dog protecting territory— and its owners—will go feral, especially once the scent of blood hits the air. But I knew my dogs. Even in a blood frenzy, they would obey. Eventually.

It was too late to save the possum by the time I got the dogs all separated out. I didn't have it in me to scold them for doing what dogs do. Kill prey. Kill trespassers. Protect their own. But standing over the torn, bloody body, knowing it had wanted nothing but to live and raise its young in safety, brought tears to my eyes. Tears for a rodent. I *was* tired.

As if sensing that I was close to the breaking point, Nana sent the girls back inside the house and found a shovel in the barn. Silent and grim, she used it to carry the possum back to the barn, then locked the animal up in the tack room. I followed her, my eyes burning, the shotgun hanging from one hand, not sure how or when I had gotten it back.

"There's no reason to bury it this late," Nana said, her voice as blunt as a mallet. "I'll send one of Moses's young'uns over in the morning to dig a hole. It's going to be a job getting a hole deep enough to keep the dogs from digging the possum up again. They seem to have developed a tendency for grave robbing."

At the words, the tears I had been holding in fell, a fast, hard scouring that left my throat aching, my eyes burning and my skin scalded as I sobbed, my face cradled in one arm and pressed against the tack-room door. Nana stood silent as I cried, once or twice patting my shoulder. More kindly, she finally said, "Don't worry about it, Ash. Life's throwing you a lot of curve-balls just now. But you'll do." It was a lot more words of comfort than Nana usually gave, and was her way of telling me I'd make it through the crisis.

I laughed shortly. But I felt better after her version of a pep talk and wiped my face, nodding when she suggested that we return to the house. "Thanks, Nana. I'm okay." I leaned into the hand she cupped on my shoulder.

"Course you are. You're a Chadwick."

When I laughed, the sound was stronger, more calm. "Yes. I am."

When we got back to the house, the girls had already gotten over the excitement of the possum. The TV was on and young voices chattered in the rec room.

Nana and I stopped in the doorway. The rec room was free of the business furniture and hunting trophies that had hung there when Jack had been alive and this had been his office. After his death, I had found a photo of Jack lying naked on the maroon carpet, with Robyn, my best friend in all the world, naked above him.

I shuddered at the memory and Nana again comforted me with a gentle pat, though she surely attributed my reaction to the possum and not to old pain. I had ripped up my husband's power-red carpet, sold his furniture, slapped a couple of coats of paint on the walls and turned the office into a teenager's party room.

In just that way, I ripped away my own reactions to old pain. Jack was dead. Long dead, years dead. And I was whole and had people who loved me, right here in this room—my nana and my daughter.

There were six girls in the rec room—young women, really, all twenty or so—but none of them hid a bottle or glass when I entered. I didn't smell alcohol or smoke of any variety, and I was proud of Jasmine. If she had experimented, I had never caught her. Which might mean that she was just more sneaky than I, but I preferred to believe that she was the perfect daughter. It was easier on my heart. Nana snorted and walked past me, carrying a lowball glass full of good bourbon to a chair in the corner, a scowl on her face. Her eyes were on the TV and her goodwill had evaporated.

The headline banner on the evening news was pink, emblazoned with bold red words, AMBER ALERT. "Turn that up," I said. Realizing I had made it an order when one wasn't necessary, I added, "Please."

Topaz extended a hand with the remote and turned up the volume. The reporter, a young man, was live on the scene in a Columbia, South Carolina, neighborhood. "It's been twenty minutes since the abduction of Sharon White, a thirteen-year-old girl who played soccer, was a red belt in karate and had just taken up white-water rafting. The young athlete's mother, a single parent, is currently with the police. They have just released this picture of the girl, who was abducted by a man in an older model station wagon." The reporter held a photo of a pretty girl with dark hair and eyes full of life, up to the camera. All I could think was *She isn't blond. She isn't blond.*

"Police do not have a license-plate number," he continued, "and the only description of the kidnapper is that he is a white male. Again, a white man in an older, white station wagon has abducted a thirteen-year-old girl. Anyone who might have seen a white wagon leaving the Dutch Square area of town is asked to call police immediately. Anyone seeing a white station wagon with a white male driver, with or without a passenger, is asked to call police." He glanced back over his shoulder.

The anchor asked a question, but I didn't hear it. On-screen, Jim Ramsey's long, lean form walked across the lawn, tension in every limb.

"We'll have more shortly," the reporter said. "The police have stated they will issue a statement at 11:45, and with the urgent nature of an Amber Alert, I expect little in the way of delays. Back to you, Shelly."

Mari had been in police custody only a few hours. Already the kidnapper had abducted another victim, and this time in a very public way. I had taken enough psychology courses and read enough mystery novels featuring profilers to know that meant he was beginning to decompensate. But she wasn't blond…. Did it matter? Was it the same guy? Was it a copycat kidnapper? I had heard of such possibilities.

"Mama? You know her?" Jasmine asked.

I raised my head and looked into my daughter's gray eyes. She was worried. Again. I had made her worry a lot after Jack had died, losing myself in my own selfish grief and I had sworn not to let that happen again. I took a deep breath. Honesty and forthright speech with my child was not second nature to me. It was downright hard, but I was learning to be honest. I met Nana's eyes and she nodded fractionally, as if she understood what I was thinking.

"The girl's body that was buried on our land, the serial kidnapper the police and FBI have been talking about, and the fact that you saw me on TV are all related." I took a seat on the edge of the big cushy couch and the girls scooted down to make room for me. "I am, marginally speaking, on the task force."

Jas's eyes sparkled with excitement. She opened her mouth and I held up a hand to stop her. "I will tell you nothing. Not one word of what I learn about this situation. Don't ask." This time when I issued an order, I felt perfectly okay with it. It was hard to know just how to act with a daughter who was on the verge of womanhood but hadn't quite reached it, but my decision to treat this just as I would any confidential patient information made it easier. Jas shut her mouth, looking mutinous.

Nana's brow lifted, letting me know she would not be included in any gag order I gave myself. I said to the girls and Nana, "I gave my word not to talk about it."

Nana's scowl deepened. She was big on keeping

one's word. "Your name and face were on the news," she said. "That means the killer knows who you are. Are you safe? Is this house safe? Is Jasmine safe?"

I looked at her in horror and scanned the room. Females in rural areas were generally safer than big-city girls. Fewer rapes, fewer assaults, fewer everything. Maybe there were simple reasons for that—less stress in rural living, fewer places to go where trouble might brew, a slower, easier lifestyle. But Nana was right. I looked at Jas. "Can you stay over at Topaz's for a while?"

"No."

My brows went up all by themselves. "I beg your pardon?"

Jas stood and held my eyes. When she spoke, it was to her friends. "Party's over, guys. See you later. Paz, will you see them all out?"

"Sure, cuz. But I'd rather stay and see the fireworks."

"Not this time," my daughter said. Behind her, Nana grinned as she sipped and swiveled her chair so she could see us both better.

"My house, y'all," Topaz said. "Bring the pizza."

Moments later we heard them clatter out the door. Silence settled on the room as Jasmine and I studied each other. I expected to see rebellion on her face, but instead I saw determination and a stubborn intensity that reminded me of Jack. Jack, as I had known him to be before all the hurtful secrets and lies had come to light. A curious, painful tension in my chest eased, as if a tight band was loosened and I could breathe. Somehow, seeing Jack's expression on Jasmine's face brought relief to my heart. A sense of peace I hadn't known I was missing. I fought a smile down and won. "*No?* What happened to 'No, ma'am?'"

"No, ma'am." Jas shifted her feet into a balanced position, as if ready to do battle. "I know you're worried about me, but I'm not leaving you alone in this big ol' house. I'm not moving out just because there's trouble. I'll keep my gun loaded and near me at all times. I have that holster Daddy got for me. I'll hang around the barn only when Elwyn is here, and I'll go inside the house and set the alarm when he leaves, if you aren't home. I'll call Nana if I think there's trouble. And the police. But I'm not moving out." Jas glanced at her great-grandmother and licked her lips. "And you can't make me."

Nana chuckled into her whiskey glass. A moment later I laughed, too, the sound rueful. "Your gal's growing up," Nana said. "I'd say she's got a spark a me in her."

"God help me," I said. "Okay. You can stay. But you keep your cell phone on you and turned on at all times. And if the press shows up, call the sheriff's department. I'll notify C.C. that you're here alone. See if he can schedule a patrol now and then."

"Lotta good that'll do," Nana mumbled.

"It's better than nothing," I said.

"Not by much."

"I'm hungry," Jasmine said. "We have pizza in the fridge. How 'bout I start a fresh one? Supreme okay?"

"Fine by me," I said. "I'm sure your nana isn't finished with me."

"I'll take my tender ears to the kitchen." Jas left, sock feet silent on the carpet.

"I gave my word I'd keep the task-force business confidential, but there's still a lot to tell," I said. "Let me get my glass of wine and we'll chat."

Nana grunted and rose to refill her glass. "Wine," she grumbled. Nana thought a real woman should drink bourbon.

When I returned to the rec room, I curled up on the couch and said, "If you think Jasmine is listening or you see her shadow at the door, let me know."

"She is a nosy little thing."

"She's a lot like you."

Nana smiled and seated herself back in the lounger. "Flattery will get you nowhere. Spill it."

So I did. I left out a lot, but most of that Nana could figure out. "They still think the kidnapper is one of us, don't they?"

"This family's a handy target. Cooperate. As soon as they rule us out, they'll move on to likelier suspects. But wear your gun, okay?"

Nana lifted her shirttail to reveal a little .38 in a belt holster. 'Nuff said.

I saw Nana off, her lithe form striding through the woods. I watched until the security light came on at her house, and went off again. When the house phone rang I answered it, her number on the display. "I'm safe," she said. "From now on, we stay in better contact. You get called in to work, you let me know. E-mail me your schedule."

"Yes, ma'am. Night."

The phone clicked off. Nana wasn't much on unnecessary niceties. When the phone rang much later, my daughter and I were having a picnic on my bed, the pizza stone on a pad of towels, her cola and my wine on the nightstands. This time it was Jim. As I answered, I took a quick peek at the TV. Letterman was on, but the little Amber Alert icon was still up in the corner of the screen.

"Hi. How's it going?"

"Not well," he said. "You know we got an Amber Alert out."

"I have the TV on. Any progress?"

"The kid's pet dog chased the car. It just dragged in, half-dead of exhaustion. Tracker dogs are on the way to follow the dog's scent. Maybe it'll give us a direction."

"The girl in the hospital?" I asked, careful not to say Mari's name in front of Jas.

"Crying. Not talking. The parents were on vacation at the beach. We just got them and they're on the way. DSS let us talk to her, but she's not cooperating until her parents get here."

I could hear the frustration in his voice and felt a twinge of remorse. I had been responsible for DSS getting to Mari. But she had needed legal protection. She was just a kid. Had they suggested she not talk to the cops? If I hadn't gotten in the way, would the cops know the identity of the kidnapper? Would the latest little girl be snuggled down in her bed?

Guilt snaked its way through me. Before I could reply, Jas slid her piece of pizza back onto the stone and took the phone right out of my hand. "Jas!"

"Hey, Mr. Big Tough Cop. My mama's name and picture made the evening news. I don't know anything about being a feeb, but that just seems stupid. Now the whole world knows who she is. A quick Internet search will show her address and heaps of personal information. You can even get an aerial shot of the house and farm. Who's gonna protect her if this nut job decides to go after her?"

I ripped the phone from Jas and glared at her. Hard. She just glared right back. Jas was once again trying to protect me. Which felt weird, but at the same time gave me a glow. "Sorry about that," I said into the phone.

"Don't apologize. She's got a point. But there's not a lot I can do about it." I heard the phone muffle and then he said, "Listen, I gotta go. When you're in town, let's do lunch. Call me."

"Do lunch?" I repeated.

And he clicked off.

"Men," Jas said, disgusted. I couldn't help it. I burst out laughing.

He watched the news off and on, late into the night, the Amber Alert, the police updates, the flyovers by the TV news helicopter, its camera shooting not much of anything except dark homes and streets. They didn't have a clue. Not one. He had bandaged his ankle and was holding an ice pack on his knee, alternating ibuprofen and Tylenol for the pain and swelling. Sitting there, the sound muted, he mostly watched for shots of her. Blond, a bit plump for his taste. But… A mother of a daughter. A widow. Ashlee Davenport. She had to be lonely. Had to be.

15

Jas landed on the bed, waking me just before seven with a blare of the television. "Wake up, Mama. Jim's on TV." I rolled over and shoved the hair out of my mouth and face. A sexy sleeper, I'm not.

I rubbed my eyes and focused on the set in the armoire across from the foot of the bed. I expected to see a press release, Jim giving a statement. Instead I saw aerial footage of cops in SWAT gear and plain-clothes cops in vests, cars with blue lights flashing, all surrounding a small house in the pale light of dawn.

Jas slid from the bed and pointed to a tiny figure in the corner of the screen, kneeling in weeds, protected behind an old Jeep on cement blocks. My heart leaped into my throat. It was Jim. He held a long-barreled gun across the hood, his head bare in the early light. "Don't cops wear protective headgear?" I said, more insult than question. *Idiots.*

"They've been in a standoff for half an hour in Blythewood," Jas said, climbing back into the bed with me. "When they tried to storm the place, the guy fought back and shot a cop. He's been taken to the hospital."

Blythewood was near I-77 and Carolina Health-Com, where any injuries would be taken. I picked up the phone and dialed directly into the Majors. Sharon, a nurse I knew in passing though we worked opposing shifts, answered. "Hey. This is Ashlee," I said. "I'm watching the TV. You guys got enough coverage or you need me to come in?"

"We got it covered, Ash. Dr. Rhea-Rhea is here and she's got everything under control. It was a slow shift, till now."

"The cop?" I knew better than to ask. The federal crime of breaking patient confidentiality and all. But sometimes there were ways around a law.

"We got a thoracic surgeon on the way in. We'll call if we need you. Later."

"Bye," I said as unnecessary adrenaline shot through me. Thoracic surgeon meant the cop had taken a chest shot. If he'd been wearing his vest—and I didn't know any cops who went without these days—that meant the round or rounds had penetrated below the vest and traveled up through the gut into the chest, or that the round had hit at a downward angle through the shoulder. Worst-case scenario, the shot had penetrated under the arm and through from side to side. Usually such a shot damaged both lungs and a good part of the circulatory system.

I wanted to be there. I wanted to help.

But Jas snuggled up next to me and I patted her arm, taking comfort in the warmth of her body heat and the scent she wore, the same night-blooming jasmine from

Revlon that she had given all her female relatives at Christmas. My gal's signature scent.

"He'll be all right, Mama," she said as she turned up the volume.

I knew she was talking about Jim, and realized my eyes were on the cop as the news helicopter hovered over the scene. My heart was pounding an irregular rhythm; my skin felt clammy. It was an intense reaction, and it both startled and distressed me. When had I become so attached to Jim Ramsey?

As if she felt my fear, Jas laced her fingers through mine and squeezed gently.

The TV reporter's face appeared as a small inset in the screen. "This is Jacqueline Omera at WIS, with an update on the breaking news in Blythewood. Police have traced a man who they are calling a *person of interest* in the kidnapping of several young girls in the Columbia area to this neighborhood. Charles Wayne Smith lives in the small house centered on your screen." Jacqueline's expression was taut with the tension of the moment, her eyes direct and piercing.

"When police went to his house early this morning to bring him in for questioning, the man opened fire, injuring one officer, who has now been taken to Carolina HealthCom. According to one source, the local police believe Smith may have a young girl, kidnapped last night, in the house with him, which is why they have called in a hostage negotiator and FBI backup." The reporter looked to the side and said, "We now have an update from our reporter on the scene at Carolina HealthCom. Let's go to Jermaine Joiner at the scene. Jermaine?"

The view from the helicopter vanished, replaced by a scene of the CHC parking lot, the ED entrance in the background. "Jermaine Joiner here, Jacqueline," the smart-looking black man said, making me think of a singing duo—Jacqueline and Jermaine. "As you can see in the background, police and ambulance have arrived with the injured cop, whose name has not yet been released. We do know it was a uniformed officer, who was working the night shift."

The scene refocused beyond Jermaine to the back of an ambulance where paramedics lifted a stretcher down to the tarmac. A fresh, unstained sheet had been placed over the body, and before the man's head could be seen, a cop unfolded a blue plasticized paper sheet, to give him privacy. Other cop cars, lights flashing, raced into the lot and cops poured into the entrance. A distraught, dark haired woman was handed from cop to cop with care and she disappeared inside, too.

The camera centered again on Jermaine. "Hospital spokeswoman Rebecca Cooke assures us there will be a press release as soon as possible, and we will be there to cover it. Back to you, Jacqueline."

The helicopter scene reappeared and the reporter rehashed all the breaking news, speaking in headlines, as if everything she said was capitalized and of world-shaking importance. Which, to me, it was. Jas muted the TV and put the remote in my hand. "Want some tea? Breakfast?"

My daughter needed to baby me, so I nodded. "Sure. Tea. Cereal would be nice. And I diced some fruit a few days ago. If it's still good, I'd like that, too."

"Coming up." Jas clattered away, once again assuming the role of caretaker. Guilt flitted through me. A daughter wasn't supposed to take care of her mother until the old lady hit eighty at least—and in the Chadwick family, eighty was young. But Jack's death had changed the dynamics of our relationship and I still wasn't sure how to change it back. Or even if I should try. I should probably watch Dr. Phil or Oprah or one of the other TV advice specialists.

Jas returned a moment later, carrying a tray of cereal, hot tea in big mugs and fruit. We had breakfast in bed and watched the stalemate on TV until the helicopter had to refuel and the morning shows came on. Jas headed off to school, her little .32 in her glove compartment and her cell phone strapped at her waist. Unable to sleep, I got up and rambled around the house.

I hated housecleaning and usually did little except straightening clutter, laundry and making the beds. The housekeepers came twice a month—which was tomorrow—and shoveled us out, but unfortunately, the clothes still piled up. I spent the morning putting things away so the cleaning crew could get at the filth, did laundry and kept an eye on the TV for news reports. I was staring at the screen when WIS interrupted a lunchtime soap with more breaking news.

Jacqueline had given way to another well-coifed twentysomething, this one blond and blue-eyed, standing before the news desk. "We are back with breaking news, a story WIS has been following all morning." She quickly recapped. "We have been informed that police believe a young girl, kidnapped last night, may be inside the house. A source tells us— Oh!" She pressed her earpiece. "Police are moving in. The reporter from the scene sees white smoke from the window, perhaps tear gas. Can we get this uploaded to our viewers? Yes, we have our news chopper at the scene, and aerial footage is available."

The scene over the house in Blythewood appeared, the view from straight overhead in what had to be a perilous position for the camera person. On the ground, police moved toward the house, weapons outstretched in two-handed grips, knees bent to present smaller targets and to give them better balance.

White smoke poured from a window at the front of the house. Two State Law Enforcement Department cops carried a battering ram. By the time they reached the back door, four SLED officers had handholds on it, and I saw the ram swing forward hard. Local and state cops in gas masks and SWAT gear disappeared inside. I was happy to see Jim behind the Jeep, where he was relatively safe. I knew that meant he was waiting for the all clear, which came faster than I anticipated.

I muted the annoying newscaster and watched the scene unfold with only the sound of the dryer going and the screaming inside my head. Jim was seventh inside and second outside, a lanky male in tow. The man was thrown to the ground and cuffed at hands and feet, another cop staying with the prisoner while Jim ran back inside.

I prayed they would find the kidnapped girl safe. Unharmed. But no one else came out of the house. No DSS van appeared on the scene. No ambulance moved in, lights flashing.

I hit the mute button, restoring sound as the anchor's face appeared again, her blue eyes wide and stern, a look an older woman might have pulled off but which made the blonde look about ten years old, a child playing TV anchor. "Our remote reporter, Jermaine Joiner, has left the hospital where veteran police officer Stanford Rickoff is still fighting for his life, currently in surgery to repair what we have been told are life-threatening injuries. Jermaine is now at the scene of the shootout. Jermaine?"

Jermaine was already speaking when his face appeared and the sound kicked in. "—is no indication that a hostage has been found. Police are swarming through the house, and we can hear the sound of walls and doors being kicked in. The officers are all over the property, searching both outbuildings and fanning out through the low scrub around the house." An officer appeared, one hand out to shield his face or to block the camera and we heard him ask Jermaine to move twenty yards farther down the street. The camera remained rolling as the news crew complied. In the background, other news vans were briefly visible, also rolling down the street.

Jim raced from the house to an unmarked car with a man in the driver's seat, radio to his ear. The car started and Jim left the scene, still talking, now on a cell phone. He turned away from the camera as the car passed, but the crew caught the side of his face, his expression clear. Fury. Failure. I knew no girl had been found. Frustration flowed over me.

I turned the television off and finished the laundry before dressing for the scheduled task-force meeting.

I wondered if they would let me in, or if the cops would appear on my doorstep to harass me again first. Not that I really minded. My words to Nana the night before had been trite but true. As soon as the cops ruled out my family, they could move on to more likely suspects.

I made it to the FBI building on Westpark Boulevard by 2:45 for the 3:00 meeting, parked a block down the street and went inside. On the way, I spotted Steven's SUV parked on the street and Jim's Crown Victoria behind secure fencing in the employees' lot.

At the desk inside, I presented ID to the woman behind the glass and waited. And waited. And waited. And finally got mad. At 3:15, I dialed Jim's cell. He answered, and before he could speak, I said, "It would have been a kindness and just plain old good Southern manners to let me know I was banned from the meeting."

Jim said, "Uhhhh."

"Well, that's a lively rejoinder. I *am* banned from the meeting, I take it?"

I heard a door close and the ambient noise quieted. "Sorry. Ash, I'm really sorry. Someone was supposed to call you."

"Uh-huh. Bow-tie Emma tell you that?" Without letting him answer, I went on. "I have better things to do than to be jerked around by a woman with jealousy issues."

"Simmons and I have never—"

"Not jealous about you and me. Emma is jealous about any woman stomping on her turf. You tell her I said so. And you tell her she better stop wasting my time." I snapped the phone shut, nodded to the officer, who was hiding a smile, and shoved open the door to the outside. I was nearing the sidewalk when my phone rang again. I glanced at the display and flipped the phone open. "She got me an apology yet?"

"Dinner at the Cock's Feathers at five?" Jim asked, naming a restaurant in an old building down in Five Points, a new one that catered to the alumni crowd of the University of South Carolina, whose football team mascot was a fighting cock. "I missed lunch and I'm starving."

"Emma?"

"Will not be joining us. Something about her dinnertime repartee gives me indigestion."

I couldn't help it. I laughed.

"That's better. I'm sorry about Simmons. I'll speak to her. Now, how about dinner? To make it up to you?"

"Yeah, okay. I'll meet you there. But I'm on call, so if something comes up I may have to cancel."

"Same here. Check your messages. Bye," Jim said.

Feeling lighter of heart, I got in my old SUV, wasting the quarters still in the parking meter and drove out toward I-77. Twenty minutes later I was walking into the disinfected confines of CHC's Majors Emergency Department, knowing I could finish paperwork if I needed an excuse to be here. It was my good luck that Lynnie Bee was working. She had been pulling double shifts to deal with what she described as "a small debt crisis," and lately I had found her working in the ED more often than not. Lynnie would dish the dirt. I stuck my head in her door and asked, "How's our patient?"

Lynnie jerked her head in a "come in" gesture. Closing the door behind me, I came inside and sat down. "Mari Gabrielle Bascomb is resting quietly after a morning of hysterics and a parade of cops that would make Macy's proud," Lynnie said, putting down her pen and sipping from a cup. She made a face and I knew her coffee had gotten cold. "That boy they caught? If he's a kidnapper, I'm Herbert Hoover."

"She ran away with him, didn't she." I made it a statement, not a question.

"I think her parents had refused to allow her to see the guy. She ran away, got knocked up. Things got hairy financially, he got stressed and she got beat up a few times. From the look of her mama's black eye, that's about what Mari expected from a man. Poor kid. Now she's got cops all over."

When Lynnie made a second face at her cold coffee, I got up, dumped the used grounds from the old stained coffeemaker on the corner cabinet, and added fresh water. "You don't have to do that," she said, but I heard the exhaustion in her voice. She was several years younger than I and in a lot better shape, playing tennis often and running in local marathons. But right now her eyes were tired, her shoulders had the it's-been-a-bad-day slump, and her hair, which stood up in short tufts on a good day, hadn't been combed in hours. She needed pampering and a calm ear more than she needed coffee, but I could give her all three.

"And that cop," she said from behind me.

My hands stilled a moment before continuing, shutting the little lid of the coffeemaker.

"He'll make it," she said, "but he's gonna be stuck

behind a desk for the rest of his career. They had to take out half of one lung." I hit the button that turned on the heating element and heard the nearly instantaneous sizzle of water. "His wife is a real trooper, though. Got some paramedic training. She held up better than the cops around him. Started right in giving orders and limiting who could see him and when. Did you see her press conference?"

I shook my head.

"She was great. Good TV presence. Calm. Refused to answer questions. Just gave a quick report and asked for prayer. Not rattled, that one." Lynnie was focused on the far wall when she smiled. "Now that you twisted my arm and got all the good gossip out of me and set me up for doing hard time, are you going to do your backlog of paperwork so you have an excuse to be here?"

I blushed and Lynnie laughed as she rose to pour a fresh cup of coffee.

"You can have the desk," she said. "I hear the overhead speaker. We got a stroke code coming in." Lynnie paused as she came around the desk and hugged me, one-armed, her coffee threatening to lap over the cup rim. "How's your family?" When I looked at her in question, she said, "You know. With the…" she paused and looked away, as if realizing what she was asking. "With the little girl you found on your farm?"

"Hanging in there," I said. "It's hard, though."

She nodded and gave my shoulder a squeeze. "Lock up when you're done."

"Thanks, Lynnie."

"OTR," she said, which was Lynnie's shorthand for "off the record."

"OTR," I quoted back at her, and she left me in the office. Feeling guilty, I sat in the still-warm chair and did paperwork, catching up on files that had lain dormant for a week or so. Nursing had once been about patients. Now it was about documentation. Paperwork, paperwork, paperwork. When I left the ED over an hour later, I was feeling righteous and more than a little excited about dinner with Jim.

He called when I was nearly there; not to cancel, as I feared, but to ask me to order for him. The wind picked up as I entered the restaurant, blowing my hair in a swirl and my skirt higher than I liked, and I was glad when the door closed me in.

The Cock's Feathers wasn't fine dining, but it had great burgers and better fries—likely cooked in lard and full of trans fats, but totally delicious. I got a bucket of fried veggies to sustain my feelings of righteousness, knowing the fat content in them alone was a week's worth of good eating down the drain. Not that there had been good eating in the last few days. Midnight pizza and wine. I'd be doing diet penance for a month.

I took a booth in back, a nook I liked that would keep us screened from sight, and set the little red marker with our order number on the table edge. A corner TV was tuned to CNN with a breaking report, and I listened to the announcer update the world on the Amber Alert.

The story of the serial kidnapper had become national news, with so-called specialists coming out of the woodwork, some telling parents how to protect children, survivalist-types recommending keeping guns loaded and ready, self-defense specialists showing personal defensive moves, and news celebs just stirring the already boiling waters. The announcer suggested that the FBI was ready to charge the man, Charles Wayne Smith, with kidnapping, and also implied that the Bureau had more information pointing to another suspect. I wondered how much of that was a way to get viewers to tune in more often, and how much of the conflicting "news" was inside-source reality.

Minutes later, Jim followed the server down the narrow aisle. The term *boyfriend* bounced around in my brain as I watched him, weird feelings shifting within me. I didn't need or want another man. I was totally fulfilled and happy in my single life, and I certainly didn't need to be hurt again. But like my blushing I couldn't suppress the little spurt of delight when his eyes met mine.

Jim was right at six-feet-tall, lanky and trim, with brown hair and eyes. Together we looked like Mutt and Jeff, me coming to his shoulder, rounder than was fashionable and older.

Jim sat. When the server left, hot grease sizzling on plates between us, he took my hand and kissed the back of it. My face, warmed when I saw him, heated to a blazing red. Jim laughed low but released my hand and sat back, sighing. "Man what a day. You blessed this yet? I'm starving."

I held his eyes, pleased that he remembered we asked a blessing in my house when we ate. Well, usually. Without lowering my head, I said, "Thank you, oh God, for this food. Bless it to our health. Amen."

Jim's brows raised and I said, "Public blessings don't *have* to draw attention, though when Aunt Moses prays, it's long and loud with fulsome praise, no matter where she is. And she likes the entire restaurant to be involved."

"Preacher at heart?" he asked, shaking a paper napkin across his lap and taking a sip of his vanilla Coke, a Cock's Feathers special.

"Missionary at heart. Old-time Baptist. She wants everyone to know her Lord like she does."

"I was raised Lutheran. She going to try to convert me?" Eyes twinkling, Jim bit into his burger and moaned softly under his breath. "Missed lunch," he reminded me through the mouthful of food.

"Probably. When I was a kid it used to embarrass me, but I gave up trying to make her be PC years ago." I took a bite of my burger and nearly moaned with him, but something about dual moaning from the hidden booth struck me as foolish, if not immoral, and I restrained myself.

Jim ate with the silent rhythm of a working man who had missed a meal. Bite, chew, swallow, sip, repeat. I ate slower, finishing half of my burger and a third of the veggies to his whole meal, and passed the remaining fries and veggies to him when he still looked hungry. He ate it all and grinned unrepentantly at the mess of greasy napkins and ketchup. "Sorry."

"No, you're not."

"No, I'm not. But I am sorry about eating and forgetting my duties as a conversationalist. My mama would be appalled. She taught me better. So. How was your day?"

"Not as exciting as yours, Mr. TV Action Star."

He made a little snorting noise through his nose and shook his head. "Local cops use those news choppers more than you would imagine, letting them coordinate chases, follow a suspect on the run. But they can be pains in the butt sometimes, too."

When he took a bite of fried squash, I broached a question that had been bothering me. "The little girl kidnapped last night, Sharon White. According to her Amber Alert picture, she was brunette, not blond. All the girls on the task-force wall were blond."

"We noticed."

"And?" I asked, my voice softer so the six business types squeezing into the next booth wouldn't hear. The after-work banking and legal crowd were packing in, with the student population close behind. By six, there wouldn't be a seat left in the place.

"I can't talk to you about that."

At his tone, I narrowed my eyes. "Can you tell me if you've ruled out my family?"

"No. We haven't. In fact, I have a few questions for you."

I felt heat start to rise, but this time it was an angry flush. I sat back stiffly and opened my handbag, "I paid for a meal with my interrogator? I don't think so." I slapped the receipt on the table. "Pay up and I'm out of here."

"No, no, no, Ashlee. No." He was laughing and waving his hands in front of himself as if trying to wipe the last few seconds off the face of reality. "Okay.

This is off the record, but here's what I have. A few members of your family are still possible suspects, yes, because they have records. But they aren't any higher on the list than anyone else. Smith, the guy in custody, is our prime suspect at this time. But some things don't add up with him. I just want to ask a few questions about your family history, is all."

"Genealogy or individuals?"

"Wicked Owens."

I snatched the receipt off the table and walked out. Chadwick T. Owens—known in the family as Wicked Owens, a play on Chadwick that was more than appropriate—had been a troubled youth in Charlotte. In and out of gangs and involved in petty crime, he had been a resident of the juvenile justice system rather than the public school system until the age of fourteen, when he'd been accused of killing a man.

Aunt Mosetta had hired a detective to clear his name. When the P.I. had been successful, Wicked had gone to work for the man to pay off his debt to the family matriarch. He'd been on the straight and narrow ever since, not that he'd had much choice against Aunt Mosetta and her plans for his life. Wicked Owens was a near legend in Chadwick lore. His mama had disappeared off the map for a time and when she'd reappeared, it was with a fatherless, troublemaking little boy in tow. Wicked was one of the lost ones brought back to the fold, his place on the genealogy map filled in, his problem-child personality properly corrected. Of course, there were dozens of places on the genealogy map still vacant.

Wicked was in business on his own now. He ran Chadwick T. Owens Security Firm, and he was one of the best in the business. He was small and wiry, weighing not much more than Jasmine, a coffee-and-cream-skinned man with the green eyes of Aunt Mosetta's branch of the Chadwicks. He'd helped me through a bad time or two when I'd needed security around the house and farm. I liked him. And he was family. Throwing a five-dollar bill at the waitress for tip, I slammed out the door and into the billowing wind.

I had reached my truck when Jim caught up with me. "Ash." He took my elbow and whirled me around, which made my mad-meter go through the roof.

I slapped him before I thought about it, the sound ringing through the parking lot. "You can talk to my lawyer. Boyfriend, my ass." I got in the cab, locked the door and took off so fast gravel slewed through the lot.

He pulled up the Chadwick Web site and clicked on the photo file. A moment later, he was staring at her. Blond. Lovely. Ashlee Davenport. He raised a hand to the screen and traced the contours of her face. She was perfect. He didn't understand why he hadn't thought about it before. The mother figure. Of course…

16

I was halfway home before I calmed down enough to think about the consequences of striking a police officer. A federal cop. Can I be any more stupid? My phone rang, and when I saw Jim's number, I considered not answering. Instead I flipped the phone open and said, "I'm sorry I slapped an FBI agent. Are you pressing charges?"

"I don't know," he said slowly. "You gonna forgive me for being an ass?"

All the tension drained out of me and I eased my foot off the accelerator. I was hitting eighty, moving with the northbound traffic but still traveling faster than I liked, and faster than my old Ford wanted to go.

"Maybe," I said. "If you know what you were an ass about and this isn't just a 'placate the little woman' ploy."

"I invited you on a date, suggested a fast-food place instead of a restaurant more suited to your refined elegance, showed up late, somehow made you pay *and* questioned the integrity of your family, obviously someone you like."

He had it all down pat. Smart man. "Wicked Owens

is a charming, kind man who got into trouble once a long time ago and has worked his backside off to remake himself. To make himself worthy of his Mama Moses and the trust she put in him. If he were white, fully white, he never would have appeared on your radar, would he?"

"I'm not a racist, Ash. I've got white Chadwicks on my radar, too."

I wasn't sure that was any better, but it seemed ornery to say so. I maneuvered around a slower-moving convertible with the top down. The driver had hair so tangled it would have to be buzzed to the scalp. "So why do you want to know about Wicked?"

"He came to me today with some information. I want to know if he's on the up and up."

Guilt snaked its way into me. I had just slapped a potential boyfriend and…oh crap. I had called him that. I had actually said, "Boyfriend, my ass." Maybe if I just didn't mention it… I took a slow breath. "Wicked is on the up and up. If he told you something, you can trust that it's the truth as far as he knows."

"Good. Thank you. We're going to charge Smith with statutory rape in about an hour. And we're holding him pending charges on the other cases. But there are things that don't add up, and the information Owens brought in is even more damning to our case."

"Thank you. I'm sorry I lost my temper and slapped you. I've never slapped a man before. Ever."

"Maybe it's because it's been a few years since you had a boyfriend. It likely made you feel a bit on edge."

I closed my eyes and cursed silently under my breath. But only for a moment. I was still going seventy.

"It's been a while since I had a girlfriend," he continued, and his voice dropped lower, a register that made my toes curl. "So to make up for being an ass, when this case is over I'd like to invite you to Charleston. There's a restaurant there that might make up for burgers and fries. Date?"

It took two tries, but I got it out. "Date."

"I gotta go now. Watch me on TV in an hour."

"Okay. Bye."

The phone made a series of little clicking noises before I flipped it shut. Dang. *I had a boyfriend.* And he was taking me to Charleston. Oh crap. Overnight? Had I just agreed to sleep with my *boyfriend?* A titter burbled through my frozen lips.

I thought, not for the first time, about Jack. Losing him, a man I had trusted and loved so totally, and discovering that he had not been the man I'd thought him to be, had to have affected me on all sorts of levels. Had to.

Jim had been gently but persistently trying to move our relationship to another level. And I had been digging in my heels, not so gently. Did I want to trust another man? Did I want to move beyond what had to be scars of grief and betrayal? Could I? And if so, was Jim the one to make that happen?

Some small flame warmed within me. Charleston…

I pulled off the interstate and passed Trash Pile Curve, crossing the bridge over Magnet Hole Creek—a creek where cars, guns, safes and other stolen things were reputed to be tossed by the county's less-than-savory crowd and where locals sometimes went fishing—with a large magnet and a hundred-pound test line, hoping for treasure. It was a beautiful evening and I figured I could work in the barn for a while with Elwyn. The trainer and I hadn't worked together in days, and I needed to see which horses would be ready to foal in a month so I could set my work schedule accordingly.

As I pulled in to the drive, the phone rang again. It was the number to the ED. Before I could say hello, Lynnie Bee said, "How fast can you get here? We got a train wreck in the middle of town. Chlorine spilled, a major evacuation, with inhalation injuries. So far everything is heading to Richland and Baptist, but we're on standby for a code 515."

515 was a disaster code. This day was never going to end.

"On my way. Let me tell Jas what's happening and grab some clothes. I'll be there in thirty."

"Make it twenty," she said. The phone clicked off. So much for manners in the new electronic world. I pressed the accelerator, raced down the drive and slewed to a stop. Running inside and back out, I carried white jogging shoes under one arm and a uniform under the other, still wrinkled from the dryer. I had forgotten to take it out.

Jas followed me to the porch railing. "Paz is coming over for dinner, bringing something Aunt Pearl made. We're going to study together."

"Lock the door. Call Pearl when Topaz is ready to come home and have her call you when she gets home safe. Set the alarm."

"Why? WIS says the cops are gonna charge that

man in Columbia for the kidnapping," Jas said, leaning against the railing.

"Something stinks about the case." I closed the door, started the SUV and rolled down the window. "Jim said so."

"Cool. CSI Carolina."

"Lock the door," I said, sounding stern.

"Yes, ma'am."

I spun the wheel and gunned the motor, heading back down the road to the hospital.

It was organized chaos in the ED. The Majors department was structured like a doughnut with the nurses' station, a mini-pharmacy, a swinging X-ray arm, pneumatic chutes to the lab, phones, the desks and various other necessities in the center and with a wide hallway all round. The patient cubicles, each closed off with doors or curtains, were in a ring beyond that. It was a standard design for Emergency Departments now.

Lynnie was administering meds to a woman in a room dedicated to cardiac patients. She looked up at me, saw I was still in street clothes and said succinctly, "Change." I headed to the nurses' lounge, listening with half an ear to the overhead speaker. In the Majors, the speaker system tied the ED team in with the ambulance staff, allowing paramedics on scene to speak to doctors without the MDs having to leave patients already in their care. Everyone could hear everything. And everything was a mess.

The tanker carrying chlorine had ruptured during rush hour and the volatile, dangerous gas was whip-

ping through the crowds as they were trying to
evacuate the downtown area. While a lashing wind
prevented a chlorine gas cloud from forming, it also
increased the area that was affected, turning anyone
with pre-existing respiratory difficulties into a prob-
able patient, and creating new patients with respiratory
damage and skin burns and a host of other problems.

Already, Richland had reached capacity. Lexington,
Baptist and Providence hospitals were close behind.
Because CHC was on the northeast side of town, we
weren't getting chlorine-damaged disaster patients,
but those who would ordinarily be sent to the closest
trauma center were being diverted to us. The place was
packed.

I pulled on the wrinkled scrub uniform, keeping an
eye on the TV in the corner of the lounge. A lot of EDs
kept the television on when there was trouble, tuned
to CNN, FOX or a local news channel. The media was
often a better way to keep up with problems than the
communication methods established by homeland
security structures.

I stepped out of the lounge and took a breath, cen-
tering myself in the melee of medical personnel. I
spotted two surgeons who weren't on rotation and
didn't have to be here, six respiratory therapists and
techs, a lab girl, doctors Farley, Mathews and Benson,
and four residents, who kept glancing at the TV with
hopeful faces. They wanted to be where the most interesting patients were, which was at every hospital in
town but this one. I picked a spot and dove in.

For two hours, while the crew in the ED continued
to grow as more employees checked messages or

heard the news and showed up for work, I dumped meds and started respiratory treatments. At some point MacRoper clocked in, and twice, in his guise of Dr. Demerol, ordered meds at the wrong dosage, mistakes caught by assisting nurses. He was limping and complaining about a basketball injury, and he looked as if he had been drinking, though I didn't detect the smell of alcohol on him. I saw Farley watching MacRoper. It looked as if the doctor's poor medical practices were drawing the attention of not just the nursing staff, but of his peers. I hoped he wouldn't be here much longer.

An EMT arrived in the ED. He had mild burns on his face and one arm, and was so stinky with chlorine that we couldn't treat him without a wash-down. Surrounded by residents with eager expressions, I doused him in the corner shower. Fully clothed.

As water gushed over him and down the drain, he gasped, "We were carrying a patient from downtown when there was an accident on I-26. It backed up traffic for miles and sent me and my partner in the other direction." His throat was raspy and strained with chlorine burns. "Straight back into a cloud of gas. We rerouted and came to you guys," he said. The cold water brought on chills and his face paled.

Both paramedics were having difficulty breathing, but their patient was none the worse for wear, having been breathing through an oxygen mask at the time. The fast-thinking paramedics had covered his skin with burn patches, which kept the fumes from damaging his skin, but they hadn't had enough oxygen or equipment to protect themselves. I turned the EMT over to the residents, who descended on him like locusts.

As they dragged him from his shower, the TV reporter broke in with news of a young girl's body found at the foot of the Confederate Monument on the state capitol grounds. Unconfirmed reports said it was Sharon White, the dark-haired child abducted in the most recent Amber Alert. Every medical professional in the Majors went white-lipped at the words.

On the 911 speakers, we heard ambulance number 718 dispatched to the scene. For a moment there was disbelief in the department, then a cautious optimism. Was a cop at the scene hurt? Had the gas cloud shifted? Or could the girl still be alive? Was it possible?

Half an hour later, the call came in. 718 had been diverted from the closest hospital. A white female, victim of assault, was being transported to the CHC Emergency Department. A soft cheer went up.

I looked at Lynnie Bee. Her eyes were angry, and when she saw me watching, her mouth turned down awkwardly. I shrugged in commiseration. Nurses weren't supposed to react on an emotional level to anything and we were both breaking that cardinal rule. Lynnie took a breath and quickly scanned the cubicles, choosing a patient who was nearly ready to be sent home. Following her lead, I went back to my patient. Lynnie rushed through paperwork and cleared a private room for the arriving ambulance. Our eyes turned often to the TV, both of us silent, hopeful and fearful.

Just before the ETA was up for the patient being shipped, I said, "I'll take any patient." I assumed I wouldn't be allowed to help with the case, even though I was the only forensic nurse on duty.

Lynnie touched my hand, silently thanking me for understanding. "Can you take the broken femur?" she asked. I nodded and slipped into the ortho cubicle.

I was right. The FBI blew in first, Emma Simmons in the lead, her face hard, shoulders bent beneath the weight of the investigation. She pointed at me and said, "That woman is to be kept out."

Understanding got squashed like a bug.

Lynnie's spine went ramrod straight and she looked from Emma to me and back. Her face was pale, and if anger could be worn, she would have been sheathed in it. "Lady," she said softly, "you may be in charge in the FBI building and on crime scenes, but you ain't in charge here. You can ask, but you can't demand. Now, you want to start over?"

I knew Lynnie would give in the moment the patient appeared on the scene, putting injuries before turf wars, but until that happened, she was ticked off. I turned back to the patient with the broken femur, hiding a smile.

"Clearly, you don't understand, Nurse," Emma said. "This is a federal investigation. Where's the doctor in charge?"

"I'm the senior medical doctor," Dr. Farley said, stepping out of a cubicle, rubbing his hands together so that the antibacterial wash he'd applied would dry more quickly. "And I'm with Lynnie. You want to start over?"

Under most circumstances, I found Farley officious, intrusive and annoying. But right now, his supercilious attitude suited me just fine. Emma, however, didn't like him much. The skin around her mouth went pale. "This is a—"

"I got that. Which nurse do you want to toss out of here and why?"

Emma pointed at me. "Her family is under investigation in the matter of the abductions of several underage females."

"The Ballerina Doll murders," he said. "Is Ashlee charged with anything?" When Emma shook her head no, her mouth so tight I thought her lips might shatter and fall off, Farley said, "Then I guess it's up to us, and Ashlee, whether she'll be part of the girl's case or not. Ashlee?"

"I'm with the patients in four and seven. Lynnie and Claudia are available for the FBI." I turned to Emma. "And that was decided before you barged in here and started throwing your weight around." I turned on a heel and went into room seven to push some morphine into the IV line of the patient waiting for an orthopedic surgeon.

As I worked, the doors blew in, paramedics running a stretcher between them. A patient lay beneath a white sheet. One medic was administering oxygen, holding a mask over the girl's face. I got a glimpse of her, skin so pale it looked like parchment and purpled with bruises. She was strapped onto a backboard with a cervical collar around her neck. Two IVs were running, but slowly, which hinted that the paramedics feared a head wound. Oddly, I thought I saw blond hair hanging out of the protective padding sandbagged around her.

Over the protests about physical evidence, Dr. Farley and the nurses pushed the feebs out of the way and went to work. Though I was kept busy, I saw the X-ray arm rocked down for head and chest shots, and caught sight of her stretcher as the girl was shipped to radiology for a CT scan, MRI and other X-rays. She might not be back. From radiology, she could be sent to a room, ending the ED's participation in her care.

As she disappeared down the hall, I saw a cop carrying evidence bags jog in the opposite direction. Someone had collected evidence for them. I kicked a gurney in passing. This was a huge thing, for the girl to be found and to be brought here. I wanted to know more. I wanted to be in on the action. I wanted to help, and here I was, stuck on the sidelines, not allowed to participate. Which really ticked me off.

I was between patients when the girl's mother raced in. I watched as the woman I recognized from the TV screen was instantly surrounded by law enforcement, both federal and local. Though she was distraught, she seemed the type to hold her own against pushy cops, and I heard her say, "Well, it looks to me like you have the wrong man in custody. Unless she drove herself to the monument." Which made a lot of sense to me, but seemed to irritate Emma Simmons. I had to admit that pleased me immensely.

At eight-forty, just as we got the last of the diverted patients admitted or sent home, a call came in about a gang shooting. There were three males down, all with multiple GSWs—gunshot wounds. And all three were coming here.

The night shift had come in and the day shift was still on duty. No one had gone home. The ED was more than double staffed and we needed every hand. The nurses and techs who had food ate it fast, and the rest of us raced to the nearest vending machine, taking a chance on the day-old sandwiches or making do with a candy bar. I was feeling righteous and went for the sandwich.

I was finishing up the last bite of a slightly stale turkey-and-cheese when the first ambulance reported in. "This is unit 428," the voice called over the loudspeaker, "transporting a male, approximate age nineteen, with four large-caliber GSWs, one mid-center chest, the others in limbs. CPR's in progress. Patient is nonresponsive, BP seventy-five, palpated with chest compressions. Patient is intubated and has two IVs, running Ringer's Lactate and O negative. Request a surgeon available upon arrival." All the jargon meant that the patient was close to dead. It would be up to us to get him back among the living and to stabilize him for surgery.

Dr. Farley called up to the OR for a surgeon. Dr. Christopher handled the EMT call. "O2 sat?" he asked, referring to the oxygen saturation as measured by a fingertip oxygen monitor.

"O2 sat is eighty-eight and falling."

"What is patient's heart rhythm without compressions?"

"Patient is asystole without compressions," the paramedic said.

Which was bad. No rhythm at all. The teenager was flatlining.

"Pupil contractions?" Christopher asked, his voice controlled and as sterile as an operating room. His questions were right on target, taking over for Farley who had been on duty for over fourteen hours.

"Pupils are equal and reactive, but sluggish," the paramedic said. Which meant that the patient still had some brain function, but it was vanishing.

"Do we know what caliber of weapon was used?" Christopher asked.

"Cops stated they have military-style, two-and-three-quarter-inch brass and shotgun-shell casings on the scene."

Someone cursed. Two nurses shook their heads. We all knew what that meant. He'd get the best medical care we could give, but the paramedic had just told us that the holes in the patient were too big to plug. The kid was a goner.

Just before the gunshot victim arrived, I caught a glimpse of the monument girl, her head free of the sandbags and resting comfortably on the stretcher, eyes closed. Lynnie Bee slashed a final line on her paperwork and handed the young girl over to a transport crew. Pointing, she directed them to the hallway and the crew shuttled the cops and family out the door, just as the stretcher bearing the first GSW was brought in.

17

The kid was stripped to his Skivvies and was so smeared with blood, it looked as if he'd been finger-painted in bright red by a dozen preschoolers. He was receiving chest compressions and being bagged with oxygen through a tube into his bronchial tubes. The paramedics wore PPEs—personal protective equipment—but large patches of bloody skin showed on both, where the blue and white plastic and cloth had been shoved aside in the heat of the moment.

I sucked down the final swig of a Diet Coke, washed my hands with fast-drying alcohol and slid into a trauma gown and gloves. The kid was going to need more IVs and a lot of luck. I spotted what might have been a vein—if the kid had had any blood to fill it—on the left arm, proximal to the one in his hand, and reached for an IV kit.

Dr. Christopher took one look at the patient and turned him over to a general surgeon standing nearby. "He's all yours, Will."

"Gee, thanks," the surgeon said. "Why didn't I leave when my wife called me an hour ago? Let's get a femoral line in, push some blood and get me a BP.

And, Ash?" I looked up. "See which thoracic guy is on call."

"That guy would be me," a tiny woman said, halting me as I reached for the phone. She was from India and barely five feet, making her even shorter than I. She was round all over, from her apple cheeks and cherry-shaped nose to her pregnant belly and swollen feet. Dr. Ishwandara, Dr. Ish to patients and medical personnel alike, took over. "Do we have an exit wound?"

"Not in the torso," the paramedic said, stripping out of gloves and a bloody trauma suit to reveal the uniform beneath. "Just the widespread pattern of the chest wound. The one on his arm took out a hunk of muscle and tendon. But he has two big mothers from the entrances and exits on his left leg. We got them all packed down but it's gonna take a miracle to save it."

"Kit?" Dr. Ish demanded, the fingers of her left hand over the patient's femoral artery.

"You sure you up to this?" the general surgeon asked, staring at her belly

"You can assist, if you will," she said. "Put in this line?"

"Sure." He held out a hand for the kit and Ish stepped aside.

· "Got another line started, right jugular," Lynnie said, dropping a long needle into the sharps container and sweeping trash to the floor, clearing the bed.

I had started another line in the antecubital site, at the left elbow vein, and got a flashback of blood in the Jelco. I inserted the plastic sheath and said, "Here, too. Want blood started?"

"Yes," Ish said, taking a glance at the general surgeon working at the femoral site. She placed her stethoscope on the kid's chest. "Stop compressions," she said, listening. Everything stopped, even the steady hands of the surgeon.

Someone dropped a chilled bag of blood into my hand as I tore tape to hold the line in place, ready to hook up a unit of blood. Someone else took the bag and slid it into a special sleeve that pumped blood through the line and into the kid's arm faster than normal.

"Begin compressions. Let's get him upstairs, stat," Ish said, sliding a stool over. "Can you give me a boost?" Every eye in the cubicle went to her. "I can't see what I need to see. Boost me up there." She pointed at the kid and placed one foot on the stool. The paramedic who had stripped down to his uniform picked her up and set her atop the patient on the stretcher. She was straddling his abdomen, her weight on her knees, her lower legs and feet close to his body, resting in his blood. The paramedic's face turned bright red, but Dr. Ish was too busy to notice. She was palpating the boy's chest and abdomen.

She paused a moment to look up. "Why are we still here, please? Go!"

Lynnie slammed the brake off with her foot and four of the gathered crew pushed the stretcher toward the bank of elevators, Dr. Ish atop the patient for the ride. They passed the next two stretchers on the way in.

"I got this one," a voice said. Olivia, an RN I had worked with several times and who knew her stuff, grabbed the one spurting the most blood and I got ready to take the other. The teams split, with Livy's group applying pressure, starting additional IVs and beginning basic life support, and mine starting neuro checks and assessments.

My PPEs were soiled, so before I could do anything, I stripped and redressed, tossing the bloody gown into a corner, washing and re-gloving as I looked over my five-man crew. I'd be team leader over Amy, an RN, Fred, an LPN, Sheldon, a tech, Willie Mae, the patient rep, plus Dr. Christopher and me. We were all well trained and no newbies. Good. They were already giving overlapping reports, voices colliding and sharing.

"BP's one-forty over ninety-seven," Fred said.

"Pulse ninety. Hey, kid, you been running a marathon?" Sheldon asked. "What day is it?"

"Tuesday. I'm hurting," the kid said.

"O2 is ninety-nine," Fred said.

"No kidding. I'd be hurt, too, if I got shot with a military round." Sheldon continued with the banter. "What's your name, marathon man?"

"We got two wounds, in and out, midline, right side, but the exit is a doozy," one of the paramedics who had stabilized and transported the patient said. He was letting us know that the wound was worse than it appeared from the front.

"Elroy Littlejohn," the patient said. "Can I have something for pain?"

"Elroy Littlejohn?" I leaned in. He had pasty skin and pale hair, glasses, khakis cut half away, brown lace-up shoes still on his feet and a laptop clutched under one arm. If it hadn't been for the kid's blood-smeared chest, he'd have been a poster boy for geek.

I knew him. He'd gone to classes with Jasmine last year. "Hi, El. It's Ashlee. Miz Davenport. Jas's mom."

"Oh. Mamash. Right?" Tears started to fall as he recognized me, and his skin went a shade paler. He reached out and I caught his hand. "Help me," he begged, panic in his eyes.

"We're helping you, kiddo," I said. To the patient representative, Willie Mae, I said, "USC student." She nodded, understanding that we might have a patient who was legally a minor. To El, I said, "Let me put your laptop over here, where it'll be safe."

He hesitated. Bloody fingers tightened with spastic reflex, relaxed and slid away. I put the laptop on the counter. "Take care of it, okay?" he said, his eyes acquiring the glassy stare of shock.

Amy said, "We need your family contact information. You live with your parents?"

"With my dad. He's Elroy Littlejohn, too. Senior." He gave the phone number, mumbling. I jotted it down on the gurney sheet, noting that Willie Mae wrote it on the paperwork, her pen following and documenting every move we made. A plainclothes cop entered the room and stood to the side, watching and listening.

"How old are you, Elroy?" someone asked.

"Twenty."

"You know what happened tonight?"

Willie Mae took the kid's clothing, shoes, laptop and watch, documenting the personal effects for which she accepted responsibility.

"I was getting off from work. I was crossing the street." Recounting the event brought some color back in his cheeks.

"Where do you work, Elroy?" Fred asked, assessing the patient's mental state and orientation.

"The museum."

"The State Museum? On Gervais Street?" Christopher asked.

"Yeah. Anyway, this car came around the corner. Cruising. You know? Ahhh!" Elroy shouted as Christopher probed in a circle around the dressing over the entrance wound on his right side.

"Easy, Elroy," I said as I looked for an additional IV site. "I know what that feels like. I was actually shot once, and I was probed the same way. It'll be over in a sec."

Christopher probed harder. Elroy took a swing at him and cursed.

"You were shot?" Christopher asked without looking my way as he stepped out of Elroy's range, his voice level.

The cop stepped closer, watching. I didn't know if it was because of the topic of conversation or to get a better view, but either way I didn't like it. I settled for a simple "Yeah. Small caliber. Upper leg. Not much damage."

"Let me see the entrance," Christopher said.

I started, until I realized that he meant on Elroy, not me. I stepped away as the crew levered Elroy's stretcher up to a thirty-degree angle. Elroy cursed again, this time a racial slur aimed at Amy, who ignored it. Christopher stepped back in and pulled away the gauze on Elroy's right front side, getting a good look at the entrance wound. It was big enough to put a thumb into. He took the time to palpate the area, which resulted in even more cursing. The doctor slid the dressing back in place and ordered a broad-spectrum antibiotic. He directed Amy to turn up the fluids going through the IV.

"The museum closes at five," the cop said, his tone as even as the team's.

"Yeah," Elroy gasped as the bed went back flat. His face, which was greasy with shock and pain, took on a bit of color. Suddenly he wanted to talk. A lot. Shock has that effect on some people.

"We had an event. An exhibit of Middle Eastern antique rugs and prayer shawls. About fifty people were in the museum when the train tanker went over. And when a car wreck jammed up traffic, we were all stuck in there. But the museum has a good air-filtration system, you know? So the air was okay to breathe. So we just all, like, stayed. And us part-timers, we're still setting up a new exhibit that's opening on Friday."

"The Grecian statuary and urn thing," Fred said. "Saw it advertised on TV."

"Right. So we just kept working. Got finished about eight. Oh, God, I hurt."

"Blood pressure now?" the doctor asked, interrupting the flow of chatter.

"One-thirty over seventy-seven."

"Better," Christopher said as he studied the readout showing Elroy's heart rhythm. He punched a button and ran a paper strip, handed it to Willie Mae for the chart. He looked up at me. "Give him five of morphine. Up his O2 to four. I need to get a look at the exit wound." Which meant moving the bandage that had stopped the worst of the bleeding, which would likely cause new bleeding and more pain. But the doc needed to assess the damage. We all understood that, we just didn't like it. "Get another line started and check the blood supply."

"We're down to two units, and the other guy needs it," Amy said.

"Let's get an H&H and type and screen."

I glanced down to see blood splattered all over Christopher's Italian shoes. When he noticed, he'd have a conniption. I just hoped he didn't slap Elroy. The mental picture made me smile and when Christopher noticed, I pointed innocently to a vein. "Got one."

The cop held up a hand to stop me from giving Elroy pain meds. "Thirty seconds?" he asked. Because he asked nicely, I nodded and stepped back, but looked pointedly at the clock, timing him. To Elroy, he said, "You were heading east, toward the capitol from the museum. On foot, right?"

"Yeah."

"And the car came around the corner." Elroy nodded. "What make?"

"I don't know. Older. White. Four doors. That's all I saw. But it was moving real slow. And then this dude, a black guy, leaned out the window and started shooting. And people went down everywhere. I dropped behind a car. My hands were all bloody." He looked at his hands. Blood had dried into the crevices and under his nails. "And I knew I was hit."

I eased past the cop and administered the morphine. The cop could talk later.

About twenty seconds after the plunger was completely depressed, Elroy sighed. "Thanks. Thanks, man." He gripped Christopher's crisp sleeve in his bloody hand and squeezed, taking in the doctor's name badge. "Hey, you're one of the patrons, right? At the museum? I saw your name on the listing. That's my job, updating the listing. You're one of the platinum-level donors. You're rich as shit, aren't you?"

Someone smothered a laugh and Christopher slid his arm away, grimacing at the long smear of blood on his lab coat. "You relax. We'll talk later." The doc looked down at his expensive shoes and I thought he'd join Elroy in the curse festival but he just sighed. To me, Christopher jerked his head and stepped back, indicating that it was time to turn the patient. Again.

Four of us lifted the sheets beneath Elroy and rotated him onto his side. Elroy flailed and cursed, but with less precision in both aim and vocabulary.

The doc raised the bed with the foot pedal until Elroy was at his waist, pulled on fresh gloves and bent over the patient. With steady fingers, he peeled back the bandage revealing a two-fist-sized wound. A jelly-like clot covered the interior of the hole, and Christopher pursed his lips. "See who's on call for urology." Elroy's kidney was possibly compromised. "And get a BMP and a PT and PTT," he said, adding lab tests to check for blood clotting and chemistries. "While you're at it, see if we have a vascular surgeon available."

He pressed the gauze back into place and reattached the tape holding it. As the rest of us lowered Elroy back to the bed, Amy labeled vials of blood, set them in the lab's pneumatic tube and pressed the button. They were gone with a whoosh of air.

I went for the call sheet, but set it aside when Dr. Peterson walked in. He was with one of the urology groups. "You want this one?" I asked, putting a chart in his hands. "Hasn't had a CT yet, but it might be a kidney. Might also be some vascular problems."

"Why not? It's only my anniversary," he said.

"Ouch," I said. "Remember to order roses."

"I did it on the way in, but they won't be delivered until tomorrow," he said, sighing. He waved to another surgeon and bent over the patient a moment before indicating that he, too, needed to see the wounds. Once again we moved Elroy, who was now having break-through pain. His word choice was pretty ugly, and Peterson ordered additional meds to take the edge off. And to shut him up, but no one mentioned that part. "Let's get him to radiology stat and I'll take him to OR," Peterson said. "When or if you get a vascular guy to call in, forward the call to me, okay?"

It was over. The ED was empty, silent, and it was time for the paperwork and the cleanup. Housekeeping was beeped and two short, stocky women arrived with mop buckets and orange-scented cleansers. Lynnie and I started on the documentation. Lynnie, who had worked her usual double shift, was exhausted, shoulders slumping, chewing her lower lip, her expression distracted and worn. I took most of the documentation while she took a break.

Several times I noticed her staring at me. She seemed about to speak, but never did. I had wondered about the "small debt problem" she had referred to. Finally, I asked, "Lynnie, do you need money? I could make you a loan."

Instantly, Lynnie burned a bright red that gave my own blushes a run for their money. She laughed, the sound almost nervous but relieved. "You're a good friend. Not just now. But if you're really making an offer, I may hit you up later."

I had money from Jack's estate, and I assured her that a loan would not be a problem. I had helped a few co-workers in the past. She patted my shoulder in thanks, heaved a sigh that sounded very tired and took the last chart.

I wondered about the blond girl found beneath the monument to South Carolina's Confederate dead. What had happened to her? It was hard being on the outside, kept on the sidelines.

We were nearly caught up with paperwork when the EMS speaker blared. Two units were coming in with victims from a multi-vehicle accident on I-77—the source of most of our accident patients. Lynnie sighed again, and I thought she might cry. Before my mind could override my mouth, I volunteered to finish the third shift.

There are a few good reasons to work third shift. Money is one. Good company is another. We ordered in pizza at 11:00 p.m. and actually had time to eat it before it got too cold, as the night quieted again after midnight. We played a few hands of rummy, until word came in that someone from administration was in the building and looking to cook up trouble. Until we got the all clear, we dawdled over charts, trying to look busy.

But the best part of tonight's graveyard shift was

when Jim came in about 3:00 a.m., after the admin chief had left.

Jim looked like something the cat dragged in—or the dogs dug up, but that analogy hurt too much to use. He was wearing the same clothes he'd worn at the shootout, the same muddy shoes, and he needed a shower, though I was far too kind to say so. He had a heavy five o'clock shadow. But hey, he brought me a rose.

I'm sure I blushed like a debutante when he whipped the flower out from behind his back, and I counted five wolf whistles from my teammates. Jim fixed it for me by saying, "I screwed up. I beat up a Moonie and stole this for you as an apology."

Everyone laughed and my blush faded as I took the tightly curled bud. "You didn't really. Did you?"

"No. I didn't beat anyone up. Unless you think that's really sexy. Then I beat him to a pulp."

I resisted a smile at his teasing and said primly, "No. It's not sexy." I pulled the water reservoir off the stem and set the flower in my foam cup. "Thank you."

"That would go over better if you were looking at me."

I met his eyes. "Thank you." My blush flamed higher.

"You're welcome."

"So. Are you going to tell me everything?"

"You mean in spite of my boss's prohibition? Hell, yeah. Can you take a break?"

I waved at Amy, grabbed my rose and cup, and led the way to the nurses' lounge. When the door closed on us, Jim leaned down and kissed me. It was a chaste kiss, but it was enough to make me want more. I remembered the Charleston invitation and my belly did a little flip-flop.

Jim walked to the machines and bought two Cokes, one diet, one high octane, popped both tops and passed me the diet. He knew what I liked, which was really nice. I set the rose to the side where I would remember to take it home. Jim's eyes measured me as we drank. I measured him right back.

"You heard about the girl at the Confederate Monument," he said, making it a statement instead of the question it might have been.

"Yes. Saw her, briefly. Beat all to heck. She wasn't left at a graveyard." I kept my eyes on him, too. The staring contest was doing strange things to me.

"No. She wasn't."

"But the Confederate Monument is sacred to a lot of locals," I said.

"Yeah. Our thinking, too. He had dyed her hair blond."

I nodded slowly. "I saw blond hair beyond the sandbagging."

"We think it's him," Jim said. "We think he left her there because he got stopped by the chlorine leak."

"And?" I asked.

"Why do you say, 'And?'"

"I'm older and wiser than you. I know things." Several years older. Which bothered me a lot.

"Like what?" he asked, his eyes going all twinkly on me. I was pretty sure I had never met a man with twinkly eyes before, but Jim had 'em. That part of me that wanted to do belly-flops was reacting with acrobatic delight.

I looked away. Which cost me points in the staring contest, but I couldn't help it. I grinned to show I lost with good grace. "Like the fact that you have a tell."

"A tell? Like in poker?"

"Yep." In professional poker, a tell was a player's dead giveaway of a good or bad hand. It sometimes took another professional poker player to interpret. "Your mouth does a little quiver on the left side," I said.

"I'll have to work on that." He kissed me again and my acrobatic insides went for the gold.

"And," I reminded him, my lips moving beneath his, "I said 'And.' So what else?"

He eased back so our lips just brushed when he spoke. "And we discovered a folded piece of paper inside her shirt, over her heart. It was a poem. On handmade, homemade paper."

The tickle made me smile. "Anyone can make handmade paper," I said.

"Yeah, we found that out. His is from a kit sold for three years over the Internet, at Michaels and at half a dozen other chain stores across the nation. The company made a blue million of them."

I eased back a few inches, still so close he was out of focus. I needed reading glasses. "What did you learn from the girl?"

"Nothing. She was diagnosed with a concussion. Last thing she remembers is winning a soccer game."

"And that's why you still have my family under the scope as suspects?"

"Nah. We have the Chadwicks under the scope because every single time we found a grave, it was either a Chadwick grave or there was a Chadwick connection."

I went still.

Jim stepped back a bit and we focused on each other. "The first girl was found in a grave plot for the Shirleys, but one woman's maiden name was Chadwick."

I digested that and something clicked inside me. I recalled the uncomfortable sensation of knowing something and not knowing what it was. At the first task-force meeting I had seen photos of a graveyard, stones standing upright nearby, and a name. Shirley.

"We have some Shirleys in the family, in the genealogy records," I said. My heart seemed to slide deep into my bowels. "And tonight? What about the girl tonight?"

"It's been suggested," Jim said, "that a lot of Chadwicks fought for the Confederates."

I nodded. "They did. Almost as many fought for the North. The war divided the white side of the family. That was before my ancestor married his half-black cousin and turned us into spotted sheep."

"Several of your male relatives are being brought in for questioning."

The sofa in the nurses' lounge was ratty, a leftover, springless, holey piece of discomfort. I sat on it anyway. My legs had turned to water. What could I say now? Some Chadwick might be involved. Some Chadwick might be killing little girls.

"I have to ask you something." His voice sounded even more tired. "Do you or any of the Chadwicks have any enemies?"

I put it together quickly. It didn't have to be one of

us. It could be someone who hated us. All of a sudden the Chadwicks were victims instead of perverts, kidnappers and killers. I smiled at him in relief.

"Thought you'd like that," he said.

"Jack had scads of enemies, but most are behind bars or dead." Including the one I had killed, but I didn't say that. "Finding this out just tripled your suspect list, didn't it?"

"You have no idea. We have to go back and interview all your family. Again. With a different slant, looking for who might want to target them. I'll be tied up in this for a while, Ash. I'm sorry."

"Don't be." I looked at him again. "Get the person doing this. And make sure he can't do it again. Ever."

Jim nodded. "Thanks." He knocked back the rest of his Coke and left, tossing the empty can into the garbage on the way out. I still sat on the dimpled cushion, holding a warm drink and staring at a rosebud. And wondering what in heck I would tell Nana.

He watched as she left the hospital. She was perfect. So perfect for his daughter. Ashlee Davenport tucked her blond hair behind her ear as she fished for her car keys in the dawn light. She was softly rounded with generous curves and the strong morals a mother should have. She slapped men with wandering hands, he remembered. She would make a perfect replacement for Mnem, his long-dead wife.

He didn't know what he would do with the other one, however. Women always seemed to become complications that had to be dealt with.

18

Thursday

I was home by 8:00 a.m., every bone in my body aching. Hungry dogs met me at the door of the SUV, and I dumped a bag of food into their bowls, not worried about the amount they each should get. I was just too tired to care. Inside, I relocked the doors and stuck my head in the rec room. Music played at a decent volume as Jasmine and Topaz snoozed on the couch. It looked as if they had fallen asleep studying. They raised their heads when I rapped on the wall. "Don't be late to class."

They grumbled and yawned, but at least they were awake. I waved and went back to the kitchen, where I tore a head of lettuce into a salad bowl and added raw veggies. Along with a glass of wine, I carried it upstairs. For someone who had once hated baths, eating in the tub was becoming a habit. And a glass of wine for breakfast sounded just dandy.

As I soaked, I watched the news on a little five-inch TV. Additional charges had been filed against the man who had abducted Mari. Statutory rape charges had been added to the federal kidnapping charge, along with a host of lesser charges. But no corollaries had been drawn by law enforcement between Smith and the girl found at the foot of the Confederate Monument or the Ballerina Doll murders. The press was speculating wildly, but most commentators seemed to think the three cases were unrelated. Others thought a copycat killer was on the loose.

Columbia, South Carolina, was making national news, and the usual man-in-the-street interviews were bringing out every undereducated redneck in town. Most talked about shooting a kidnapper on sight. The more educated and culturally responsible responses were probably left on the cutting room floor. Not sensational enough for New York or the West Coast.

One local reporter with sources in the police department suggested that a poem had been found in the shirt pocket of the latest girl, the one brought to the ED yesterday. I figured Emma Simmons would have a hissy fit at that being released to the media.

After my bath, I checked on my daughter and Topaz again and found both girls packing snacks for school. Satisfied that they were able to repeat back orders about personal safety, and far less satisfied that they had enough sleep to drive, I nevertheless saw them out, called Nana to report in and hit the sack.

Six hours later, I woke to find my hair defying gravity on one side and sheet wrinkles on my face. I looked like a six-year-old—or like a woman facing middle age. I didn't know why my age had put such a lock on me, but I wasn't enjoying my remaining years as a fortysomething, even though I wouldn't be hitting fifty anytime real soon.

I showered, dressed, considered going to the Clip N Curl for highlights, and decided to go to the barn instead. I knew Nana needed help with the farm, and I hadn't offered much in the way of assistance in the last few days. I mucked out a few stalls, then put in four full hours in a field, overseeing a crew of migrant workers who were making hay while the sun shone. By dark, we had two bare fields studded with this year's first, huge, round hay bales. I was sweaty and tired and feeling a lot better about life.

Following a quick shower, I started up the grill and put steaks on to cook, while potatoes baked and I tore up more lettuce. Jim had left a message that he was heading this way. I figured I could repay him for the opening rosebud on the kitchen table. Anyway, I was in the mood to stay home. So I set the table on the porch and lit candles for ambience.

When Jim arrived, I was sitting in the porch swing, watching the night sky, which was a deep purple velvet, and listening to early mosquitoes buzz around the screened porch.

Jim parked his ugly gray Crown Victoria—the unmarked car of choice for most law-enforcement departments—and climbed the short steps to the deck. He moved as if he hadn't slept in days, though I saw his face was cleanly shaven when the porch light hit it and he was dressed in fresh clothes. He had at least been home to clean up, or maybe he kept clothes at feeb headquarters.

He sat in a chair at the table—fell into it, actually.

"Evening, Miz Ash. If that's a steak I smell cooking, I'm your eternal slave."

"Hope you like them medium rare or rare. I don't burn good meat."

Jasmine and Topaz roared up in the drive before he could reply, slammed doors and ran squealing onto the porch.

"We passed the midterms!"

"Both of us. I got a ninety-three and Paz got ninety-seven." Jas stuck out her tongue at her cousin. "Teacher's pet."

"Not me. I'm just smarter than you. Do I smell steaks? And double-stuffed potatoes? Oh-ho yeah!"

They grabbed plates and began to load them up, chatting about a friend who had been shot. Elroy, but of course, I couldn't say that I already knew all about it. Nor could I correct the inaccuracies they had heard through the gossip lines. El had been shot five times. He was near death. The shooter had been a jealous ex-girlfriend. I kept my expression bland and let them babble.

As they chatted, I handed Jim a plate and indicated the rapidly diminishing food. He dished up salad and took two of the remaining three potatoes. I always made more food than I needed, as I never knew who Jas would bring home.

"Gimme some salad. Mamash makes the best salad in the state."

"Hey, Mr. Cop." Jasmine kicked his foot lightly. "You found that assho—that evil excuse for a human being that's killing those girls? Sorry, Mama."

Topaz snorted and reached into the bowl of ice,

withdrawing two diet drinks. "I bet your mama heard the term before."

"Not from my girls, I haven't. I'm glad you did so well on the exams and made it home in one piece. Now go on in the rec room and eat. I'm too tired for your energy."

"Yeah. We got music to listen to." Topaz slid her eyes at me. "So, you and Mr. Cop can smooch."

"Paz!" I said.

Giggling, the girls raced inside and slammed the door. Not that it did much good in terms of noise. Jim laughed softly and popped the tops on drinks for us as the stereo came on and John Mayer floated out to us. At least they had good taste in music.

"I like rare," Jim said, picking up our last conversation. I placed a steak on his plate and took one, leaving two for steak sandwiches tomorrow, finally sitting down to his left. We ate in silence as owls hooted back and forth, their territorial calls floating on the night air from somewhere near Nana's house and the back forty. Near my ancestors' family graves.

When we had eaten, he stood and took a seat in the swing, his long legs moving the creaking chain. I just waited. I may not be psychic, but I know when a man has something on his mind. Finally he said, "The poems the girls have on them when we find them?"

"On the homemade paper."

"Yeah. They're weird."

"Want to tell me how weird?"

"Yeah. I do. But Emma would take me off the case if she knew I was talking to you."

"But she knows you're here now." I made it a statement, but I had a bad feeling about where this was going.

"She knows."

I got up and poured us both a glass of wine. That he took it let me know he wasn't on duty. Not exactly. But he was here for something other than my great steaks. "Let me guess," I said. I retook my chair, though there was a lot of empty seat on the swing, and his arm stretched out across the wood back looked awfully inviting. "Despite the possibility—no, the *likelihood*—that the killer may be of no relation to the Chadwicks at all, she wants you to question me, unofficially, about who in my family might be a killer." He nodded. "People don't look like killers, Jim. They don't go around with marks of Cain tattooed on their foreheads that says, Child Killer. They look just like anyone else."

"Seen a lot of killers, have you?" Humor laced his voice.

"Enough. Where do you think they come for patching up when they get hurt being arrested or in jail? To hospitals."

Jim leaned forward, sensing there was more I wasn't saying. I had never told him about the night I'd nearly died. The night a man had shot me. The night I'd shot him back and killed him, his blood all over my kitchen floor. I thought for a long silent moment, the owls falling quiet, the stillness broken by horses snorting and the sounds of hooves milling. Could I tell him this? Did I want to? Did I want to go off with this man, get to know him better? Maybe intimately? Did I trust him?

Ahhh. That was it. Did I trust him? Had I healed from Jack's infidelity and death or was I still twitching mentally from the wound.

I studied Jim across the porch, his face illuminated by flickering candles. His eyes were steady, determined, caring. Something slid into place inside me, some indefinable tiny something that had been out of place or missing. Or maybe just waiting for the right moment, the right stimulus.

Damn. Damn, damn, double damn. I *did* trust the man. I sipped my wine to moisten my unexpectedly dry throat. "My husband, Jack, got into some really bad business dealings. When he died, they came back to haunt me. A man named Alan Mathison shot me." I watched Jim's eyes in the night. "Emma wants you to ask me about that night, doesn't she?"

Jim nodded. "But I won't. I will listen, though, if you want to tell me." His voice was firm, and I realized that he'd tell Emma some cock-and-bull story about it to protect me, if he had to.

"Have you read the official reports?" I asked.

He nodded again. "Simmons dropped them on my desk today."

I drank, the merlot an astringent, biting tang, and held the glass up to the light, concentrating on the way the wine swirled and clung to the glass. Far too casually, I said, "Made some snarky comment about me, too, didn't she?"

Jim just grinned and drank his wine.

"He was a business partner of Jack's. He had already killed a man to cover up a problem on a development project," I said. "A multimillion-dollar problem. He tried to kill me. To save myself, to keep him away from my child who was due home within minutes, I stabbed him with a pitchfork." Jim didn't react. He was wearing his cop face, giving nothing away. "I left him in the barn, after knocking him into Mabel's stall."

I half smiled in the night, but it was laced with sorrow. "Mabel was Jack's horse. She never really cared much for other men. I heard her when she went at him." I remembered that night, remembered the smells of the barn, the faint taint of human bowel on the air, the sounds of Mabel snorting and striking out at him to protect her last foal.

"I thought Alan was dead, and I was bleeding pretty badly," I touched my thigh. "Not thinking straight. But I made my way back to the house. I called 911 on my cell. I was in the kitchen, talking to the dispatcher, when I looked up and he was standing there."

I turned the wineglass around and around, the stem sliding in my fingers, my hands sweating with the remembered fear of the night. Oddly, what I remembered most clearly was the feel of my teeth that night, dry and rough when I tried to talk. Yet, I could see it all in my memory with a high-definition clarity, the clarity of post-traumatic stress syndrome.

"Alan was standing in the doorway to the kitchen, bleeding, clothes torn. There was a faint stench of feces from where I stabbed him in the abdomen with the pitchfork." Had I said that part yet? I couldn't remember. "The skin on the left side of his face was gone. Ripped away in a wide swath." It was the face of a dead man, pale, bloodied, bruised. I blinked away the image, but the chill that it always brought shivered along my skin. "He wavered, bloody and trampled, holding the pitchfork in his left hand. He stepped into the room."

Terror again flooded through me, as sharp as if he stood there now. "Having him there alive meant that Jasmine was in danger, my baby who was due home soon.

"I set the phone down. I could hear the dispatcher's voice from the tabletop. I picked up the gun. It was Alan's. I had carried it from the barn, I think. I rested it on the table. The blood on my hands made me clumsy and the gun was slick. I was fighting throwing up. I remember the taste of acid and bile." It had been overpowering, a fresh, burning tang, the taste of old blood and vomit. Everything had moved so slowly.

"The holes across Alan's abdomen were down low. Evenly placed, two in the lower right quadrant. Two in the lower left. A neat row of them. There wasn't much bleeding, just the scent of feces to tell me I had punctured his intestines, torn something inside. The blood came from his cut hand and the torn place on his face.

"He said, 'Remember, Ash. I never lose. Never.' And he came at me, holding the pitchfork to kill me. But he stumbled and slipped in my blood." I didn't watch Jim, now. I stared out at the night. It had been nighttime when Alan had died. It had been a long time after that night before I had the guts to look into the dark again. "His feet left red smears. And I was going to die.

"The room tilted and I knew I was falling. I fired the gun."

And though I knew I couldn't have, I seemed to see the round leave the barrel, travel through the air in slow, slow motion and enter his body. Just below the sternum. I touched my own chest at the memory, mid center. I couldn't have seen the round. Couldn't have. But the memory was there, always in my mind, hard as stone.

"I hit the floor and the gun went off again. The shot went wild." Hit the cabinet, I found out later. "I landed on my bad leg. The pain was…"

I took a breath that stuttered, and Jim pulled his legs under himself to stand, tenderness and compassion in his face, guilt for making me remember it all again. I held out a hand to stop him. He had wanted to hear this. Well, he'd hear it from across the porch. He slowly sat again.

"It was bad, and I was passing out." A slow-moving cloud of blackness, like the shadows in the night outside. I had wondered which would take me over first. The pain or the darkness. "Before I passed out, I saw him fall." He had landed in this long, graceful tumble, bounced on the bloody floor and settled there, his eyes on mine.

"The pitchfork fell beside him. I couldn't hear the clatter, beneath the gun blasts. But he writhed there, his face close to mine, his body curled into a tight ball." His eyes had been bewildered. Confused. And I still saw them in my nightmares, though I had less of them these days. "I saw his lips move and I'm sure he said, 'I lost. I… I lost.'"

The motion of the swing had stopped. "I'm sorry," Jim said.

He leaned in, placing his wineglass on the table, and he seemed to come to some decision. "The girl buried on your farm. She was a poet. A prodigy." When I didn't respond, he went on. "The poems that the girls have in their shirts are strange. This last one was titled something like 'u-terp.' One was titled a word for an accordion or merry-go-round. And none of them make any sense."

"Eu-ter-pe."

Jim looked up fast. Jas was leaning in the doorway, a cola can dangling from her fingers, her face blank, watching me. I knew she had been listening to me tell my story, but she didn't refer to it. Instead, she said, "And it wasn't an accordion, betcha. It was a Calliope."

Jim's whole body tensed. "How did you know that?"

"I've been to college, Mr. Cop. I took a course in Greek mythology last year. Euterpe and Calliope are Muses."

"What the bleeding hell are Muses?" Jim asked.

"Come on. I'll show you." Jas turned and walked away. Without speaking to me, Jim followed. I debated going, too, but the dirty dishes wouldn't get clean by themselves. I stacked greasy plates and carried them inside, adding the girls' dishes to the heap. When the kitchen was clean, I turned on the dishwasher and followed my daughter and my maybe-boyfriend to the rec room.

19

They were bent over Jasmine's open laptop. "The Muses were the daughters of Zeus," Jas said, her voice taking on a tone of teacher to student. My lips softened into a smile, but Jim was too tightly focused on the laptop to notice. "The number of Muses varied, but usually there were nine—Calliope, Clio, Erato, Euterpe, Melpomene, Polyhymnia, Terpsichore, Thalia and Urania."

"I'll never be able to pronounce all that," Jim murmured.

I curled onto the couch and watched Jim with my daughter. The sight brought a bittersweet sadness close to the surface. Jack should have been the one leaning over her, encouraging her, teasing her. Jack, who had died. And now Jim, who... I trusted him. It was a strange feeling.

"Apollo became their leader in Delphi and Parnassus, which were their favorite places," Jas said.

"Man, I should have taken that course with you," Paz said. "Does my cousin get a reward for this?"

Jasmine laughed abruptly and turned to Jim. "Do I?"

"I don't know," Jim said, nudging Jasmine aside

and taking her seat. "Not very likely. This stuff is in the public domain. But it's a big help to me. I'll take you and your mom to dinner some day."

"Not as good as cash, but food is good," Jas said.

"Calliope was the eldest and most distinguished of the nine Muses," Jim read. "Her emblems are a stylus and wax tablets." He stopped and whispered, "Oh crap."

I remembered the melted candle found with the little girl on the farm. Not a melted candle. A piece of wood covered with wax, and a stylus. Jim scrolled down. "Clio, the Muse of history. Usually associated with a parchment scroll or a set of tablets. Erato, the muse of lyric poetry, particularly love and erotic poetry, and mimicry," he read. "She is usually depicted with a lyre. Euterpe. Here she is," he said, his voice growing excited. "The muse of music, she is also the muse of joy and of flute playing…." He paused.

"Melpomene, Polyhymnia, Terpsichore." He stumbled through the names. "Thalia and Urania," Jim continued, scrolling down and hitting Print. "Son of a bitch. There's nine. Nine. I have to get back to the office. Wait. Who is Mnemosyne?" he asked.

Jas looked at him, puzzled. "She was the mother of the Muses, the goddess of memory."

"It all fits. Son of a flaming duck, it all fits." He stood and studied the screen as if memorizing it. He looked at the girls. "You can't talk about this. Not until I give you permission. The lives of little girls depend on it."

"They'll keep your secrets," I said, spearing both girls with the "mother" look. They nodded, though I could see mental crossing of fingers taking place. We'd have to talk. "You going to give a Chadwick credit for this?" I asked Jim.

"Yeah. I am." He looked at me hard. "But not until I catch the guy." He leaned down and gathered up the papers from the printer. "Jasmine Davenport? You are my hero."

"Dang skippy," my daughter said.

Jim's car hadn't reached the curve toward the street before Jas and Paz were back at the computer, searching out sites about Muses. I was surprised they waited that long.

"Girls?" My voice was stern. When I had at least part of their attention, I said, "You may not speak of this to anyone but your parents and to me."

They exchanged a glance, bursting to tell the secret.

"I mean it. This family is still considered the main suspect in the kidnapping and murder of more than one little girl. You're nearly adults. You have a responsibility to protect the Chadwicks." That caught their attention. Responsibility to family, church and community were pounded in to Chadwicks from the cradle up. "Make Nana, your Mama Moses and me proud." I left the room, knowing I had guilted them into keeping the secret and not feeling remorseful about it at all.

Not sure I had remembered to feed the dogs their evening meal, I dumped food into their empty bowls. They didn't seem very excited about it, but then I wouldn't be excited about dog food either. I set the coffeemaker, locked up the house and went to my room.

Lying curled up in my bed, the TV remote in one hand, I flipped between FOX, CNN and David Letterman and I thought about all I had learned tonight. About the case, about my daughter and my niece, about Jim, and about myself. It was flattering to have a younger man interested in me. Flattering, yet painful.

I knew what time and good eating was doing to my body. I had seen the cellulite starting, the sagging arms and flabby thighs, the little tire around my middle. I wasn't fat, but I was no skinny, svelte swim-suit model either. Before Jack had died, I'd had a good body image. But finding that he'd conducted a many-years-long affair with a woman taller, thinner and more willowy than I had put a big dent in my self-confidence. The idea of Jim seeing me naked was more painful than exciting.

Lovely bedtime thoughts. I tried to concentrate on Letterman's Top Ten list, and fell asleep with the TV on and the remote in my hand. I woke when Jas raced down the hall, feet thumping, and jumped onto the bed. "Wake up, Mama. You have *so* got to see this!"

I looked blearily up at my daughter as I clicked the TV off. "Not at nearly 2:00 a.m., I don't. Go away and go to sleep."

Jas threw the covers off me, grabbed a wrist and pulled me to the edge of the bed. "Jasmine Leah Davenport, you stop that right now!" When she tugged me half off the bed, I shrieked, "Stop it! Jasmine!"

"Get up, Mama. I think we found those dead girls." She was serious, her face set, her eyes sparkling with a mixture of horror and excitement. "They're on the Internet."

That woke me up in a hurry. I pushed her away and straightened myself in the bed before rolling off the side to the floor. "Okay. Let's see it." I followed her to the rec room and found that Paz and she had changed into flannel pj's and made a nest for themselves on the big couch. The room smelled of popcorn, the food of choice for late nights.

I crawled next to Paz in the center of the blankets, tossed a handful of popcorn into my mouth and rubbed my dry eyes. "Okay," I said around the mouthful, "this better be good."

Paz turned the laptop to me as Jasmine settled against my other side. Any thought of sleep fled at the sight. It was the opening page to a site, the graphics and art featuring a Grecian temple and a statue of Zeus. The photography was grainy, as if the designer had used pictures with too few pixels.

"We should be the cops," Paz said. "This stuff only took a couple hours to find. Why haven't the cops found it yet?" She hit a key and the home page disappeared to reveal a woman in Grecian clothing, an off-the-shoulder gown that puddled around her feet. She held a flute in delicate fingers. Her face had been cut out, leaving a black silhouette where her head should have been.

Below her picture was the word *Mnemosyne*. Below that was a poem, the first line reading, "Mnemosyne, my life, my love, the woman who was my home. Dead thou art and ever shall be, till the underworld thou dost roam."

"The poetry sucks," Paz said, and I had to agree, not bothering to read on.

Paz scrolled down and stopped on the image of a young girl, standing beside a huge Grecian urn, the kind that transported oil on sea voyages. She was dressed like the older woman but held a lyre in one hand, a flute in the other and a rolled parchment in the crook of her arm. Her smile was tender. A stylized black ribbon had been added at the top of the picture, the ends trailing down around the photo like a border or a frame. Below the photo was the single phrase, "My Muse." I looked at my two girls, one on each side. "So?"

Paz gave me a triumphant look and hit another key, revealing another photo of the girl in the off-the-shoulder gown. This time she was sitting in a thronelike carved chair before a backdrop of the Mediterranean Sea, holding dancing slippers and a lyre. Below her photo was the single word, *Terpsichore,* and below that, a poem that began, "Terpsichore, joy and dance, siren of the stage…" *The slippers were pointe shoes.* Chills that had nothing to do with the room slid down my back.

"It's them, isn't it?" Jasmine asked.

I pulled the laptop closer and studied the photograph. "Go back to the first page," I said. Paz hit a key and I memorized the child's face. "Back to the second one." The face was narrower, the lips thinner. The expression sadder. It wasn't the same girl. But I had seen her before, and recently. On the wall of photos in the FBI office.

"There's more," Jasmine said. Paz hit a key and the page changed again. The photograph on this page was a child, standing, the dress longer or the girl shorter than in the previous standing shot. But the backdrop was the exact same as the sitting child, the Mediterranean Sea, suggesting a wall-size photograph or a background added afterward. This child wore her hair upswept in a loose chignon, earrings at her ears. There was fear in the tightness of her features, her haunted eyes. At her feet was what looked like the scroll from the original photo of the older woman. In one hand she held something. It was hard to tell in the poor quality photo, but I was pretty sure I had seen it before. A wax tablet and a stylus.

I was breathing hard, too fast, feeling the tingling in fingers and toes, the result of stress and hyperventilation. I leaned in, studying the photo. The earrings looked like knots, and she wore a bracelet. The word *Calliope* was beneath the photo, followed by another bad piece of poetry that began "Calliope, beautiful voice, arbitress in the argument…"

"Back and forth," I said, waffling my fingers. The pages went back to the home page and slowly forward. Each girl wore a bracelet. "Two girls," I breathed.

"Five," Jas said softly.

Paz hit more keys and the first photo came up. "My Muse," she said and hit a key. "Calliope." She hit another key. "Terpsichore." Hit a key. "Euterpe." Key. "And Clio."

"Five girls," Jasmine said.

"I have to call Jim."

Jasmine put her cell phone in my hand. My mind went blank. As if she understood, Jasmine shoved out of the entwining blankets and raced from the room and back, depositing my cell in my hand and jumping back onto the forgiving couch.

With nerveless fingers I hit speed dial, ignoring my girls' shared glances. He answered, sounding awake, though tired. "Ramsey."

"Sorry to call you so late," I said, "but you need to get on the Net."

"Why?"

"Because Jasmine and Topaz found a site with the missing girls on it." Jas and Paz leaned in and I tilted the phone so they could hear. "Three of your original girls, not counting Mari, and two new ones."

I heard the sound of a body rising and springs protesting. "You're sure?" I heard buttons being snapped and a chair scooted across a hard surface. Microsoft's signature music floated over the airwaves.

"Yes. I'm sure. Go to www.myvisionquest.net. No spaces, no dashes."

A moment later, Jim said, "Ah, hell. Ah, hell."

"Yeah, that's what I thought. You said something about poetry. How about, 'Terpsichore, joy and dance, siren of the stage. Pirouette, gavotte, ballet, lyre and song, the gods will rage. War and death and dance and sway…' It just gets worse."

"How did they find this? How did they find something with information only the cops have seen?"

"They're children of the electronic age. And they're nosy."

The girls bumped fists and shared a grin. "We're the best," Paz whispered.

A long pause followed before Jim spoke. "I gotta go to the office. If I can find a way to keep you and the girls out of it, I will. Otherwise, a cruiser will be at your door to escort you in."

I felt myself flush. "You'd have us brought in for finding a site with the missing girls on it?"

"Not me. Simmons. Her first thought will be that you set up the site, kidnapped the girls and were manipulating us the whole time."

Jas took the phone right out of my hand and said, "That's the last help you getting from me and mine, cop." I pawed the air trying to get the phone back but Paz got it instead.

"Yeah. You screwed with the wrong family. Screw you." She closed the phone with a hard snap. "That's the last time I help the cops solve a murder case," Paz said. "Can you believe that?"

I clenched my fists, closed my eyes and sighed, the sound long-suffering and weary.

"We should just switch to criminal justice and become cops. Show them boys how to do it right," Jas said.

"Huhn. I got no use for a system that assumes people are guilty instead of innocent. That's against the Constitution," Paz said.

"The *court* system assumes people are innocent until proven guilty," I said, my eyes closed. "And, on paper, law enforcement does, too. But the reality is that cops work from a different perspective. Everyone is guilty. All the time."

"We're not guilty," Jas said, her tone stubborn. "You let that Emma come after us. Nana and Aunt Mosetta will have her job. Probably have her stuck somewhere like Guantanamo Bay, get her tortured or something."

I wanted to laugh at the thought of Emma and Nana butting heads. Nana had the harder head and the bigger friends, but Bow-tie Emma had a gun. Opening my eyes, I said, "Let's see it again." We went through the site, studying the photos of the girls. "The cops will find who made this Web site and bring him in," I said. "You girls did a good thing."

"Not gonna be so easy," Paz said.

I looked at her in surprise.

"I looked at the HTML code. It's a basic site design, with really primitive coding. Anyone could have designed it. So I went to Whois, thinking it would be just as basic, you know, listing all the Web site info."

"Who is? Topaz, you are light years ahead of me on Internet stuff."

"Yes, ma'am. I'm supposed to be," she said knowingly. She was majoring in computer studies or whatever they called it these days.

"Whois is a Web site that tracks all the owner's and site's info, if you know how to get in and use it. I do. The designer, administrator, hosting site—everything—is anonymous, listed as corporations in different parts of the world. The only address is in Thailand."

I thought about that for a moment. "So the Web site is basic but the way it's set up is intricate."

"Juicy. Really juicy."

I figured that meant she was agreeing with me. "Maybe the guy paid someone else to set up the site and get it registered, then he took it over and built the site himself."

"Maybe. He can upload new pages from anywhere. All he needs is a laptop and any open Wi-Fi. He can drive around any town and look for a Wi-Fi connection, log on and shoot an upload to the site." At my blank look, she said, "Trust me. This guy's invisible. He could live two blocks over and we'd never be able to trace him. And he can work the site from anywhere."

I sighed and rubbed my eyes. "Okay, girls. Tomorrow—today—is a school day. Go upstairs and get some sleep. And leave the laptop in the rec room. I mean it. No more of this tonight."

"When this case is over, I'm writing a paper on it," Paz said with satisfaction. "And I'll get an A."

Back in my bed, I lay in the dark and stared at the ceiling. Moonlight filtered through the blinds and curtains, throwing whispery shadows above me, shadows that moved with the bushes beyond the windows, as they were stirred by the night wind. It was soothing, comforting, like the mattress beneath me, and the soft sheets and blankets.

The Web site Topaz had discovered was connected directly to the case and the kidnapper. The man in jail for kidnapping and Mari were not connected to either. That meant that the police still had pertinent missing persons reports on four girls, including the one who had been found beneath the Confederate Monument. Which meant that they had two unaccounted for. Two more children taken by this monster and probably already killed. Tears filled my eyes and I rolled over and closed them, hoping sleep would come and that there would be no further interruptions in the night.

20

Friday Morning

Knocking woke me. I stumbled to the back door to find Nana standing there with a shovel in one hand, a pair of gloves in the other, and dressed in bib overalls. She scowled at my state of dishabille, and said, "I've been up and working for over five hours. You still in bed?"

I yawned and leaned into the doorjamb, smelling flowers, coffee, clean-turned earth and dog. Big Dog bumped my hip, long-haired tail wagging. The coffee scent was from behind me and I glanced over at the ancient Mr. Coffee. "We were up till two-something solving murders. Want to hear about it over coffee?"

"What I want is someone to watch the wetbacks in the field on Tyler Road," she said, propping the shovel and following me inside. "They do okay on the hay yesterday?"

"You don't hire illegal aliens, Nana, and *wetback* is not PC. They did fine." I poured two mugs and passed her one. Nana drank it black—"Straight up, just the way I like my whiskey," as she put it. I added both cream and sugar to mine—a lot of each—and poured a bowl of Special K.

"Spill it. I don't have all day," Nana said, sitting at my breakfast table. "You gonna take the haying or do I have to do it all by myself?"

I sat beside her and propped my feet on the chair opposite. "You want to gripe a bit more first, get it all out of your system? Make yourself sound a bit more martyred?"

Nana glared at me and I smiled sweetly. She chuckled under her breath and took a loud sip of the too-hot coffee. She cut her eyes to me. "Not many of mine would say something like that to my face."

"I used to be scared of you, too, but I'm not anymore. I'll take the haying until two. I have to be at the hospital at four this afternoon."

"Better than nothing. I'll stick one of Mosetta's youngsters over it after school. I got to train one or two of them up to be foremen. I'm getting old, need to be prepared to turn the farm over to the next generation."

I didn't reply. Nana had said the same thing for decades. The next generation was now in their sixties. Mine were in their forties and early fifties. The generation who might be interested in farming were the greenies, still in public school, learning about the waste of land, erosion and global warming. Instead, I told her about the Web site and about waking Jim at a bit before two. Nana frowned when I repeated Jim's reactions to her. "He hasn't called me back, so I don't know if it panned out or not."

"If it does, and if he wasn't able to keep the girls' names out of it, this family will be in the police spot-

light again." Nana drained her cup and stood. "You tell
me if I need to do something." Which sounded vaguely
ominous. She set down her cup and headed for the
door, adding, "That possum is three feet under. You
owe a tip to Mosetta's Thomas Spires. He's twelve."
The door closed behind her.

That was when I realized I hadn't had to disarm the
alarm system when I'd opened the door. I looked at the
door, pretty sure it had been unlocked. I took in the
girls' vehicles parked behind the house and heard giggling and a monotonous bass from upstairs. There
were no breakfast dishes out, so Jas hadn't been down
yet. Jas always ate first thing when she came down the
stairs. And yet the door was unlocked.

I stepped to the bottom of the stairs and called up.
"Jas? Paz?"

The music went silent and both girls stuck heads out
of opposite rooms to look down at me. "Sorry about
the music, Mama," Jas said.

"No problem with the music. Have either of you
been down here yet this morning?" Two heads shook
no. "Did either of you go out last night after I went to
bed the first time?" Two more head shakes. "Okay.
Don't be late. I'll put cereal bowls out for you."

"What's the matter, Mama?" Jas asked.

"Nothing. I guess I didn't set the alarm."

"You set it. I looked when we went up last night.
The little red light was on."

Apprehension waltzed its way along my spine. "Oh.
Thanks." I turned away before she could see my expression. Jas could read me far better than I could read
her these days.

I stared at the green light on the alarm pad. Someone had unlocked the door and turned off the alarm without waking us, which meant that I had slept through the soft warning tone that had sounded. It meant that someone had been inside the house during the evening and had turned off the alarm before leaving. Or someone was still here.

I raced to my room and grabbed the little gun off the top closet shelf, then changed my mind and took the shotgun instead. On instinct, I broke open the weapon and checked the load, brass shells shining in the closet light. I still hadn't cleaned the guns since the police had confiscated and returned them. With a snap, I closed the breach, which effectively cocked both barrels, and thumbed off the safety, set the stock firmly against my shoulder, ready to fire.

Methodically, I went from room to room, checking the house. There was no one here. But in the small room off the rec room, the small space that still stored Jack's business papers, building and development plans, a small section of floor had been cleared, papers pushed to the side and the carpet beneath exposed. Someone had sat here.

Fear gripped me hard. Someone had been in my house. Last night. While the girls had studied and played here? Or later, after we'd gone to bed, a quick in and out? I couldn't be sure.

I backed out of the room and called a locksmith, paying extra to get the husband-and-wife team out today to change all the locks. I called URSafeWithUs, the company that handled our security system, and had them check the automatic security log. What I discov-

ered terrified me. Someone had disabled the alarm
system at 3:00 a.m.. Had we shared our evening with
someone? If so, they knew everything we did. Everything we had told the cops. Or had someone entered
at 3:00 a.m. and left before I'd woken, without reset-
ting the alarm?

I stared at the clear space on the floor and the piled
papers. Was this a connection to the Ballerina Doll
murders? I had to consider the possibility. But it could
also be something more mundane. Something ordinary.
I felt my hackles drop and I took a breath, smooth and
steady. Okay. Someone with security knowledge,
perhaps specific only to my house, had been here.
They—no, he or she, not more than one. The space was
too small for two people. He or she was here to rob. I
came home and they hid in the vault room for us to go
up to sleep. "Yeah," I said aloud, breathing easier. "That
makes more sense."

Along that line was the possibility that my intruder
was one of the young cousins, intent on mischief,
testing the waters of thievery. Yeah. That felt right.
Wicked Owens had started out that way. One of the
cousins might have learned the security code by
watching us come and go. My fear receded further
with the thought.

Nevertheless, I arranged to have the security company come look the house over for listening equipment
and change the code. You aren't paranoid if they really
are after you.

I spent the remainder of the morning driving back
and forth from the hay field to the house, overseeing

the lock changing and the hay baling. When the security team left, I was reasonably satisfied that the bad guy or girl couldn't get in, not without waking me. The warning tone announcing that the door had been opened was now set to eardrum-blasting volume. I wouldn't sleep through it. Not again.

The security team had also taken fingerprints and physical evidence from the little vault room. They assured me they could process it, and while they couldn't promise speed, they would give it top priority, whereas the cops would put it on the bottom of their list because no property damage or loss of possessions had occurred, and no lives had been lost. They could even run the fingerprints through AFIS, which law enforcement used to ID fingerprints. The company had a man on the inside who did work for them under the table. Which sounded like a good way to lose a job, but I wasn't complaining.

Near noon, I was eating my lunch in the front seat of my SUV, parked on the side road near the hay field. The growing season had started early this year, and the clean smell of fresh cut hay mixed with the less agreeable scents of gasoline and diesel. English and Spanish dialects carried on the air. The temperature was warm. It was a perfect day.

From behind the partial concealment of a rotted three-board fence, I spotted a familiar gray Crown Vic. It rocketed down the adjoining state road, shaking my vehicle in its wake. Three heads were visible inside, at least one of them female. I considered the road they were traveling. There were four Chadwick families within a two-mile radius. All of them had a white or mixed-race male living in the house; some more than one. I dropped my chicken sandwich in the zippered chiller packet on the passenger seat, flipped open my cell and called Nana as I pulled out and followed them. The Crown Vic was nowhere in sight, but I knew where all the Chadwicks lived. I wasn't in a hurry.

The backup I had called would be nearly a half hour getting there, and I wondered who I could channel to get through the next thirty minutes without getting arrested. Josephine wouldn't do. My mama wouldn't be caught dead in jeans, T-shirt, boots and a straw hat. I couldn't do Nana if my life depended on it. But maybe I could do me, the me that handled irate doctors and drunk patients. Hmm. Maybe so. And for once, it might be fun.

I arrived shortly after the cops knocked on Erasmus Wilcox Chadwick's door. From the street, I called Nana's cell and said three numbers. "Three-oh-eight." The address. I snapped the phone shut.

Heads turned toward me as I cruised into the yard. Fully aware that I was about to kick a hornet's nest, I stepped from the truck, stuck my thumbs in my jeans pockets and walked up the five steps to the wide porch. I looked at Erasmus, standing protectively, half-hidden behind the door. "Howdy, cousin," I said.

He nodded to me. He was from Aunt Mosetta's side of the family, a well-educated professor. He had taught history at an all-black college up North and had returned to Dawkins to retire. He was a light-skinned black man, or a dusky-skinned white man, and his green eyes were like emeralds in his narrow face. "Cousin," he acknowledged me. "Welcome."

"No. She is not *welcome.*" Emma Simmons's voice vibrated with fury. She looked at me with enough sparks in her eyes to set off a good-size forest fire, then turned them to Jim.

I knew what she was thinking and who she was about to accuse, so I said, "You folk from the big city should slow down when you travel country roads. You might see interesting things on the byways. Like a friend's SUV parked in a hay field, overseeing the workers. Jim didn't call me, Emma. I saw your car. I'm pretty sure it was speeding." I looked at Jim and raised my brows. "Shame on you. Besides—" I transferred my gaze back to Emma "—you couldn't spit in a ditch in this county without my nana hearing about it, if she was of a mind to know it."

"You can't do this, Ashlee," Jim said, and I knew he meant it. I knew I was putting pressure on a man in ways no girlfriend should. I should step back, walk away. Julie Schwartz watched me quizzically, a half smile on her face. I inclined my head at her.

"You are impeding a federal investigation," Emma said to me.

I narrowed my eyes. This was family. I'd stay. "Well, that's one way to see it, Emma. Another is that I'm visiting my cousin. And he might invite me in. Erasmus?" I pulled off my wide-brimmed hat and dusted it against my leg.

"Happy to have family." He held the door open and I preceded the cops into the room. "When will Nana be here?" he asked, knowing that I would have called in the big guns.

"Shortly. With Macon." I sat in the wingback chair

in the corner and smiled at the feebs as they filed into the room. I could tell that nothing was going according to their usual plan. I had presented them with a quandary. I glanced at my watch. Twenty-two minutes to go. I was sweating, but they didn't know it.

"Mr. Chadwick doesn't need a lawyer," Emma said. "He's not being charged with anything."

"He's a good boy, our Macon," Erasmus said, looking from me to the cops. "What should I do, until Macon gets here?"

"You tell them that your lawyer is on the way and you'll be happy to talk with them. That you'll answer any questions as soon as he arrives. Till then, Nana suggested that you offer the cops something to eat, maybe some coffee." I looked at Julie and smiled. "Erasmus makes a great espresso. And his homemade doughnuts are to die for." Julie's lips twitched.

Erasmus's shoulders relaxed and he sent me a relieved smile. "As my students would have said—" he jutted his chin at me "—*what she said.* Coffee? Espresso, anyone?" He turned to his compact kitchen and started fresh grounds. Emma, Jim and Julie fidgeted and looked from the furniture to each other. The seating was sparse. Julie took a comfortable chair with the air of a woman at a Broadway play. The other two sat on the couch with ill grace.

The petite brick house was of a style last built in the sixties, four rooms and a bath, a few small, high windows, with the only comfort being the large screened porch out back. I had never been here, but I had seen houses like it and knew it would have two bedrooms in the rear, with a bath and the back hallway between, and the kitchen as part of the dining room, just off the living room. I shifted in my seat, following Erasmus as he bustled in his kitchen, and spotted the laptop open on the dining-room table, its screen marked by geometric forms floating in the darkness. I had no doubt that the cops had seen the laptop, too.

Seventeen uncomfortable minutes later, two cars arrived from opposite directions. Macon pulled in from DorCity, the name the locals called Dorsey City, the county seat. Nana eased into the drive in her old truck from the direction of the farm. Erasmus stood, looking uncertain in his own home.

My grandmother walked into the room without invitation and without greetings, her boot heels sharp and purposeful on the wood floor. She took a seat on the couch next to Emma, jostling her quite deliberately. Macon stopped at the door and surveyed the group. His eyes lingered a moment too long on Julie, and I read volumes into the gaze.

Though I wanted to stay and watch, Nana looked at me with quiet purpose and then at the door. It was a clear order to leave. I got up and touched Erasmus's shoulder; he bent so I could kiss him on the cheek. He smelled of coffee and newspaper ink and faintly of aftershave. Patting my back, he walked me to the door and whispered in my ear, "Never mess with Chadwicks. We stand together."

"Always," I said. I looked at Nana. "Give 'em hell, Nana."

Julie smothered a chuckle. Jim finally almost smiled. Nana and Macon laughed. Emma nearly swallowed her tongue, her face taking on a hue that looked distinctly unhealthy. If I lost Jim over this, the expression on Emma's face made it all worth it.

As I walked across the porch, I heard Nana say, "The Chadwicks number in the hundreds. In Dawkins County alone there are nearly two hundred of us. Within the next hour, each and every one of them will have been notified that Macon Chadwick will be available to represent them during questioning by the local police or by the FBI. Should you wish to speak with any of them, they will refuse to do so until they have Macon by their sides. You will be wasting your time and ours to show up without an appointment unless you have an arrest warrant or intend to take someone in for formal questioning. And even then they will not talk until Macon gets there. We will help the FBI and any other law-enforcement agency to solve this case. But we will not be targeted. Do we understand one another, Miss Simmons?"

I had reached the bottom step and missed the SAC's comments, but I headed back to the hay field comfortably sure that my family had proper representation. It was only after I had reopened the remains of my lunch that I considered why they had chosen Erasmus. My cousin, second or third or fourth, I never could remember which, had taught advanced studies in old-world history. If any Chadwick had the knowledge and skill to make the Web site and to know about the Muses, it was Erasmus.

A cold chill whispered through me. It had to be someone who hated Chadwicks. Had to be. Or, at the worst, one of the Chadwicks who had left Dawkins and never returned. Every family had them. Chadwicks called them lost sheep.

* * *

He pulled his car into the strip mall where the new tae kwon do gym was, and watched through the lit front windows. She kicked high, the right leg bent at the knee, the left heel extended. She missed the black belt she was sparring with, but he knew that was by intent. Had she wanted the kick to land, it would have, and with amazing force for such a small body.

He would have to take great care with this one. The bruises from the last one were only now beginning to fade, and this girl would pack much more of a punch. The previous girl had been a dismal and horrifying failure. He would make sure that this one would be perfect. He had learned with each, and the lessons—and fate—had led him here, to this perfect girl.

The sun was setting behind the building, and the glare made it hard to see. Pulling his hat low on his brow, he slid from the car and moved to the front window to watch. No one noticed him. Why should they? He was just one more parent waiting to pick up his daughter—the girl who had just won her brown belt.

I was finishing up a stroke code, sending the patient to a room in ICU, when Rhonda sidled up to me and whispered, "There's another Amber Alert. Another blonde." I nodded to show I had heard and handed my patient over to the crew to transport him to his room. I washed my hands and went to stand in front of the TV. It was overhead in the back corner, volume turned low. With three others, I stood and stared, listening as the local commentator brought breaking news, her voice overlaying a night scene in front of a strip mall.

"The child, who had just finished a tae kwon do class, walked out of the building and disappeared. According to a source, her mother had a flat tire and called the class to tell them she would be late. But the teacher forgot to pass along the message and allowed the little girl to leave the building anyway. Her name is Jennifer Burton, a blond, blue-eyed girl who recently won her brown belt. Police have already confiscated the security camera and have taped off the entire parking lot. We'll be showing the girl's picture as soon as we have one."

The camera angle widened and slid to the side to reveal the entrance to the gym. Police cruisers cast flickering blue lights and the people at the doorway resolved into individuals. It looked like a mob scene, with two people exchanging blows, or one hitting and another blocking each strike. "We believe the distraught woman seen attacking the instructor is the mother of the missing girl," the reporter said. "If what we have been told is true, she did everything right in calling the martial-art school to say she would be late."

On impulse, I said, "I'm taking a break." In the lounge, I activated my cell phone and listened to messages while getting a Diet Coke. Jas was ticked off. She had been met at the door by Nana and given the list of changes in the Davenport household. All of them. The one she was most angry about was the one Nana had come up with on her own. "Nana says I can't leave the house *without notifying you first.* I have to call my *mommy* to leave the house like a *four-year-old kid?*" she complained, her voice rising. "I am *twenty years old,* Mother. You have to talk some sense into that old woman. She may be the family matriarch, but she isn't queen."

My lips twitched, but my humor faded when she continued. "*And* she said I have to call you and her when I get home and hold on while I walk through the house, carrying my gun. So I did that. I called her. I'm home.

"But I'm not stupid. You change the locks and the security code and the way I have to operate. Somebody got into the house, didn't they? You better call me, Mama. I'm ticked off that you didn't let me handle part of this. That you didn't tell me yourself." She paused and I could hear her breathing. "I'm not a little girl, Mama. I'm a grown-up. You have to start being honest with me." She hung up.

I sat on the worn couch, popped the top of my cola and took a long gulp, feeling the Diet Coke burn its way down. Jas was right. I was being unfair. I would continue to protect her as long as she lived, but I could be more up-front with her. I could treat her more like an adult. She had certainly acted like one on the phone, no sulking, no hysterics. I smiled and took another drink. My baby, my Jazzy, was growing up. Jazzy. A baby nickname.

On the lounge phone, I dialed my daughter. When she answered, the first words out of my mouth were "You're right. I am sorry."

"Oh," she said. With mild surprise, she added, "Mama?"

"Yes. You are grown up." Tears gathered in my eyes, blurring the room. "And I love you very much, and I am so very proud of you. I will endeavor to treat you as an adult, as a grown-up." I set down the can and wiped my nose. "Do you want to know what happened?"

Softly, Jas said, "Yes. I do."

I told her about the disarranged vault room, and the alarm system being off, and that I had the security company checking in with us two times a day. I told her everything.

Jas listened silently. When I finished she said, "Mama, you think whoever was in the house was after me, don't you?"

I breathed through my mouth as my nose clogged up. Yes. I had been thinking that. I had *believed* that.

"I'm too old to be one of the kidnapped girls," she said. "He could be after you just as easily. If it was the kidnapper at all."

Which had been my thoughts as well. I was worried over nothing. Then Jas ruined my fledgling sense of safety.

"He could be wanting to hurt a Chadwick, any Chadwick. So you be careful. And you follow all the rules that Nana set up for me. We'll look after each other. And we'll get through this just fine."

I chuckled. "I feel like the kid, and you sound like the mother. Okay. We'll both take precautions. Love you, baby."

"Love you, too, Mama. Oh—Paz and the other girls are bringing pizza over. If I have to be in jail, they're going to keep me company. And Nana's buying," she added smugly.

"You're just milking this for all it's worth, aren't you?"

"Oh yeah. Later."

"Later," I said.

I hung up the lounge phone and my cell rang almost instantly. Nana's number was displayed in the view screen, so I flipped it open and said, "Evening, Nana."

"You see the Amber Alert?"

"I saw it," I said.

"Mosetta and I started calling every one of ours the moment it went out. I called all of the men the FBI visited today. Erasmus isn't answering." She stopped for a long silent moment. Softer, she said, "I rode by his house. His car is gone."

A sense of disquiet settled in my chest. "Have you called Macon?"

"Macon was supposed to meet him at seven-thirty at his office in DorCity. He didn't show. Did we... Did we make a mistake?" Nana sounded broken, lost, as if the world had pulled the rug out from beneath her feet. "Is it one of ours?"

I stuffed my own fears deep inside and lied. "Nana, he could have cut his finger cooking and gone to the all-night clinic in Ford City. He could have forgotten he had an appointment with his barber, and left Macon an e-mail. You know how unreliable the Internet provider is in Dawkins County. Macon is always griping about it. That's why so many of us switched to AOL. It could be anything. Just be patient, Nana. He'll call. You know he will."

Nana heaved a long sigh. "Thank you, Ash. You're right, of course. It's nothing. Erasmus is good as gold. I just got worried when I saw the way he looked when that woman took his laptop."

The apprehension that had been whispering to me

all day became a roar of worry. I gripped the little phone tighter. "Emma? She had a warrant for the computer?"

"Oh, yeah. Pulled that outta her briefcase like it was a rabbit and she was a magician. And Erasmus got a mighty strange look on his face when she did. I thought he was gonna hit her. He said it held all his research. Did you know he was researching a book on the history of the Chadwicks?"

"No, Nana," I said, pressing a hand to my stomach. Research on the family history would include where the burial plots were, wouldn't it? Like the rest of us, he would have the genealogy chart with all the missing family members and access to the family Web site.

Farley stuck his head in the door and said, "Two codes on the way in."

I gave the okay sign with finger and thumb, and he closed the door. "I have to go, Nana. Will you call me when Erasmus shows up?"

"So you can say I told you so?"

I chuckled, hearing the false note in my fake laugh.

"Fine. I'll call. Crazy old man. Cause me to have a heart attack. Bye, Ash."

"Bye, Nana. Love you."

We hung up and I stood. I looked at the phone. Should I call Jim and tell him Erasmus was missing? If I did, all the law-enforcement attention would focus on one old man, a man I trusted totally. Didn't I?

Through the door, I heard a commotion. The first code had arrived. Slowly, my thumb lowered, to hover over the cell's off button. Deliberately, I depressed it. And went out to deal with my patient.

21

"**Y**our mother is not someone you can trust. You must not expect her to help you. She's an evil woman who wanted to take you away from me. She tried. She tried." He nodded slowly.

The girl in the corner stared at him with huge eyes. Her tae kwon do uniform was wrinkled and dirty. Her hair hung in straggles, and he wanted to brush it back and up, securing it with combs, but it was too soon. He had to win her over first.

She had put up a fight, but he had been prepared this time, and the duct tape had been perfect for holding her still. No wonder maintenance and construction types praised it so highly. But he would have a hard time getting it off her favorite blanket. The velour held tightly to the sticky tape.

"You're that crazy man the TV has been talking about," she said.

He smiled gently. They were always this way, but it would be harder now, he knew, with all the media attention. He had expected that. "I'm your father. The courts and your mother have been trying to keep us apart. But I fixed it and we can be together now."

"You're not my father," she said, standing taller. "My father was killed in Iraq. He was a marine. And he'd have kicked your ass, you pervert."

He ignored that. "Would you like to see your mother? She's right next door."

Her face went through a series of changes. Shock, disbelief, pain, hope. Her little body quivered with need. "You have my mama?"

"Right next door. Do you want to see her? I'll take you to her, if you promise to eat your supper, take a shower, put on your nightgown and go to sleep."

She quivered harder but she nodded, acquiescing as always. He stood and opened the door. The dark hallway beckoned. He waited as she measured the dark beyond, the open door and the man who stood between. Hope and fear warred within her, his little warrior. She took a deep breath and let it out.

Moving with the jerking, measured steps allowed by her shackles, she left her corner and came toward him. Toward the dark. He stepped back, allowing her to walk past him, sorry that events and the media had forced him to apply the restraints. It had been so much easier to win their trust when he could befriend them slowly and safely. The press had also forced him to move up his ultimate timetable. He didn't have a choice now.

She moved into the hallway and he rewarded her by turning on the light. She blinked, the tension in her shoulders easing at the sight of the ordinary white-painted walls, the three doors, the carpeted floor, the stairs up to the next floor. Shelves lined the hallway, each containing a memento or an artifact from his travels. Urns, statues, one broken horse he had not been able to repair when the severed hoof went missing. Many statues of the Muses, reproductions mostly, though not all. Ordinary things. There was no devil with a pitchfork or wild man with an ax. The door from the basement was locked, so that if she tried to get away, she wouldn't get far. She stopped and looked up at him, questioning with her eyes. Beautiful eyes.

He walked to the other door and turned the knob, pushing the door wide. She stepped forward, hesitant. When she was framed in the doorway, he flipped on the light. The room within lit up instantly.

The girl screamed.

And screamed.

And screamed.

After a long moment, he knelt and pulled her gently to him. He held her, smothering her hysterical screams against his shoulder. Patting her back soothingly, he muttered gentle nonsense words as the screaming went on and on, finally breaking, to slide down the slope from fear to exhausted tears. It was always like this, and he felt so guilty at crushing them with so much pain, but there was no other way. Slowly the wails subsided until she shook in his arms, silent. He could smell the sweat, the stench of fear caught in her hair and in her gym uniform. Beneath it was an odd sweetish perfume, vaguely familiar.

He rubbed her shoulder. "As long as you do what I tell you, as long as you are a good girl, I won't bring your mother here. I won't be forced to do to her what I had to do to my Mnemosyne. I'll allow your mother to live. Understand?"

She nodded, tension once again vibrating through her.

"But if you act up, if you disobey, I'll do to your mother just what I did to the lovely Mnemosyne. Now, go get your shower, and I'll bring you some soup and a sandwich." The girl nodded and stepped back. He let her. He was so proud. This one would surely be the one. Surely.

At 1:00 a.m., Jim walked in the door of the Majors and rested a hip against the desk. Robert was on the phone, chatting to his significant other, and he pointed to me in cubicle seven. Because I had no patient privacy to protect, I continued to change the soiled sheets, gather up the trash and spray the bed with antibacterial cleanser. RNs are usually too valuable in terms of time to clean rooms, but on third shift, we all pitch in and do a bit of everything.

Jim paused in the door, his face unreadable, the cop mask showing nothing. He was wearing a mixture of fresh and old clothes, his shirt and tie starched and neatly tied, his slacks wrinkled from hours of sitting. When I finished the room, I snapped off the blue non-latex gloves and washed my hands at the sink, using plenty of hot water and soap. My hands were cracked and red as usual, the constant hand washing straining the ability of normal human flesh to keep up. Standing at the sink, watching him, I pulled a tube of hospital-approved moisturizer out of my pocket and squeezed a generous portion out, rubbing it into my skin.

Finally he sighed and his face softened. "You're not going to make this easier on me, are you?"

"Not planning on it." I tucked the tube away.

"I'm a cop, Ash."

"And I'm a Chadwick. Born and bred. We protect our own."

"Even if they're guilty?"

"You show me proof that a Chadwick took those girls and I'll get a gun and shoot him myself. And Nana and I'll bury him in a cesspit. And the Chadwicks will dance on his grave."

A sound that might have been a strangled laugh stuck in his throat. "Are all the Chadwicks so bloodthirsty?"

I ignored his question as rhetorical. "Do you have proof that one of us did it?"

He measured my expression, my body language, using skills gained from years as a cop to evaluate me and my reactions. "No," he said finally. "Not yet. But your cousin Erasmus has accessed several sites on graveyards in research for a book. In light of what we know, that's suspicious. He'll be contacted in the morning and asked to come in for questioning. With his lawyer," he added with a small smile. "Another cousin—you are all cousins, aren't you?"

"Second, third, fourth, twice removed. All cousins." I was pretty sure I kept the belligerent tone out of my voice, the one I carried from school days when some redneck called one of us zebra or Uncle Tom. We stuck together, standing toe to toe, black and white and mixed, Chadwicks against the rest of the world. It hadn't been easy.

As if he read my mind, Jim said, "I've never heard of a family like yours. Half black, half white, sticking together for generations."

When I didn't reply, he scrubbed his face and

seemed to come to a decision. Again. "We've made some progress in refining the investigation. Smith, the guy charged with statutory rape of Mari, wouldn't know a Muse if it bit him. He's been removed from the list of suspects, and his case has been turned over to local law enforcement.

"Based on the Web site Jas and Paz discovered, we've widened the search criteria for the missing girls. We have a total of seven possibles on the map now, five confirmed." He shifted at the door and slid his hands into his slacks pockets. His exhaustion seemed to intensify, pulling at his face. When he blinked, even his eyelids looked tired. "I want to tell you that we have eliminated your family as suspects, but I can't. We cemented the common denominator with most of the missing girls. All but one of the seven has a Chadwick ancestor. All but one, Ash. It might be back a generation or two or five, but it's there, and we're still looking for the family association with the other girl. There must be a thousand people in the South with a connection to your family. This guy, the unsub, has researched your roots back as far as he can go and turned it sideways and upside down. If he isn't one of you, then he has some powerful reason to hate all of you. I know I've asked before, but can you think of anyone who has a grudge against you? Against your family? Anyone at all?"

"No." I closed my eyes and turned to the wall as I worked to bring myself under control. *Erasmus...* I wrapped my arms around my waist and held myself. This would kill Nana and Aunt Mosetta.

Jim continued to speak to my back. "The girl he left

beneath the Confederate Monument had been dyed blond. Her mother says she thinks that the girl's paternal great-grandmother was a Chadwick."

I shook my head, not in negation, but in horror. The silence stretched between us. In the center of the Majors, two nurses were talking about a man they had both dated and now hated.

"She hadn't been sexually assaulted," Jim said. "So far as we can tell, none of them were."

Some of the fear gripping my chest eased, and I was able to take a breath.

"Her bruises were facial and upper body. Most looked defensive, according to the doctor. No sign of restraints. Mostly blows, not necessarily sexual in nature, but more likely to be signs of a struggle. And a couple on her hands and feet that might have been offensive."

There was an admiring smile in his voice, and I knew he was thinking about his own daughter and how she might fight off an attacker. I hadn't met his daughter yet. Once again, I wondered why.

"Unfortunately, she still doesn't remember anything. We're hoping that changes, but her mother won't let us near her except for short periods of time. An hour here and there."

Good for her, I thought. But I didn't say it.

"We're speculating that both of them, the one we got back and the girl taken last night, from the strip mall dojo, were to be Melpomene, the Muse depicted holding a mask and a knife or a club."

Still, I remained with my back turned. I stood and listened without speaking, facing away, and he kept on talking, telling me things he probably shouldn't.

My breath sped up. I felt blotches break out on my neck. I kept myself from making fists, but only barely. I felt trapped, Jim Ramsey standing between me and the door.

"Most of the postmortem results are back on the girls," he went on, his voice soft, sounding so reasonable. "None had been sexually assaulted. None died violently. They were given something that slowed their metabolism. Slowed their heart rates. They were smothered."

I flinched, only slightly, but I knew he had seen it. Cops were trained to notice little things like that. And they were trained to use information to herd their prey where they wanted it to go. That was what I had just understood. I was being herded.

"Having one alive helped. We'll be able to discover what he drugged them with."

The feebs wanted me for something, so they had sent Jim. And he had come.

"The docs pulled enough blood and urine for us to test for most anything. They tell us the reference lab will have a definitive answer by morning, and our own lab is doing parallel testing."

Emma had sent him, and he had obeyed like a well-trained dog. I knew it. I schooled my face to stony and turned to him. Beyond him, two EMS workers were wheeling in a patient. Her struggle to breathe was apparent even across the room. Other nurses and Farley dove in to help. I had to get back to work. I said, "The Web site with the photos isn't helping?"

Jim shook his head. "It originates in Thailand," he said, offering the information freely and corroborating Topaz's assessment. "It can be uploaded from anywhere. Identifying the owner is like dancing in quicksand. But we did discover a number of child-pornography sites connected to it, so we're still running with it."

"What did Emma send you here for, Jim?"

His eyes widened fractionally.

"You wouldn't be here if she didn't send you," I said, shoving all the anger, all the betrayal, and all the… The word *infidelity* flashed through my mind, and I knew that the ghost of Jack's treachery was sparking some of this. That was something to deal with later. Much later. I shoved all the anger down, out of the way, deep inside. When I spoke again, my tone was almost gentle. Almost calm. "You wouldn't be telling me all this, if you didn't have her blessing. Some of it, maybe, but not all of it. So you're here on official business. What is it?"

Jim didn't react. His cop's face as hard as stone, he said, "We want a complete family tree. There are empty spots on the family Web site and we know some of your cousins are working on adding to it. They may have information that we need. We want a copy. Can you get it?"

"Yes. What else?"

"Will you call off your nana? I think we can make some headway if she'll just bow out. Macon's not so bad. He knows the score and the law and we can work with him or around him." Jim rubbed his face again, the gesture of a weary and burned-out man. This case was getting to him. Despite myself, something inside me softened. Emma may have sent him to me, but I knew better than to think she would have approved of him telling me everything about the case. And, if I were being honest, I'd have to admit that it was possible that a Chadwick was the kidnapper and killer of little girls. Drugging them and smothering them.

Erasmus? God, please, no.

"Your nana and Aunt Mosetta are causing trouble, Ash," he went on. "Simmons is going to charge them with obstruction of justice for interfering in an investigation if they don't back off. And Simmons didn't send me to say that," he added quickly. "I'm asking for myself. And for you. And for the little girls. We may step on some toes, but we need to get this guy. Please. The last little girl he took? She's a diabetic. She can last a couple days before she starts having major problems with her sugar level. We can't afford to—"

"I'll call her." I watched him as the words stopped whatever he was about to say. "Nana is like a force of nature, so I can't promise that anything I say will affect her, but I'll call. Would you be in trouble if Emma knew you were telling me all this about the case?"

"She'd shoot me herself."

I chuckled softly, and the anger and hurt seemed to steam out with the sound, a splutter of foggy pain that dissipated into the air and disappeared. "Since you've been so honest with me, I want to tell you two things. One, Jas and Paz found newspaper and online photos of some of the girls who were taken. The guy may be doing research on his victims through the family tree, but he may also be correlating it with news photos."

Jim's gaze narrowed as he processed that information. "This guy's dedicated to making things complicated. Thanks. Get Jas to send me the dates the girls appeared in the paper. I'll keep them out of it until this is over. Afterwards, if they want it, I'll give them credit. What else?"

I held up an index finger and pulled my cell phone out, activated it and dialed Nana. It was the middle of the night but she would be up. The woman wouldn't sleep until this threat against her family—or perpetrated by it—was solved. When she answered, I said three words. "Is he back?"

"No," she said, her voice tinny in my ear. "He isn't answering anywhere. No one has seen him."

"I'm telling Jim. And I'm asking you to back off. Let him do his job."

Jim's eyes widened and he stood straighter, knowing that I knew something. Maybe something important.

"Yes," she whispered, sounding more anguished than I had ever heard her. "I won't stand in the way of law enforcement doing their jobs. Not against someone who would hurt these children. How can it be one of us, Ash?"

"We don't know it's one of us. But I can trust Jim to find out. To make sure he gets the right man. And Nana, get the keepers of the family genealogy to make copies of all the old records. The FBI needs it. Whether or not this guy is a Chadwick, he's targeting Chadwicks." When she agreed, I said, "Thank you. Night, Nana." I closed the phone when she clicked off.

"Ash?" he said, a question and a warning in his tone.

I swallowed and rubbed my chapped hands together. There was no way to put a good spin on this, but I had done the best I could until now. And I wouldn't do anything to get Nana in trouble. Maybe he'd understand. Maybe not. My palms started sweating but I met his eyes squarely.

"When the Amber Alert went out, Nana and Aunt Moses started calling all the Chadwick households with grown men in them. Macon had told Erasmus not to leave his house without contacting either him or Nana so one of them could go with him, be witnesses and alibis. He didn't call them. And when Nana phoned his house, he didn't answer. So she went out there. He's gone."

"Son of a flaming whore," Jim swore, his face dark with rage. "How long have you known this?"

"She started trying to find him right away. I just got confirmation that she wasn't successful. You heard me."

Jim pointed a finger at me, barely contained rage in every nuance of the gesture. "You call FBI headquarters right now. If you can't get put through to Simmons, you leave a message with that information. No more of this, Ash. I'm not your lying, cheating husband or his murdering business partners. I'm a cop. A good one. And I care about you. Either you trust me and work with me, or we call it quits. Your call."

Without waiting for my reply, he turned and walked away, moving with the jerky pace of a man who had just been backstabbed by his best friend. Or by the woman he trusted. *What had I done?*

I rested my head against the wall and tried to find my sense of balance, tried to remember my place in the world. Everything was off-kilter, out of whack.

Nothing in my world was right anymore. Not right in any sense of the word. I had been raised to be a Chadwick, to put family first before anything and anyone else except God and country, and sometimes even them. That way of life had worked for over forty years. But it wasn't working now. Everything I was doing was coming out wrong.

A soft voice whispered in the back of my mind. *Maybe it never worked. Maybe that's why Jack cheated on you.*

Tears sprang to my eyes. I stood straight and smoothed my scrubs. Later. I could think and worry and live in guilt about it all later. Later, I could remember that I hadn't told Jim about the prowler in my house. Later, I could remember the look on his face, fury and hurt and abject…betrayal.

The thought sang deep inside me, like some primal note of truth. Jack had betrayed me, ripping my world to shreds. And now, this time, *I* had betrayed someone else….

I had hurt Jim by not trusting him enough to tell him everything. But to do that, I would have to be well and truly over the damage done to me by Jack. A catch-22 I wasn't sure I was ready to deal with.

Right now, I had patients.

22

Saturday

By 7:27 a.m., I was on the way home, drained by more than just the hours, the codes, the misery and the blood from the shooting that had come in at 5:05. A young father, who had lost his job, his family and his hope, had shot his young son, his ex-wife and himself. We'd worked for thirty minutes to save the child, before turning him over to the OR crew, thinking him stabilized, believing him savable. The seven-year-old boy had died on the table at 6:18.

Any sense of accomplishment and hope I had died with him.

When Jas called me, I was pulling out of the employee lot, tears streaming down my face. My voice was calm when I answered, however, and Jas never knew that I was upset. Which was the way I wanted it. I never wanted any of the darkness I faced day in and day out to taint my baby.

Jas was excited—*hyped,* she called it—her words and sentences running over each other in her enthusiasm. "You can't tell anyone, 'cause they'll get in trouble, but we found another site underneath the first one and it has Muses and the little girls and it's called Melete. It has a poem dedicated to Apollo, who tried to bring Zeus down and failed, and three of the photos are girls whose pictures appeared on the other site and it says they were abducted by Zeus to protect them from Apollo, and it has lots of poems about 'She will awaken, she will return.'

"And honest to God, Mama, there's a photo of a woman in the pose of a Grecian matron, and she's blond and identified as Mnemosyne, the wife of Zeus, and she looks just like—*just like*—Aunt Winnie, if Aunt Winnie was white and not mixed, and we think we can figure out who he is, the guy who is taking these kids, and we need to talk to the FBI and Jim and what do we do? What do we do? We can't get my pals in trouble."

While she jabbered, I had pulled off the road into a drop-off zone, giving the policeman sitting in his cruiser on the corner a little finger wave. I might be in trouble if the cop saw me driving and using the cell phone and fighting tears all at the same time. As I parked, I latched on to the one thing that seemed to be the most distressing to my daughter. "Jas, honey, what friends? Why would they get in trouble?"

"We had some of the guys over and they hacked the Web site. The one with the little girls who were kidnapped."

Putting aside the thought that my daughter had "some of the guys" over when I wasn't home, and that, if her tone and the background noises were any evidence, they were still there, and not considering the idea that they had hacked into an Internet site and that Jas had, therefore, told more people that she was part of an FBI investigation, I fastened onto the other important bit of information. "Jasmine? You have to call Jim."

"But, Mama they hack—"

"No 'but Mama.' Children are in trouble. Call Jim, right now." An eighteen-wheeler blew through the intersection and the SUV rocked. The cop eased out into traffic and turned on his blue light, following the speeding transport truck. "Jim can protect you from trouble about hacking into the site. But you *will* call him. It's the adult thing to do. And if you aren't adult enough to do it, I will."

"That was a low blow, Mamash," Topaz said, clearly having stolen the phone. "Smart, but a low blow."

"Put Jasmine back on, Paz."

"I'm here, Mama. Stop it, Paz. You sure he'll keep us from getting in trouble?"

"Yes." He would, wouldn't he? "Call him." I gave her his cell number. "Call me back after you talk to him. And stay home from school today, okay? So we can talk."

"It's Saturday, Mama. No school. But anyway, we're on the way to see Elroy. He's taking visitors in the hospital and he *has* to know something about Muses. He works at the museum, right? And there's a show coming, right? Which is just too big a coincidence, right? You *have* to see how it is! Something could be connected here, so we're going to talk to him, Mama."

"Jasmine, you will not—I repeat, *not*—leave the house today."

"Umm. Mama, we're almost there. We left right after six." The background noises I had heard were music and car sounds, not rec-room sounds.

The background noises changed. There was a long, total silence, indicating a lost signal or disconnected call. Had Jasmine hung up on me? Or had she entered the no-man's-land of I-77, an area of no coverage that lasted for about ten miles. If I'd been a cussing kind of woman, I'd have cussed a blue streak. As it was, I settled for a very unsatisfying "Damn." It didn't help at all. "Damn, damn, double damn!"

I held the cell in one hand while I whipped back into the employee lot, hitting Redial. I got Jasmine's voice mail and left a terse message. If the girls had left at six, they should be far beyond the stretch of road that was no-man's-land. Jas was right. She should be nearly here. Which meant that she was ignoring my call. I began hitting redial.

I couldn't stop my nails drumming on the steering wheel as the phone rang each time. And rang. When the voice mail answered the fifth time, I gripped the wheel so tightly the chapped skin stung across my knuckles, and said, "Jasmine Davenport, I am not playing games. You will call me back in the next sixty seconds or I will give Johnny Ray your truck." I hung up and watched the second hand on my watch.

The cell rang at forty-seven seconds. I pressed the send button and said tightly, "I am not so stupid that I'll fall for *any* excuse for you not answering the phone. Only an apology is acceptable."

"Sorry, Mama," she said softly.

I took a breath, trying to calm myself down. I leaned my head on the wheel. "You are an adult, despite some of your actions, and I am trying to honor your growth into adulthood. If you want to see Elroy, that's fine. But—" I took a steadying breath "—I'm asking you not to go alone. If you don't mind, I'll go with you. Where and when?"

"That would be great, Mama. Topaz and I are parking now."

Thoughts of my bed and a good four hours of sleep were instantly squashed. I stifled my sigh. It was, after all, my big idea. I wheeled back into a parking spot, turned off the car and said, "What room number?"

As I walked to the patient room, the door opened and a stout woman in too-tight polyester clothes stepped into the hallway, a pocketbook under one arm and a satchel hanging on the other. She waved at me on the way past and said, "Morning, Ms. Davenport." I figured she was either psychic, or I knew her from someplace and had forgotten her entirely, or the girls had described me to her. I hoped it was the latter. Psychics scared me and my own bad memory was not something I wanted to cultivate. I knocked, listened to the faint reply, pushed open the door and entered.

The girls had stopped at a gas/fast-food combo place and picked up a box of fresh Krispy Kremes and three large coffees. They were on the patient's table, coffee steaming, box open and one third-empty. There were traces of sugar on Topaz's face and Jasmine's shirt, and

Elroy was stuffing a cream-filled doughnut into his mouth, the filling squishing out around his lips.

I was sure Elroy's doctor would not want him eating fats, sugar and caffeine this soon after surgery but I kept my mouth shut. The kid looked miserable, pasty-faced, dark rings under his eyes, hair hanging in strings. He was reclining on the hospital bed, turned on his side, a hospital gown over padded bandages and soiled sweatpants. But his eyes were glowing and I guessed this was the first time pretty girls had given him much attention.

"Mama!" Jas jumped up from a chair and ran to me. Hugging me, she whispered, "Play along." In a louder voice, she said, "Elroy told us he remembered you from the emergency room, so that's why I called you." She closed the door behind me and pulled me toward the boy. "I really appreciate you coming to check his bandages. Right, Paz?"

"Mamash is the best." Paz shot me an amused grin as I dropped my bag on the table beside her. The girls were dressed nearly identically in jeans and T-shirts with denim jackets and boots. The uniform of American girls everywhere.

"Elroy," I said, "nice to see you again. And looking so good." Fishing, since I couldn't ask him outright about the nature of his injuries. But I shouldn't have worried. While Elroy was clearly in pain, he was in an expansive mood.

"The shotgun missed everything vital except the top part of my liver. They had to take out part of that, and my gallbladder. Here, wanta see?" He raised the gown up, revealing a swollen, pasty, purpled torso and bloodstained bandages taped into place at front and back.

Because I was being called upon to play nurse, I washed my hands and dried them before bending over the bandage.

"They won't let me take a shower. Sorry about the BO," he said.

He was a bit rank. But the skin around the two wounds was clean, not particularly swollen or hot to the touch. I pulled the gown back over his stomach and patted his hand. "I'm glad you're okay," I said. "You had a good surgeon."

"Sorry about my mouth in the E.R.," he said. "The doctor told me I was rowdy but I don't remember much."

I smiled at him and said, "People in shock and pain often say things they don't mean." I hoped he didn't mean the racial slurs. Amy had taken a mouthful of them.

"Tell us what happened," Jasmine said.

Elroy walked us through the events in front of the museum, the car full of gangbangers, the shots fired. The blood on his hands. The pain and the voices of people who came to help. His mother's face when she got to the hospital. "She just left," he said. "You mighta seen her."

"I did," I said, taking a seat in a plastic chair. It was just as uncomfortable as it looked, hard, molded too sharply and pressing against the outer part of my hips. Chairs in hospitals were designed by sadists, I was sure of it.

"Bet they're gonna miss you at the museum," Jas

said. I thought that was a strange—or nonexistent—segue, but Elroy didn't miss a beat.

"Big time. We got that Grecian exhibit opening soon, one we negotiated over for years. Four of the artifacts were damaged in transit." He rolled slightly and his face tightened with pain. In sympathy, Jas handed him another doughnut. He took a bite and drank the coffee.

I couldn't help myself. I raised my brows and said, "Aren't you supposed to be on a liquid diet?" My tone came out sounding like a nurse and not a mother, but both of my girls rolled their eyes. There was no NPO sign on his door forbidding food and none over his bed, but I was pretty sure Elroy shouldn't be eating solid foods.

Through a mouthful of doughnut, he said, "Dr. Peterson was here at five and said I could eat. But when they brought my breakfast, it was still liquid." He pointed at the covered tray on the window ledge. "The nurse said she'll get me something but it hasn't come yet and I'm starving. Coffee?" He held out a hand to Paz. She handed the cup to him and took it back when he finished slurping.

"The show from Greece?" Jas prompted. She looked at me significantly. "What was damaged?"

"Two urns and two small statues," he said. "When we unpacked them a week ago, the curator discovered it. Some deckhand probably dropped a crate on the ship or in port." He took another doughnut and pushed the box away. "Thanks. I'm good now. Anyway, the museum was lucky to get the show because the Greeks never let their artifacts out of the country. I don't think they would have let a no-name museum like us have it if Dr. Poulous hadn't pulled some family strings."

I remembered the horse's hoof, broken off a statue. Couldn't be… But that had been buried with the child months ago. "Elroy? Was one of the statues a horse? With a broken hoof?"

"Nope. Two vases and two small household gods. Man, this coffee's good. Hospital coffee sucks, you know. No offense, Mamash."

"None taken," I said.

"Dr. Poulous," Jas said, sounding far too casual. I looked at her quickly. "He married a local woman, didn't he?"

"Yeah. Not a Greek. And believe me, that caused a stink. His mother wanted him to marry a woman she picked out like last time, and she was pissed when he married an American."

"A South Carolina girl," Jas said, sounding certain rather than questioning.

I felt the small hairs rise up along my arms. *A Chadwick?*

"Yeah, she was." Elroy looked around as if searching for unseen listeners and leaned in a bit. "A divorcée."

Jas snorted, the laugh she uses to signify derision. "How evil."

"And a dedicated Baptist, with no intention of converting to Greek Orthodox. I was there when his mother came to the museum and let me tell you, she raised hell." Elroy glanced at me. "Sorry. Heck." I waved it away and he went on. "You could hear him through the door of his office, shouting at her that he had done his duty the first time and he was doing what he wanted this time."

"What was her name?" Jas asked. "The new wife. Do you remember?"

"Clarisse Johnson. I think."

Jas smiled like a barn cat with a mouse, all predatory and pleased with herself. I looked the question at her and she gave a minute shrug as the door behind us opened and an aide entered. "Breakfast," she said. "Looks like you had the good stuff already."

I moved my bag and the aide set the tray down, pushed it to Elroy and lifted off the plastic top. The scent of bacon and eggs mingled with the coffee and the doughnuts. Elroy moaned and took a piece of bacon, chomping half a strip in one bite.

"Well, we gotta go," Jas said. "We'll try to get back before Monday. Let us know if you go home, okay?"

"Yeah, sure. Leave me your number?"

They exchanged numbers and I followed the girls out of the room, pulling the door tightly behind me. "Clarisse Johnson?" I asked instantly.

"Clarisse Anne *Chadwick* Johnson. Now Clarisse *Chadwick* Poulous," Jas said smugly. "And we have our killer. A man who knows more about the Greek Muses than almost anyone in the whole state."

"I remember Clarisse Anne," I said. "She came to the last family reunion…." With her new boyfriend. I had met him. Nick Poulous. Dr. Nick Poulous, curator of the state museum. A mid-fifties man with a paunch, who drove a Porsche, wore suits worth more than most people made in a month and who just happened to fit the police profile of the killer. And who had been in a position to go with the small group of relatives out to the old family homesite and burial ground.

I looked from Jas to Paz, their excited, satisfied faces, eyes filled with certainty. "Okay. Come with me. We're going to call Jim."

I led the girls to the ED and into the office I shared with the charge nurses, forensic nurses and others with job titles and hectic lives. I closed the door, pointed each girl to a chair and took the swivel seat behind the desk. I dialed Jim's cell and waited through the rings.

23

Jim knew all about Poulous. The curator had already been questioned, in his home, by police. Jas was deflated at the news, and sat back, arms crossed tightly, her legs twisted and wrapped around each other in an impossible position only a teenager or a yogi could attain. She stared at me with mutinous eyes, telling me without words that the police had missed something.

Knowing my daughter, I had to call her off or she would hunt the curator down and question him herself. So I said into the phone, "Jim, there's something else. Paz hacked into the Web site with the Muses and found another Web site beneath that one." The girls did that identical eye-roll thing. "Or inside it or beside it or something." Jas held out her hand for the phone and I shook my head. "It shows additional photos."

"Yeah?" Jim said, sounding interested and amused. "You know those girls are going to cause you major trouble, don't you?"

"Going to? One headache after another," I agreed. "On the new Web site, there are photos like the one of the adult that's cut out on the pages you saw. Will you talk to the girls and keep them from getting into trouble for hacking the site?"

"Yeah. Better yet, keep them at home today and I'll be by around lunchtime. I'll bring Chinese."

He looked at the girl. She wasn't cooperating. She was causing trouble, even worse than the last one. He stared through the one-way glass at the hole she had made in the wall. She had promised to be good, and so he had taken off the shackles. Then she had used a blunt nail file to dismantle the frame of her bed and beat through the paint and the wall board, sending construction debris, wall-board chips and mess across the room. He had hoped that when she found only concrete block beyond, it would discourage her. She stood there now, her back to the window, staring at the wall, trembling. Slowly she turned her head, and stared at the window as if she could see him. And she snarled.

In a fury, she whirled and raced to the window, the short metal rod taken from the bed frame held like a baseball bat. Like a weapon. At a dead run, she attacked the glass.

I had a precious three hours of sleep before Jasmine stuck her head in the door to wake me. "He's here. He brought mu shu, sesame chicken and lots of veggies."

As my daughter watched, I rolled out of bed, fought for balance until I found it, stripped off the T-shirt I'd slept in and pulled on the sweats I had left at the foot of the bed. I ran my fingers through my ash-blond hair and started to the doorway. Jas held up a hand. "I don't think so," she said.

Groggy, I blinked at her. "Don't think what?"

"Go brush your teeth and comb your hair and put on some jeans. And some makeup."

I couldn't help it. I laughed. The laughter helped clear my head and I looked at my daughter, studying her where she stood, blocking my doorway. I didn't say it, but I was pretty sure my suddenly grown-up baby was matchmaking. "Keep the food hot," I said instead. "Nothing worse than cold sesame chicken."

Ten minutes later, I emerged from the bedroom in jeans and a button-down shirt, hair combed and blush and lipstick in place. I felt better and I no longer looked like an extra from a teenage-kegger movie. In fact, I looked pretty good—as good as a late-fortysomething can in the presence of two college-age, skinny, pretty girls. I left my feet bare because this was not—*not*—a date.

As I entered the kitchen, Jim looked up in the middle of asking a question. "And you found the site—" he stuttered a half beat, holding a spoonful of rice over Topaz's plate. The half beat was the biggest compliment he could have given me. I'm pretty sure I blushed. Jasmine grinned at me with satisfaction and Topaz looked back and forth between Jim and me, almost as pleased as my daughter. Dang. They were both conspiring against me.

The conversation went on. "Paz, you have to tell me who you told," Jim said. "I have to know, so I can contain the information spread."

"Not gonna do it, Mr. Cop."

Jim put on his cop face and his voiced dropped into interrogation mode. "It's not an option."

"Ooooh. Mr. Cop turned into Mr. Bad Cop." She did a little head wiggle and raised her hands in "scary movie" pose. "Who you gonna get to play Good Cop? Mamash?"

"Not me," I said, accepting a plate from Jim. "I'm just going to call Wallace and Pearl and tell them you and Jasmine are interfering in a federal police investigation, talking to friends about the case, hacking into Web sites on the Internet and staying up all night with boys in the house. You and Jas can spend the summer with no cars, no cell-phone privileges and no fun."

My girls' jaws dropped. Ignoring their reaction, I took a bite of sesame chicken and groaned. I loved this stuff.

"You wouldn't," Paz said.

"Um-hum," I said smiling, mouth closed around the food. I swallowed and said, "I would and I will." I was usually too easygoing to put my foot down, but when I did, I put it down hard. "Shall I call Wallace now?"

"Crap. Mamash, I promised not to tell on my buds."

"Too bad. Spill it." I ate another bite.

They met one another's eyes as the silence lengthened. Jas finally shrugged. Paz sighed and gave Jim the names, addresses and phone numbers, then detailed the way into the Web site's hidden area so he could reproduce it. He copied the information in a little spiral notebook that made the electronic-age girls giggle. He went to work on the meal with a single-mindedness that let me know he hadn't been eating regularly. When he finished his lunch, he sat back with a cup of hot tea Jas had made and watched us. "Anything else I need to know?" he asked.

Jas and Paz looked at each other again, a surreptitious slide of eyes.

"Spill it," I said. I had been saying that a lot lately and couldn't help the anger I heard in my voice. My girls were fast becoming troublemakers.

Topaz said, "We been doing some research on the girls, the ones they say the kidnapper took? And we found every one of them in the news."

Jim nodded. "After Ash mentioned it, I went looking at the possibility that he chose the girls from media sources. But not all the girls had their picture in the news. They all did have Chadwick connections."

"Maybe not *The State* paper or on TV. But I'm telling you, we found them all. Every one."

"Yeah?" Jim said, interested now.

"Yeah, Mr. Cop man." Paz said triumphantly. She cocked her head and said, "Two were in school newspapers, you know, like the ones students put out. We found 'em posted on the school's Internet sites. But we found 'em *all*."

"I want to see the pics and let you walk me through the new site you found," Jim said. "After I talk to Ashlee." He looked at us all in speculation, one hand holding the tea, the other on the table. The silence lengthened. His study was unnerving. It must have been to the girls as well, because they gave another communicative glance and excused themselves. They went to the rec room with a promise to show Jim the site as soon as he was ready.

As they disappeared, Jim set his cup down and eased back, reclining at an angle, an arm stretched along the chair back, elbow bent, hand dangling. The fingers of his other hand were poised over his mouth as if he was hiding a secret, but his eyes were solemn. I took my last bite, freshened my hot tea and his and waited. This was one of those "Men are from Mars" moments that another man would have had no problem with, but that drove any normal woman up a wall. Jack Davenport had played the I'm-thinking-so-wait-on-me game after meals, too, and I had learned to be patient until he was ready to start speaking. Trying to draw out what I wanted to hear had been a waste of time.

Finally, Jim dropped his fingers and said, "Sarah— my daughter—is four. Am I going to have all that—" he nodded his head toward the rec room "—to look forward to?"

"If she's well behaved and smart. Otherwise you may have problems."

He laughed, the breathy sound coming through his nostrils. He sat up, steepled his fingers as if preparing for bad news, and said, "Okay. What else do you have to tell me?"

I filled him in on the fact that Nana had not yet gotten in touch with Erasmus. I told him about the un-expected visitor in the vault room. I finished with the fact that the security company had changed the locks and taken fingerprints and would get back to me.

Jim's eyes darkened steadily throughout my narra-tive. When he spoke, his voice was too soft, too calm. "And you were going to tell me this when?"

I stiffened at his tone. "I was going to call but I saw you all on the road to Erasmus's house. It got put on the back burner. And at the time, I was pretty ticked off at you and Bow-tie Emma. I didn't exactly want you in my house for any reason, especially when Emma would brush it off as nothing."

"She might. I wouldn't," he said shortly. "Someone may be targeting you."

"Maybe. Maybe it's just coincidence. That does exist, you know. Maybe we startled a robber and he hid there until he could leave. Maybe it's a family member on drugs, targeting those closest to him for money."

"That's supposed to make me feel better?"

"I'm not trying to make you feel better," I said tartly.

"I noticed. Let me see this room." He stood. I didn't.

I simply looked up at him, standing above me, and I steeled myself for what I needed to say. "Jim, once upon a time, I waited for a man to make decisions, to handle family safety measures, to buy and pay for cars and to do household repairs. I'm a widow and a single parent now. I no longer have that luxury. And I no longer want those things to be taken care of in that way.

"This is my house. Jas is my daughter. I killed a man once, for threatening her. For trying to kill me." Tears of exhaustion sprang to my eyes, too little sleep making me weepy. "And it nearly killed me, trying to live with that. But I learned. And I took up the reins of my life and took control. Of *my* life," I said distinctly. "I will make my decisions based on the knowledge I have and not on any man's desires or preferences. I know you're angry that I didn't call you about the person in the vault room. But I won't call you for things I can handle. And I handled the invasion of my home.

"I've changed the security code, upped the volume on the alarm, changed all the locks, had the finger-prints in the room taken." Before he could ask, I said, "And I have a shotgun and several handguns loaded and stored in safe places. Now, you tell me. Did I miss anything? Anything that would keep us safer?"

"No," he said. But he still sounded annoyed.

I narrowed my eyes at him. "Okay. Let's go see the girls." I stood and he stopped me with an outstretched hand on my arm.

"You guys are out in the middle of nowhere. Too few sheriff's deputies, too few neighbors. Only a couple of old women within close range. I agree it's unlikely that the person who invaded your house is the guy we're looking for. But it is remotely possible, what with you being a Chadwick and being identified by the media on television. I worry."

I felt my face soften from the hard mask I hadn't known I was wearing while speaking my piece. "Thank you."

"And I want you to know that I trust you, even if you don't trust me." He must have sensed my confu-sion because he said, "You *don't* trust me, Ash. You don't trust me or any man, at all. I understand why. Your husband was an SOB. But I'm not." I stiffened but he went on. "And to prove all that I'm saying, es-pecially the part about trusting you, I'll tell you this. Erasmus and his deceased wife, Ellen, owned some property, three rental houses. None of them are rented out at this time, and so getting warrants for them was easy. We have teams going in, taking all three houses at once, in a little over an hour. I'll be with them. I'm asking you to trust me enough to not call your nana and tell her."

He was telling me something that would get him in trouble if I revealed it. The last of my animosity melted away beneath his words. His hand was warm on my arm through the thin shirt fabric. I turned up my hand and clasped his. "I won't call Nana. If Erasmus is guilty of taking these girls, I want him put away."

"Thank you. And you should know, too, that Poulous was being questioned by Simmons early this morning. Someone found some more damaged statues in the state museum. One was a horse, missing all its feet."

I took a quick breath and gripped his hand hard.

Jim smiled at me. "Thought you might like to know that the Chadwicks aren't the only ones under a microscope."

Wryly, I said, "No. You're also looking at enemies of Chadwicks and people who married, divorced or did business with Chadwicks. Bet that sent the possible suspect numbers through the roof."

Jim sighed. "You have no idea."

He slapped his open hand against the wall and looked at the hole in the broken one-way mirror. It was ugly now, covered with a scrap of wood and duct tape. The room beyond was ugly now, too, with wall board scattered all over the pretty pink carpet, and the four-poster bed taken apart, the frame separated, the mattress on its side, and linens everywhere.

She had hurt him. He tested his weight gingerly, leaning on the leg she had kicked. His other knee was tender now, too, and would be for a while. Not that she would be around to notice. He had made sure of that.

He hated to punish them. For most, that was the worst part of it all, having to cause them pain. But this one had left him no choice. The anger of failure rose up in him, hot and rancid. He slammed his hand into the wall again, and when he heard her moan, he shouted, "Shut up! Shut up, shut up, shut up!"

She started crying. Her sobs were muffled in the dark of the closet where he had locked her. "I want my mama. I want my mama," she cried. "I need my insulin," she whimpered more softly.

Insulin? He stepped to the door of the closet and opened it. She was curled on the closet floor, her face bruised. He could smell the sweet scent of a diabetic, strong in the enclosed space. He needed a nurse. Needed Ashlee, to mother and care for his daughter. But until then, until she came to help them, he would have to trust the other one.

Jim's phone rang, a tinny sound. He pulled it from his belt with one hand and stood. He had been bending over Topaz at the laptop, inspecting the new site, asking questions about the woman in the Greek toga. She undeniably resembled a Chadwick family member, but none of us knew who she was.

"Ramsey," he said into the phone. "Yeah… Yeah." He flipped open his spiral notebook and took the pencil Jasmine passed him. "Coordinates?" His voice held a peculiar tone, part old anger, part resignation, part something I couldn't name. He scratched on the pad and flipped it closed, saying, "On my way." He paused, then said, "Maybe three hours. I'll push it." He closed the little phone.

To Topaz and Jasmine he said, "Thanks, girls. I'll keep your friends out of it. But if I hear about any hacking in the state, I'll know who to come see."

Paz and Jas squealed happily and jumped up, hugging him, leaving Jim Ramsey, special agent of the FBI, nonplussed. When he peeled out of their arms, distinctly uncomfortable, he said, "I gotta go. Ash, want to walk me out?"

I followed him from the room, through the kitchen and out onto the porch. "Thank you for lunch," I said.

He leaned down and kissed me on the cheek. "You may not see me for a day or two," he said. "I'll be working out of the Charleston office." His gaze swept the porch for teenagers. Finding it empty, he went on, "They found another girl down near there. She was buried in a shallow grave in an abandoned cemetery. She had been there awhile." He moved off the porch to his car, spun and walked backward, watching me. "I'll be in touch."

I nodded and crossed my arms. "Be safe," I said. He flipped me a wave and climbed into the ugly gray Crown Vic, then started the car and pulled down the long drive and out of sight. I saw the reflection of blue lights against the trees and he was gone. Moments later, I heard his siren begin to wail. In the distance, thunder rumbled. At last I became aware of rain clouds overhead. I hoped that the storm front didn't extend all the way to Charleston, threatening the crime scene discovered there.

The next morning I was called into the Dawkins County Hospital for a rape workup. The ob-gyn who often handled them for the local police was in surgery, and Dawkins was part of my territory.

I was exhausted, but I dressed and stuck the yellow emergency light on the SUV's dash. I made it to the hospital in twenty minutes.

The workup was routine. Though I always had to strive hard for an unemotional approach in rape cases, all I usually wanted to do was hug the victim, tell them that things would be okay, that they could recover both emotionally and physically. But I couldn't. That was the job of the rape-crisis volunteer, not the forensic nurse. I was there just to collect physical evidence. That was all.

When the samples had all been taken and the cops were questioning the woman, I stopped in the E.R. lounge and visited with old friends. It was shift change, and four nurses, my cousin Wallace and Dr. Rhea-Rhea were all waiting on coffee. "Ashlee!" she shouted. Rhea Lynch, affectionately known as Dr. Rhea-Rhea, was my favorite doctor of all time, and was one of the doctors I'd lured to CHC for part-time hours, two days a month. We worked opposite shifts, though, and I seldom saw her. She grabbed me and swung me around in an unaccustomed display of exuberance, then shoved a box of doughnuts at me. "Eat. I picked 'em up fresh this morning."

I took one and sat, taking a bite. I was never going to get the weight off my thighs like this. "When you marrying that good-looking cop?" I asked Rhea-Rhea, needling. The doc dated a local cop, but rumor suggested she was loath to set a wedding date.

She crossed her arms and looked down at me from

her five-nine height. "If *you're* ready to settle down, we can make it a double ceremony."

Three of the nurses made "Oooohhhhh," sounds.

Gleefully, Wallace said, "Catfight."

"No fight," Rhea said, holding her hands up in the universal peace-and-surrender sign. "I did good introducing you to a younger man. Admit it. You think he's hot. All your friends at CHC are talking about him stopping by the ED to visit all the time, bringing roses…"

"Ooooh, Ash's got a maaan in her life," one of the RNs said.

"You'll have to walk down the aisle by yourself, Rhea," Wallace said. "I'm sure Nana and Mama Moses have already set a date for her wedding. Ash needs a younger man to keep up with her."

The nurses all chortled. I blushed ten shades of red and glared at Wallace, who just laughed evilly. Still getting me back for the bathing-suit incident when we were kids, I guessed. I stuffed the rest of the doughnut into my mouth and stood. Pointing at my lips to show I couldn't talk, I walked backward from the lounge to the ambulance-pad doors.

Rhea stuck her head from the room and called, "Chicken!"

I nodded and held up my hand, gesturing the okay sign, showing that I was indeed a coward, and left the building. Sometimes I hated living in a small town.

24

After a Sunday off, when I missed church and spent the time catching up on sleep, I was back at work, finishing up a shift with Lynnie Bee. We were sharing cups of caffeine—she had coffee; I had hot tea—in the office. Lynnie sniggered into her cup. "I can't believe they said that."

"They did." I raised my pitch into Jas's higher range, imitating our conversation. "'But Mama, they weren't *boy* boys, they were geek boys—and not cool geeks who might become rich computer geniuses someday. They were *gamer* boys.'"

Lynnie laughed. "Sounds like some of the guys I used to date."

"I know. Me, too." I lifted my teacup to Lynnie and we touched rims. "In Jas and Paz's way of thinking, they weren't breaking the major number-one rule about having boys stay over at night because they were geeks, not boys. I reminded them the geek boys had penises. I thought they were going to die, right there in the rec room."

"Well, Mamash shouldn't use such foul language."

"We both know they've said worse. Anyway, they seemed to get the point."

"Oh, honey, this is too rich. Thanks for sharing." Lynnie checked her watch and drained her cup, rinsing it at the small sink and putting it away in the cupboard wet. Her body tightened just a bit as she said over her shoulder, "I'm sorry about the girl they found. She was a member of your family?"

The laughter drained away and I closed my eyes for a moment, thinking about the TV pictures of the newest graveyard crime scene, the camera's glimpse of the decayed body. "Yeah," I said. "She was. My Aunt Mosetta's great-granddaughter. Her father didn't even know she was missing. Not like that." I finished my tea and passed her my cup, which she rinsed as well, her back still to me. "He thought her mother had come back and taken off with her. Over twenty months ago. She was so much older than the other girls that no one put it together with the Ballerina Doll murders."

Lynnie turned from the sink, her face pained. "They think one man did everything, don't they? All the murders?"

I walked to the sink, the two of us in the tiny space, hemmed in by desk and cabinet and chairs. I slipped an arm around Lynnie's shoulders and she put hers around my waist. Side by side, we stood in the office, surrounded by clutter. "Yes," I said. "One guy working alone. Cassie was sixteen, but looked fourteen. Not an early bloomer, our Cassie." I remembered the girl, dusky-skinned and green-eyed, unlike the blond, blue-eyed girls the murderer usually took. Jim had said it was most likely a "trial run" to see how it went and refine his technique. It was sordid, horrific, and I grieved for the young girl.

"This is awful," she said softly, sounding as upset as I felt.

I nodded, my head against hers. "Thanks for being my friend," I said.

Lynnie laughed, a breathy sound, and squeezed me in a hug. "I got to work. See you tomorrow," she said, grabbing a chart. I followed her with my eyes out the door and to the pharmacy, the small nook in the Majors where meds were kept.

I shook my head. Time for the pill and med count, documenting every single drug prescribed in the last shift. More paperwork. With Lynnie gone, I finished up and gathered my bag, fishing out the keys. I waved to the night crew as I passed through the door, and Christopher waved back. He and Farley had the schedule out on the counter, their heads close together. They seemed to be negotiating days off. MacRoper was standing nearby and seemed surprised to see me still around. He looked at the clock and frowned.

I took the elevator and stopped in at Elroy's room, telling him that Jas and Paz would be back in a day or so. He had taken a shower and shaved and was looking better. He would be going home soon, he informed me. "I'll pass it along to the girls," I said, and headed out, trying not to think about the way his eyes had lit up at the thought of their visit and hoping that my girls wouldn't hurt him.

It wasn't dark in the parking lot. Rather, the soft, gloomy dusk of spring, shadows pooled in odd places, cast in peculiar patterns by the security lights. It was a comforting sight, the evening air warm on my skin.

The older SUV didn't have an automatic unlocking system and getting the key in the lock was never easy in less than perfect lighting. I bent over the door. I needed reading glasses. Could I date a younger man if I needed reading glasses?

The breath thudded out of me. I slammed into the asphalt. Skidding. My knees and palms ground into the pavement and pain shot up my limbs, white hot. My bag hit my hip and whipped past me.

I've been hit. I'm on the ground. The thoughts lightning fast. I tried to shift upright.

The second blow took me on the shoulder. My face hit the tarmac. Dusk became night-dark. Something draped me, smothering, covered my head and shoulders. I sucked in a single breath, hot and panicked. Adrenaline blasted through me.

Hands wrenched my shoulders back. The cloth tightened around my head and upper arms. I struggled, hitting out. Hard. I felt an impact, heard a grunt. But I was on the ground, at a disadvantage. I kicked, screamed. I fisted my hands, lower arms still free, and swung them. Beating into the attacker.

"Damn it, Mnem, stop fighting."

Screaming, I redoubled my efforts. He cursed. Abruptly, he whipped the cloth off me and he was gone, footsteps receding. I whisked back my hair and blew it from my mouth, sucking in a breath.

A second man was running toward me, a silhouette

between cars. He had drawn a gun. "Stop!" he shouted, extending the weapon in both hands, pointing it at the running man.

His steps faltered when he saw me in the dark between cars. The security light behind him shadowed his face into a dark mask in the rapidly falling night. His form towered over me. Instinctively, I cowered back, fear bubbling up fast. He cursed before holstering his gun and bending over, hands on his knees, breath huffing.

His face resolved into human. I recognized a security guard.

The bubble of fear popped. He was maybe mid-sixties, out of shape. He looked up once more, as if tracking the running man, and then at me. "You okay?"

"Yes, thanks to you." I looked down at myself. "He tore my new uniform," I said, and I burst into tears.

The security officer laughed, the sound shaky. Abruptly, I was laughing with him through my tears.

"Yeah. It's like that sometimes," he said, of my whiplash emotions, "laughter and tears." He pulled out his radio and said into it, "He got away, but she's hurt. Send EMS."

"No. I'm fine." I wiped my nose, bloodying my face in the process.

"I'm convinced," he said dryly, the tone of the career cop beneath the words. "You got hurt on hospital grounds, so you have to be seen in the ED. Company policy. And I have to fill out a ton of paperwork."

"Can't I just walk back in?" I asked.

"Nope. But you can sit in your car until they get here." He extended both hands and I held up my bleeding palms. He gripped my wrists and levered me to my feet, found my keys, which had been knocked away into the shadows, and opened my SUV door. One handed, he helped me into the seat.

"Did he get anything?" he asked.

My bag was still looped over my arm, and I shook my head. "He didn't take my stuff."

The guard nodded, thoughtfully. "I thought I saw something over your head."

"A blanket or something. He—" I stopped as fear flared through me, belated. I forced a breath into my lungs and it exhaled as laughter, the sound edging toward hysteria. The security guard reached in and patted my shoulder. His touch was calming, and I took another breath, forcing down the panic. Softer, I said, "He wanted *me*. He was trying to take me."

Red emergency lights flashed at the entrance to the lot. After that, it was a lot of medical mumbo jumbo, putting me on the stretcher, which I argued against, taking my blood pressure, which was up a bit, pulse ditto, respirations ditto again. Frustrated, I pushed them away with my bloody hands saying, "I just got beat up. What the hell do you expect?"

Lynnie Bee's shocked laughter floated across the lot and I spotted her at the back of the crowd, pushing her way through. I realized I had just cussed a paramedic, which let me know, better than the tests, just how upset I was. I looked up into the paramedic's face, realized I knew him in passing from dropping off patients, and said, "Sorry, Chayo," sounding as overwhelmed as I felt. Tears pooled as my hands started shaking. *Stress reactions,* the professional part of my mind informed me.

"No problem," the Latino man said, amused. Opening a bottle of sterile water, he brandished a pair of scissors. "Let's get your pants legs out of the way and flush your hands and knees, okay?"

Lynnie pushed in, her face strained, took the scissors and cut through the thin cloth exposing my knees. I cried harder, knowing I looked like a ten-year-old who had taken a fall from a bike.

They carted me in the ambulance to the ED, bypassing the Minors, which was where I should have gone, and wheeled me directly into the Majors, where I could be properly fussed over. There are benefits to working in a hospital, and preferential treatment is one of them. I got the premier cubicle, the head of my stretcher up at a forty-five-degree angle so I could see and be seen by the crowd of co-workers who streamed by, their images wavering in my tears, which were falling now, unchecked. I knew from their expressions that I must look pretty beat up. I wiped my nose on the back of one wrist and accepted the tissue Lynnie handed me. Even Dr. Death walked by, looking me over. Of course, he was probably gloating at my being beaten up in the parking lot.

My wounds were being cleaned when the cops showed up, two in uniform and one in plainclothes. Lynnie shooed them out as she washed my cheek and applied antibacterial salve. "It's only a tiny bit of road rash," she assured me, tears bright in her own eyes. "Please stop crying. It'll heal with no scarring. I promise." She hugged me, my face tight against her shoulder.

"I don't care about my face," I whispered to her.

"Not really. It's only a scratch. I might have been dead." Lynnie shuddered with me, rocking me like a child before wiping her own face and returning to the job of cleaning my wounds.

In short order, the FBI entered—Bow-tie Emma and Julie Schwartz. Standing in the corner of my cubicle, they took a statement from the security guard, whose name was Hickson, and who, it seemed, had called them. I listened in as I was bandaged with burn pads and cling wrap—not the kind used in kitchens but the sticky gauze wrap used for bandages. Someone thought I deserved the pretty stuff, so one hand was wrapped in purple, the other in fuchsia. My knees were done up pale pink and lavender, to match.

Hickson said, "That other agent, Ramsey, said to keep an eye on her, coming and going. We were watching on the camera monitors and saw it right away, when she was attacked. I took off to help and my backup called Ramsey. I guess he called you?"

Jim had asked hospital security to watch over *me? Or to watch me? There was a mighty big difference.*

"Yes, he did," Emma said, sounding just as ticked off as she looked. She glared at the local cops and said, "We'll handle it."

The plainclothes guy shrugged and said, "Less paperwork for us." They left without a backward glance. I would rather have been under the focus of the locals than have the attention of Emma.

Hickson gave the bow-tied feeb a detailed but succinct version of the events while Julie watched me, taking in every scrape, cut, tear and road rash. When the medical part of the entertainment was over and I was bandaged up like the Michelin man, Julie moved in closer and opened an evidence kit. She put on gloves and began picking bits and pieces of things off me. I had never been conscious while a forensic investigation was done on me and was surprised how awful it made the recipient beneath the examination feel—unimportant, and somehow more of a victim.

Julie bent close to me, her body still. She raised her voice. "Supervisory Special Agent Simmons, would you take a look at this?"

With ill grace, Emma left Hickson, came close and bent over me, inspecting my shoulder. Her face tightened a fraction and I watched as she moved around the stretcher to my other side, studying my scrub shirt, my hair and my face. "We'll need her clothes."

Residual fear blasted into anger and my tears stopped. "For what, Emma?" I demanded. "Being mauled isn't enough, you have to steal my clothes, too?" Okay, I had gone from feeling pitiful to snarky.

Emma gave me a real, honest-to-goodness grin with no attitude in it at all. I flinched, I was so surprised. "The cloth your attacker used to cover you left a number of short black fibers on your shirt," she said with satisfaction.

Instantly, I understood what she was thinking. This may not have been a random attack, a man on the lookout for any available female to kidnap, rape, torture and kill. Oh no. Nothing so horrifically mundane. The kidnapper of the little girls may have been after me. Me, specifically. A Chadwick. One who had been on TV and whose house had been violated. "Oh," I said, a world of meaning in the word. "But I'm an adult…."

Lynnie grabbed my wrist, dark eyes wide. I thought she might pass out, she looked so pale. To give her something to do other than think of me, her friend, as a victim of assault, I said, "I have a clean set of scrubs in my locker." I was satisfied when my words came out sounding almost normal. "Would you get them, please?"

The breath rushed out of her. "I'll get them. Be right back."

"Sorry," I said to Emma before I thought. I was saying it a lot lately, and this time, I wasn't sure what I was apologizing for anyway.

"No problem. Too bad we weren't really expecting an attack on you. We could have used you for bait and *had* the son of a bitch." With that pithy comment, she left the room, followed by Julie.

Special Agent Schwartz flashed me a smile on the way out of the room. "I'll be back to get the clothes," she said.

"Whoopee," I said to myself. But I was feeling calmer. More steady. More myself.

Moments later, she was back, excited and agitated. "You know a Denise Abercrombie?" she asked.

"Distantly."

"We just found out she's a Chadwick," Julie said, jubilant. "Someone broke in to her house yesterday and tried to kidnap her. She fought him off. He got away."

I held Julie's gaze. "Why is he taking adults now?"

"*That* is the million-dollar question."

Jim raced around the corner of my cubicle, long legs flying, and nearly skidded into Julie. My heart jumped in my chest, then plummeted. How did he get here so fast? How did any of them?

"Hold up there, cowboy," Julie said. "The little lady's doing fine." She laughed as if that were an inside joke.

Jim chuckled dutifully but the sound was strained, and his eyes swept me as his hands took my bandaged ones. He curled my fingertips out, inspecting the wrappings. He was breathing hard, a sheen of sweat beading his forehead. He leaned in and brushed something hard and sharp from my cheek. "Ash?" he asked. "You okay?"

"Don't touch her," Julie said belatedly. "I have to get her clothes for fiber analysis. I don't want to be getting results from another site."

Jim backed off and I managed a smile for him, uncertain, shaky. "You got security to watch me?" I asked, careful to keep any accusing tone out of my voice.

"I had a feeling," he said. He blew out a hard breath and bent over for a moment, his hands on his knees, his head down, in odd imitation of out-of-shape Hickson. He must have run hard and fast to get to me. He stayed bent over, breath strident. At last he stood, his face folded into some resemblance of the cop mask, tucking his hands in his pockets. "Nothing to go on. Just a hunch," he said.

"Too bad it wasn't official," Julie said, her tone acerbic. "Simmons would have used her for bait."

"Simmons can go fu—" He caught himself but not before Julie laughed and looked at me from the corner of her eye.

So he had been worried about my safety, not my guilt. The thought warmed me, taking a bit of the sting from my heart, if not my palms.

"Step outside the curtain and I'll get her clothes," Julie said. "Then you two can go kissy kissy, okay?"

"Yeah. Sure," Jim said, and he pulled the curtain around the bed, though I could see his shoes on the other side, lace-up leather in need of polishing. He was easing his weight back and forth from foot to foot, antsy. He was worried about me. Which, I decided, I really liked. It brought me down another notch from the adrenaline rush of the attack, though tears still threatened with every other breath.

Julie spread a blue plastic cloth on the floor and motioned me to step on it. I slid my legs off the bed and stepped on the blue evidence cloth. Julie bent and unlaced my shoes.

"My shoes, too? They're brand new," I complained.

"Yeah." She met my eyes from the floor, patiently waiting. "Tough break."

"I'll never get them back, will I?"

"Probably not," she said, sounding totally indifferent. She could have at least faked concern. It would have made me feel better. And they were comfortable shoes, too. Now I'd have to make time to go shopping. I sighed, resigned, and eased my feet out one at a time. Julie placed the shoes in an evidence bag.

Next came the socks, then the torn and cut scrub pants. Julie rolled them down and placed each in a bag, which she labeled. She pulled my scrub top off over my head and put it in a bag, holding me bent over until she had a free hand to shake out my hair before gathering up the blue cloth and folding it carefully, putting it in its own bag. She plucked several hairs from my scalp, put them in their own tiny evidence bag, and all the bags went into a large bag, which she labeled as well. "Done," Julie said. "Thanks."

From the other side of the curtain, Lynnie said, "I got your clothes. Ready?"

"Yes," I said. "Hope you brought socks and shoes."

"Got it all," she said, easing through the split. She set pants, top, shoes—old and scuffed—and socks on the stretcher, all except for the pink socks and white shoes. Easter colors. I'd forgotten I had put old pink scrubs in the locker. I took the socks and tried to pull them on my feet, the bandages making me clumsy. Fingers still quivering, Lynnie brushed my hands aside and helped me put them on. Helped with the pants and the top too, and even tied my shoes for me.

By the time she was finished, I was crying again and this time I didn't know why. Whether it was receding shock, or the feeling of helplessness, or another emotion that came from a friend doing a personal chore with such loving care, I couldn't have said. I sniffed and said, "Thank you."

Lynnie hugged me hard, kissed my uninjured cheek and said, "You'd do the same for me. MacRoper wrote you out for a few days. Soon as the questions are done, go home."

"He didn't even see me," I said, sniffing once again and wiping my nose on my bandaged wrist.

"He didn't have to. He disappeared to the toilet without telling anyone where he would be. I covered for him, so when I put the scrip pad in his hands and told him what to write, he did. You up to being questioned by the cops and to helping security fill out paperwork? They have a ton of it out here."

I sighed again, taking in a breath that wasn't quite steady yet. "Sure. But my hands are really starting to hurt and I'm thirsty. Can I have a Diet Coke and some graham crackers and…" I tried to look pitiful, "a shot of Demerol?"

Lynnie looked at me with concern. "Are you hurting somewhere besides your knees and hands?"

"No. But I'm a patient. They get the free food and the good drugs. Right?"

Realizing I was joking, Lynnie finally relaxed and swatted my shoulder. "I'm so glad you're okay. I'll bring you the food and some Tylenol."

"Tylenol's good," I said, easing back on the stretcher. I sat up straight. "Jim?"

He poked his head through the curtain, face strained, full of fear beneath the cop face. "The guy, he called me Nem. He said, 'Damn it, Nem, stop fighting.' The 'm' in Mnemosyne is silent…. Could 'Nem' be a short form?"

Lynnie stepped back. "Mnemo— What? What's going on?"

Jim cursed, nodded and left, dialing his cell phone.

I held up a hand to Lynnie to delay her and called out, "Jim, wait." When he stuck his head back around the cubicle wall, I said, "If he wants me, he might want Jasmine, too. Call Nana. Get her some help? Please?"

He nodded and finished dialing, his face still the cop mask that was so unexpectedly comforting.

I met Lynnie's worried eyes and said, "It's a long story."

"You gonna tell me?"

I sighed again and rested my head back on the stretcher pillow. "Eventually. Over coffee and something sinfully sweet."

"Deal," Lynnie said. Looking back over her shoulder at me, her eyes dark with fear, she disappeared into another patient cubicle.

25

I couldn't drive, bandaged as I was, so Jim put me in the passenger seat of my vehicle and drove me home, Julie following in his Crown Vic. Though I was hurting, I felt amazingly good. I didn't know if it was the aftereffects of the attack or being with Jim. Okay, maybe I did know, but I wasn't ready to look at that yet. I rode the miles with my hand in his, knowing I was safe, my daughter was safe, and I could, at least for a moment, relax and close my eyes. The tires hummed on the interstate and soft music played on the radio. Some small, romantic part of me thought it was wonderful.

Partway there, the night pressing against the windows like a living thing, Jim said, "You awake?" I nodded sleepily. "He's decompensating. He's falling apart. Now he'll start making mistakes. Now we'll catch him." His tone held something, some chaotic, shadowed quality that brought me fully awake.

"Yeah," I mumbled. "But will you catch him before he kills that last little girl? The diabetic?" I felt Jim quiver once and grow quiet. I had a moment of understanding, one of those intuitive leaps that the mind can make in times of stress or worry or fear. I opened my eyes in the night and whispered, "You're going to kill him, aren't you? If you can. When you catch him, you're going to kill him."

Jim's entire body tightened and shook with a minute compression. "Go to sleep, Ash."

I laughed softly, the sound knowing and defeated all at once. "You've never had to pull the trigger, have you? Never had to…kill someone."

The SUV's lights picked up the flight of a large bug, surfing over the hood in the slipstream. Jim reached down and cut off the radio. "No," he said finally.

I lifted a hand to the steering wheel and touched his knuckles with the tips of my fingers. "It's not so easy to kill, Jim," I said, my voice a breath of sound. "To hold a gun on someone and look in his eyes and pull the trigger. It's not so easy."

"You had no choice," he murmured back, his voice barely audible above the drone of the tires.

A flurry of insects beat the air above the road with thousands of wings, an instant of chaos caught in the headlights. "I had no choice," I repeated, my tone reconciled to the past but not forgiving of it. "If I wanted to make sure Jasmine was safe, I had to stay alive. Which meant killing Alan. He threatened her." The breath caught in my throat. "Threatened her life. If not for her, I might have quit. I might have stopped struggling and just…died. But instead, I shot him." Tears crawled across my cheeks, burning through the salve, melting into the pink scrub top. "And I watched his eyes as the life sputtered and went out." My breath was painful as I saw Alan's eyes again, pupils widening, emptying, face going slack and inert. "It's still hard. So very…very hard."

The road beneath us had taken on a steady sound, the occasional car or eighteen-wheeler passing in the night, close and comforting. "That's the way I feel," he said. "That I'd kill for my daughter. Or for you."

I smiled and closed my eyes again, soothed by the drone of the engine and the feel of his hand in mine.

"Oh," he said, his tone sharp enough to rouse me slightly. "The prints in the vault room? Except for yours, from when you took the forensic course, none are on any record anywhere. Preadolescent finger-prints don't take well, and some of the smudges suggest it was a kid, like you thought."

I yawned. "Much ado about nothing, then." And I was asleep, feeling utterly safe even in my dreams.

Jim woke me with soft words. "Pretty lady, wake up. We're home."

I smiled. *Pretty lady… Whose home? Ours?* But I didn't say it, knowing it was far too soon to think in terms of taking our relationship to a higher level. "I'm awake," I mumbled.

Amused, he said, "Your eyes are still closed. Want me to carry you inside?"

"That would be very romantic," I murmured.

"Even with your nana and aunt Mosetta watching?"

"No!" I sat up fast, blinking, scanning. Aunt Mosetta and Nana were standing outside the SUV, watching me. Jas was pressed against the passenger window, fear etched in her face, her posture. "I'm awake, I'm awake. Ohhh," I groaned as the pain hit me, throbbing up from my hands into my spine. "I'm awake, but I'm not happy about it." I rubbed my eyes with my bandages, avoiding my damaged face, the cling wrap abrading my skin.

"Okay," I said. "I'm ready." I reached for the door and Jim leaned past me, lifting the handle. The door opened and I slid out against Jas's taut body.

She wrapped me in her arms, holding me too tightly, her face against my head, her body racked in sobs. I patted her, hugging her just as hard. "It's okay," I murmured. "It's okay. I'm fine. Well, a little beat up, but, really, I'm fine."

"Nana came over and sat on the porch and I knew something was wrong and you were in trouble but she wouldn't tell me why, and I was so scared." Her arms constricted around me and she rocked our bodies, shifting from side to side.

I peered over her shoulder at Jim, who had come around the SUV, and at Nana, who stood, feet braced, dour in the bright security light. The scene was surreal, all shadows and light, the smell of horses and dog. Big Dog thrust his muzzle into my hip.

Jas's fingers clenched in my shirt. "What happened? Are you okay? I love you, Mama."

"I love you, too, Jazzy," I said, using the name I hadn't used in years. I eased her back and she touched my injured cheek.

"Nana wouldn't tell me—" She stopped, wrenching a breath so hard it scudded in her throat. Jas gripped my upper arms and set me away from her. Her face suffused with anger. She pivoted away from me to face Nana and pointed a finger at the stern old woman. "You!"

Nana raised her brows.

"You let me worry." Jas advanced on Nana, her stance menacing. "You let me *worry.* You let me *cry.* And you knew she was okay. You knew she was *on the way home* and *you didn't tell me she was okay!*" Jas screeched, her arms out as if to do battle.

Nana studied her great-granddaughter, her expression dispassionate. She tucked her hands in her jeans pockets, watching.

"How—" Jas's voice stopped as if her throat closed up. "How *dare* you!" Hands fisted, her voice strengthened. "You had no right to make me worry!"

"Jas!" I said, not certain what was going on. Nana flicked her eyes at me and away. They said, quite clearly, *Let me handle this.* I stopped, remembering another time, another place, when Nana had looked at me as she was looking at my daughter.

"You wanted to be told?" Nana asked. "You want to be treated like an adult? Like a grown-up Chadwick?" Her chin lifted in challenge.

"Yes," Jas said. "Yes! I'm tired of being treated like a child! Like I'm too stupid to make decisions, to be trusted with the truth, like I'm too young to *think.*"

Nana grinned, a strange type of victory on her face, an expression I remembered. "Fine. Next time, I'll tell you everything. 'Bout time you grew up. Now you can take a bigger responsibility for things around here. This farm don't run itself." Nana looked past my daughter, whose body was still poised for combat. "I'll see you in the morning, Ashlee. We got things to talk about." She looked at Jas. "You can be part of that. If you're awake."

"I'll be awake," Jas said, her voice vibrating with emotion.

"We'll see. Night, Ash, Topaz. You, too, Jim. Julie." Her heel ground on the rock driveway as she turned, joined by Aunt Mosetta. The two women moved into the night toward their house, its lights just barely visible through the woods.

Silence settled on the yard. I scratched Big Dog's head and he sniffed at my bandages, trying to decide if the smell of my blood was reason enough for him to go into attack mode. "It's okay, boy," I murmured. His tail wagged, but he looked around, inspecting the small party just in case. In the distance, an owl hooted. From a different direction, another owl answered, the calls of the mated pair lonely in the dark.

Jas shifted and faced me in the night, her expression defiant, her body still poised for combat. "I will *not* apologize to that old woman," she said.

"You will not refer to your great-grandmother as 'that old woman,'" I said back. Jim moved in beside me, as if he thought I needed support. I appreciated it, but I stood on my own two feet, steady and strong, as my daughter grew up before my eyes.

"Fine," she said. "I will not apologize to *Nana* for speaking my mind."

I rested against Jim, letting him put his arm around my waist. "I was about your age when Nana put me in a position to stand up to her." I smiled slightly. "It's her way of gauging if you're grown up enough to be considered a Chadwick adult."

Jas tilted her head, the movement stiff in the harsh security light. "You mean it was a…a *test?*" she spat.

"Your whole life is a test to Nana."

"Well… That just sucks."

I chuckled and yawned. The abrasion on my face pulled with the muscles, but I ignored the discomfort. "Yes, it does. Get used to it. She's been training us all up for the role of Chadwick Elder for years. You ready to play in Nana's sandbox or you want to gripe about it?"

Jas thought about my words. Finally her shoulders eased and her feet shifted. "I guess I can see her point."

"Good. I'm hungry. You got dinner ready?"

Jas crossed her arms. "How'd you know Nana made me put chicken breasts on the grill?"

"I can smell them. And 'cause she would know I hadn't eaten and I'd be hungry. Are you going to feed me?"

"Yeah. You and Julie and Jim and Paz and me. Six breasts. That old woman is either psychic or crazy."

"Like a fox," I said, and my knees gave way.

Jim half carried me, half dragged me to the porch and sat me on the swing. His hand lingered on my shoulder and he whispered in my ear just before he stepped away, "How long before she realizes her nana just gave her an unpaid summer job?"

"I give her an hour. Tops."

Jim chuckled softly, his features indistinguishable in the night. "You want to meet Sarah, my daughter?"

I said, "I'd be honored to meet her. Bring Sarah over anytime. Nana and Aunt Mosetta and I will make her feel right at home."

Laughing, he said, "Part of me thinks that would be great for her. The other part of me is scared to death at the thought."

* * *

The special agents seemed to appreciate the downtime; they hadn't had much of that since the day my dogs had brought me a red sneaker with a child's toe inside. Over grilled chicken breasts, steamed asparagus and salad, they chatted with the girls about school and the farm and future plans. I was mostly silent, carefully handling my fork with just my fingertips and hoping I didn't dump my whole plate in my lap. Jim only looked at his watch once, and Julie told him in no uncertain terms that even Simmons expected them to eat. But I was worn to a frazzle and ready to be alone. It was nearly midnight when we finished the meal, and only a bit before that when Jas realized the price she would pay for being recognized as a Chadwick adult. I didn't bother to hide my amusement when Paz laughed at Jas's spluttering.

Something of my fatigue must have shone in my face, because Jim and Julie left quickly after that, driving off in his unmarked car while Paz and Jas cleaned up the dirty dishes. I locked the doors, set the alarm, checked the location and readiness of the guns and talked Jasmine through sliding bread bags over my hands and taping them over my knees so I could shower. No way was I going to bed covered with nasty hospital germs and road dirt.

I stood, alone at last in the big shower stall, hot water streaming over me, and had a good long cry, full of self-pity and fear, emotions that I would never admit to anyone. Feeling better, I peeled off the bread bags, dressed in flannel pjs, took my painkillers—not Demerol, but still better than Tylenol—and went to bed.

* * *

The next day I awoke at nine to find Wallace at my bedroom door, Jas behind him and Nana behind her. He didn't look happy. The females looked like an amused conspiracy. Many people might be nonplussed at finding visitors standing in their bedrooms, but it wasn't the first time with Nana. She had respected my marriage to Jack, knocking on doors and calling before dropping by, but that had ended with Jack's untimely death. Now she barged in whenever she wanted.

"Morning," I said as I crawled from bed, glad that I didn't sleep au naturel.

"Yes. It is," Wallace replied. "Nana said I needed to change some bandages?" He had clearly worked all night, still dressed in the hospital scrubs he wore on duty, and sounded grumpy. "Where are you going?" he asked as I stumbled away.

"Potty, brush teeth, put on clothes and comb hair. Meet you in the kitchen." I closed the bathroom door on them. When I met them ten minutes later in the kitchen, I was more chipper, Wallace more dour. He wanted his bed and he wasn't too happy to be doing nursing chores, work he normally delegated to others in the E.R. of Dawkins County's small hospital. He didn't mind snarling at me to make his point. I wasn't sure how he managed to gripe while surrounded by breakfast smells but he did, pointing to a chair and saying, "Sit."

Jasmine and Topaz, who had stayed over again, cooked bacon and eggs and baked biscuits while he worked. Nana just drank coffee and watched us. Wallace opened his black bag and set supplies on the table, donned gloves and peeled off the dressings on my hands. Some of his animosity slid away at the sight of the damage. My left hand was the worst, gouges deep and swollen. "This has to hurt," he murmured, pressing gently on the deepest laceration. "I'm surprised they didn't put a couple of stitches in it."

I didn't reply. My cousin cleaned my wounds and redressed my hands, this time in bright yellow cling wrap. When he was done, I said, "Not bad. Almost as competent as a first-year nursing student."

Wallace laughed softly through his nose, a sound that came out much like a snort, and turned my hands over, studying them as if he had wrapped a secret up in the bandages. He met my eyes, his greenish ones fierce. Softly, so the girls couldn't hear him, he said, "They catch the bastard who hurt you, he better not need treatment in my E.R."

I colored. "Thank you," I said. Nana just grunted.

Wallace removed the dressings on my knees and left them off, saying, "These are fine. You hit harder and skidded farther on your palms than on your knees. Let them air." He smeared some antibacterial ointment on my cheek and put the tube in my pocket. "Keep this moist and clean."

"Yes, Doctor," I said primly, sounding like a nurse on a soap opera. "Right away, Doctor."

"Yeah. Keep it up. I'm for bed." He kissed me on my forehead, patted Nana's shoulder and hugged Topaz to him, pulling his daughter out the door with him while she squealed and pretended to fight him. Suddenly there were only three of us for breakfast.

We ate in silence, serving ourselves from a pile of

food meant for five. I remembered that Nana had said she wanted to talk to me today. When she was finished eating, she leaned back in the chair, the wood creaking, her eyes thoughtful and worried. "What is it, Nana?" I asked.

"They found Erasmus," she said. "We got a problem."

"What?"

"About two this morning, a sharp-eyed highway patrol officer saw tire marks off the shoulder of the road, through some brush along an old fence near Campbell's Truck Stop. They found his car in a creek. He was dead."

"Oh no," Jas said, softly. "I liked him."

Nana stared at my daughter and said, "He had a trunk full of porn. Child porn. Magazines, photos, movies. Stuff he had collected. Probably for decades."

"Erasmus?" I couldn't keep the shock out of my voice. My skin raised in slow prickles. I remembered the way he had looked over at his laptop when the federal agents had been in his house. He'd claimed to be working on a book about the Chadwicks. But…

Erasmus was a child-porn collector.

"Was he leaving town?" I asked. "Running? Was the little girl with him?"

"He was alone. No suitcase in the car. C.C. seems to think he was taking his collection to a safe storage place. Now we have to figure out if he had the little girl, and where he hid her. The cops are all over his house, looking into his background." Nana looked down at her grease-smeared plate. "Seems there were complaints when he was younger. About him touching little girls. That's why he moved around so often, from school to school. Maybe he tried to stop. Maybe that's why he ended up in a college setting, where the girls were too old to interest him. Maybe that's why his wife died young. Too hard to be married to a *pedophile*."

Clearly Nana had been thinking about this a lot.

"They didn't put him in jail?" Jas asked, horrified.

"Back then, people thought it would ruin the lives of the victims to have it known they had been abused," I said. Jas looked at me as if I were crazy, so I explained. "Until recently, educators, priests—important people in the community—were quietly fired, with no blemish on their records. They'd get a job in another school district or church and go on abusing. Things are getting better, but until a few years ago, that was the way things were done, Jas. No police involvement, no legal brouhaha."

"They're looking into his job history." Nana stopped, cutting off the words as if they pained her, and closed her eyes for a moment. "He was one of ours. And he was evil." She made a slashing movement with one hand, stood and walked to the window, staring out at the spring morning. I knew she wasn't seeing the bright sun or the horses and barn out back. "I protected this family," she said to the window, her voice fierce and as hard as old stone. "I told the cops there was no way one of mine was kidnapping and killing children. Seems I was wrong."

She turned to us, bracing herself on the counter. "We need to help the cops figure out where he kept the girls. So far they haven't found anything." She focused on Jas, and I saw my daughter sit up straighter in her chair. "Can you go to the records office at the county courthouse and look up properties in Erasmus's parents' names and his wife's family names? Find out what they owned in the past and whose names the properties are in now? All the cops have are the rental houses. They were clean, ready to be rented to tenants. I know it's a school day—"

"I'll do it," Jas said.

Nana looked at me with penetrating, sad eyes and I fought sitting straighter. It was a losing battle. "And will you go help the cops? See what you can learn, what information they need to help them in the search? Let me know what they need and I'll get it for them."

"Yes, ma'am," I said. Nana nodded once, a sharp jut of chin, and walked to the door and out into the day.

Fortunately, Wallace had bound my hands with less cling wrap than Lynnie and my friends in the ED had, and there was enough movement in my fingers to let me drive. Fortified with the grease and protein of a good country breakfast, a strong cup of tea in the cup holder beside me and extra-strength Tylenol to hold back the discomfort, I eased down the driveway toward Columbia. I had reached the entrance to Chadwick Farms and was turning onto Mount Zion Church Road, heading for Trash Pile Curve, when I noticed the truck behind me. It was speeding, going too fast to take the turn.

I glanced right and left quickly. The road was empty. I wrenched the wheel and pulled hard onto the soft shoulder. I looked into the rearview and had a moment of shock. The truck behind me seemed to speed up.

I braced myself. The sun glinted off the oncoming truck's windshield. Its engine roared. And it rammed me.

I was thrown forward and back, hit the seat belt with my chest, the steering wheel with my forearms, and bounced off.

Metal screeched; tires squealed. The SUV spun toward the road and around. Sunlight on glass and metal blinded me. When the vehicle stopped, I had one clear thought. *This is not an accident.*

My old SUV was still rocking. I spotted movement outside, a form racing toward me. Male. I unlatched the seat belt and slid to the right, opened the glove box. Grabbed the 9 mm's box. Hands shaking, needing better access and fewer bandages in the way, I shredded the worn cardboard and grabbed the pearl-handled gun.

The driver door was locked and I heard the handle jangle. The tap-crack-rattle of breaking safety glass. The door was ripped open. I turned, seeing something black, spreading out like wings, coming at me. I fired.

The cloth spiraled toward me. It hit my hands, covering the gun. Slapped against my face. I fired again. And again.

26

A weight landed on me, trapping my hands between us. Trapping me under the black cloth. Over the concussive deafness, I heart grunts and sobbing. "You shot me. You shot me."

Time seemed to slow with the words, each bright and sharp like shattered crystal. I knew the voice. I was sure I knew the voice.

Through the covering of the black cloth, I struggled to get the gun up. "Get away from me," I panted, nausea rising in my throat. "Get off me."

He rolled toward the steering wheel and away. Collapsing down and back, toward the ground. His body pulled the cloth with him. It slid from me, measured and surreal. Like stop-action photography. It skimmed along my body, pulling my hair in a static charge as light found me. Exposing my shirt, my bandaged hands holding the gun, my slacks.

His body slithered to the ground, taking one of my shoes, twisting my leg. I raised up, pulling my legs into the cab to uncertain safety, free. My attacker was propped on the street, sprawled half-under my SUV, a black velour throw draped over and beside him.

He was wearing a mask. A ski mask in spring.

Heart thudding, hands quaking, I aimed the gun at him. He looked at me through the holes in the mask. "You shot me." He touched his chest, and his hand came away bloody. "Why did you shoot me, Nem?"

My hands were shaking so hard I couldn't keep the gun aimed at him. I set it on my lap and scooted back, curling hard against the passenger door. I could hear my panting breath as my hearing came back. Help. I needed help.

My bag was on the floor and I reached for it.

Groaning, he rolled to the side and vomited. There was blood in the vomit. Blood on the road. I couldn't see the cell phone in the bag and grabbed its bottom, emptying the purse's contents onto the floor in a disordered pile.

The man made it to his knees. I spotted the phone.

He made it to his feet. I opened the phone and stared at the buttons, my mind frozen.

He stumbled against the SUV and caught himself on the open driver's door. I remembered the numbers. Punched in 911. Hit Send.

The man reached for me. For the gun. I dropped the phone, sending it bouncing, and scrabbled for the 9 mm. We fought for it, his hands slippery with blood, mine wrapped in cling and burn pads. He grabbed the gun by the barrel. My hands landed on the butt, finger on the trigger.

For a moment, everything went still. His eyes met mine, wide and shocked. Blood on the mouth of his mask. His breath was rank with vomit.

"Don't make me do this," I whispered.

From the phone on the floor, I heard a voice say, "Nine-one-one."

He jerked the gun, pulling it. I lurched forward with him.

Terrified, I fired. The report was almost silent.

He blinked and looked down, between us. The barrel was buried in his belly. His hands fell away. He pushed back across the seat and out the door. Into the sunlight. Bonelessly, he slid to the ground.

I looked at my hands, holding the small gun. The cheerful yellow cling wrap was splattered with blood.

From the floorboard, I heard the voice of the 911 operator and I said, "Help. Help me." I sobbed hard, the sound as jagged as broken bones, my eyes as dry as a skull-littered desert. "I just killed a man."

Holding the phone, keeping the line open per the order of the dispatcher, I sat in the corner of the passenger seat, shaking with cold and the aftershock of violence, the gun beside me on the driver's seat. Hours went by. I was sure it had to be hours, though no one passed me on the street. My hearing cleared. I heard birdcalls. Heard the sound of the running engine in the truck nearby, the truck I had been rammed with. Saw two hawks soaring overhead, their flight a lazy grace, a languid dance of freedom. And finally I heard the sound of sirens. Several of them.

Two marked cars reached me first, both of them sheriff deputy cars, black and silver, lights flashing. The deputies pulled close, putting their cars between mine and themselves, tires squealing to stops at almost the same time. The deputies opened their doors and pointed guns at me across the hoods of their cars. I raised my bandaged hands.

"Get out of the car and lie on the ground," one of them shouted, "hands over your head." I lowered my right hand and tried to open the passenger door. It was locked. The door being locked broke something inside me and started the tears that hadn't come. I pressed the lock button and lifted the handle. The door opened. More sirens were coming. Tears poured harder and I sobbed, my breath abrading my throat like rope burns.

"Come around to the front of the vehicle," the other cop shouted. "Keep your hands where we can see them."

I nodded and raised my hands higher. Easing from the SUV to the ground, my one shoe and bare foot sank into the soft earth. I walked around the cab and stood, knowing I couldn't kneel. Not on my injured knees. I should have made Wallace leave them bandaged. That made me laugh, a hysterical sound mixed with the sobs.

"Down! Down on the ground!"

"I can't," I said. "I'm hurt."

One of the deputies said, "Ash? Ashlee Davenport?"

"Yes." I sobbed harder when the deputy said something to the other and put away his weapon. He stepped from the protection of his unit and walked toward me, my tears hiding his identity until he was up close. It was Randy. Randy Bollington. We'd gone to high school together.

He put an arm around me and led me to his patrol car, my gait uneven, the pavement burning my stocking-clad sole. He sat me in the back seat, my legs dangling to the pavement. Three other cars pulled up close. And when one of them was an ugly gray Crown Victoria, I stood up and collapsed, right into Jim Ramsey's arms.

The questioning and paperwork took the rest of the day. The FBI was in charge, but Jim wasn't part of the team that brought me in. He was relegated to the sidelines, his face furious as Emma Simmons took over. Lucky me.

She confiscated my cling wrap, took my clothes, impounded my damaged SUV and infuriated my lawyer. I thought Macon would pull out a gun and shoot her when she suggested that I had lured the man to the street and shot him in cold blood. I laughed at that one, standing there in the FBI interrogation room in sweatpants, shirt and sock feet. "Yeah. I lured him in," I said. "And made him hit me with his car. And made him throw a black cloth over my head. A black velour cloth similar to the one you feebs are looking for in the kidnapper and killer of the little girls."

"You shot him at point-blank range," she said.

"He didn't give me a choice." The words were true. He *hadn't* given me a choice. And with that realization, that acceptance of a truth, some of the guilt eased away from me.

She was watching my face when the understanding and acceptance hit, and seemed to see the emotions settle under my skin. She sat and said, "Tell me what happened. Again."

I did, thoroughly, comprehensively and exhaustively, over the course of the afternoon. After that, they left me alone for several hours.

It wasn't until nearly dark that I found out who I had killed.

On my way to the bathroom, escorted by Julie Schwartz, we paused at a desk so Julie could sign some papers. There was a television in the corner, tuned to a local news update.

The announcer's voice caught my attention. "Prominent Columbia doctor, Paul Christopher, was shot today by one of his nurses in what some are calling a crime of passion." I turned to Julie and met her eyes. Julie was as still as marble, watching my face. "Ashlee Caldwell Davenport, who was working with the FBI on the Ballerina Doll murders, shot and killed Dr. Christopher on the street today in Dawkins County. Sources suggest that the divorced doctor and the widowed nurse had been secretly seeing one another for some time. More on this developing news later in our program."

I looked up at Julie. "Dr. Christopher?" *Dear God. Did I shoot an innocent man?* Her eyes gave nothing away and I searched her face as she watched me, evaluating.

"No," I said softly. "He was wearing a mask. He rammed my SUV. He came at me with a black cloth. He was going to…kidnap me." Uncertainty hit me and I whispered, "Wasn't he?"

"Let's get you to the restroom. Come on." She took my arm and it occurred to me that this had been planned, letting me find out this way, so she could watch me react to the news. While I had no doubt that

Bow-tie Emma put her up to it, it was Julie who carried the charade through. Julie, who I had liked, and had half hoped would end up with Macon. At the moment, I hated cops.

I walked beside her to the restroom, a special place just for prisoners, a room with no stall, just a toilet. I sighed.

"Sorry about the lack of walls," Julie said, not sounding as if she meant it at all.

"I had a baby when I was not quite twenty, with half my female relatives standing all around, cheering me on. I think I can pee in front of you."

Julie chuckled under her breath as I sat. "Lord, spare me from that."

Knowing I was exposed and vulnerable, and that looking harmless often made people more forthcoming with information and truth, I asked, "Do you really believe I killed Dr. Christopher in cold blood?"

She looked at the door, as if weighing her response. "No. But Simmons is running this show, despite everything the Chadwicks are throwing at her."

"Nana's calling in the big guns?"

Julie pursed her lips, speculation on her face, and decided to share. That made me marginally less antagonistic toward her. "We had a visitor from the governor's office and a phone call from Washington. Your nana knows some important people. Simmons had to tell them you were being held in protective custody, pending resolution of the accident and shooting. She's not very happy at the political interference in her job."

"Ladder climbers seldom are." I finished my business and rearranged my clothes, then lifted a roll of toilet paper off the dispenser and handed it to Julie. When she looked confused, I said, "Wrap my hands so the pads don't fall off. The Wicked Witch of the Feebs took my cling wrap. I'm hurting."

Julie took the roll and looked at my hands. Shrugging, she unrolled a length of paper and began to wrap my right hand, tucking the end under to hold it in place. When she was finished wrapping my left hand, she set the roll on top of the dispenser and studied me. "Thank you," I said, and I meant it.

"On another topic, SLED arrested your cousin's husband," Julie said. SLED meant State Law Enforcement. I looked my question at her and she added, "Nicolas Poulous. Curator of the biggest museum in the state?"

"For what?"

She gave me a small, tight smile and opened the bathroom door. "For a lot of things. Mostly for trafficking in antiquities. Seems he had a gambling problem and a few rich clients. He's been filching stuff for years and selling them off. Interesting family you have, Ashlee Davenport."

"A lot more interesting than I thought," I said, my tone sour.

Shaking her head, Julie led me back down the hall. When she opened the door of my room, I stopped in the doorway. With all the sarcasm I could muster, I said, "Home sweet interrogation cell." I looked at Julie. "Wait, I forgot, it's a protective custody cell now. Funny how one looks so much like the other."

Julie didn't respond to that at all. She pulled out my

chair for me and sat across the table, a folder open but angled away from me on her lap. I was bored and hurting. I wanted Tylenol. I wanted to go home. I wanted to *not* have killed a man. Another man.

I closed my eyes against the truth of it. I had killed two men in my life. I had to live with their souls on my conscience. Had to live with the memory of their dying faces.

I didn't know if I could do it; I didn't want to do it. I wanted to turn time back and stay home for the day, not leave on Nana's errands. Not get rammed. Not kill. But for now, I had to put away my grief and guilt and concentrate on getting free and home to my baby.

Macon joined us soon after the bathroom break, opening the door to the dour little cell, his face satisfied and slightly smug. I sighed with relief, knowing that meant he had found a way to get me out of here. Emma followed him in, looking considerably less cheerful, and took the chair next to Julie. I was sure I was the only one who caught the look Macon and Julie exchanged across the table. Things were going well in someone's life, it seemed.

Emma looked at me with unfeeling eyes, her mouth pursed. The expression was giving her smoker's lips, wrinkles in vertical lines. She needed a good facial peel. Funny how every time I saw her, I thought of spa treatments. Maybe because Emma Simmons, while the antithesis of my spa-going mama, seemed to look down on me the same way Josey did. As if I wasn't good enough. Somehow that brought out all the meanness in my soul. I'd have to pray about that one.

Maybe later.

"Sorry about the wait," she said. I bit my tongue against saying she didn't sound sorry at all. "Things have been moving quickly around here since you killed Dr. Christopher." I flinched. "We found where Christopher was keeping the girls," she said, and paused to watch me.

"Ohhhh," I breathed. I couldn't help it. I closed my eyes in thanksgiving, feeling all the animosity accumulated by several hours in a cell drain away. If they had found the girls, it was all worthwhile. All of it. Even death.

"We found two partially mummified adult female bodies, but not the missing girl." My eyes snapped open. Her eyes were hard and fierce.

"The women were stretched out on tables in his basement, lying on their backs, their heads positioned so they were facing the door. They were wearing togas and were tied in grief knots from their toes to their mouths. Pending forensic identification and postmortems, we're positing that it's his wife and her sister, both missing for two years.

"Next door to the room where we found them was another room decorated for a young girl. Pink. Dolls, toys and a one-way window so he could watch them without them seeing him." Emma watched me, watched the tears gather in my eyes, and kept talking.

"Someone had done some damage to the room recently, took the bed apart and used the metal frame to bust through the wall and the window. Jenny's mother says her daughter liked tools and building things, almost as much as taking them apart. We think it's possible that he held her there until she was close to breaking out.

"Right now, my forensic team is dismantling the house and the basement. We think, with trace evidence, we can prove that he held all the girls in that one room, one after another. And there's some evidence that he kept at least one of them in a closet for a while."

"Why are you telling my client this, Special Agent Simmons?" Macon asked, leaning forward, his hands between his knees, fingertips spread and touching. "It isn't customary for the Bureau to tell civilians anything. It's usually more like pulling teeth without painkillers."

Emma's mouth turned down as if she were sucking on a bitter pill. "Some *unnamed source* released this information to the media. We know it wasn't your client, but we think it might be a family member or friend on the local Dawkins County police force."

She looked at me. I hoped Nana hadn't started a vendetta against the agent, pulling out all the stops. Nana on a rampage was a force of nature, a forest fire, an avalanche of snow and ice, a volcano erupting. Hard to stop, impossible to control.

Voice sour, Emma said, "We want you to put a stop to the release of unauthorized information."

"My client has no authority over her extended family, Special Agent Simmons," Macon said.

"Ask my nana," I said. Emma's eyes flicked to me. "Call her on the phone and ask her, politely, to work with you. Not for you or against you, but with you."

Emma looked at Julie. "Do it."

"Not her," I said. "You. Big dog to big dog. If you'd asked for her help in the first place, she would have given it."

"It isn't the policy of the Federal Bureau of Investigation to ask for help in cases like this."

"Big mistake in small-town, rural America. Nana could open doors for you."

Emma put her hand to her bow-tied blouse, fingers fluttering the loops and strands. She cocked her head at me. "We can't find any family tie between Christopher and the Chadwicks. Would she help with that?"

"Yes."

Emma nodded, once.

In short order, I was freed and hustled out of the FBI building through an underground entrance. Macon drove me home in his sporty truck. I no longer had a vehicle to call my own and I wasn't certain that I wanted my old one back—even if it could be repaired—once the police released it from the impound lot.

Rain tapped slowly against the windshield, the wipers a soft shush of sound. The lights of oncoming cars on I-77 came at random intervals. Not much traffic tonight. Macon was of a mind to let me rest, which was nice. But I wished I were driving myself. I missed the autonomy, the feeling that I was in control of my life. This was twice that I had been driven home, twice that my freedom had been taken away from me.

We were nearly home when Macon said, almost offhand, "Nana talked with Simmons. She had amassed quite a bit of info that the feebs wanted, and

Nana gave it to her the minute Emma asked. Just like that. And Simmons thanked Nana for the help."

"Good," I said.

"Nana thinks that Christopher's wife could be one of the lost cousins. A Chadwick who disappeared after a divorce or death, and wasn't seen again. She's offered the full family genealogy to the FBI, including the parts not yet uploaded to the Web site." He glanced at me. "Even some stuff that she had withheld on general principle, though I'd never tell that to anyone but family. I can't decide if Nana is devious, just plain old mean or the salt of the earth."

I smiled. "Nana ticked off is like a runaway bulldozer. In a generous mood, she's like a genie in a bottle. Make a wish and watch it come true."

Macon laughed. "On my ninth birthday, she asked me what I wanted. I told her I wanted a pony. But Mama and I were living in Columbia at the time, smack in the middle of the city. Nana bought me a pony, then arranged for Mama to get a job offer in Dawkins at better pay, found her a house and moved us back, lock, stock and barrel." He glanced at me, his face greenish in the dash lights. "All so she could grant my wish."

"That's Nana. Take over and take charge. And even God better not get in her way."

Macon's cell rang. He answered, sounding all business, but his voice changed to a low murmur, calculated to keep me out and his tone gave everything away. Julie Schwartz. No doubt about it.

When the quiet conversation was over, he flipped the cell phone shut and glanced at me again. "I forgot to tell you. Nana is sending one of Mama Moses's young'uns over to apologize." I raised my brows and he said, "One particularly devious twelve-year-old spent the night in your safe room. The name Thomas Spires mean anything to you?"

I thought a moment. "He buried a dead possum for me. I was supposed to tip him but I haven't seen him."

"He decided to take a tip for himself. Snuck in and got stuck there overnight. His mama found some papers with Jack's old business name on them, and she and Nana figured out what had happened. He got his butt beat." Macon seemed pleased by that.

Without segue he said, "According to records, Christopher had a daughter. There was an accident a few years ago, and the girl is in a chronic vegetative state in a private hospital. Want to visit her tomorrow?"

"Will the cops let me?"

He laughed softly, something odd in his tone. "Let you? The private hospital where the girl lives is making a stink about letting the cops in without a warrant. A judge refused to grant one, told the cops they could go through her guardian first and if she refused to let them in, he'd reevaluate." Macon shot me a calculated look. "They have to ask *your* permission to see her. Christopher made you her legal guardian in the event that something happened to him."

My mouth fell open.

"You're also his legal heir. A will and the necessary papers were signed yesterday." Macon's voice hardened. "Looks like he intended to marry you. Whether you wanted to or not."

27

By 7:00 a.m., I stood in the doorway of the small room with the administrator of Sunnyvale Acres, a full care facility for the disabled. The cops stood a few feet behind me and the feebs were across the hall at my request, to give me space and a moment with my charge.

The private room was painted a pale pink, with pink linens and drapes, and a soft pink-and-peach plaid chair in the corner. The colors should have jarred but they didn't, instead making the room warm and inviting and girlish. A soft light burned beside the bed, and sunlight, weak and dull this early, came through the window, revealing flowers planted just beyond.

Dolls, books and stuffed animals were on shelves against the walls. I instantly noticed the preponderance of dancing dolls of all kinds, from large porcelain dolls swathed in silk, some standing en pointe, to small dancing dolls dressed as if to perform *Swan Lake*. Grief knots held back the drapery.

All over the walls hung framed photographs and cards. When I looked closer though, I saw the cards were actually single sheets of handmade paper, covered with calligraphy. Poems. I was pretty sure they were the same poems on the Internet site Dr. Christopher had dedicated to his daughter.

"Ms. Davenport?" Emma said from behind me, impatient.

"In a minute," I said. I walked into the room and stood over the young girl who slumbered in a permanent vegetative state. The hospital bed had a bulky box at the foot and the thick mattress pulsed steadily, the rhythm signaling that air moved up and down the length of the bed to prevent bedsores.

The girl was curled beneath a single sheet and a thin blanket, slack-faced, her arms and legs drawn up, feet pointed in a permanent ballet position, as if she tried to dance while curled like a fetus in the womb. Her blond hair was brushed back and secured in a ponytail. She smelled sweet, like talcum powder, and showed every evidence of being well-cared for. Blue eyes rocked back and forth beneath curled lashes. Her name was Aloise. She was sixteen.

Her mother had been confirmed in the genealogy. She was a Chadwick, as was this young woman. Four bronze statues were lined along the head of the bed, miniature females with their arms lifted, fingertips touching over their heads. They were dressed in Grecian robes, hair long and flowing, faces turned to the sky.

Muses? I looked closer to see a lÿre in one's hand, a bow in another's. I shivered. I didn't look closely at the other statues.

Instead, I touched the girl's head gently with my fingertips. "I'm sorry," I said. "I'm so very sorry." I tucked my hand in my jacket pocket and turned slowly, surveying the room, wondering if Christopher had left funds to cover this level of care indefinitely. I'd know soon enough. I had an appointment with his lawyer this afternoon. I needed to see the document that turned his estate over to me. Had to see what financial provisions had been made. Had to sign papers. And according to South Carolina law, I had to plan his funeral. The funeral of the man I'd killed. That was an irony I could have lived without.

I walked back into the hall and looked up at Emma. "Okay. I'll sign for you to have access to her. But she's not to be touched beyond what we discussed." Looking at the administrator, I said, "I'll sign the permission form, if you have it ready."

The middle-aged woman extended a clipboard. It was a pretty straightforward form but I passed it to Macon for approval. Once he agreed that it was acceptable, I took the pen in my bandaged hand and signed the forms, in triplicate, knowing that, for now, it was time to walk away. Macon was going to stay and make sure the feebs followed the permission I had given them to dust for prints in her room and copy her medical records.

My part was done, but I looked back into the room once. It was now swarming with busy people carrying arcane bits of equipment; in the center of the human storm was a bed with an unmoving form on it, breathing so shallowly that the covers didn't move. She might have been a mannequin. Or dead.

I turned to move down the hall when I spotted a photograph just inside the door of Aloise's room. It

Gwen Hunter

was of a young girl standing beside a table, holding a pottery horse. I stepped back into the room, to the photograph. "Emma?" I said. When she glowered at me, it occurred to me that she might resent me calling her by her first name, instead of Supervisory Special Agent Simmons. I smiled at her frown and said, "This looks like something you might want to see."

She stepped up behind me. "This doesn't look like Aloise," I said of the girl in the photo. "It looks like someone else. One of the other girls. And the horse looks like it might be a good source for the hoof in Lorianne Porter's pocket."

"We'll be taking all the photos and the poems," she said. "We'll ID everyone in the photos."

"Yes. I know." I looked at the girl curled on the bed. As her guardian, I could hang new things on her walls. I'd get the Chadwicks to help.

"I'll walk you out."

I looked up into Jim Ramsey's face, almost gaunt at the end of this investigation. Some of the tension eased from me. "Thank you." We turned and walked away, leaving behind the official-sounding voices, the hiss of spray cans and the click of plastic and wood. "I was afraid you were off the case because of me," I said.

"I was for a while. Now I'm supposed to hang around you and Nana and see what I can pick up."

The cynicism in his tone told me a lot about his feelings. I didn't look his way when I said, "Babysitting duty for an experienced field agent? Is that going to make trouble between us?"

"Nope. It isn't." He stretched out his arms, laced

his fingers together and popped his knuckles. "Standard procedure is that I'd be reassigned to Kalamazoo for the duration. But your nana pulled a few strings, so I'm staying."

I thought about that as we exited the building into the brightening dawn. The temperature had started out in the sixties but was warming. Birds were singing and a few puffy clouds rested supine in the sky, as if still sleeping. It was a beautiful day. "Nana's sticking her nose into your career? Should I tell her to back off?"

He shrugged and lay an arm around my shoulders. "Not yet. I'll have a talk with her and we'll see what happens."

"*You're* going to talk to Nana?"

"Mano a mano, as it were. Think I'll survive?"

"If not, I'll be there to comfort you as you lick your wounds."

"Sure you don't want to lick those wounds yourself? It might make the suffering worthwhile."

At his teasing tone, I blushed, feeling as if I were twelve years old. I tilted my head forward, hiding behind my hair. "Maybe. In Charleston. We'll see."

Jim leaned down and tightened his arm, making a noose around my neck, pulling me closer. He kissed the top of my head. With no more words between us, he walked me to my rental car and saw me inside. When I was belted in, he said, "We've begun interviewing friends and acquaintances of Dr. Christopher and his former wife. A co-worker of Christopher's wife told us that they were on the verge of a divorce two years ago, because he was having an affair with her sister. The wife and sister disappeared. They didn't have any other family, and the sister's co-workers thought the two had made up and taken off together. Which explains the presence of both bodies in his basement."

Sordid and tawdry, I thought. But I said, "So sad. All of it."

"Christopher had no friends, so far as we can determine. But we think he was living with someone."

I looked up at that one. "Dr. Christopher had a girl-friend?" I couldn't imagine the man having a normal life. "With a basement full of dead people and kid-napped girls? No way. He couldn't keep all that a secret."

"We don't think it was a secret. We think the live-in was a guy, his partner. Two toothbrushes, one bed, two colors of hair on the pillows. Some medium-sized, men's flannel shirts and T-shirts in the closet. No girlie stuff in the bathroom."

"Partner?" I said, trying to make it all fit.

"Yeah. Current theory is they were working together, but the partner cleared out before we got to the house. Left a few things behind, but got away." Jim stroked my hair, in a gesture that was both tender and somehow very intimate. "So I'll be sticking close until we catch him. Hope you can live with me."

With that cryptic statement, Jim closed my door and walked to his Crown Vic. When I recovered, I inserted the key and turned the ignition. Close behind, Jim followed me the thirty miles back home.

Around my kitchen table, Nana, Aunt Mosetta, Jim and I studied the genealogy charts and family photograph albums over a late breakfast of pancakes, syrup and several pots of hot coffee and chai tea. My waistline and thunder thighs would surely suffer for all the carbs, fats and sweets I had been eating lately, but I was too tired and too much in need of comfort foods to care. Twice, Jim's phone rang, and I understood that someone was keeping him apprised of developments in the case. The investigation was taking place at breakneck speed now, because there were leads aplenty, two sites for forensic workup and evidence pouring in like water over a falls. If the missing girl was still alive, she had perhaps been alone, without food, water and her insulin, for days now. They had to find her.

Jas had uncovered a lot of useless information about Erasmus, information the local cops were checking out, just in case. My daughter had been stricken with the investigative bug. Now she wanted to be a P.I. and raise horses on the side. I sent her on to school with orders to pass this semester and we'd see. I figured a summer spent working the farm and part-time with a security firm, like the one conveniently owned by Wicked Owens, would either cure her or convince her. Sometimes—other than Christmas, birthdays and other gift-buying times—it was really nice to have a large family.

As we ate, Nana traced the exact lineage of the girl who was now my ward. Aloise Christopher was related to me through my father's half brother.

I was cleaning away the dirty dishes when Jim said, "Ash. Look at this."

I set down the plates, washed syrup off my fingertips and crossed to the kitchen table. He was looking at an old daguerreotype of my great-grandfather, one of those stiffly posed, stern-faced, sepia-toned pictures. He was sitting in a wingback chair. Behind him was a statue of a horse, the same horse I was sure I had seen in the photo hanging on Aloise's wall.

"Did they find the horse statue? Was it the source of the broken hoof in Lorianne Porter's pocket?" I asked.

"No," Jim said, studying the old photograph.

"Nana, who got this statue when Great-grandpa died?" I asked "Do you remember?"

Aunt Mosetta answered for her. "Wasn't it that wife of his? Almetha Chadwick. Went on to marry again and moved her kids with her."

Jim looked at me, knowing we may have just drawn a direct line between the teenaged Aloise and the broken hoof found on the body buried on Chadwick Farms. He pulled his phone, ready to report in.

Mosetta's next words stopped him. "They got some land in that will, too, not far from here. Somebody builded hisself a huntin' house on it 'bout ten year ago."

"Hunting house?" Jim asked.

"A shack to use during hunting season," I said.

"Cardboard and sheet metal?" he asked.

"Now you're getting the picture," Nana said, laughter in her tone for the city cop.

"Where near here?" Jim asked, his phone still open but undialed.

"I can draw you a map," Aunt Moses said. She looked at me, her face creased in a thousand wrinkles. "You know where the old Felix's Texaco is?"

I nodded and set the last dirty plate in the dishwasher.

"There a two-rut track behind it. Or once was. Take two turns offa that, you find it. Back behind nowhere, it is."

"I remember that," Nana agreed. "I tried to buy the land. Wanted it for the farm. The owner didn't even bother to reply to my lawyer's query."

Dutifully, Jim called in all he had learned in the last few minutes. The conversation was short and sweet. When he hung up the phone, he said, "Feel like exploring? Simmons says I should take a field trip."

"Sure," I said, draining my teacup.

"Take along a picnic," Aunt Mosetta said. "Nothing for young lovers like a picnic."

At the words, the tea went down wrong and I choked. Jim just laughed.

We borrowed Johnny Ray's old clunker truck, Nana whispering in my ear that she put my shotgun under the passenger seat, Aunt Mosetta adding that she put sandwiches there, too. Jim was dressed in street clothes, *city* street clothes—button-down shirt and slacks, with brown oxfords. Not the best attire for searching backcountry property. But maybe his recent experience walking Chadwick land had made an impression, because he left his tie and suit coat draped over a kitchen chair, though he still wore his holster strapped around his shoulders. He whistled appreciatively when I emerged from the house in T-shirt, jeans and western riding boots. "Remind me I need to keep casual clothes in the unit," he said, which I thought was a pretty good idea, though awfully belated.

Taking the roads to Felix's Texaco, we passed the skid marks and torn earth of the accident that wasn't an accident. I couldn't help but look, and saw that there was no sign of blood on the highway. I had worked with the county's emergency services for years and knew that someone had opened a two-liter bottle of cola and washed down the street. The phosphoric acid and carbonation in colas dissolved blood from asphalt and washed it away. Jim didn't mention it, so neither did I, but it put a huge damper on a day that was emotional and melancholy at best. I knew from experience that one could expect emotional swings after taking a life.

Jim passed me a water bottle as he drove and I drank, mentally thanking him for reminding me that life went on. I don't know if that was what he intended, but the simple act of kindness had that effect on me. When I passed the bottle back, he lifted it to his own lips and drank, and I felt a bit of warmth return at the sight of his mouth on the bottle where mine had been. When it was empty, he tucked it beneath the seat.

It was a long bench-style seat, with deep dips to mark where people sat, and the springs had given way. The tires were bald, the bumpers missing; the lights were held in place with duct tape and baling wire, and the truck was rusted inside and out. If one of us touched something wrong, we'd need a tetanus shot. Heck, we might need one just for riding in it. Neither one of us mentioned the strong smell of cheap alcohol, old vomit and cigarettes that permeated the cab, but by unspoken agreement, we rode with the windows down and the warm breeze snatching at us, sweeping the odors away. Clearly, Johnny Ray did a lot of living in the old truck.

The cling bandages I wore were now no more than a couple of layers thick. My hands were healing fast, which was good because the truck had no suspension, and I had to hold on, grinding my hands against the filthy metal door frame.

Jim handled the beat-up truck like a pro, though, and we made good time, weaving behind the old abandoned service station and along a two-rut trail into scrub brush, onto land where I had never been before. The second turnoff should have been overgrown or well used. Instead it looked as if it had been deserted for years and then driven recently. Once.

Jim got out and studied the overgrown, washed-out drive, last year's dry foliage, the relative obscurity of the place. When he got back in, he threw the old truck in reverse and said, "I'm taking you back."

"No, you aren't," I said, insulted. "No way. You're going to drive along this rut and see what's at the end. If you need backup, you'll call for it. I'll wait in the truck like a good little girl and the good guys can storm the place."

Jim turned to me, amusement and tenderness in his gaze. "I like you a lot, Ashlee Davenport."

My brows raised all by themselves in surprise. "I like you a lot, too, Jim Ramsey."

"If I fall in love with you, are you going to be this easygoing about everything?"

"No," I said, feeling the usual blush-burn. I stuck my nose in the air. "If you cheat on me, I'll make you regret it for the rest of your natural life."

"Yeah? How so?"

"I'll sic Nana on you."

"Ouch." He looked at the road, thinking, a small smile pulling at his mouth. "Okay. I can live with that. When we get to wherever we're going, stay in the car."

"Deal."

28

We followed the rambling trail along a winding, rain-gutted course, Jim banging his head once on the cab roof when the truck hit a particularly deep dip. After ten minutes of jouncing and bouncing, I pointed to the left through the trees. "There," I said. Jim stopped the truck quickly, skidding over a patch of bare, potholed ground.

Up a slight incline, about a hundred and fifty yards away, was a shack, but only by the most slim definition. The hut had been built of scraps, things that might be left over from a construction site. There was rusted sheet metal, plywood that had separated and buckled, two old windows with the panes busted out, sheets of rippled fiberglass and tar paper on the roof. Everything had been camo painted to blend in with the environment. Out front, half-hidden by the dry and spring vegetation, was a small red car. If it had belonged to a serious hunter, the vehicle would have been camo painted, too, so the car belonged to someone else.

Jim flipped open his cell phone. "Son of a bitch," he said, without apology. "No reception. Nothing. Not even a bar. How do you people live like this?"

"Welcome to the rural South," I said. "Feel free to back out and drive toward the traffic-clogged interstate, the pollution, the crime and the overpopulation. You'll find reception."

His eyes on the shack, taking in the terrain, Jim laughed shortly. He slapped the phone into my hand. I winced at the pain but he didn't notice. Throwing the truck in reverse, he backed into a three-point turn. "Watch the bars. As soon as you see some, let me know."

It didn't take long. The property was not too far from the I-77 corridor and the cell towers that lined the highway. We were still in brush when I handed him the cell. Jim reported in, giving our location and directions, and asked for uniformed backup. He never said a name, but whoever he was talking to left him unhappy about the outcome. He said, "You got to be kidding. Half an hour is too long. He might have heard the truck and decided to book. I'm going in to check it out…. Yeah, yeah, I know. Right." He closed the phone and dropped it on the seat. He held out his hand and I raised mine to take it.

"Backup will be here in half an hour. You sit tight. I'll walk back in and check it out."

"And if it's just a hunter scouting out the fall's deer hide, or a couple of teenagers indulging in a private moment?"

"Then I'll risk being mistaken for a buck or walking in on kinky, redneck sex."

I laughed, and Jim laughed with me. He reached out, wrapped his hand about my neck and pulled me to him. His lips were warm and gentle on mine and everything in my life, good and bad, vanished in an instant, leaving only him, only Jim and this single touch. His tongue touched mine and he pulled me closer. Into his lap. I wrapped my arms around him and melted into him. He breathed against my mouth, and the breath turned to soft chuckles, which I returned.

He pulled slightly away, until his lips were just barely touching mine, and said, "What if I more than like you, Ashlee. Will you run away from me?"

Despite the heat, prickles rippled along my skin. "Chadwicks don't run."

He kissed me again, briefly this time, and eased me back into my seat. He climbed from the truck and reached into the back, pulling out a Kevlar vest and a navy T-shirt with FBI emblazoned on it. I hadn't noticed when he'd put them in the truck bed. Jim strapped on the vest and pulled the T-shirt over his head, his appearance now bulkier and solid looking. "Wait here. If I'm not back in fifteen minutes or if you hear gunfire, drive out and get help."

"Sure," I said. "Sure. Be careful."

Jim nodded and walked away, through the brush.

Fifteen minutes is a long time sitting in a stinky truck while a man I might be falling in love with is out stalking down possible bad guys.

I wasn't happy, alone with my thoughts. I began to feel exposed, sitting there in the truck, sunlight streaming in the dirty windshield. I no longer had my pearl-handled 9 mm. I was pretty sure I'd never get it back, now that the cops had it. I had also been pretty sure I never wanted to see it again, until now. I was alone, starting to sweat, and getting fidgety.

Against Jim's suggestion—I refused to think of it as orders—I slid into the driver's seat and turned on the truck, the old engine cranky and hitting on too few cylinders. I hadn't driven a stick shift in years but it came back to me, and the truck lurched forward, clutch grinding as I turned around again and headed back up the ruts. When I came to the spot where Jim had made our first three-point turn, I stopped, pocketed the keys and eased the truck door open. Sliding into the sunlight, cowboy boots on the washed-out earth, I pulled the double-barreled shotgun out and checked to see the safety was on. I followed the ruts into the brush.

I was halfway to the shack when I heard gunshots and the roar of an engine. It was coming my way fast, a red blur along the track. Right at me. I ducked, dove to the side. Landed in the dry scrub, hard on my injured hands. The shotgun spun away. I rolled, my limbs windmilling around me. My momentum stopped when my hip hit a small tree, jarring my spine. An electric charge of pain shot through me.

The red car raced past, taking bumps and potholes hard. All I saw was the top of the driver's head, short sweaty hair and pale forehead.

An instant later, I heard more shots. He was shooting at the truck. The truck I was no longer in. Engine gunning, the car took off again and was gone. I heard footsteps, running hard, slipping on the brush. Jim, cursing foully under his breath.

I called his name, sitting up in the dirt. "I'm over here," I shouted, rubbing my hip, immediately wishing I hadn't. My hands were bleeding again.

Jim spotted me and ran, fighting for traction in his slick-bottomed city shoes. Breathless, chanting my name and swearing, he fell over me, his face frantic, his hands searching my torso. Despite the pain in my hands, I grabbed his head and forced him to look in my eyes, and said, "Jim. I'm okay. I'm fine."

"I heard more shots," he said, eyes wide with fear. "I heard more shots." His eyes changed, focusing hard on me. He took my wrists, pulling my hands away. "I told you to stay put."

"Good thing I didn't," I said indignantly. "I think he tried to kill Johnny Ray's truck." Jim burst into startled laughter. I grinned ruefully back.

Jim didn't say anything when he took the shotgun, just looked from me to the gun, speculation and a sort of amused resignation in his eyes. He broke the shotgun open and removed the double-ought buckshot rounds, inspecting the load before reinserting them and bracing the open weapon over his arm.

I had seen Jack carry the shotgun the same way, open, unable to be fired, but easy to ready with just a slight lift of the arm. I stared at the weapon and the man in my life, feeling all sorts of strange things settle deep inside me. "Nana put it under the seat," I said.

"Uh-huh. Of course she did," he said, no inflection in his voice. "Those are two very dangerous women."

Since I agreed, I just shrugged. What could you really say about women like my family matriarchs? They were unique, and they did things their own way. End of story.

While Jim questioned me, we made our way back along the two-rut drive, the shotgun still open. I had to admit that I hadn't seen anything except the top of the shooter's head. And Jim had to admit that he'd seen even less. "I was moving up around the back of the shack when I heard the car start up. By the time I got to the front, it was pulling out. I did manage to get a partial license-plate number, which I'll run later, but that's about it."

Jim slid an arm around my shoulders, pulling me close beneath his arm. The Kevlar around him was unyielding, a reminder of the shots fired. I put my head against his shoulder.

"What was the gunfire about?" I asked, remembering the sound of the shots.

"I shouted for him to stop. He had other plans," Jim said. "He fired out the vehicle window without looking."

We got to the truck to find it had taken a half-dozen rounds in the grille, passenger's door and through the windshield into the interior. Jim looked it over, grim-faced, and climbed in. He said, "Even money says it's dead." He turned the key. Despite his dire prediction, the rusted hulk started up on the second try, no more cranky than usual.

I took my place in the passenger seat, sticking a finger into a hole in the door beside me. "Good thing I wasn't sitting here," I said.

Jim didn't reply, but his mouth tightened, and the look in his eyes was deadly. It promised retribution.

The shotgun back under the seat, we drove slowly toward the hunter's shack, a farther distance than I had thought, as the poor excuse for a road made several twists and turns in the last half mile. The truck was steaming and I figured at least one round had hit the radiator. Not good.

Jim stopped the truck just beyond where the rutted drive curved hard to the left, turned off the engine and got out. He opened the hood, letting out a small cloud of steam. "Unless we find a couple gallons of water, we could be stuck here until the backup arrives," he said. He looked at his watch. "If they show at all."

A muffled scream sounded. Jim crouched and drew his weapon all in one move, then shoved me down and jerked me behind the truck in another, his body bent over mine. The sound came again. It could have been a crow or a wildcat, but it was human. And it was coming from the shack. "Stay put," he said against my hair.

"No," I said. I opened the passenger door and felt under the seat for the shotgun.

"You know how to use that?" he asked, his voice hard and indecision on his face.

"I've fired it a time or two."

The scream sounded again, this time softer, breathy and panicked. I looked at Jim. "Sitting in the truck would have gotten me shot last time. I'll stay right behind you, but I'm going with you."

He looked at the truck, taking in the bullet holes, and shook his head. "Stay close. Point that thing way off to the side. Let's go."

Jim raced from the protection of the truck to a large tree, his weapon held low and close to his leg. I followed, tight on his heels, the sound of our feet in the dry, dead scrub giving our position away. From the tree, we moved laterally to the side of the shack and around back. The overgrowth was thicker here, dry kudzu vines draping from nearby trees over the house, nearly encasing it. In summer, the shack was probably not visible for the greenery.

Jim pushed his way through the rotten vines and knelt at a back window, his head below the ledge. A doorway with the door half off its hinges and open to the elements was only a foot away. The shack had no floor, only bare earth, the door resting on it at an angle.

The sounds from inside were stronger now, truly terrified, the intonation of a child in danger. I wanted to rush in, but Jim put his hand on my arm. "There could be someone else inside," he said softly. "Waiting on us to charge in."

I whispered in his ear, "If they have ears at all, they know where we are."

Jim nodded, vine dust and an old kudzu leaf falling from his hair. "I'm going in. You stay here. Please."

"Okay. But if anyone but you comes out, I'm shooting." I closed the action and set the stock against my shoulder, then flicked off the safety, sliding the switch on the tang between the barrels, above the trigger.

Jim glanced around again, looked at his weapon and walked in a crouch to the door. In a single fast move, he whirled inside and disappeared. I waited, hearing the faint scuff of his shoes on bare dirt as he moved through the house. It didn't take long. "Ash."

I looked in through the open door to see Jim, his back to me. A breath I hadn't realized I was holding escaped me in a long hiss. I reset the safety, broke open the weapon, and stepped inside. My mind didn't understand what I was seeing at first, or didn't accept it. A trench was freshly dug, about a foot deep and three feet long, a shovel still buried in the ground. Beside the hole was a small body, hooded and bound in rope.

Jim met my horrified gaze with his cop face, cold and hard. He opened a pocket knife. When he touched the child, she screamed and fought to get away. Jim said, "It's okay. I'm cop. Be still, okay?"

"Take off her hood so she can see us," I said.

Jim reached for the hood and pulled, but it was caught under the ropes, which were wrapped around her. I moved to her other side and took the hood in both hands, pulling with him. The hood came free.

It was Jenny, the girl from the tae kwon do gym. She was screaming, panting, her eyes wide and unfocused. The scarf in her mouth was wet with saliva and blood, and was tied so tightly, her lips were pulled back, exposing her teeth.

I came around and knelt beside her, my body blocking Jim from her view. As if he understood that I didn't want her to see a male, he eased away and moved to the window. "Jenny? Jenny, it's okay. The cops are here. They've rescued you. Okay? Jenny?" I didn't try to touch her now, just kept saying her name and telling her help had arrived.

After long moments, she finally looked at me, finally *saw* me, and her panting terror became something else. With a twist of her hips, she threw herself at me. I caught her, holding her close, my nostrils full of the smell of old urine and fear and unwashed child—and the sweet stench of a diabetic crisis. I stroked her hair with my bandaged hands, murmuring softly, "It's okay. You're safe now. You're safe." She shivered with tremors and shock and almost unbearable relief.

It took time, but eventually Jenny's respiration slowed to forty. Her pulse, which I had estimated at 140, dropped to 120, and I figured she was calm enough to accept help. I eased her off my lap and back to a sitting position. "Jenny, I'm going to take off your gag, okay?"

She nodded.

"I have to use a knife. You have to be still, so I don't hurt you."

She nodded again. My hands clumsy, I opened Jim's pocket knife. It was sharp, but the scarf in her mouth was pressed into her skin, and it had been there long enough for the flesh to swell above and below it. Her lips were swollen, too, and I worried about damage to her mucous membranes and circulation.

But she was alive. Everything else could be dealt with later. I sawed through the scarf, and at last it parted, falling away.

Jim handed me an open bottle of water and I held it to Jenny's mouth, but her lips were so swollen she could barely swallow. Most of the water dribbled down her shirt. But she looked at me and her eyes smiled. She nodded and I saw her swallow, so I knew she had gotten some down.

"We need to get these ropes off you. Okay?"

"Yeash," she said. "Wheash." Which I took to be "Yes. Please."

Jim was again nowhere near and so I began to saw

through the ropes. I worked up a sweat, but I had success, freeing her hands, which were an alarming shade of purple. She had been tied far too long and I didn't know if she would regain use of her hands, but I didn't let any of that show on my face.

"Wa-er," she said, and I helped her to drink again before starting in on the knots holding her feet together. No grief knots here. Tight, double-tied square knots. I set the water bottle in Jenny's lap and began to saw.

"Eesh going to kill ee," she said.

I looked up from the rope. Jenny's eyes were on the trench and I realized what I hadn't in the surprise of finding her. The killer was digging a grave. For Jenny. And she had understood what he was doing.

"Well, he wasted his time, didn't he?" Jim said.

Jenny looked up at him and laughed. I hoped that someday, she might laugh like a child again. But for now, it was the half-mad laugh of the survivor, a sound far too mature for her years. To keep her a bit more calm, I told her my name and who Jim and I were and how we had managed to find her, chattering to keep her attention focused and her mind settled. But I was worried about the sweet smell coming off her. I didn't know what she had been eating or drinking or when, but her blood sugar had to be high.

Soon after I had the last rope off, Jenny began to shiver, showing clear signs of going into shock. She needed hospital care desperately. Her pulse was thready and her respirations were increasing again. The flesh around her eyes was sunken, and she looked badly dehydrated. There was no telling what other injuries she had sustained. I said to Jim, "We need to get her out of here. Can you carry her?"

He looked at his watch and said, "Yeah." He pulled off the police T-shirt, ripped the Velcro straps loose, and handed the vest and the shotgun back to me. He knelt at Jenny's side and said, "My name is Jim Ramsey. I'm a cop. Is it okay for me to carry you back to safety?"

Jenny looked from me to Jim and lifted her arms. I was satisfied to see both the aching trust and the change in her hands. They were slightly less purple. Maybe we could save them.

I carried the shotgun and Jim's supplies down to the old truck; it had stopped steaming. Jim placed Jenny on the front seat and turned the key. The engine came to life. He glanced at me. "I found one last bottle of water and poured it into the radiator. Maybe we can make it back to the Texaco station."

I nodded and climbed in beside Jenny. Jim made a circle through the brush, back toward civilization, the truck wheezing and clattering and jerking as if it were having seizures. Though it was steaming and creaking, the old truck held up all the way back to the turnoff. There was a sheriff's patrol car waiting in the parking area, the deputy sitting with his head back, taking in the afternoon sun. After that, it was short work getting Jenny to Dawkins County Hospital, lights and sirens running, Jenny and me sitting in the back of the patrol car because I didn't want to wait for an ambulance. Jim stayed behind, calling in the FBI crew to the shack for a full forensic workup.

* * *

The media converged at the small hospital, but it took them a full hour to get there, during which Jenny's mom was ferried in by the highway patrol and followed closely by the feebs. Dr. Rhea-Rhea took care of Jenny, ordering tests, starting fluids and administering insulin. She pulled a chair up to Jenny's bedside, entering notes into a portable computerized notation device, refusing to leave her side.

Hospital administration showed up for a brief confab and disappeared to set up the conference room for police and the media. I stood back, taking in all the action but not part of it, watching from a corner, silent and pretty much useless.

When the cops brought Jenny's mother in, the dark haired woman raced into the trauma room, her face streaked with tears and worry, tremors gripping her body. Jenny, who had been flagging and pale, lit up like a party light, threw off the covers and seemed to fly through the air to her mother. The two fell across the gurney, tears running like twin fountains. There was hugging and squealing, Jenny shrieking, "Mama, Mama, Mama," and her mother crying, much more brokenly, "Jenny. Oh, Jenny."

Emergency rooms seldom see happy events, being a place of injuries and despair rather than joyful reunions, and every tech and nurse made it a point to come by the doorway and glance in. Mother and daughter were the center of attention. Dr. Rhea-Rhea stood to the side. Her arms were folded tightly around herself and her face solemn, but her eyes danced. I saw it all through a thick sheen of tears.

I managed to call Nana for a ride and sneak away without anyone being the wiser.

By dusk, I was back home and was soaking in a tub of hot water when the doorbell rang. It was the mellow ding-dong that signified the back doorbell, the one only family and close friends used. I pulled myself from the tub. Wrapped in an oversize terry robe, my hair in a striped towel, I went to the door. The shotgun was still on the kitchen counter where I had laid it when I'd entered. As I passed, I slid the morning newspaper over it.

At the door, I retied the robe and looked through the window, spotting Lynnie Bee. She was turned to the side, staring out over the barn. I opened the door and said, "Lynnie, come on in! I wasn't expec—"

She turned to me. And I saw the gun.

29

"Lynnie?"

"Get inside," she said, her voice sounding bruised and breathless and cold.

I backed away and she followed. With the gun, she waved me to the table and said, "Sit." I did, and she shoved the chair beside mine out, and eased down into it.

She was filthy, her face smeared with grime and dried gore. She stank of sweat and old wounds. She was wearing jeans, a man's button-down shirt and dirty sneakers, all crusted with blood. There was a bullet hole in her jeans' right lower leg and in her shirt, upper chest, near the collarbone. Blood stained her clothes. Two GSWs. At least.

It all fell into place.

"It was you, today, wasn't it?" I asked. When she didn't answer, I said, "You and *Christopher?*"

She laughed, the sound half agony, half disbelieving. "I tried to get you to date him, but I fell for him myself."

"He was kidnapping little girls," I said, stunned. *"Little girls."*

"Not like that," she said, resting an elbow on the table so she could square the gun on me. The wound in her upper chest oozed blood, bright against the darker blood drying around it. "Not like you think. Not like a pedophile. He was just…just…"

"A little crazy," I whispered.

"I loved him." She looked at me, her eyes begging me to understand. "I didn't know about them until Jenny. And this was the last one. He promised. He promised." Her voice broke on the word. Whispering, she said, "This was the last one he was going to take. He knew it wasn't working. He finally…" She shuddered with pain and closed her eyes tightly.

I tensed to stand, ready to grab the shotgun from the counter, but her eyes opened, bright and laser-sharp on me. "He understood that she wasn't coming back no matter what. He was accepting it, at last. He was…"

She took a hard breath and grimaced with pain. "He knew she wasn't coming back. That she was in a permanent vegetative state and that nothing was ever going to change that. But you *had* to get involved. You. My *friend*," she said bitterly. "You *shot* him." Tears slid down her face, washing clean streaks through the filth.

She looked away, to the side, as if she couldn't bear to see me. "Why couldn't you just stay out of it?" she whispered. "Why? He's dead and you…you killed him." She wiped mucous from her nose. "I don't know what to do."

"You need help," I said softly. "You need a hospital."

"I'll go to jail. And I'll be alone forever."

I had nothing to say to that one. The silence in the

kitchen was brittle, harsh, no longer the silence of friendship. My mind focused on that thought. Lynnie was holding a gun on me. I struggled to accept that one simple concept. One of my best friends was holding a gun on me. Just as another best friend had slept with my husband…

The image of Jenny, tied and squirming beside a grave, flashed into my mind. Would she shoot me? My…*friend?*

My voice calm and soothing, I asked, "Lynnie? Today? The little girl?"

She shook her head, oily hair sliding over her forehead. "I didn't know what to do with her. She saw me. She could maybe describe me. To the police.

"I just thought that if I got rid of her, I could go back to the way it was. And Paul had shown me the land. We were going to build a house on it. Near you. Near the Chadwicks. And I was going to live just like you. Like I always wanted to. But now it's all ruined." Her eyes raised to me, pleading, unfocused, staring at a reality only she saw.

"I couldn't steal any more insulin. Someone was going to notice soon. I had to get rid of her. I had to put her where no one would find her." She met my eyes and her grief was ripped away by fury. "And then you showed up. With that cop."

"Lynnie, let me help you. Let me call an ambulance."

"No."

Voices sounded from outside. Nana and Aunt Mosetta, chatting. Getting closer. Coming here. Shock quivered through me like lightning. It was dusk. Time for an evening chat and a drink on the back porch. Lynnie swung the gun that way, panic on her face. And the door opened.

I dove at the arm holding the gun, shoving it hard, following through with my whole body. Lynnie's chair rocked with the momentum, back on two legs. It crashed to the floor. The world spun, tilting drunkenly. Our bodies hit, mine on top of Lynnie. She grunted with pain. The gun went flying. In a single blink, I saw it airborne. Heard it fall. It clattered across the floor.

Suddenly Nana was there, her .38 pointed solidly at Lynnie Bee's head.

Aunt Mosetta took my arm and pulled me away. I scooted away with her, crying. My eyes were locked to Lynnie Bee's as she curled in a fetal position on the floor. Tears crawled down her face. "I just wanted to be like you," she said. "That's all."

"Oh, Lynnie," I said. "I'm so sorry."

"Moses, call the police," Nana said.

"Whatchyou think I'm doing?" Aunt Mosetta said as she dialed. "You think I'm stupid?"

It took half an hour for Jim, three cop cars and an ambulance to get to the farm. Half an hour for Lynnie to bleed. The fall had opened the wound in her upper chest, tearing something inside. She went into shock, her pulse fluttery and fast, her skin pasty and wet with a slick sweat. I wrapped her in blankets, washed and packed her wounds with sterile gauze from my supplies and padded over them with kitchen towels. I taped them all down with clear body tape, supporting her legs with pillows from the rec room.

She was still alive when the ambulance came, and I helped the EMTs to stabilize her, inserting IVs and opening up fluids, volume expanders in one arm. The pulse in the other was diminished, possibly due to the gunshot wound high in her chest.

And it was over. Lynnie was on the way to the hospital, the crime-scene techs were finished taking pictures. Once again, my clothes had to be confiscated by the cops.

Jim waited outside my door while I changed. If my family hadn't been so close by, I was pretty sure he'd have been in the room with me. He couldn't bear to be away from me. We talked through the door as I washed off the blood and dressed in jeans and a sweatshirt.

"I knew it was Lynnie," he said, his voice so tight it ground like glass on raw granite. "I ran the plates. We had put out an APB on her. I just didn't expect her to come to you."

"I'm okay," I said. "I'm fine. Really." But I wasn't. Lynnie was one of my very best friends. Just as Robyn had been. Lynnie had known when Christopher had kidnapped Jenny. She had known that he'd killed the other girls. And she had been willing to kill the last one. She had shot at Jim. Had held a gun on me. And now...

Dressed, I opened the door and handed Jim my robe. It would go in as evidence, along with all the other clothes the cops had taken. After the last few days, I nearly needed a new wardrobe. He accepted the robe and took me in his arms, holding me close. "I've taken the rest of the week off," he said against my hair.

"You have time off. So I booked us a room at a bed-and-breakfast in Charleston. Let's go for some R & R."

I laughed and the sound was shaky, muffled in his shirt. Was it only days ago that we had planned our trip? "Sure. Why not? I got nothing I'd rather do."

"And when we get back, I'm bringing my daughter to meet you and your family. You may well ruin the sweetness and gentleness that make up so much a part of her. But I can't think of anyone better to teach her the value of family and self-protection."

I laughed against his chest. "We can turn her over to Nana."

Jim huffed a laugh that sounded oddly like a groan.

Epilogue

Standing in front of the open window, I turned my face to the sun. The light was brighter here—near the ocean and the Battery—than at home. I could smell the salt of the ocean, the damp, slightly sour scent of the old harbor city, the faint scent of horse droppings mixed with car exhaust, and coffee and bacon—the mélange of morning smells in Charleston.

It was breakfast time and guests of the bed-and-breakfast could eat in their rooms, or dine out on the front porch. Jim and I had chosen to eat on the porch. We had reserved the little corner table under the arch for eight-thirty; the same table we had shared the weekend we stayed here back in the spring. "Living in sin," as Aunt Moses had said, when we got back. And Jim had agreed with her, dropping to a knee on her screened-in porch and proposing on the spot.

Memories of the B&B, and this bed, and the little table waiting for us were all mixed together, part of the whirlwind our romance had become. Engaged and married in less than three months, it was almost a Chadwick record, and totally against Chadwick tradition, as was our ceremony. No huge wedding on the front lawn of Nana and Aunt Moses's house with a hundred or so family members standing around to cheer. Just a few dozen Chadwicks, and the minister, and all the food.

My stomach rumbled.

I'd have to wake him soon or we would miss the scones and the muffins, and after the wedding night he had given me, I needed the calories. But for now, I wanted only to lean into the sunlight, and just…be. I couldn't remember when I had felt so peaceful. So content.

Sheets rustled, feet padded softly across the rugs, and Jim's arms came around me, his skin warm and smooth. I leaned back against him, this husband of mine. He clasped his hands together in front of me, his chin on my head, looking out the window with me at the city. "Morning, sleepyhead." I said.

"Morning. Smells hungry out there."

Jim said the strangest things sometimes. "I could eat," I agreed, my head nodding against his chin.

"Then a walk around the Battery, lunch at some small café, and an afternoon…nap."

I smiled wider. "I could nap," I said, knowing sleep was not likely.

But my happiness faded. Today was the day Lynnie would be sentenced. She had elected against a jury trial, pleading guilty to a small host of charges in a plea bargain that got her five years and then probation. She had lost her nursing license, her home, everything. And we hadn't spoken since she was arrested. She refused to see me when I visited. My mail came back unopened.

As if Jim knew what I was thinking he said, "I forbid you to be sad today. It's our honeymoon. So stop."

"Not married two days and you're already being a *man*," I teased, "ordering me around again."

"You didn't mind me being a man last night."

I elbowed him gently in the abdomen and he gave out a mighty whoof as if I had poked him much harder. But his banter had the desired effect. The melancholy that had threatened was gone.

"We better go eat," he said, his meaning clear, "or we'll miss breakfast."

"I could lose a few pounds."

"Umm. Sex or food…" He considered, making a little humming noise in the back of his throat. "No. I like you the way you are." He released me, slapped me on my butt, and walked to the bath, pausing to stand naked in the doorway. "Breakfast, a walk, then sex. Besides, we only have a few days to ourselves before Sarah and Jas and Paz get here. I want to see the city with you, just the two of us."

"Are you sure you want to be a part of this family?" I asked for the hundredth time.

"Family? You mean me, my daughter, your horse-loving, Internet-hacking, slightly whacky girls, the horses, the two crazy women in the house out back, the nearly three hundred family members, most I've yet to meet, the country life on the farm? That family? I've got to be nuts, but yeah. I do. I love you, Ashlee Ramsey. And I want you to be happy."

"I am," I said. "I am happy."

A heartfelt story of home,
healing and redemption from
New York Times bestselling author

SUSAN WIGGS

International lawyer Sophie Bellamy has dedicated her life
to helping people in war-torn countries. But when she
survives a hostage situation, she remembers what matters
most—the children she loves back home. Haunted by
regrets, she returns to the idyllic Catskills village of Avalon
on the shores of Willow Lake, determined to repair the
bonds with her family.

There, Sophie discovers the surprising rewards of
small-town life—including an unexpected passion for
Noah Shepherd, the local veterinarian. Noah has a healing
touch for anything with four legs, but he's never had any
luck with women—until Sophie.

Snowfall
at Willow Lake

"Susan Wiggs' novels are beautiful, tender and wise."
—Luanne Rice

**Available the first week of February 2008
wherever paperbacks are sold!**

MIRA®

www.MIRABooks.com

MSW2493

New York Times Bestselling Author

STELLA CAMERON

Annie Duhon knows all about nightmares that shatter life's dreams, and the need to escape the past. But her fascination with Max Savage—the new surgeon—grows, even when disturbing rumors start to surface and her darkest visions seem to play out in living color. Can she trust Max with her secrets and her deepest desires? Or is he the specter she sees when she sleeps—a killer stalking women with his cleansing fire? Is she about to become his next victim?

"If you're looking for chilling suspense and red-hot romance, look no farther than Stella Cameron!"
—Tess Gerritsen

A Marked Man

Available the first week of February 2008 wherever paperbacks are sold!

NEW YORK TIMES BESTSELLING AUTHOR

KAREN HARPER

Briana Devon knows her twin sister would never deliberately leave her—but when she emerges from under water, Daria and their boat have vanished. Fighting rough waves and a fast-approaching storm, Bree doesn't have time to question: if she wants to survive, she has to swim.

Exhausted and terrified, Bree barely makes it to a tiny barrier island, where Cole De Roca revives her. Bound to Cole by the harrowing experience, she turns to him as she struggles to understand what happened to her sister. What really transpired that terrible afternoon? And what secrets lie dormant...below the surface?

BELOW THE SURFACE

"Harper keeps tension high...providing readers with a satisfying and exciting denouement."
—*Publishers Weekly* on *Inferno*

Available the first week of February 2008 wherever paperbacks are sold!

New York Times Bestselling Author

JENNIFER BLAKE

They are the pride—and scourge—of
New Orleans: a dashing fraternity of
master swordsmen whose infamy
is matched only by their skill, their
allegiance to each other and their
passion for the fairer sex.…

The New Year begins with alluring
widow Ariadne Faucher's request for
private lessons from Gavin Blackford,
a rakish sword master, in order to
challenge her sworn enemy to a duel.
Ariadne proves a quick study, her resolve
fueled by a vendetta that is all she has
left in the world. Their lessons crackle with undeniable
electricity…but the secret of her all-consuming vengeance
may have rendered her heart impervious, even to such a
virtuoso as Gavin.

"Beguiling, sexy heroes…Well done, Ms. Blake!"
—*The Romance Reader's Connection*

GUARDED HEART

HARLEQUIN

More Than Words

"Jeanne proves that one woman can change the world, with vision, compassion and hard work."

—**Linda Lael Miller,** author

*Linda wrote "Queen of the Rodeo," inspired by Jeanne Greenberg, founder of **SARI Therapeutic Riding.** Since 1978 Jeanne has devoted her life to enriching the lives of disabled children and their families through innovative and exciting therapies on horseback.*

Look for "*Queen of the Rodeo*" in
More Than Words, Vol. 4,
available in April 2008 at eHarlequin.com
or wherever books are sold.

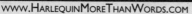
MTW07JG2

GWEN HUNTER

32221 BLOODSTONE	__ $6.99 U.S.	__ $8.50 CAN.
32130 SHADOW VALLEY	__ $6.50 U.S.	__ $7.99 CAN.
66669 DEADLY REMEDY	__ $6.50 U.S.	__ $7.99 CAN.

(limited quantities available)

TOTAL AMOUNT	$ _____
POSTAGE & HANDLING	$ _____
($1.00 FOR 1 BOOK, 50¢ for each additional)	
APPLICABLE TAXES	$ _____
TOTAL PAYABLE	$ _____

(check or money order—please do not send cash)

To order, complete this form and send it, along with a check or money order for the total above, payable to MIRA Books, to: **In the U.S.:** 3010 Walden Avenue, P.O. Box 9077, Buffalo, NY 14269-9077; **In Canada:** P.O. Box 636, Fort Erie, Ontario, L2A 5X3.

Name: _____
Address: _____ City: _____
State/Prov.: _____ Zip/Postal Code: _____
Account Number (if applicable): _____

075 CSAS

*New York residents remit applicable sales taxes.
*Canadian residents remit applicable GST and provincial taxes.

MIRA®

www.MIRABooks.com

MGH0208BL